Tying the Scot

HIGHLANDERS OF BALFORSS

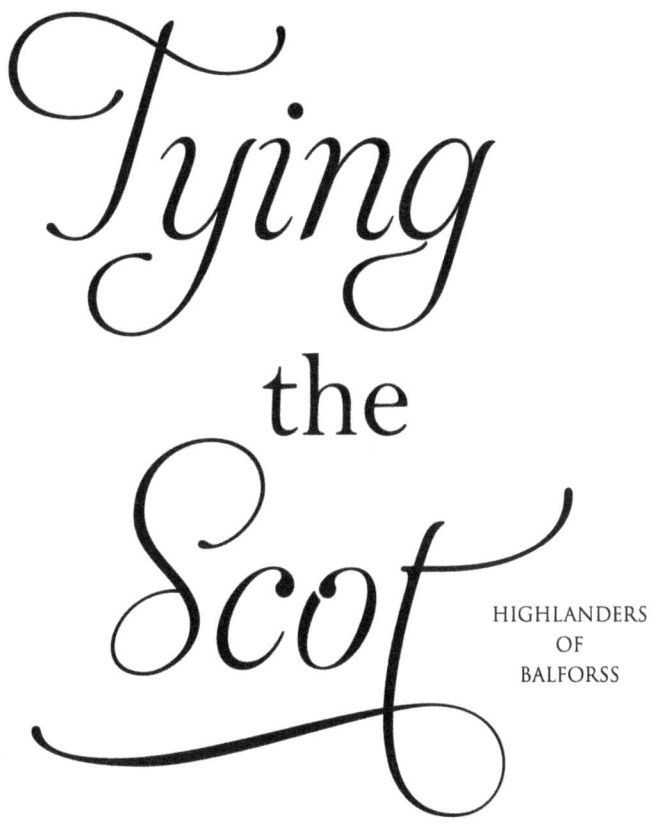

Tying the Scot

HIGHLANDERS OF BALFORSS

JENNIFER TRETHEWEY

This book is a work of fiction. Names, characters, places, and incidents are the product of the author's imagination or are used fictitiously. Any resemblance to actual events, locales, or persons, living or dead, is coincidental.

Copyright © 2017 by Jennifer Trethewey. All rights reserved, including the right to reproduce, distribute, or transmit in any form or by any means. For information regarding subsidiary rights, please contact the Publisher.

Entangled Publishing, LLC
2614 South Timberline Road
Suite 105, PMB 159
Fort Collins, CO 80525
Visit our website at www.entangledpublishing.com.

Amara is an imprint of Entangled Publishing, LLC.

Edited by Erin Molta
Cover design by Erin-Dameron Hill
Cover art from Romance Novel Center and DepositPhotos

Manufactured in the United States of America

First Edition November 2017

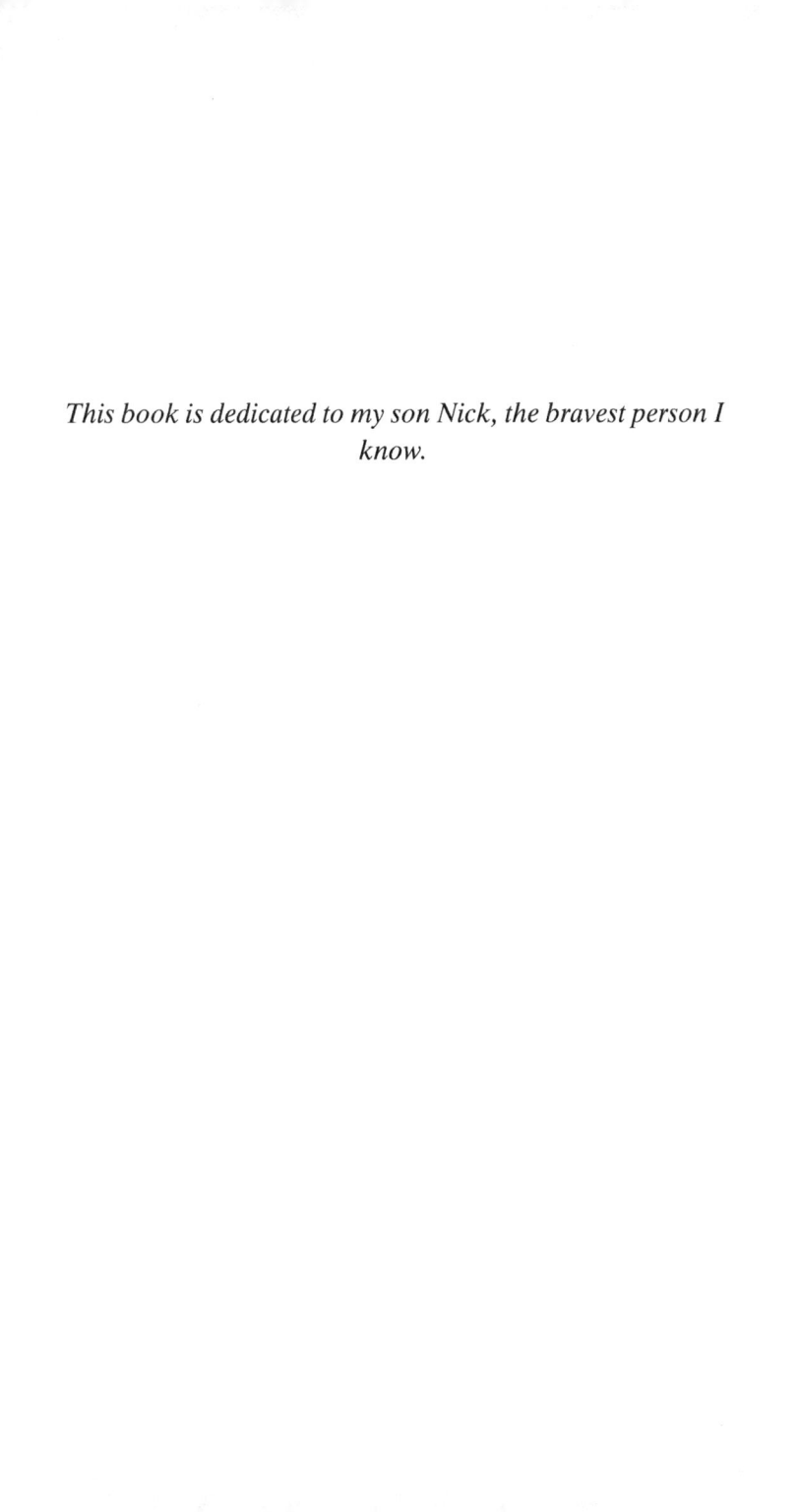

This book is dedicated to my son Nick, the bravest person I know.

Prologue

SPRING 1805, MAIDSTONE HALL, KENT, ENGLAND

Alex Sinclair's ears flamed. Not because of the heat of the day or the fight he'd just had with an older boy. His ears went hot because a pretty girl favored him with a smile. A smile worth a dunk in the pond. A smile worth a split lip. A smile worth the beating he would get for brawling with her brother.

Alex waded out of the duck pond, boots and kilt soaked to the waist. He made a courtly bow to the girl, then handed her the treasure he'd rescued, the yellow ball her brother had tossed into the pond.

"It's a bonnie wee thing," he said.

The girl tilted her head. "What's your name, boy?"

"Alexander Sinclair, son of Laird John Sinclair of Balforss." He wanted to touch her shiny dark curls, but he knew better than to try.

"My name is Lucy. It's my birthday today. I'm nine years old."

"My da is a friend of Lord Chatham."

"Lord Chatham is my papa. That makes us friends, too." A dimple formed on her smooth cheek.

In that moment, though only eleven years old, he understood what it was to be a man, to attempt the impossible, to risk everything, even death, for a lass's smile.

"Alex!"

He flinched. The tone in his father's voice held the promise of a tawsing he would not forget.

William Harris, Duke of Chatham, strode shoulder to shoulder with Alex's father, their tall bodies blocking the sun and casting long shadows on the garden path. The duke's son George trailed behind, holding his bloody nose with one hand and pointing with the other.

"There he is, Father. There's the red-haired devil who attacked me."

Alex probably shouldn't have hit the boy so hard, even though the numpty had deserved it. He faced his accuser and, to his surprise, Lucy moved to his side—his shield arm—like a fellow warrior. He stood tall, steady. Ready to take his punishment like a man.

His father snaked a long arm out, grabbed him by the collar, and cuffed him.

A satisfied "ha-ha" burst from George's blood-streaked mouth. The duke cut him off with a slap to the back of his head.

"Go back to the house. Now." The duke's tone was low and deadly. The kind of voice only a dafty would ignore.

"But Papa—" George protested.

One hard look from the duke and George ran for the house.

Alex's father gave him another shake before releasing his collar. "Come along, ye wee gomeril. It's the back of my sword you'll get for brawling with His Grace's son."

"No. You mustn't punish him." Lucy grabbed the duke's

coat and tugged. "Please, Papa. Don't let him punish Alex. He rescued my ball when George threw it into the pond. He's my protector, you see."

Alex hid his smile. Like a knight in a heroic tale, he had won the devotion of a beautiful lass, a prize worth every blow to his backside.

"Is this true, Alex?" the duke asked.

He made himself as tall as he could without standing on his toes. "It's true, Your Grace. I fished Miss Lucy's ball from the pond. But George wouldnae stop vexing the lass. I lost my temper and smacked him. For that, I am truly sorry, sir." He felt his cheeks color. The "sorry" part was a lie.

The tall Englishman and Alex's father suppressed laughter at what seemed a private joke. He deflated a little. Were they laughing at him?

"The apple doesn't fall far from the tree, John," the duke said, dabbing at his eyes.

"Aye. His mother is an honest woman," his father chuckled. "He's mine. I've nae doubt." He inclined his head toward Lucy. "I'm glad my son could be of service to you."

The dark-haired lass plucked at her blue skirt and bobbed a curtsy.

"Come with me." The duke led Alex by the shoulder toward the house. Would His Grace be giving him the tawsing?

The four of them assembled in the study, a room much like his father's library, but twice as big. The duke removed his ceremonial sword from its place above the mantel and unsheathed the long blade. The mood in the room instantly turned somber.

"Alexander Sinclair, kneel before me."

Back ramrod straight and shoulders squared, he stepped closer to the duke. The thought crossed his mind that he was about to be executed. He struggled to remain stoic, determined to face death like a man, if need be. Alex did as His Grace commanded, kneeled and bowed his head. Perhaps he should say a last good-bye to his father.

"Alexander Sinclair, son of John Sinclair of Balforss, in recognition of your chivalry, I, William Harris, Duke of Chatham, confer upon you the title of Champion and Protector to my daughter Lucy FitzHarris." The duke tapped his right then left shoulder with the tip of the sword.

Alex's cheeks *and* ears flared.

The duke nodded for him to stand, and he did. He should say something. Something noble. Words worthy of a man.

"You have my solemn oath I shall protect and serve Miss Lucy with my life, Your Grace."

The duke dropped his formality and slapped him on the shoulder. "Thank you, Alex. I accept your oath."

Lucy peered from behind a blue-and-gold striped chair, her yellow ball cradled in one arm. He crossed the room to repeat his oath to her, but the lass skittered to her father and hid her face inside his coat. She had been bold before he gave his oath. What made her shy of him now?

He turned to his father, unable to stop himself from grinning like a fool. His father flashed him a brief smile then lifted the dreaded eyebrow. "Dinnae think you'll escape the tawsing you're due for brawling."

Chapter One

Spring 1814, Maidstone Hall, Kent, England

Lucy FitzHarris tested her bowstring once again. What was it her instructor, Stevens, had said? *Relax your mind and body. The only thing that should be tight is your bowstring.* She selected an arrow and inspected the fletching. Satisfied, she whispered to herself, "Nock…draw…loose."

A short *ffftss* sound and then a soft *thunk*.

"Bulls-eye."

Lucy smiled down at her tiny white-and-brown spaniel whose tail was waggling. "Come along, Hercules."

She walked across the practice field toward the straw bale target, with Hercules bounding along at her side. Five of her six arrows had struck center. Lucy had proven herself a far better archer than her brother or his friends, yet they had never allowed her on a hunt. "Hunting is for men," George had said. "The sport is too rough for girls."

"One day, Hercules. One day we will take down a stag with a single shot. That will wipe the sneer off George's face once and for all."

Hercules broke into wild barking at an approaching threat—Lucy's maid, Nounou Phillipa, puffing and grunting up the hill, her wide frame swaying from side to side. *Merde.* She must have run all the way from the house to the shooting range. She had her skirt hitched up to her knees with one hand, and the other hand waving madly.

"*Viens. Viens.*"

Lucy met her half way. "*Qu'est-ce que c'est?*"

"*Votre père veut vous parler.*" Phillipa bent over to catch her breath.

"What does Papa want to talk to me about?"

"*Oh mon Dieu.*" Even Phillipa's wheezing sounded French.

"Tell me. Is it Langley?" Lucy gave her shoulder a quick shake. "Has George brought Lord Langley home to Maidstone with him?"

"*Je ne sais pas.*" Phillipa gasped and fanned herself with a free hand.

Lucy started for the house, calling over her shoulder, "Hurry. I can't receive him in my morning gown. Hurry, I say."

Triumph swept Lucy along the gravel path through the gardens toward the house. She had been waiting for this day for many months. Viscount Langley was the son of the Earl of Bromley, and he had finally come to ask for her hand.

A schoolmate of her brother's, the handsome and charming Langley had visited Maidstone many times. Although he had never professed his love, she was certain of his affections. He had kissed her in the garden. Everyone knew a gentleman never kissed a lady unless he intended to marry her. No doubt, he'd been waiting for her to turn eighteen. Now that she had, they would be married, and she would be a viscountess.

"Remember to act surprised when you see him, Hercules. We don't want Langley to think we're too eager." She lifted her skirts and took the back staircase two at a time. She paused at the top to call down. "Phillipa, where are you?" No answer. She let out a growly huff. "I have to do everything myself."

Lucy pawed through her gowns hanging in the wardrobe. A look of casual perfection would be most appropriate. She held the blue satin to her body, consulting Hercules. "Too fussy?" Rejecting the blue, she tried the green velvet. "Too formal?" The tiny spaniel cocked his head, confirming her assessment. Lucy swiped past two more. "Definitely not the pink or the burgundy. Far too frivolous." She needed something sophisticated. A gown that conveyed effortless grace.

At last, Phillipa appeared at the bedroom door, red-faced and winded.

"Where have you been? I have nothing to wear." Lucy pointed to the offensive wardrobe, her voice teetering between a whine and a wail.

"*Le jaune est parfait.*"

"Of course." Lucy wanted to collapse with relief. "The yellow muslin. *Merci, ma chère.* But hurry. *Vite. Vite.*"

After a flurry of fluttering shifts and stays followed by fastening, brushing, pinning, and draping, Phillipa held up the glass for inspection.

"*Voilà.*"

Lucy touched the small cameo tied around her neck. It had belonged to her mother, Genevieve, a French noblewoman whose family had been displaced during that awful business in France. She had died of fever soon after Lucy's birth. It would have been nice to have her here today, the biggest day of her life. Langley had come to propose. In a matter of minutes, she would be engaged to the future Earl of Bromley. Her life would never be the same.

"*Suis-je prête?*" Lucy asked.

"*Oui.* You are beautiful," Phillipa said in her halting English. "You look so like your mother." She was the only person who ever spoke of Lucy's mother. The only person to keep Genevieve alive in George and Lucy's memories. "*Je t'aime, ma petite.*"

"I love you too," Lucy said.

Hercules bounded off the bed.

"*Non, mon cher.* Not this time. You stay here with Phillipa."

Lucy stepped lightly down the hall with *Lady of the Lake* in hand, a recently published poem popular with London Society. Evidence of her sophistication. Spotting her brother below, she arranged her composure into what she hoped looked like pleased indifference. She took a breath, and floated down the grand staircase as she had practiced many times.

The viscount was not present to witness her entrance.

"Where's Langley?" she asked, her voice airy, careless.

George shrugged.

George lived to make Lucy's life difficult. Or at least that's what it seemed like to her. She tried a different tack. Sweetness. "Did he come home from school with you?"

He shook his head. She could tell he was being deliberately obtuse. *Patience*, she reminded herself. To show frustration would fuel her brother's mischief. "Is he arriving later?"

"Father awaits you in the library."

George gave her the look he often wore when he was about to spring an especially nasty trick on her, but she refused to fall prey to his nonsense today. She lifted her chin, picked up her skirts, and swooshed into the library.

"Lucy. You're looking lovely as ever." Her father favored her with his best smile. The one she knew he saved only for her.

He kissed her on the cheek and motioned for her to sit. She chose a place on the loveseat where her gown might be best displayed. The library was Lucy's favorite room in the house. Small compared to what had been her mother's parlor, yet warm and welcoming. Tall shuttered windows, comfortable leather chairs, shelves overflowing with books, papers, and oddments. A decorative reflection of the duke—stately, elegant, masculine.

"Ah, *Lady of the Lake*," he said, seeing the book. "Like it?"

"Oh yes, indeed." She loved Scott's poetry. So romantic. So heroic. "I didn't care for the ending. I would have preferred Lady Ellen marry King James and live happily ever after as queen." She handed her father the small leather bound volume, and he frowned at it.

"Not every story has a happy ending, my darling." *Is he thinking of Mother? Everyone said he grieved like a madman when she died. If he loved her so much, why didn't he marry her?*

A moment later, her father's face cleared. Setting Walter Scott aside, he moved a mahogany *bergère* close to Lucy and sat. Taking both her hands in his, he leaned in and said, "I have momentous news."

Lucy tilted her head, a coquettish look she had practiced. "Really? How wonderful."

"News I am certain will make you very happy."

"Don't tease me, Papa. Tell me."

"You, my beauty, are to be married."

Lucy inhaled her joy. "Oh, Papa. I am so, so happy. I am glad you approve." Lucy gave her father's hands a squeeze. "Did he write to ask you, or did he meet you in London?"

The duke rose and crossed to the spirits trolley. "I made arrangements with his father by messenger. But I assure you, your fiancé is most in favor of the union." He poured them both a finger of brandy. Handing her a glass, he said, "Lucy, dear, you haven't even asked me whom you are to marry. Don't you want to know?"

She could barely contain the giddy sensation rising in her chest. "Stop your teasing. Did he say when the wedding would be? Will we hold the ceremony here at Maidstone Hall or in London?"

"At his father's estate, of course."

"I see." The disappointing news dampened her spirits. She had hoped for a London wedding. With renewed enthusiasm, she asked, "Did Langley say when he will arrive? I mean, he should ask me himself, oughtn't he?"

"Langley?"

She rolled her eyes. Her father was such a tease. "Yes, silly. Who else?"

Her father looked blank. "Langley who?"

Lucy's heart began to beat faster. Her casual tone faltered. "Lord Langley. The Langley I am to marry."

"Lucy, dear, what makes you think Lord Langley asked for your hand?"

Her attention sharpened on her father. "He…he didn't?"

"No, dear." The duke shook his head. "You are to marry Alexander Sinclair of Balforss."

She dropped her glass of brandy on the carpet and bolted to her feet. Blood pounded in her head, the cameo tied around her neck now strangling her. "What? Who?"

"Alexander, the son of my dear friend, Laird John Sinclair."

"I don't know any Alexander Sinclair. I've never heard his name before in my life. Papa, how could you?" Her hands curled into fists.

The duke chuckled. "Of course you know him. You met him when you were a little girl. You liked him very much as I recall. Insisted he was your protector. Don't you remember?"

Why on earth would she remember some dirty little Scottish boy? "This is your fault!" she shouted. How could her father do this to her? Ruin her life without a care. Not a trace of remorse on his face. "It's because you never married our mother. We're an embarrassment to you, I suppose."

At last, she saw a crack in her father's impenetrable facade. "Darling, if it had been possible, I would have married your mother. I loved her very much."

The room began to spin, and she clutched the back of the *bergère* to keep her balance.

He started toward her, a conciliatory gesture she staved off with a hand. "I'm doing this for you. You're miserable here. London Society is cruel, and I can't bear to see you hurt."

She shook her head. A few pins fell out of her hair and pinged on the floor. "Stop it! Stop talking." Lucy straightened and lifted her chin. "I'm supposed to marry Langley. I can't marry someone else. I won't." She stormed out of the library before her father could say anything else to upset her.

Lucy collided with George in the hallway. He was stuffing a chunk of cake in his mouth and laughing.

"What's the matter, Lucy Goosey?"

She despised the pet name, one he had tortured her with since childhood. "Shut up."

"Did you think the future Earl of Bromley would marry the illegitimate daughter of a duke?" George coughed and pounded his chest with a fist.

"I hope you choke on that cake and die." She ran up the stairs to her room, flung herself onto her bed, and screamed into her pillow.

"*Ma chou chou. Ma chère. Qu'est-ce que c'est?*" Phillipa sat on the edge of the bed, rubbing her back.

Coming up for air, Lucy wailed, "He's a monster."

"Langley?"

"No. Papa. He's making me marry some horrible man." She took a breath to yowl, "From *Scotland*."

Insisting the bedroom door remain open so her father could hear the full measure of her misery, she shrieked and howled and wept while Phillipa did her best to console.

She must marry Langley. London Society barely tolerated the illegitimate sons and daughters of nobility. As such, she had no real title. She'd learned to deal with the ugly remarks made behind pretty fans, never allowing people to see how their words wounded her, what their nasty comments cost her. But a title, especially the title of viscountess, would stifle all such remarks for good. It was essential she marry Langley.

"Oh, Hercules. How could Papa do this to us? *Scotland*. Of all the detestable places on Earth." Even worse, he was sending her to live in the Highlands.

She'd heard her father's guests speak of the Highlands at parties. "Untamable," one man had said. "Savages incapable of civilized behavior." Lawless was another term bandied about. Lucy shuddered. How could her father send her somewhere so vulgar?

She heard a light rapping and lifted her face from the soggy pillow. George stood in her bedroom doorway, the look on his face apologetic, rather than his usual sneer.

He swallowed hard. "Lucy, Langley was engaged to Miss Whitebridge two weeks ago."

She sat up straight. All the crying had left her ears plugged. She hadn't heard her brother properly. "What?"

"Sorry. I thought you knew. There's been talk of nothing else. You know, the sea of broken hearts he's left in his wake, and all that rubbish."

"You're full of rubbish. Langley plans to marry me."

"Did he tell you so?" George asked, his voice uncharacteristically sympathetic.

"Yes." Lucy swallowed a gulp of air. "No. Not in words. He kissed me. Everyone knows a gentleman doesn't kiss a lady if he doesn't intend to—"

George shook his head. "No, Lucy. You misunderstood. I'm sorry." George left, closing her bedroom door behind him.

She sat motionless, numb, wanting to believe George was playing another one of his childish tricks, yet knowing he told the truth. She felt broken inside, her dream of becoming Countess of Bromley shattered. Langley's kiss had been a lie.

She gasped as another thought, more horrifying than the last, hit her square on. She had told Caroline Humphrey of Langley's kiss. She'd told Caroline, the most notorious gossip in London, that Langley intended to ask for her hand. How could she have been so stupid?

Oh God, everyone must know.

Everyone must be talking about foolish Lucy, the silly girl who misinterpreted a kiss. She was ruined. She dropped her face into her pillow and wept, and wept, and wept.

Exhausted and congested, she lay on her back, hiccupping, one arm draped over her eyes, the other cradling her only solace, darling Hercules. Phillipa removed Lucy's boots, pulled the drapes, and left her to wallow in the very worst kind of unhappiness, self-pity.

Her life in London Society had come to an end. She could never show her face again, doomed to a lonely life at Maidstone Hall. As the years passed by, she would watch her brother marry and have children. She would become the sad aunt who was never loved and lived the life of a spinster. Over time she would slowly become invisible, forgotten, like an old shoe.

Or she could go away. Far, far away.

Lucy uncovered her eyes and stared at the pleated pink canopy above her bed. With this new perspective, the arranged marriage her father had foisted upon her so rudely didn't seem as awful as it had earlier.

Lucy had told Papa a fib. The Scottish boy had made a deep impression on her at the time. His strange Highland costume and his fierce behavior had frightened her at first.

"Bonnie wee thing," the boy had said.

He was referring to the yellow ball her father had given her. George had tossed her gift into the duck pond, but the Highlander boy had rescued her ball. He'd waded back to shore, smiling, unperturbed at having soaked his clothes to the waist. He had handed her the ball and said, "It's a bonnie wee thing."

Walter Scott's *Lady of the Lake* was the most romantic poem she'd ever read. He made Scotland and its people sound exciting. Would the Highlands be like the poem? Full of heroic princes and dashing knights?

No. Scotland was no place to live. It was a social wilderness, a cultural desert. Her father's friends had called it the land of the barbarous tongue.

Lucy scooped Hercules into her arms. "He was a nice boy," she whispered. The dog's floppy ear twitched. "No doubt he's grown into a beastly man. We can't let Papa send us to Scotland."

• • •

Late Summer 1814, Balforss, Caithness, Highlands of Scotland

Alex stretched out on the summer grass and watched the fickle Scottish sun disappear behind a grey cloud. He pulled the painted miniature from his pocket and examined it again. If the artist was true, Lucy FitzHarris was a real beauty. Raven curls, alabaster skin, blue eyes. She looked defiant. Her brows and chin lifted as if she challenged the looker to doubt her loveliness.

When the duke's letter had arrived five months ago, memories of the day he'd spent in the gardens of Maidstone Hall had come to him quick and vivid; the pretty little girl he'd showed off for, thinking that he was very grown up, smacking her brother in the nose and wading into the pond to rescue her wee ball, expecting a tawsing and instead, making an oath to His Grace to serve and protect his daughter for life. Even now, nine years later, remembering the pride shining in his father's eyes made him flush with happiness.

A similar look had appeared on his da's face when he had agreed to the duke's proposal. Reminding him of his oath, His Grace had offered Lucy's hand, a substantial dowry, and the duke's added promise that Balforss be the exclusive wool provider for his two mills in Leads, a contract that would ensure the financial stability of Alex's family for years to come.

"Are you sure?" his father had asked. "The duke willnae hold you to an oath you made when you were eleven."

"At what age is a man obligated to abide by the oaths he makes?" Alex had smiled.

"I see your point. You are an honorable man and one who doesnae shirk his duty. Ever. But marrying for duty alone willnae make for a good marriage," his father had warned.

True, yet, how could he let his father down? Balforss needed this union. With the wool contract, his father could buy more land, more sheep. As the oldest son, he would be laird one day. If he could make this union work, he could prove himself ready to take on the yoke of responsibility. If not, if he failed, then… Well, he wouldn't fail.

His decision to marry Lucy had been difficult. At the time, he had been in love with Elizabeth Ulbster, the daughter of a distant cousin. Elizabeth had not, however, returned his affections. Even so, he had been reluctant to walk away, certain he would never love another woman as much as he loved Elizabeth.

He was surprised, therefore, at his eagerness to meet Lucy FitzHarris again. As much as possible, he maintained an appearance of relaxed indifference. Inside though, he battled with his twin demons, self-doubt and uncertainty.

The sun came out from behind the cloud. Within seconds, he was sweating. He got to his feet and replaced the miniature in his pocket. In less than two weeks, he'd look upon the real thing—real woman, he corrected himself. Alex felt a hard thump in his chest. A real woman. A wife. Bloody hell. Now that the day of reckoning was nearly upon him, doubt niggled at the back of his mind. Would they make a happy life together? Would they, over time, come to love each other? Or would Lucy, like Elizabeth, reject him?

He'd known more than one man who, after making an arranged marriage, found life with his spouse unbearable. The unhappy man often found the love he craved in the bed of a mistress. He didn't find that prospect appealing. He wanted the kind of loving marriage his parents shared. Although theirs had been an arranged marriage, according to his father, he had fallen in love with his mother the instant he saw her. Even now, after being married twenty-five years, Alex would often catch glimpses of the passion his Da had for his Ma. Would he find that kind of love with Lucy?

Probably not. She was, after all, English. She was English *and* nobility, albeit illegitimate. He would most likely be saddled with an opinionated, spoiled, and selfish wife. So used to a large household staff of servants, Lucy FitzHarris would expect to be waited upon rather than contribute to the running of Balforss. His new wife would have a rude awakening. She was about to be introduced to the Highland way of life.

LATE SUMMER 1814, MAIDSTONE HALL, KENT, ENGLAND

Lucy tried everything to change her father's mind during the months following his horrifying announcement. Tears, tirades, tantrums, declaring she would as soon throw herself into the sea than set foot in Scotland. She even tried sweetness. But nothing worked. Her father kept repeating nonsense about familial bonds, political ties, and duty.

Duty. How she hated that word. Ridiculous people were always talking about duty like it was some holy act of sacrifice. *Merde.* Duty simply meant having to do something you didn't want to do.

She retreated from London Society, refusing to attend public events, accepting no invitations to social gatherings. There would be talk, of course. Her appearance at such affairs would rekindle gossip. Perhaps, after a suitable length of time, people would forget her blunder, and she might gracefully re-enter Society. But until then…

Lucy secretly hoped Langley would appear at Maidstone Hall, declare his love, and carry her away to Bromley. Surely, when he heard of her forced marriage, he would break his engagement and save her from the savage Scot. She fantasized how Langley might rant and rail like a man possessed, then jump on his horse and ride to Maidstone Hall to rescue her just like in romantic novels. Just like James in *Lady of the Lake.*

But Langley never appeared.

A week before she was to leave for Scotland she tried one last gambit. Lucy marched into the breakfast room and announced to her father she was on a hunger strike.

She shook her head. "I would rather starve to death than move to the Highlands and marry a Scot."

Refusing breakfast, she retired to her bedroom where she ate nothing all day. Well, she ate a little, but not much—only a few crumbs of this and that, and some hot chocolate, for medicinal purposes only. After eight hours, weak from starvation, she came down to her father's study. He was relaxing on the settee, reading the paper. A kind father, an understanding father, a merciful father would see her pitiful condition and beg her forgiveness.

But no, the duke lifted his nose from *The London Times* and smiled. "Lucy, darling, if you've finished with your amateur dramatics, would you please sit down and talk to me?" He patted the spot next to him.

She was tempted to storm away, but something about her father's demeanor made her obey.

He folded his paper and set it aside. "Do you think I don't know how painful it is for you when people say unkind things?"

She shook her head slightly, her curls bouncing on her shoulders.

"I would do anything to take away that pain, to shield you from those who would harm you for sport. I know it's my fault. I should have married your mother."

"Why didn't you?"

He took her hand in his. "I wanted to, but your mother refused me."

"She didn't love you?"

"She wasn't a member of the peerage and she thought our marriage would harm me socially. You see, darling, that's what people do when they love each other. They put the needs of their loved one before their own." He swallowed hard. "I thought in time she would change her mind, but then…we ran out of time." His eyes had become watery. He put an arm around her and kissed the top of her head. "One day, when you have children, you will understand how much it hurts my heart to see you go."

"But why Scotland? It's so far away."

"I've been told the Scots judge a person by his actions, not by his pedigree. I've known Laird Sinclair for many years. He's a good man, and I think his son is equally as honorable. I believe you will be happy at Balforss."

Lucy sniffed. "What if I'm not?"

"All I ask is that you give it a try. If you don't like it there, you can come home. You can always come home, darling."

She wiped her eyes.

"What do you say? Will you try? For me?" he asked.

Lucy mustered a smile and nodded. "I'll miss you, Papa."

"And I will miss my little girl, but you, my darling Lucy, are a woman now."

...

Balforss, Caithness, the Highlands of Scotland

The night before Alex was to leave Balforss to collect his bride he paced in front of the peat fire in his father's library. He and his cousins, Declan and Magnus, were discussing the risks involved with the journey over a dram or two or three of whisky.

"We'll have no difficulty in Inverness or Caithness. But traveling through Sutherland is another matter," Alex said. "The county is rife with highwaymen."

"Displaced crofters, most of them," Magnus said. "You can thank Lady Sutherland's factor for that."

"Patrick Sellar, ye mean?" Declan asked.

"Aye. He's run most of her tenant farmers off Sutherland land to make way for pasture." Magnus shook his big head of black hair and made a grunt of disgust. "Greedy bastard."

"It's rumored Sellar burns cottages to the ground and leaves the families to starve," Declan added.

"Not rumors. Fact." Alex struggled to keep his temper in check and his voice low. "Sellar's treatment of his tenants is criminal. If we find further evidence of the man's cruelty on our journey, there's a chance we can bring the man to justice."

"What about the British soldiers?" Declan slumped down in his chair, hands clasped around his belly, his long legs stretched out, and ankles crossed. "Sellar's established a garrison in Golspie to protect Sutherland's land. We'd do best to avoid them. I hear the soldiers get bored and harass residents for entertainment."

Redcoats. Nothing more dangerous than soldiers drunk on power and whisky. "Dinnae fash. Between Uncle Fergus and us three, we'll keep Miss FitzHarris safe. Just be sure to wear your uniform. I ken Redcoats and highwaymen alike will be less inclined to trouble a party accompanied by three soldiers of the 42nd Highland Regiment of Foot." He raised his glass to Declan and Magnus.

They toasted in unison. "*Slainte.*"

The golden liquid made a slow voyage down to Alex's belly where it lit a small fire. "Miss FitzHarris will arrive aboard the *Arbroath*. Uncle Fergus will meet her at the dock in Inverness with the wagon while we wait for them on the road outside Inverness."

Magnus, well named for his size and appetite, released a soft belch. "But why wait outside the city? Why not meet her at the dock with Fergus?"

"Never mind why." His nerves bubbled up from his stomach and burned the back of his throat.

"I ken why." Declan pointed his empty whisky cup at Magnus. "He's waiting to see if she's an ugly cow. Aye, you're a canny one, Alex."

"Shut up. That's not—" He held back an overwhelming urge to smack Declan. "She's no' a cow."

"How do you know? You've never met her." Magnus

poured the last of Laird John's good whisky into Declan's cup.

"Look." He pulled the ivory miniature from his pocket and handed the tiny painted portrait to Magnus. "See for yourself."

Declan dislodged his backside from his chair for a keek over Magnus's shoulder. Their appreciative whistles pleased him.

"Oh, aye. She's a beauty all right." Declan giggled like a girl, as he always did when he was soused.

A stab of possessiveness sank into his right side. "Enough." He snatched the miniature from Magnus, rubbed away his cousin's grimy prints, and returned the treasure to his pocket. "And I have met her before." An unreasonable need to defend what wasn't even his yet pecked at his liver. "She was only nine, but she was pretty even then."

"I still dinnae ken why you willnae meet her at the dock," Magnus said.

He hedged for a moment, not wanting to reveal his plan. "I want to…see what she's like. Get to know who she is from a distance…before—" Alex ground his teeth. "Bloody hell. It's my business. Just do as you're told."

"I hope you know what you're doing," Magnus said.

They fell silent, lost in their own thoughts, staring at the dying peat fire for several minutes.

Magnus scratched his head. "I ken your da is pleased with the match. Illegitimate or not, Miss FitzHarris brings much to the union. But why is the duke so keen to give his daughter to a Scot?" He squinted like the question hurt his brain.

Irritation with his cousin dissolved instantly when he recalled the duke's letter. "His Grace believes Lucy—Miss FitzHarris—will be better off away from the stress of London Society."

"No doubt her illegitimacy has made her an easy target

for wagging tongues," Magnus said with no lack of sympathy. The big man's most appealing quality was his kind heart.

"The whisky's gone. We drank it all. You best get to bed. We'll have an early start tomorrow." Alex said his good nights and went upstairs.

But he couldn't sleep. He kept picturing what Lucy's face might look like when he met her. Dismayed, disappointed, disdainful?

Early the next morning, he stood outside the stable, anxious to be underway. He had taken leave of his mother after breakfast. Flora Sinclair, more than anyone, was enthusiastic about his impending nuptials. With his sister Maggie married and gone to live in Edinburgh, and his brother Ian away in the army, his mother was thrilled at the prospect of having someone new to blether with.

Peter, the newest and youngest groom, led Alex's horse from the stable, a huge chestnut gelding named Goliath. Alex checked the girth. Loose again. Small for a groom, Peter didn't have the strength required to pull the strap as tight as it needed to be.

"Sorry, Mr. Alex," Peter said, seeing him tighten the strap.

He placed a big hand on the dejected looking boy's narrow shoulder. "It's all right, lad. Remember, asking for help doesnae show you're weak. It shows you're canny, aye?"

"Thank you, sir."

"Go and have your breakfast, man." He gave Peter a gentle shove toward the kitchen and the boy dashed off.

Alex joined his cousins in front of the house and waited for his Uncle Fergus to bring the wagon around. John Sinclair appeared at the door. His father would want a private word with him before their departure. This was an important mission. No doubt his father was worried he might cock things up.

"Are you ready, son?"

Alex attempted to make light of his serious business. "As ready as I'll ever be." He rested a hand on his horse's rump, assuming a casual pose.

"You mind what we talked about. Make your way through Sutherland with caution. Dinnae bring attention to yourselves. And guard Lucy with your life."

"Aye. I will."

"There's still time to change your mind." His father was dead serious. "If you like, we can postpone the wedding until spring. You would have more time to get acquainted with your bride."

As usual, his father had no confidence in him. "No need. I have a better plan for getting to know her."

John swiped a hand over his face. "Son, your ideas, although creative, have on occasion, ended in calamity. What exactly do you have planned?"

"Nothing but an innocent diversion. Dinnae fash."

Chapter Two

The day the *Arbroath* took sail, Lucy felt as though she stood upon a tiny bit of England that had broken away from the mainland and floated north. Today, though, they would make port in Inverness. Then she would step ashore and say goodbye to England. Possibly forever.

Lucy braced herself on deck, the North Sea wind whipping her skirts and threatening to tear off her bonnet. She cradled Hercules in her arms. He whined, and she hugged his warm body closer, nuzzling her face in the soft fur of his floppy ears. Hercules was the only companion she'd brought with her to Scotland.

She loved Nounou Phillipa. Their parting had been tearful. The woman had been Lucy's nanny since forever, and in many ways, was the only mother she'd ever known. But Phillipa was old now—close to her pension—and not always well. The cold, wet Scottish winters would be bad for her rheumatism. The poor woman would be miserable. So, out of love, she'd left Phillipa behind. Trembling on the deck of the *Arbroath*, however, Lucy regretted her decision. She would not feel half so frightened if she had her maid by her side.

The four-day journey to Inverness had been blessed with good sailing. Lucy had spent whatever time she could on deck, as the cramped quarters below stank of unwashed humans, vomit, and ordure. It had been so awful she'd had to lie with a bundle of dried rosemary close to her nose in order to sleep at night.

Her brother George had delivered her into the hands of the ship's captain, Benedict Honeyweather, a kind, older gentleman, and a friend of her father from his days in the Royal Navy. The captain and his wife had invited her to dine at their table each night. Her hosts had provided dull conversation and even duller food, but a break from her solitude.

Inverness loomed in the distance under a grey sky. She turned up the fur-trimmed collar of her pelisse to shield her cheek from the wind. So cool in September, what would winter be like in this wretched place?

And what kind of man was this horrible Scot she would have to marry? This Alexander Sinclair? He didn't even have a title. Her father had said he was a man of honor and would be Laird of Balforss one day. She had a vague recollection of that day in her father's study when Alexander had made an oath to protect her. Would he still honor that oath?

"Beg pardon, Miss FitzHarris." A gangly young sailor named Bailey approached her. Like a puppy, he had not yet grown to match the size of his hands and feet. He pawed at his unruly hair, a fruitless endeavor in the wind. Lucy found his attempt to groom for her sake touching.

"We'll be dropping anchor in an hour. Captain wants to know if you're packed and ready to go, miss." The boy's Adam's apple bobbed up and down.

"Yes, thank you. You can tell the captain I'm ready."

She had said the same thing to her brother before she'd

boarded the *Arbroath*. Papa had sent George in his stead, explaining with a laugh that he didn't trust himself not to blubber in public when they said their good-byes. She'd seen the tears in her father's eyes and knew he spoke the truth, so she had tried doubly hard to be brave for him.

At dockside, she had braced herself for George's mischief. He would most certainly gloat over her misfortune. Yet, he hadn't, which had been odd. He had behaved very unlike himself. Even his sneer had disappeared when he'd spoken to her just before she went aboard.

"Lucy," he'd said. "I am sorry to see you go, you know. You might not believe it, but I am."

She'd waited for the sharp end of his jibe, but George's voice had softened.

"You must never regret not marrying Langley. Trust me. He is not a good fellow. He's a rather despicable person, to be honest."

She eyed George with suspicion. Why would he lie about Langley?

"May I give you some advice?" he asked with a sincerity Lucy had never heard him use before.

She nodded.

"It's something Stevens told me before they sent me off to school. He said, 'Don't let fear and anger rule you. Instead, think of this as a great adventure, and value each moment—good and bad.'" Then her brother had leaned down and given her a tender kiss on the cheek. After a moment, he'd said, "Ready?"

"I'm ready."

"Good-bye, Lucy Goosey." And he'd winked.

Lucy contemplated the exchange. Why had he said those things? Was it his way of making up for all those years of teasing and tormenting? Was he finally growing up, finally learning to behave like a gentleman? A sharp pain lanced through Lucy's chest. If it had been George's way of showing his brotherly love, she hadn't returned the sentiment. She might never again see him to put things right.

The *Arbroath* dropped anchor in Inverness Harbor just after ten in the morning. In an awkward but gallant gesture, young Bailey offered to take Lucy's gloved hand, and then guided her down the gangway to shore. His help was much appreciated for it took her a few moments to adjust to dry land. When she set Hercules down, he, too, staggered on sea legs.

"Thank you, Bailey. You have been very kind." She removed a shilling from her reticule and handed it to him.

"Thank you, miss. It's been my pleasure." Bailey stood a little taller in his ill-fitting coat. "Captain said I was to stay with you until you were met by your escort."

She scanned the docks crowded with men loading and unloading ships, foremen shouting orders, sea gulls screaming. She held an inkling of hope that Langley would have come to his senses, broken his engagement to Miss Whitebridge, and secretly stolen away to Scotland to meet her here. But there was no Langley.

Merde.

What on earth did he see in Virginia Whitebridge beyond her money? She was as timid as a mouse and terribly nearsighted, for goodness' sake.

"Miss FitzHarris?" a voice asked in a soft Scottish burr. She found the sound of it pleasing.

"I am." She turned to face the voice. Hercules barked. The little dog didn't like it when strange people got too close. "Quiet, Hercules."

"Welcome to the Highlands, Miss FitzHarris. I am Fergus Munro, Laird Sinclair's factor. I've come to escort you and your companion to Balforss."

The man made a polite gesture, more a dip of the head

than a bow. She bobbed him a curtsy. He was an older man with greying hair and skin like cured leather. Although he didn't smile, he struck her as a kind fellow.

"Hercules is my only companion."

"You traveled alone? Unescorted?" Mr. Munro's brows buckled with disapproval.

"Didn't my father tell Laird Sinclair? The wife of the ship's captain was my escort aboard the *Arbroath*. I assumed Laird Sinclair would provide a lady's maid to act as my companion."

"Forgive me, Miss FitzHarris. I brought no lady's maid, but you have my assurance, you will be in no danger. The rest of our escort will join us outside of Inverness."

"And my fiancé, Mr. Sinclair? Where is he?" she demanded.

Mr. Munro rolled his shoulders as if his jacket was too tight. "Waiting for you at Balforss, miss."

Anger rushed to her cheeks. Instead of meeting her in Inverness, her intended had sent men to collect her like baggage. Exactly what she expected from these Highland savages—a complete lack of propriety. How could her father have sent her to this place? Imagine not even bothering to meet one's betrothed when she'd traveled so far. Lucy had never been so insulted in her life.

She pressed her lips together and gave Munro a curt nod. Turning to the young sailor, Lucy felt a sudden bond with her countryman, maybe the last she would see for some time, and was reluctant to leave Bailey.

"Best of luck, miss." Bailey made a clumsy bow.

She experienced a moment of panic.

The boy met her gaze with eyes wise beyond his years and said, "You'll do fine, miss."

His sweet reassurance buoyed her spirits. Lucy bobbed him a low curtsy then followed Mr. Munro to the carriage.

She had promised her father she would try to make this work, and so she would.

Lucy's shoulders sagged. Carriage? More like a large wooden crate on wheels. Instead of a roof, the conveyance was covered with a tarp, an afterthought. Lucy doubted the fabric roof would actually shield a person from the elements. The side openings—she wouldn't call them windows—had no coverings at all. In place of elegant carriage horses, one gigantic black draft horse pulled the wagon. Lucy inwardly shook her head.

Mr. Munro hoisted her trunks onto the back of the wagon and tied them securely, then lifted the wooden case that held her bow and quiver to do the same.

"No," Lucy said, too sharply.

Mr. Munro froze.

"I'll keep that with me, if you don't mind." For some reason, she felt safer with her bow at hand. If something disastrous happened—and there was every likelihood that something bad would happen in this wilderness—she'd be armed. Mr. Munro placed the case in the wagon and helped Lucy and Hercules inside. After he latched the door, Lucy asked, "How long before we reach Balforss?"

"Maybe three days, if the weather holds. We'll stay in Golspie the night." He hopped aboard the front and whistled. The wagon lurched forward, toppling Hercules off the seat and giving him a terrible start. The tiny darling scrambled into her lap, shivering.

"It's all right, little man. Everything is all right. We're on our own now. We must be brave."

They traveled north along the coast. The appearance of homes and villages became less frequent until all traces of civilization disappeared. Through an occasional break in the trees, she spotted the sea, its surface sparkling in the sun like a carpet of diamonds. To her left, mountains towered in the distance. She'd seen paintings of landscapes such as this, but to see the mountains, the sheer magnitude of them, was something altogether different. Tremors of apprehension or excitement—she couldn't distinguish the two feelings—rippled across her arms and shoulders. This was the Highlands, a wild place.

Lucy was reminded of Harrington Wells, a retired captain, who had served in the King's army as a young man during the Jacobite Rising. He had regaled guests at one of her father's dinner parties with tales of the rebel Highlanders. Unlike other people who spoke with authority and disparaged the Highlanders, even though Lucy had known they had probably never visited Scotland, Captain Wells had a profound admiration for Highlanders, particularly their courage and fighting ability.

"Sir John Cope marched us north to Preston where we set up camp." A rapt audience leaned into Captain Well's story. *"It was to be a short foray into Scotland. A week or two, Cope told us. Arrest the troublemakers, make an example of them, put an end to the nonsense once and for all. It was hardly seen as a rebellion at that point."* Several of the men at the table made noises of agreement. *"Little did we know the lot of us were about to be on the receiving end of the Highland Charge."*

Several ladies emitted titillated oooh *sounds.*

"It was the drums we heard first. A dead sounding dum-dump…dum-dump. *The kind of sound you expect to hear at the gates of hell."* The captain's voice was as low as the guttering candles.

More gasps from the ladies. The ancient fellow was an excellent storyteller. Even the hairs on the back of her neck prickled.

"I'm not ashamed to say, I nearly soiled my britches. We scrambled out of our tents into the night. We could hear

them, but we couldn't see them. At dawn, the call came to fix our bayonets. The drums picked up pace. Thump-a-thump-a-thump-a-thump-a-thump. *Then we saw them. They boiled over the hill like devils. Running like madmen, swords drawn, hair flying in the wind, half naked, and shrieking like banshees."*

The captain paused for effect and surveyed his wide-eyed audience.

One of the ladies asked with a tremulous voice, "And then?"

Captain Wells pounded on the table, causing all the women to jump and squawk. "We ran," he bellowed, and gave a hearty laugh.

Lucy smiled at the memory. What had become of Captain Wells in the four years since that dinner party? The duke had admired the captain, having been a navy man himself, and she had always been attracted to men in uniform. Phillipa had once told her that all women liked men in uniform.

Phillipa. She sighed. *Oh, my dear Phillipa.* Something clutched at her heart and her mood turned melancholy. Was this how it would be from now on? Would the memories of home only bring her pain?

The regular clopping of the draft horse changed cadence. There was another horse...no...*horses* following them. A rider came up from behind on the right side of the wagon. He leaned down. The instant she saw him peek inside the wagon she turned her head away, her bonnet brim shielding her face. She did not like being on display. The rider continued to the front of the wagon. Out of the corner of her eye, she glimpsed a bare knee. He was wearing a kilt. Who was he? A brigand? Were they about to be robbed?

Lucy poked her head out of the opening. The rider posted alongside the wagon, exchanging words with Munro. They seemed to be on friendly terms. No need for concern.

The rider was a broad-shouldered man seated tall in his saddle. Rather than sporting the shorter cut that had become the fashion in London, his reddish-blond hair was long and plaited in a tight queue.

Two more riders wearing similar clothing and bristling with weaponry passed the wagon on her left. Were they military men? Yes, of course. Mr. Munro said the rest of their party would meet them outside the city. And they wore uniforms, not livery. Alexander Sinclair had sent Highland soldiers to escort her to Balforss. Better than mere footmen, she supposed.

She peered out of the wagon opening at the first rider. This time, she got a good look at the man's profile when he turned his head to speak to Munro. A strong chin, long straight nose, and sandy colored brows. He was what they called a ginger. He turned his head in her direction, and she sat back in the wagon seat out of view.

Why on earth is my heart pounding?

...

Alex guided their party into Golspie by nightfall and arranged for rooms above a local public house. The village of Golspie lay on the coast of the North Sea about a mile southwest of Dunrobin Castle, home of Lady Sutherland, one of the largest and most powerful landowners in all of Scotland. Alex nodded a greeting to the proprietor of Ogilvy's Tavern. Neil Ogilvy was a big man, both in size and in character. Ogilvy's wife, although not as tall, outweighed her husband by two stone or more—a testament to her good cooking, no doubt.

Having visited Ogilvy's Tavern many times, he had been treated to Mrs. Ogilvy's venison sausage in autumn, smoked fish in winter, roast lamb in spring, and hearty beef stew in summer. Declan and Magnus sat across from Alex, industriously shoveling Mrs. Ogilvy's summer specialty into their mouths.

Alex had positioned himself to allow a clear view of Lucy, who shared a table with his Uncle Fergus in the opposite corner of the tavern. She picked at her bowl of stew, occasionally hand feeding bits of meat to her wee dog. At least, he thought it was a dog. It barked like a dog, but looked like no dog he had ever seen. He speculated the animal's life might be short at Balforss. If his father's wolfhounds didn't mistake the dog for a large rabbit, a hawk would surely make off with the beastie.

Uncle Fergus made several attempts to engage Lucy in civil conversation. Each time she responded, then fell silent, seeming to prefer interaction with her pet. She called it Hercules. She must enjoy irony. That was the second discovery he'd made about her. The first discovery: she was indeed beautiful. More beautiful than her miniature, to be sure.

She held her head with the same haughty defiance she displayed in her likeness. However, the eyes portrayed in the miniature Lucy were different from the real Lucy's blue eyes. The real Lucy's eyes betrayed sadness. Alex had thought his fiancée might be contrary, difficult, even unpleasant. He hadn't prepared himself for an unhappy bride.

Magnus lifted his head from his bowl, glanced over his shoulder at Lucy, then back. "This is a terrible plan, Alex. Why not reveal yourself to her? You could be sitting at her table now, talking to her, instead of staring at the lass like a lovesick loon."

"Quiet, ye numpty." Declan elbowed Magnus. "It's like reconnaissance, is it not, Alex? He's got the advantage of watching her operate when she's off her guard."

"I ken that," Magnus said irritably. "But what happens when we get to Balforss, and you reveal yourself? Will she no' be angry about your deception?"

"In case you havenae noticed, she hasnae looked in our direction once," Alex said. "We're invisible to women of that rank. When we get to Balforss, I'll put on my breeks, Da will introduce me, and she willnae ken I was the man riding at her side for three days."

Declan laughed, but Magnus looked skeptical. At that very moment, Lucy strolled over to their table and all three shot to their feet.

"Good night, gentlemen." Her fair face displayed the haughty superiority Alex had expected.

He and his cousins mumbled a chorus of, "G'night, miss."

She inclined her head slightly to Declan and Magnus. Then turned and nodded to him. She lingered for a moment, eyes narrowing as if trying to place where she'd seen his face before. Alex's heart thumped hard in his chest. Bloody hell. Would she recognize him from nine years ago? When they were but children?

Magnus broke the connection when he said, "Good night, wee Hercules." For his attention, Lucy gave Magnus a brilliant smile.

"Thank you, Mister...?"

"Magnus Sinclair, miss. But you can call me Magnus."

"Thank you, Magnus." She swept away from the table and headed upstairs.

Once she was out of sight, Alex punched Magnus in the arm.

"Ow." Magnus rubbed away the pain. "So much for being invisible," he said, looking vindicated.

Blast Magnus.

His third discovery: be nice to Hercules and Lucy will be nice to you.

The next morning, Alex and Magnus entered the tavern room after having readied the horses for their journey. He found Lucy chatting amiably with a table of British soldiers. Bloody hell. They had to be Sutherland's men. They were the only Redcoats around these parts.

"Where the hell are Fergus and Declan? They were supposed to be looking after Lucy."

"I saw Fergus headed for the privy," Magnus said. "I imagine Declan is making time with the kitchen maid."

Alex bit back a curse and strode over to Lucy. "May I have a word, miss?" Hercules immediately started barking his head off. Alex took Lucy by the elbow and led her to a table on the far side of the tavern.

"I beg your pardon." Lucy sounded affronted. He didn't care. "Hush, Hercules. It's all right, sweetheart." She whispered a furious, "Why did you do that?"

Alex ground his back teeth together and breathed through his nose. When he was sufficiently calm, he said, "I would ask you to please refrain from conversations with strangers."

"Why? They aren't strangers. They're my countrymen. I was glad to see friendly faces."

"Oh. So you think just because someone is English, he cannae mean you harm?" Alex's words were trimmed with more sarcasm than he had intended.

"But those men are soldiers."

"My point exactly." Again, that sarcastic edge he couldn't control.

Lucy pressed her lips together. Fire raged behind her sparkling blue eyes. A fire he had ignited. A fire that heated his blood.

His fourth discovery: she was a feisty wee bizzum.

At last, she said in prim tones, "As you seem to be the person in command of our party, I will abide by your wishes. But I resent your implication that all Englishmen are untrustworthy." She handed him her wee dog. "Look after

Hercules while I see to my personal needs."

Alex fumbled with the animal wriggling in his hands. He shifted Hercules until the dog settled into a crook in his arm. Alex watched Lucy's back as she stomped through the rear door of the inn.

"Follow her," he said to Magnus.

Magnus strode out the door, shaking his head and chuckling to himself. Alex resisted the impulse to kick Magnus in the arse on his way out.

The dog gazed up at him with large bulging brown eyes and emitted a plaintive whine. He scratched the wee beastie behind the ears. "Good dog."

He took a seat at a table where he could keep an eye on the soldiers. All five cast furtive looks his way. One of the Redcoats mumbled a comment, and the others laughed uproariously. Alex narrowed his eyes at them. Only another twenty miles before his party would reach relative safety inside the borders of Caithness, Sinclair territory. These soldiers would have no authority there. Until then, his party was still a target for their devilry.

The dog wriggled in his arms again. Alex removed a piece of dried beef from his sporran and offered it to Hercules. "Here. Stop your footerin' and settle down."

After finishing the treat, Hercules stood on hind legs and placed his forepaws on Alex's chest. The dog craned his little domed head up, bobbed tail wagging his whole body, and licked him on the chin. He smiled involuntarily.

The swish of a woman's skirts announced Lucy's approach. "I suppose if Hercules likes you, you can't be all bad." She sat across from Alex before he could rise.

Through the yeasty miasma of peat smoke and fried sausage, he caught her delicate fragrance—salty, citrusy, and rosemary.

His fifth discovery: she smelled nice, like something one

would want to taste.

He yanked his thoughts from the carnal back to conversation. "I suppose you think we Highlanders are all savages and barbarians?"

"I'm sure you care little about what I think." In a lowered tone, as if speaking to herself, she added, "No one seems to care about my opinion."

Mrs. Ogilvy placed bowls of porridge in front of them. "I'll be back with some ale."

Lucy stared down at her bowl. "What is this?"

"Parritch," Alex said. She gave him a blank look. "Cooked oats. Eat up. It's good for you."

"I'm not very hungry this morning."

He salted his porridge before taking a bite. Hercules wriggled in his lap, desperate to get a sniff. "That's no' for you, ye wee gomeril." He swallowed a spoonful and stole a glance at Lucy through his eyelashes. "You didnae wish to come to Scotland?"

"I hardly had a choice in the matter. In any case, it's none of your business."

His sixth discovery: she didnae want to be here. Which meant she didnae want to marry him.

Lucy furrowed her delicate eyebrows. "What is your name?"

"Sinclair."

Her eyebrows lifted and Alex was quick to add, "We're all three Sinclairs—my two cousins and I. It's a common name in Caithness."

Her brow relaxed again. "Oh. I see."

Throughout their trip, Lucy had maintained a cool countenance. He was surprised when he saw her hands tremble. They betrayed nervousness behind her thin veneer of calm.

"You neednae be afraid," Alex said.

"I'm not afraid." She was too quick to respond and seemed to realize it. "I'm not afraid," she said again. "I'm tired. I didn't sleep well."

He ought to tread carefully. He had piqued her anger, antagonized her with his questions. He gave her a lopsided grin. Perhaps an apology might mollify her. "I'm sorry. I didnae mean to be so harsh about the Redcoa—erm, soldiers," he said. "But I'm responsible for your safety, ye ken."

"I will tell my fiancé you executed your duties admirably." Again, to herself, "As he didn't care enough to attend to my safety himself."

Her words hit him like a blow to the chest. She was offended. No, worse—hurt. Her fiancé had not come to escort her. Christ. He was an ass. Of course, she would expect her fiancé would meet her. And he *had,* but how could she know?

This was his doing, or his undoing, unless he ended his ruse and set things straight. If he didn't reveal himself now, everything he said from here on would be a lie. If he told her now, as he knew he should, sparks would fly, but he could pass the deception off as a mere misunderstanding.

Conscious of the soldiers on the other side of the room, now would not be a good time to have a heated disagreement with his charge. And, in any case, she had roused his curiosity. He couldn't resist a few more minutes of this delicious conversation with Lucy.

"Are you fashed about meeting him?" he asked.

Lucy looked up at him, her eyes sharp, hawklike. "What does fashed mean?"

"Oh, erm, fretful. Worried."

She relaxed back in her chair. "No. My father assured me he is a decent man. He once made an oath to protect me with his life."

So, she remembers my oath.

She tilted her head and asked, "Do you know him well?"

"Aye. I ken him." Not a complete untruth. He knew himself very well.

"Why didn't he meet me in Inverness?" There was no guile in her question. It was an almost child-like appeal. He rubbed at the plucking sensation in his chest.

"Erm...he's a very busy man." He cursed himself for saying such a stupid thing. He had just implied her fiancé didn't think she was important enough to merit his attention.

Lucy emitted a disgusted huff. She looked down at her small hands, soft and unmarked by hard work. "Is he the kind of man who would beat his wife?"

"God, no," Alex said, shocked that she would harbor that fear. "No, miss. He would never raise a hand to a woman."

She heaved a deep sigh of relief. "Good." Her lips pursed. She was preparing another question. He waited. Her questions revealed her thoughts and fears. They fascinated him.

"Is he, um, disfigured in any way?"

Alex burst out laughing and Lucy flinched. "Sorry. Sorry." He was a heel for having startled her. "No, miss."

"Is he handsome, would you say?"

"Dinnae ken. He looks a lot like me." It was a reckless thing to say, but so worth her brilliant smile.

"Oh. Good."

Seventh discovery: *she thinks me handsome.*

Alex tensed when the soldiers rose to leave. As they filed past, they each bid Lucy good-bye, bowing and murmuring, "G'day, miss." She nodded pleasantly at them.

The last soldier, their captain, paused and said, "That's a ferocious dog you've got there, Scotchy. Take it rat hunting, do you?"

Alex shot to his feet, blood surging through his arms and legs, ready to take the insolent bastard apart. His hand flew to the hilt of his sword at the same time as the soldier's.

"Gentlemen," Lucy shouted. "Behave yourselves."

Alex glared at the mirror image of his contained rage. He remembered his father's caution not to draw attention to their party and checked himself.

The soldier broke away first. "I do beg your pardon, miss." He made a deep bow before turning on his heel and marching out of the tavern.

Had he been alone, Alex would have beaten the man bloody and gladly suffered the consequences. However, his primary charge was his betrothed's safety. When he had recovered his breathing, he thought, *now is the time I should tell her who I really am*. But she looked far too irritated with him. *Best wait.*

Mrs. Ogilvy returned to their table with two tankards of ale. "Something wrong with the parritch, lass?"

"No. It's delicious." Lucy lied for the woman's benefit. A kindness Alex appreciated. Only she wasn't very good at lying. "I...I just..."

"The travel's curdled her wame," Alex said, offering a plausible excuse for Lucy.

"Poor thing." Mrs. Ogilvy's voice was laden with genuine sympathy. After she turned and walked away, Lucy mouthed the words *thank you* to him.

The moment felt intimate. He liked the feeling. Very much. And he would have lingered there indefinitely, but Magnus poked his fat head through the door and cleared his throat.

"I must check on the others. We'll be going soon." Alex handed back her pet. "He's a bonnie wee thing." She gave him her dazzling smile. His ears flamed. God, he hated that he had no control over that aspect of his anatomy. And what the hell would she do when he told her *he* was her fiancé?

...

"Bonnie wee thing," she murmured to herself as she watched the tall Scot leave the public house. The Highlander boy who had come to Maidstone Hall had used that phrase. That's why she had taken a liking to him.

The Highlander boy with the tawny-colored hair and freckles was now a man. A man she would soon marry. The tall Sinclair escort—he hadn't offered his Christian name—had the same coloring as the boy. Light red, almost blond hair, and blue-grey eyes. He'd said her fiancé looked a lot like him. The tall Sinclair was very handsome. If she were honest with herself, she wished Alexander Sinclair looked exactly like the tall one. That would suit her just fine.

She lifted the tankard of ale and sipped. She'd never drunk ale for breakfast, but the brew tasted smooth and seemed to settle her stomach, or her wame, as Mr. Sinclair had put it.

Back on the road again, the wagon jolted and jostled her until her teeth hurt. Sometimes the going was so rough she had difficulty staying seated. Tiny Hercules had no easier time, rolling off her lap a half dozen times. During the short stretches of smoother terrain, Lucy thought of Maidstone Hall, her brother George, Nounou Phillipa, and Papa. Her father would be in his library, reading the paper at this time of day. Was he thinking about her? Was he wondering if she was safe? Would he write to her?

A pang of loneliness prickled the corners of her eyes. Papa said she could always go home, but how? She'd never fit in. Even if she acquired a title through marriage, she'd never be accepted by London Society. Papa had said as much. But it was clear from the start, Scotland was no place for her. These people had no manners, no sense of propriety, no knowledge of what was considered civil behavior. She hugged Hercules tighter and wondered if she'd ever find a place where she felt accepted, admired, at home.

She hadn't slept well the night before at the tavern. The mattress had been lumpy and smelly, and she'd been plagued by a recurring nightmare in which Langley and Virginia Whitebridge were laughing at her. When she would turn to run, a crowd of faces would block her way, all laughing, taunting, making rude remarks. There was no way to escape her humiliation. Twice she had awoken, calling for Nounou Phillipa. Each time, Hercules had comforted her with his little body.

The wagon slowed to a stop. She heard unfamiliar voices. Curious, Lucy leaned out the window opening to see what was amiss. The tall Sinclair man had dismounted to talk to a family of five—a man, two children under the age of ten, and a woman carrying an infant. She couldn't make out their conversation. They all seemed to be speaking another language. Gaelic?

Magnus stopped his horse near her window and dismounted. "It's all right, miss."

"What are they saying?"

"They were ordered off their land. When they refused to leave, men set fire to their cottage. The family barely escaped with their lives."

"What have they done to be treated thusly?"

"Nothing. They're not the first to be cast out of their home. The whole of Sutherland County is being converted to pasture for sheep farming."

"Why?"

"Wool brings in more money than tatties and neeps."

"What?"

"Sorry. Potatoes and turnips."

"Where will they go?" Lucy asked.

"They're headed for a rocky patch of shoreline called Helmsdale. It's where many of Sutherland's homeless end up."

Lucy let out a sigh of relief. "Thank goodness they have a place to make a new home."

"I've seen Helmsdale, miss. It's a place of misery and poverty." Magnus's cold and empty voice gave her the shivers.

The baby cried, a weak, pitiful sound. The two children looked bone thin and wretched. The tall Scot reached into a bag hanging from his saddle, retrieved a cloth wrapped bundle, and handed it to the husband. Food. The woman blessed the tall one.

His gesture of sympathy spurred her into action. She must do something. Papa would help were he in her position. She opened her reticule and counted out ten pence.

"Magnus. Give these to the family. Tell them it's a gift from…from the Duke of Chatham."

Gleaming white teeth shone through Magnus's burly black beard. "That's kind of you, miss," he said, and strode over to the family. As Magnus passed on her gift, the tall Sinclair fastened his eyes on her and made an approving nod. Good. She'd done the right thing.

Moments later, the wagon rattled past the family, their stunned faces turned up to her. She made a mental note to tell her future husband of this injustice once she reached Balforss. Perhaps he would do something to help the people of Helmsdale. Or was Alexander Sinclair the kind of laird who treated his tenants similarly?

Chapter Three

Alex relaxed fractionally once they were well within the borders of Caithness. They stopped for mid-day meal in Latheron, a village situated at the crossroad to Wick and Thurso. After their dinner, they would head north toward Balforss. Any chance of arriving there by nightfall had passed. They would have to make camp along the way.

Lucy FitzHarris had probably never slept rough in her life. He was rather looking forward to the temper tantrum she would undoubtedly throw when she found out. His pretty bride's protest might prove entertaining. And yet, she had surprised him, even moved him, with her generosity toward the Sutherland family. At least she acknowledged her privilege through acts of charity. That weighed heavily in her favor.

He paused inside the tavern door of the Latheron Inn. After his eyes adjusted to the dark interior, he forgot how to breathe—Lucy was talking to Patrick Sellar, Lady Sutherland's factor. He stood motionless, his right hand twitching above the hilt of his sword while the rat-faced bastard smiled and fawned over his woman. Sellar's dull black eyes flicked his way. When Lucy turned to look at him, her delicate eyebrows drew together for a moment. Then she turned to Sellar again.

"Shite," said Uncle Fergus, who had materialized beside him. "Best bide here, lad. Sellar may give you away. I'll see to Lucy."

Beads of sweat broke out on Alex's brow. Uncle Fergus took Lucy's elbow, made excuses, and then led her away from Sellar with far more grace than he had demonstrated with the soldiers this morning. He scrutinized Lucy's behavior from afar for signs Sellar had revealed his identity. When Fergus and Lucy were seated at a table in the far corner of the tavern, and he was certain he hadn't been betrayed, he made straight for Sellar.

The man greeted him with a false smile. "Mr. Sinclair, I believe felicitations are in order." How could a man make such words sound hateful?

"We met with one of your tenants on the road this morning. Said you burned them out of their home. Left them with nothing."

Sellar shrugged and sat down to his meal. "Likely a disgruntled crofter seeking sympathy by making up outrageous stories of my cruelty." The rat-faced Sellar bent to his plate and shoveled a large chunk of sausage dripping with gravy into his foul mouth.

"If I find their accusations true, I'll—"

"What? What will you do, Sinclair? What exactly will you do?" Sellar challenged.

What Alex wanted to do was find a way to make the man suffer—preferably in front of an audience of Sellar's victims. But he had promised his father he would adhere to the law on this matter. That meant evidence. Testimony. Trial. Things they did not yet have.

"I'll make you pay dearly for your crimes, sir."

"I've heard similar threats from your father." Sellar shoved another piece of sausage into his mouth and talked around the food. "I don't take kindly to threats, laddie." He wiped his greasy chin with the back of his hand. "When I'm threatened, I get angry. And when I get angry, bad things happen."

Alex placed a palm on the table and lowered his head to Sellar's level, taking in his stench and the rosewater scent Sellar used to hide it. "Then take what I say not as a threat but a promise." His voice, low and deadly, rolled out of him like the tide. "So help me God, you will answer for your treachery if I have to take you down myself."

Sellar smiled, displaying a mouthful of rotting teeth. "You have a lovely little bride, Sinclair. Mind her carefully. The roads are crawling with highwaymen. I wouldn't want any harm to come to the Duke of Chatham's daughter."

The veiled threat to his woman was more than he could stand. Sellar must die.

Unfortunately, Magnus pulled him away from the table before Alex's fist found the bastard's face. "Not here, man. Not with Miss Lucy watching," Magnus rumbled into his ear.

He shook Magnus off and held onto his rage long enough to make it out of the tavern without striking anyone. Declan, unaware of what had transpired inside, was the unfortunate recipient of Alex's wrath.

"We're leaving as soon as the lass finishes her meal!" he shouted. "And for Christ's sake, keep her away from Sellar!"

• • •

A disagreeable-looking gentleman named Mr. Sellar introduced himself to Lucy as the manager of Lady Sutherland's estate. He expressed his fond wishes for a happy wedding. She held a handkerchief to her nose, a discreet attempt to shield herself from the man's body odor.

"My dear Miss FitzHarris. What a pleasure to meet you. I must have you 'round to lunch with Lady Sutherland."

She recognized the name Sutherland. Magnus had said those unfortunate people who lost their house were from Sutherland.

Mr. Sellar prattled on, "I had the honor of meeting your father some years back. It was at the Barley Corn, a gentleman's club, I think...." And on, and on, and on. His fawning behavior—the tilt of his head, the elongation of each vowel, the insipid smile—was so tiresome, she thought she might actually yawn in the man's face. She was about to extricate herself when he spotted someone behind her and said, "Ah, there's your man, Alex, now."

Lucy turned toward the doorway, her heart stumbling a few beats. Had her intended come to meet her halfway?

No. It was only the tall one. Apparently, he hadn't exaggerated when he'd said Alexander Sinclair looked a lot like him. Mr. Sellar had mistaken the tall Sinclair for her soon-to-be husband.

Merde.

The tall Sinclair's face had darkened. What could he be angry about this time? Mr. Sellar wasn't a soldier. He wasn't English. He wasn't even a stranger. Indeed, he seemed to be well acquainted with the Sinclair family.

Before Lucy could correct Mr. Sellar for his mistake, Mr. Munro appeared and said, "Pardon us, sir. We must eat and be on our way."

Happy to be rescued, Lucy followed Mr. Munro to a table on the opposite side of the tavern room. She was relieved to be away from the tedious man, but something about the recent exchange pestered her. She pretended to listen to Mr. Munro's nattering, all the while replaying scenes in her head.

"Ah, there's your man, Alex, now," Mr. Sellar had said.

"He looks a lot like me," Mr. Sinclair had said. "Bonnie wee thing." Tawny red hair, just like the boy's...

The truth crystallized all at once and her entire body went up in flames. The blasted Scot had played her the fool. Lucy said a very bad word.

"I beg your pardon, miss?"

She struggled to contain herself. Every organ inside her body shook with the need to sink a dagger into the heart of the tall Sinclair, Alexander Sinclair, the lying bastard who would be her husband.

"Are you all right, miss?" Mr. Munro asked.

Fortunately, Mr. Munro didn't seem to notice that she had incinerated before his eyes. Taking some calming breaths, she regained her noble demeanor and gave him a brittle smile that hurt her cheeks and made her teeth feel funny.

"I'm fine, thank you. Perfectly fine."

...

Alex waited outside atop Goliath, anxious to leave this place, this trap. Lucy exited the tavern with Uncle Fergus. When Magnus offered to hold Hercules and help her into the wagon, the act triggered a jealousy in Alex that only added to the churning sensation in his bowels. He shot a look at Magnus hot enough to melt the bampot. Magnus fired back an I-ken-how-to-treat-a-lady look.

Magnus would pay for that.

He was about to tell him as much when Lucy leaned her head out of the wagon. "Oh, Mr. Sinclair."

All three Sinclair men swiveled their heads in answer to her call.

"Magnus, I mean." She favored Magnus with another one of her sweet, dimpled smiles. Alex knew what it felt like to be on the receiving end of that smile. That she gave what should have been exclusively his to Magnus made him want to remove his cousin's bollocks with a dull knife.

Magnus trotted back to the wagon, all ears and bright eyes. Christ, the man was like a dog performing tricks for his mistress. "Yes, miss?"

"Would you be so kind as to ask the cook for a spare bone for Hercules?"

"With pleasure, miss." Magnus tossed a smug grin his way before dashing back into the tavern.

"Be quick about it," Alex shouted. "We're late as it is."

While they waited for his doaty cousin to complete his errand, he spotted a familiar figure strutting toward him and cursed under his breath. Liam Ulbster, stepbrother of his former sweetheart Elizabeth, and stepson to his mother's beloved cousin Diana Ulbster. He did not like Liam Ulbster. Liam was a bawfaced bastard with very little substance to his character.

"Alex." Liam's special talent was the ability to smile with his mouth full of shit.

Oh God, will this day never end?

He sighed and remained in his saddle, with the hope his exchange with Liam would be brief. "What brings you to Golspie, cousin?"

"Your wedding, of course," Liam said. "My parents and I have returned from London for the single delight of attending your nuptials. You'll be pleased to know my lovely stepsister Elizabeth will be there as well."

Alex slumped in his saddle. He hadn't considered how he would feel upon seeing Elizabeth again. Would his previous feelings for her resurface? "We look forward to your visit," he lied.

"Is that your bride in the carriage? You must introduce us."

Liam's request brought him to full attention. The

mingin' clotheid would expose his identity to Lucy and ruin everything. "No!"

• • •

Liam startled at Alex's outburst. What the devil had gotten into the loon?

"I apologize, but she's requested solitude," Alex said. "She's exhausted from the trip, ye ken. I beg your indulgence."

"I understand, cousin," Liam said, bowing.

The giant they called Magnus barreled out of the inn with a bone that looked larger than the man's forearm. He handed the ghastly thing through the wagon opening to its passenger.

Perhaps Alex's fiancé is a dog?

Alex nodded a curt farewell and spurred his horse on. The wagon rattled forward with the two other Sinclair men trailing behind. He waited until the Balforss party was well down the road and then strolled into the Latheron Inn. He found the man he was looking for finishing his meal.

"You're late," Patrick Sellar said without looking up from his plate.

Liam attempted to lighten the moment. He preferred pleasant over terse conversation, even if he had to pretend. "I do apologize, but I was detained by my stepsister. She insisted on accompanying me as she wanted to visit a dressmaker here in town."

"Sit down."

Apparently, Sellar did not wish to participate in pleasantries. He wiped off the chair opposite the man and lowered himself into it. "I must say I'm very curious. What is it you so urgently needed to speak with me about?"

"You owe a great sum to a certain moneylender in London."

He felt his public face vanish for a second, then recovered.

Keeping his tone light, to disguise his irritation, he said, "I don't see how that is any concern of yours, sir."

"Oh, but it is my concern. My employer, Lady Sutherland, has purchased your debt. You now owe *her* a great sum of money." Sellar leaned back in his chair and gave Liam his full attention.

"Why would she do such a thing?"

"Lady Sutherland requires a favor of you."

He tugged at his collar. The stock tied around his neck was suffocating. "May I ask what kind of favor?"

"It's very simple, really." Sellar used his sleeve to wipe the grease from his fat lips.

The company of this exceedingly unpleasant man made Liam's gorge rise, but he listened. Carefully.

A quarter of an hour later, he climbed inside his black lacquered carriage. He flopped down on the leather bench across from his stepsister Elizabeth and rapped on the roof, signaling the coachman to drive on.

"What did Mr. Sellar want with you?" Elizabeth asked. She made a face like she smelled something noxious and flicked open her fan. His stepsister hated him. She'd always made that clear.

"Nothing much. I saw Alex on my way into the tavern. He was escorting his intended to Balforss for the wedding."

"Did you see her?" Her eyes sharpened on him.

"I caught a glimpse. Pretty little thing. No comparison to you, my beauty. But our dear cousin, Alex, seems to have rebounded nicely after your rejection. Marrying the Duke of Chatham's daughter. My, my."

"*Illegitimate* daughter," she corrected.

"No matter. I doubt very much the wedding will take place."

"What makes you say that?"

"You remember Lord Langley?"

"Doesn't he belong to your club of deviant layabouts?" Her upper lip curled into an ugly sneer.

Liam cocked a knowing eyebrow at her, hoping to elicit a response. "Yes. The viscount is a member of my private social circle. We enjoy our pleasures of the flesh on occasion."

Elizabeth crinkled her nose again. He loved to provoke his stepsister. He especially liked the way the tops of her breasts pinkened when she was riled.

"So?"

"Apparently, Miss FitzHarris is mad for Langley and Langley is mad for her."

"Who on earth told you that?" She pulled a perfumed handkerchief from her reticule and held it to her nose as their carriage jangled past a pig farm.

"Patrick Sellar. Just now."

"Nonsense. Lucy FitzHarris made a laughingstock of herself over him. He never made any overtures toward her. In fact, last I heard, he was engaged to marry the very dull Miss Whitebridge and her piles of money." She shifted away from the open window of the carriage and fanned herself.

"Well, you are mistaken. Lord Langley is Lady Sutherland's relation, and she is quite fond of him. According to Sellar, he's desperate to stop the wedding and retrieve Miss FitzHarris. He's turned to Lady Sutherland for help and is on his way to Dunrobin Castle as we speak. I have agreed to lend a hand."

"I see. And what do you get in return for your *assistance,* pray tell?"

"Why, Elizabeth, you wound me. I'm simply helping out my dear friend."

His stepsister burst out laughing. "That's the biggest lie I've ever heard you tell." She narrowed her eyes. "You forget I know you well, stepbrother. You don't have an altruistic bone in your body."

"Lady Sutherland has requested a favor of me for which I will be paid handsomely." He hedged for a moment before adding, "And I need your help."

"Ha. I knew it. You need something from me." Contempt dripped from Elizabeth's pink lips. God, she was gorgeous. "What do I get in return?"

He leaned back, wondering how much he dared disclose. He'd left London under the pretense of attending the wedding of Alex Sinclair and Lucy FitzHarris. In truth, he'd fled the city to avoid his creditors. His reckless gambling, extravagant lifestyle, and eccentric sexual appetite had overreached his meager allowance. If his father discovered his shameful pecuniary situation, he would cut him off entirely. He was in a delicate position, to say the least.

Lady Sutherland's offer to forgive his debt in exchange for a simple service was the answer to his financial woes. Success could set him right again. But he needed his stepsister's help, and she would be loath to help him without sufficient inducement. Fortunately, Liam had the proverbial carrot in his breast pocket.

He edged forward in his seat and placed his hand on her knee. "I found your letters."

Elizabeth slapped his hand away with her fan. "Lying lout. I don't believe you." Doubt rippled across her brow.

He had planned to use her letters to extort a different kind of favor, but they would do nicely for his new purpose. "I thought Lord Toremount was a married man," he said, feigning confusion.

Elizabeth's eyes widened when he withdrew her letter from his coat pocket and waved it at her. She tried to snatch it from him, but he held the letter out of her reach.

"You thieving little worm. Give it back or I swear I'll—"

"You'll hurt me? Oh, dear heart, do you promise?"

She lifted a slender booted foot and aimed for his groin.

Before she connected, Liam grabbed her ankle and held her still.

"You're a feisty little minx today, aren't you?" In vain, she struggled to free her foot. "Relax my pet. I will return your letters to you as soon as we finish our errand of love." She stopped squirming, and he released her ankle. He found his stepsister particularly attractive when she was agitated. Her lovely eyebrows pinched together and her sweet pink lips pursed into a pretty pout. Even now, he could feel his todger pressing against the front of his britches.

"What do you mean, errand of love?" she spat.

"It's simple, really. Langley has written a letter to Lucy, declaring himself. Upon our arrival at Balforss, you will deliver the letter to Lucy, and I will deliver Lucy to Langley."

"You're going to steal Alex Sinclair's bride? Have you lost your mind? The man will surely kill you."

"Not if you reignite Alex's interest. One kiss from you and he will happily forget his mousy bride."

Elizabeth tilted her head and tapped the tip of her fan on her chin. "Easily done, I suppose. But what if I don't want to?"

"Fine. I'm certain there are plenty of people who would love to know about your most intimate affair with Lord Toremount."

"I hate you."

"I absolutely adore you, dear one." The tops of her full breasts pressed against the front of her stays. He wanted very much to fondle them. Liam struggled to maintain focus. "Flirting with our cousin shouldn't be a chore. I thought at one time you entertained the idea of marrying Alex Sinclair."

"I did until I realized the fool wanted me to leave London and live with him among the peasants and sheep." A new thought seemed to occur to her. "What if Lucy FitzHarris doesn't want to be delivered to Langley? What if she's unwilling to leave Balforss? What then?"

"Don't be thickheaded. You think she would choose Highland gentry over the future Earl of Bromley? By all accounts, Lucy FitzHarris is in love with Langley. I don't think we'll have any difficulty. Besides," he gave her an impish grin. "It'll be fun."

The crack of the driver's whip made Liam's todger stand at attention. Interesting how his appetite for carnal pleasures soared whenever he visited the Highlands. It must be something in the water that made men want to rut like animals.

He leaned back in his seat to relieve the pressure in his lap. "Tell me, dear heart, you wouldn't feel like lifting your skirts, would you?"

Elizabeth's boot connected with his right shin.

"Ow!"

Chapter Four

"Nasty, filthy, kilt-wearing Scot."

Lucy scooped Hercules into her lap, her arms and shoulders shaking from the effort of disguising her fury. Finally alone, she could bare her teeth to her anger.

"He's a beastly, beastly man and we hate him."

All of them. *All of them*—Munro, Magnus, and the one that looked like a ferret—they were all in on Alex's piece of mischief.

"Scottish bastards."

How they must have laughed when her back was turned, a jaw-tightening, tooth-grinding thought.

She had experienced anger before—anger at her brother for teasing her, anger at her father for sending her to this vulgar place—but never, never, *never* had she known the full force of her fury until today.

Oh, yes. She knew well how to deal with foolish boys and their knavery. She would get her due. She would make them pay. Nothing short of seeing Alex Sinclair grovel would douse the fire raging in her chest. She suddenly felt a murderous kinship with Lady Macbeth.

"We wait, Hercules. And when the time is right, we get even." Hercules licked her hand, and she stroked her tiny spaniel's domed head and smiled. "Mr. Alexander Sinclair wishes me to believe he's a common soldier at my service and we shall treat him as such."

The next stretch of road was all uphill, and the going was slow. When they reached the summit, Mr. Munro stopped the wagon to water and rest the horses. Lucy leaned out of the wagon and called to the tall Scot. "Oh, Mr. Sinclair."

Alex trotted to the wagon, his face open, smiling. Handing him her wiggling pup, she said, "Take Hercules for me. He needs to do his business."

His jaw dropped. "Erm...certainly." A few minutes later, he returned and handed Hercules through the wagon window. "Here's your wee beastie." He started to walk away.

"A moment, please." She handed him her boots. "Clean these. I'm afraid the mud may ruin the leather."

A pained expression crossed the Scot's face. He poked the inside of his cheek with his tongue then responded with a tight, "Right then. Straight away." The other men snickered and Alex shouted a sharp, "Quiet."

Yes, I will have my revenge.

When he returned with her clean boots, she extended a dainty stocking-covered foot through the wagon door and waited. When he made no move, she glanced up. Alex stood motionless, examining her with cool grey eyes like a wolf considering its prey. *Have I gone too far?*

Lucy smiled prettily and batted her lashes. He gave a heavy sigh that could only be described as defeat and bent to one knee. His broad shoulders flexed and bunched as he slipped on her left, then her right boot, and tied the laces. She had the handsome soldier, now her lackey, right where he belonged—at her feet.

Sweet satisfaction.

Their party did not stay at an inn on the second night of their journey because, as Mr. Munro informed her, no inn existed between Latheron and Balforss. Apparently, they had left civilization behind altogether. When Mr. Munro added that they would be sleeping rough, she experienced a feeling dangerously close to full-blown panic. For the first time in her life, she would urinate in the woods and sleep in her clothes out of doors, under the stars with strange men.

Mr. Munro relieved some of her concern when he demonstrated how the benches inside the wagon flipped open to create a sleeping pallet. Thank goodness. She would have some degree of privacy while sleeping. Nevertheless, Lucy struggled to tamp down the fear threatening to leak out through the cracks in her facade.

The men chose a quiet glen surrounded by a thick stand of pines for their encampment. She and Hercules strolled the clearing to work out the aches and pains in her legs and bottom. Magnus and Mr. Munro set about supper preparations while the other two Sinclairs—the one with the sharp black eyes and the bastard who would be her husband—collected firewood from the edge of the forest lining the clearing. When Alex returned to the fire pit with an armload of wood, Lucy set to putting the arrogant son-of-a-bitch through his paces.

"Oh, Mr. Sinclair, be a dear and retrieve my largest trunk from the back. I want to wear my yellow bonnet in the morning."

Alex sighed and dipped his head, most likely so she wouldn't see his exasperation. After he had untied the trunks, he waited while she removed her yellow bonnet. Then he returned the trunks to the back of the wagon, retied them, and stood before her only mildly winded.

"I've changed my mind. I believe I'll wear my light blue bonnet."

He repeated the exercise, his lips pressed in a thin grim line.

She watched him, hands on her hips, foot tapping.

Task completed, he bowed.

She gave him her sweetest smile. "I would like my tea now."

His shoulders hunched up around his ears. Was that a growl she heard before he spun and marched away?

Magnus and Declan broke into fits of laughter. Alex barked out, "You two bampots, shut up and see to the fire, now."

"And a little something for Hercules to eat, if you please," she called.

He whipped around, anger clearly blazing in his eyes. He pointed a finger at her. "May I remind you, Miss FitzHarris, I am not your personal—"

"Oh, but you are..." Lucy lifted a victorious eyebrow. "*Alex.*"

She resisted the urge to laugh when his face went perfectly blank. He looked so stupid with his jaw agape.

"Close your mouth, Alex."

...

"Bloody hell." His oxters instantly soaked his shirt with sweat and his mouth went dry. She knew. Sellar must have told her this afternoon. Instead of causing a great stramash in the tavern, the conniving wench had waited, plotted her revenge, and then exacted retribution by humiliating him in front of his men. He would have laughed at her cheek if he weren't so horrified by her cunning.

Declan and Magnus had fallen silent, frozen still as rabbits, no doubt waiting for the storm to break. Shit. What should he do?

Apologize to her, you idiot.

"Lucy, I'm—" Alex's voice stalled out when he saw her mouth pinched shut and bloody murder in her eyes.

She picked up her skirts and headed for him. The closer she got, the sicker he felt. He waited to meet her fury. Without a word, she wound up and slapped him. He saw the blow coming but didn't bother bracing himself. Just took it. He deserved her ire. Christ, he'd earned it. She must have put her entire weight into the slap, too, because it stung like hell and left his ear ringing.

"I'm truly—"

"Don't say another word. Don't speak to me. Don't look at me. Don't even come near me, you lying knave."

He swallowed audibly. The deadly calm in her voice actually frightened him for a moment. Lucy marched back toward the wagon. He was about to start after her when Uncle Fergus appeared at his elbow.

"Best do as she says, lad, and leave her be. Trust me, there'll be no reasoning with a woman in that state of mind. You can crawl to her on your knees tomorrow as you know very well you should." Fergus slapped him on the back harder than was necessary.

When Alex returned to the fire, Magnus mumbled, "I told you so."

"Shut up."

His cousin was right. His ridiculous ruse had backfired on him, hurting not only him but Lucy as well. Yet, however ill conceived, his plan had worked. He had witnessed her cope with her new life for two days under difficult conditions at best. Yes, she had been, at times, an intolerant, spoiled, and demanding woman. But she had also been a gracious and generous lass of great dignity. He was the one guilty of bad behavior. Sick with shame, he knew he wouldn't be able to sleep until he made things right with Lucy.

Declan handed him his flask of whisky.

"Thanks." He took a long pull and let the golden liquid slide down to his gullet. He wanted to be drunk.

Declan squinted at something. "What's she doing now?"

Lucy withdrew a child-size bow from her wooden case, bent it against her knee and strung it, then collected a fistful of arrows. Jesus God. Was she that angry?

Magnus stepped forward. "I ken she's going to shoot you with her bitty bow."

...

Merde.

Slapping Alex had been enormously satisfying, but Lucy suspected she had hurt herself more than the Scot. She ducked behind the wagon where no one could witness her agony and shook her right hand delicately. When the throbbing in her fingers subsided, she took a deep breath and rolled her temper into a manageable-sized ball—like a fist inside her belly.

Hercules whined at her feet. She collected him off the grass, hugged him to her breast, and said, "We showed him, didn't we, *mon cher*? He'll think twice the next time he tries to play a trick on us."

There was plenty of daylight left. Why not entertain herself with some target practice? Besides, these Scots probably looked upon her as a helpless woman who sat indoors all day doing needlework or some such nonsense. Best put them straight.

Lucy set aside her bonnet. She took out her case and removed the lady-sized bow custom-made for her. With practiced ease, she strung it, tested it, and gathered a handful of arrows. She glanced back at the four men now grouped together around the fire. Good. She had an audience.

She chose one arrow and stabbed the others into the soft ground at her feet. A tree trunk approximately twenty yards away made a suitable target. She smoothed the fletching on her arrow and notched it. Drawing back, she whispered, "Nock…draw…loose." The arrow hit its mark and vibrated. She turned. The men stared back open-mouthed. She drew another arrow and breathed again. "Nock…draw…loose." A satisfying *ffftss* sound and the arrow stuck barely an inch above the first. "Bulls-eye," she whispered. This time, the men burst into applause, all but Alex, who was pretending not to look.

"That's a pretty shot, lassie," called Magnus.

She sucked in her bottom lip so they wouldn't see how pleased she was. Lucy notched a third arrow with the intention of putting aside all doubt as to her superior bowmanship when she saw movement in the trees.

She lowered her bow and called over her shoulder. "Do you see something in the wood?"

"What, miss?"

"There." She pointed. "I know I saw something move."

A thunderous crashing and thrashing resounded from the wood. Animals? Men?

Alex yelled, "Lucy, run!"

His call spurred her heart to a gallop. Cracks of gunfire echoed in the glen followed by plumes of smoke. There were men in the trees firing on her party. But why? Why would anyone do such a thing?

The metallic *zing* of swords being drawn rang through the air. The Sinclair men made horrible screeching, howling sounds—sounds that weren't human, sounds that split the night and made the hair on her arms stand on end.

Hercules crouched at her feet, barking like a maniac. Two men burst through the smoke and ran straight at her, one with a sword held high. Dear Lord, they were going to kill her. A blur of movement from her left, and she saw Alex engage one of them, his sword flashing and *clang-clang-clanging.*

The second man paused, rested a huge pistol on his left forearm, and took aim at Alex.

Without thinking, she raised her bow, aimed at the man with the pistol and released. The arrow hit him solidly in the chest. He immediately dropped his firearm and grabbed at the arrow. Surely an arrow imbedded so deeply would stop him. But no. He drew his sword and headed for his target.

Engaged in a furious fight for his life, Alex didn't see the danger.

"Look out!" she cried.

Alex brought his sword down, cleaving a deep, gory gash at the juncture of the man's neck and shoulder. In one fluid motion, he drew his dirk and buried it in the second attacker's throat. Both slain men dropped, legs thrashing, arms groping, helpless to staunch their wounds now gushing life from their bodies.

Lucy heard someone scream. A woman. Oh, God, it was she. She was screaming.

Alex sheathed his dirk and ran to her, his face and shirt bloodied. He grabbed her by the waist and tossed her in the general direction of the wagon yelling, "Get inside and stay there."

But she didn't. She couldn't. All she could do was watch while Alex joined the other men hacking and slashing at their attackers. The quiet glen had become a bloody nightmare.

A third man dropped, skewered by Mr. Munro's sword. Outnumbered, the remaining two attackers took flight into the woods. Suddenly, the violence was over. The acrid smell of the dissipating gun smoke bit the inside of her nose. Hercules ceased his barking, and an unnatural quiet fell. The only sound the heaving breathing of the Sinclair men.

Three lay dead or dying. Thank the Lord, none of them

a Sinclair. Mr. Munro lifted one by the hair and asked for his name, but the man spit blood, convulsed, and went still.

Alex approached her, a deranged look in his eyes, his face and shirt spattered red with blood. He had grown another foot taller, looking dangerous and wild, like a berserk warrior sent by Satan himself. Lucy backed away.

"Are you injured, lass?"

"Stay away," she shrieked.

"It's all right now. It's over. You're safe," he said, his calm, rumbling tone quite at odds with his fearsome appearance.

"You killed those men. You cut them to pieces." Lucy dropped her bow, walked away a few paces, and vomited in the grass. When she was certain she had turned out the entire contents of her stomach, she staggered to the fire, careful to avoid Alex. She wanted out of this hellish place. She wanted to go home to Nounou Phillipa and Papa.

"Here, lass," Mr. Munro said. "Rinse your mouth with this, then take a good swallow." She accepted his flask with a trembling hand. When the liquid hit her empty belly, the whisky threatened to come back up, but she willed it to stay down. The men, bloodied and perfectly silent, were focused on her. She must keep herself from dissolving. It was a matter of pride.

She handed the flask back to Mr. Munro and walked trance-like toward her bow. Something compelled her to look at the man she had shot. She should look at his face. Remember it.

The dead man. She recognized him. Though he wasn't wearing his silver gorget and red uniform jacket, the doeskin breeches marked his profession.

"The English soldier I spoke to at the public house," she said.

A voice made her jump. "Aye. I recognized him just the now."

Having wiped his face clean of the blood, Alex no longer looked so frightening, but the memory of the brutal way in which he had dispatched both men made her shudder.

"Why did they attack us? And why is he out of uniform?"

The Scot shook his head, bewildered. "Dinnae ken. Perhaps they thought to rob us."

He spotted the large pistol lying on the ground near the dead Englishman and reached for it. "Did he aim this at you?"

She shook her head. "He aimed the gun at you."

Alex's eyebrows arched. "And you shot him? To spare me?"

She nodded.

He stuffed the pistol in his belt. To her horror, he pulled the arrow from the Englishman's chest, wiped the blood off on the dead man's shirt, and handed it to her. The ground beneath Lucy tilted slowly, and she started to slide off the earth.

Oh God, I'm fainting.

Chapter Five

A tickling sensation brought Lucy to her senses, Hercules delicately licking her fingers. Her eyelids fluttered open. The heads of four worried-looking Scots hovered above her, blocking out the remaining sunlight.

"What?"

"It's all right, lass. Everything is all right."

She was lying on the grass, cradled in the tall Sinclair's arms, head resting on his solid chest. He smelled of wool, dust, and man. She hadn't been this warm and comfortable since she left Maidstone Hall.

Her rational mind made a halfhearted effort to cut through her foggy thoughts. He shouldn't be touching her. It was thoroughly improper for him to hold her so intimately in public. What was more, he should not be calling her lass.

There was something else that bothered her about the tall Scot. Something he had done. Something very nasty—

"Release me this instant." Lucy struggled to her feet with considerable help from Alex.

"Are you sure, Miss FitzHarris? You've had a start," Mr.

Munro said.

"I can stand on my own now, if you please." She looked pointedly at the hand Alex had wrapped around her shoulder in an all too possessive manner.

He let his hand drop and walked away, his head lowered.

Mr. Munro guided her to the wagon. She saw three bodies lying on the grass and averted her gaze.

"We cannae stay here. We're moving on as far as the light will allow." Mr. Munro helped her climb inside. "Will you be all right, miss?"

"I'm fine. I'm perfectly fine."

Bumping and rocking along the road inside the wooden crate, Lucy shivered. Even with the blanket wound tightly around her shoulders, she was unable to get warm. She couldn't stop thinking about the massacre she had witnessed. Three dead. Cut down violently. And Alex looking like a monster, all blood-spattered and wild-eyed.

That monster is the man you are to marry.

How could she? How could she marry such a savage man? She was meant to marry a gentleman. A man like Langley. A man of breeding and good manners. Alex had neither. He was a soldier. A man of blood and violence. She had seen him kill two men. He'd practically cut one of them in two, for heaven's sake. All the Sinclair men, every one of them, were killers. Her father had delivered her into the hands of murderers.

"Papa, how could you make me marry such a beast?"

Lucy heard the duke's answer as clearly as if he were sitting in the wagon across from her.

He saved your life, Sweetheart.

True. Alex had made an oath to serve and protect her. Acting on his oath, he had fought to save her life. Valiantly. Like any princely knight. Of course, the deed would be gruesome. One cannot kill without getting blood on one's hands. She should be thankful.

An image of the man she had shot with her arrow came back to her, the blood spurting through his fingers, his face twisted into a frightening grimace of pain. Then his death face, blank and open-eyed. Oh God, had she been the instrument of that man's death? Lucy curled up on the seat and closed her eyes tight.

Despite the frequent jolt and jump of the wagon, she slept.

The next time she woke, she was alone in the dark, in the pitch-black dark. Now still, the wooden wagon seemed like a coffin. Was she dead?

"Help." Her call sounded like a wounded bird.

From a distance, a familiar male voice asked, "Are you all right, lass?"

She cleared her throat. "Yes. Yes, I'm fine."

A moment later, a pale oval face floated in the opening of her wagon coffin. "Do you need to make water?"

Lucy gritted her teeth. She was not ready to be pleasant with this man. She had not yet forgiven him.

"Yes, actually," she said stiffly.

Hercules hopped to the ground. A little unsteady on her feet, she allowed Alex to help her out of the wagon. When her eyes had adjusted to the dark, she looked around. Shadowy humped figures of sleeping men framed the dying embers of the campfire. Their camp was situated on a gentle slope of tall grass. Starlight illuminated a treeless expanse of moor in every direction. Never had Lucy been in a place so devoid of humans. As if they were the only people left on earth.

"This way." Alex took her elbow then placed his other big paw on her back to guide her. The heat of his hand radiated all the way through her coat, gown, stays, and shift. "Just this way and you can have your privacy behind this patch of gorse. Be careful. It's a prickly thing, gorse. I'll wait for you over there. Call when you need me."

After she'd finished, she made her own way back toward the light of the fire.

"Hercules?"

"I have him," Alex said.

She hated Alex for playing such a nasty trick on her. She feared him for being a killer. Yet, she was drawn to him. She flushed at the memory of his body, solid but warm and so… male.

Merde. He will have no kind thoughts from me. Not until we're even.

Getting even reminded Lucy of her brother and the advice he'd given her before she boarded the *Arbroath*. "Think of this as a great adventure, and value each moment, good and bad," he'd said. Today had been no adventure. More like a nightmare. She failed to see any value in taking a life. The sickening image of the dying man flashed through her memory again, and she blinked hard.

"Are you hungry?" Alex asked. "I saved you a bannock."

"What's a bannock?"

"An oatcake. Here."

He handed her a white square of linen. His handkerchief. Wrapped inside, she found a cold, hard wad of…well, no point in trying to examine the thing in this light. She took a bite and chewed the tasteless grainy mass, swallowed, choked, swallowed again, and managed to croak out, "Thank you."

"Come and sit down. I'll warm the tea for you."

Alex led her to a spot near the fire where the men lay snoring, and he motioned for her to sit on a tartan. While she waited for him to organize the tea, she fed what was left of the oatcake in bits to Hercules. He wasn't particular about the things he ate.

"Are you troubled by what happened this evening?" Alex asked.

"I've never shot anyone. Or *any* living thing." She recalled how her arrow had entered the man's chest and momentarily experienced what must have been the agony of the man's last few seconds of life and winced.

"I took the man's life. Not you," he said, sounding grave.

A kind gesture. To take all the blame.

"Had you not stopped the blackguard with your arrow, he would have killed us both. There's no sin in what you did." She gazed up at him, the light of the dying fire shining in his eyes and his face, normally inscrutable, filled with tenderness.

Alex handed her a wooden cup of warm, sweet tea. He sat beside her on the tartan so close she could feel the heat of his body—a pleasant feeling. Why was she drawn to this tall tawny-colored Scot? He was most certainly a knave. Perhaps, it was his kindness or his easy manner or—

No. She wouldn't let herself think that.

Too late. The thought had already taken root and blossomed in her brain. She was attracted to Alex because he was very handsome. A devilish voice inside Lucy's head said, *Be happy the tall Scot is your fiancé.*

Lucy hadn't let herself think about what lay before her beyond fulfilling her duty. At least she wouldn't be marrying a doddering old man. Her friend Jemima had been forced to marry Lord Ellington, a decrepit old fool. She remembered Jemima walking down the church aisle looking like she was on her way to her execution. Poor girl. But Jemima had done her duty, and the marriage had salvaged her father's estate from certain ruin. She sent a prayer up to heaven for Jemima, the friend she would never see again.

"Are you worried those men will return?" she asked.

"Nae," he said. "And you mustn't fret. I willnae let anyone harm you."

"That's right. Papa said you made an oath to protect me. Did your oath include playing juvenile tricks?"

"Lucy, I'm sorry. That's not what I intended."

His voice was soothing. Warm and smooth, like velvet. Nounou Phillipa used to say, *La langue du diable est douce.* The devil's tongue is sweet.

Lucy reclaimed her anger. "I don't want to hear your apologies. Come, Hercules." She struggled to her feet. "We'll take our tea alone." She made a hasty retreat to the wagon, but the tall man followed on her heels.

"Lucy. Please. Won't you let me explain?"

She whirled around. "Leave me," she said, using her sternest voice. "I do *not* want to speak to you until we arrive at Balforss. Then I will decide if..." She was about to say, *if I will marry you*, but said instead, "...if I will forgive you."

• • •

His eighth discovery: she was a prideful woman.

Alex spent the night seated on a rock on a brae above their camp, keeping watch. He tried to puzzle out why soldiers would disguise themselves and attack their party like common highwaymen, but he could make no sense of it. His mind was too preoccupied with worry over Lucy. More than anything, he wanted to comfort her. Every muscle in his body twitched with the need to take her in his arms, stroke her hair, and assure her she was safe. He would never let anyone harm her. Ever.

But, of course, he couldn't. With his asinine plan to pass himself off as an anonymous soldier, he had angered the lass beyond reason. She wouldn't let him near her.

Bloody, bloody hell.

And what would his father say? For he'd surely cocked this up, proving once again he wasn't fit to take on the responsibility of managing Balforss. He simply didn't have the temperament or the patience for being a laird. Not like his father, who always knew what to do, how to act, who to trust. Not like his younger brother, Ian, either, who never lost his temper. Ian was the one who should be laird. Not a hotheaded numpty like himself.

Jesus.

Fergus came to him at sunrise. "What bothers you, *macpeather*?"

Alex smiled half-heartedly at his uncle's use of the Gaelic for nephew. "I've done a terrible thing, Uncle. I dinnae ken how to make it right."

"An apology is best, aye? Even if it comes late."

"I tried to tell her I was sorry last night, but she wouldnae hear it."

"She's awake now. She's had her breakfast. Perhaps she'll be more agreeable with a full belly. I'll tell her you wish to speak with her. Prepare yourself." His uncle started back toward the camp.

"Uncle Fergus." The older man paused to glance back at Alex. "Will you make sure she's unarmed before you send her to me? I ken she's a dangerous woman."

His uncle lumbered away through the tall grass, chuckling to himself.

Alex watched the dumb show between his uncle and Lucy from his perch atop the brae. Lucy folding her arms across her chest. His uncle holding a bowl of porridge out. Lucy shaking her head. His uncle pointing up to Alex. Lucy jamming her fists on her hips, then accepting the bowl.

She seemed very angry, marching up the brae. He got to his feet. Perhaps he shouldn't have asked her to come to him. Was this a mistake? Closer now, he could see the fury in her eyes. This was definitely a mistake. For an instant, she looked as if she had it in mind to throw the hot porridge in his face.

He reached out to take the bowl. "Thank you."

She dumped his porridge on the ground, spun around,

and started back down the brae.

Anger like he had never felt before practically lit his hair on fire. He lunged forward and grabbed Lucy by the arm whipping her around to face him.

"Look who's being juvenile now," he shouted.

"Get your hand off me." Her outrage was sharp enough to cut his flesh.

He bared his teeth. His words came out low and threatening like a mongrel's growl. "You'll stop acting like a spoiled child and listen to my apology."

Her eyes went wide—the same fearful expression when she'd seen him kill those men.

Oh Christ, she's terrified of me.

Alex released her and turned away, his entire body vibrating, shaking, trying to rid itself of his anger. He couldn't trust himself in this black mood. He might say something to make the situation worse, if that were possible. He heard no movement behind him, only her trembling breath. After a few agonizing seconds, the grass stirred as Lucy marched away.

His ninth discovery: she hated him.

・・・

Lucy avoided making eye contact with the other men when she returned to the camp. She didn't want them to see how the exchange with Alex had shaken her. Once inside the safety of her wagon, Magnus handed Hercules through the window opening.

"Here's your wee beastie, miss. Do you need anything?"

Finding it difficult to speak, she shook her head. There had been no humor in the man's voice. No hint of amusement. In fact, no one was laughing this morning. Apparently, last night's skirmish had quashed the hilarity of Alex's little prank.

How dare Alex call her a spoiled child? After all she had endured, how dare he criticize her? She had tolerated bad manners, bad food, bad men, and a very bad joke. Then Mr. Munro had sent her to Alex with his breakfast like some maidservant. Of course she'd dumped his blasted porridge on the ground. How dare he act as if she was in the wrong? He was lucky she hadn't flung the porridge in his face. Which was what he deserved.

She remembered the rough manner in which Alex had put his hands on her. She'd never been handled in such a fashion. Shocking. Frightening, too, but also…thrilling. She'd never provoked her father or brother so easily. What did it mean to be able to trigger such a fierce reaction from the tall Scot? She closed her eyes, recalling the look on his face, a wrathful Highlander, magnificent in his savage outrage.

Lucy leaned her flushed cheeks toward the window opening for a cool breeze. After a while, she eased back on the seat and contemplated her situation. Mr. Munro said they would make it to Balforss by late afternoon. Most likely she would meet Laird and Lady Sinclair, acquaint herself with the household staff, and suffer through supper with Alex present at the table. During all this, she would act as if nothing had happened. Alex would get no more satisfaction from vexing her.

She sighed. Tonight she would sleep in her own chamber. At least, Lucy hoped she would have a bedchamber. She wouldn't be surprised if these savages all slept on the floor of one big room. And what would his people be like? Would they accept her? Respect her? Or, knowing her parentage, would they treat her shabbily?

"Huh." Lucy laughed bitterly at her brother's words of advice. "Value each moment, good and bad." Not very likely.

They stopped to rest and water the horses. She relieved herself behind a thatch of prickly bushes. Gorse is what the tall Sinclair had called them—what *Alex* had called them, she corrected herself. She still had trouble reconciling the fact that the tall, tawny Scot was also the beast she would have to marry. And to think, she had even felt kindly toward him yesterday morning when they'd spoken before breakfast. Recalling their conversation rekindled her feelings of betrayal and resentment.

"Is he handsome, would you say," she had asked.

"Dinnae ken," he'd said. "He looks a lot like me."

Scottish Bastard.

After seeing to Hercules's needs, she remained in the wagon for the duration. Mr. Munro brought her some cheese, bread, and a cup of bitter tasting ale. The mood among the men was somber. No more laughter, no one speaking, save simple commands. She stole a glance at Alex sitting atop his mount, stone-faced and grim. He was troubled.

Good. Let him suffer.

She could, of course, demand to be returned to England, to Maidstone Hall. Surely, when her father learned of this appalling business, he would release her from her duty. He wouldn't make her marry a wicked man like Alex Sinclair. But where would that get her? Tossed back into the viper pit that was London Society. Only this time, she would be twice failed at marriage. First with Langley, and second with a bloody Scot.

Hercules made fussy noises and rolled over in her lap, demanding a belly scratch. "Alex probably thinks I'll forgive him just because he's handsome. He's not nearly as handsome as Lord Langley. He's a gentleman. He'd never vex a woman. That beastly Scot has no notion how to treat a lady."

Yesterday afternoon, though, Alex had exhibited the lethal grace of a warrior, and Lucy had found it awe-inspiring. Heroic even. He had terrified her, but frightening and bloody as the battle had been, she had been left with the overriding feeling of safety. She would be safe with Alex Sinclair. He would defend her with his life, she had no doubt. That had to count for something in this dangerous land. For all the viscount's social graces, Lucy wondered how well he would have fared in last night's deadly skirmish. Would Langley have been able to save her life? Did he even know how to use a sword?

On the last leg of their journey, she imagined several scenarios featuring Alex on his knees before her, begging for forgiveness. In one scenario, he lavished her with gifts, all of which she refused. When at last he presented her with a simple handful of daisies, her favorite flower, and told her he loved her, she forgave him, and let him kiss her.

In another scenario, Alex had to duel Langley for her hand. After a long sword fight in which both men were gravely wounded, she demanded that they stop. But both men declared they would rather die than live without her. In the end, Lucy told Langley to go home to his Virginia, then forgave Alex, and let him kiss her.

There was one in which Hercules was kidnapped, and Alex had to travel all the way to Italy to fetch him. In another, she was lost in a forest and attacked by wolves, but at the last minute, Alex saved her. After a while, Lucy realized that all her scenarios ended with her forgiving Alex and letting him kiss her. She supposed she would eventually forgive him, but not until he suffered humiliation equal to her own. Not until he got to his knees and humbled himself.

Magnus rode up beside the wagon, smiling. "Balforss up ahead, miss."

She poked her head out of the side opening of the wagon, and her heart dropped to her stomach. Two small stone buildings with thatched roofs, looking more like something in which one would house livestock rather than people lay ahead.

"The other side, miss."

She tried the opposite side of the wagon. To her relief, in the distance, stood a stately, three-story stone house with glass windows and a slate roof nestled in a grove of mature trees. Not as large as Maidstone Hall, but substantial nonetheless. The sight of the lovely home served to allay some of her fears about accommodations. Life at Balforss *might* be tolerable, after all.

"Look, Hercules." Lucy held the dog up to the opening. "Balforss. Our new home." She stifled the thrill she felt upon seeing Balforss and rearranged her composure into that of righteous indignation. Alex had wronged her, and he would not be easily forgiven. Although, if she were honest—*really* honest with herself—a twinge of happiness that the tall, handsome, tawny-colored Scot was indeed the man she would marry, tickled her heart.

Chapter Six

Alex took the last half mile to Balforss at a trot, figuring it was best to get there ahead of Lucy and brace himself for unpleasantness. His stomach still roiled after this morning's altercation with the lass. Things were likely to get worse once his father found out about his folly.

Peter scurried out of the stable and took Goliath's reins. "Welcome home, sir."

"Thanks, man." Alex dismounted and stretched, enjoying the satisfying pop and crackle of his spine. "Rub him down good, aye? It's been a long journey. And have the smith look at his right front."

"Aye, sir."

"Wait." Alex rummaged in his sporran. He handed Peter a paper-wrapped sweetie. "One of Mrs. Ogilvy's molasses drops."

The towhead broke into a wide grin, revealing a gap where he'd lost a front tooth. "Thank you, sir." Peter stuffed the sweetie into his mouth and led Goliath off toward the stables.

He was more than happy to see his mother and father waiting outside the house, looking well, but he was apprehensive about what would follow. Lucy had not spoken to him since dumping his breakfast on the ground. Most likely, she would immediately tell his father of his inexcusable behavior and demand to be returned to England. Why not? The lass had every right.

Alex strode toward the house to meet the wagon. When he opened the door to help Lucy out, she handed him Hercules, saying nothing. He tucked the squirming dog into the crook of his arm, held out his other hand to help her down, then led her to his waiting parents.

"Mother, Father, Miss Lucy FitzHarris." Alex was momentarily stunned by her sweet smile. Recovering, he continued with introductions. "Lucy, this is my father, John Sinclair, whom you met many years ago."

"It's a pleasure to see you again, Laird Sinclair," she said, and bobbed a curtsy.

"It's a great pleasure to see you come, my dear."

"And this is my mother, Flora Sinclair."

Lucy released Alex's hand and reached both of hers toward his mother. Drawn to each other by some magical female force, they embraced without a word. His mother smiled and heaved a weighty sigh.

After a moment, Flora circled her arm around Lucy's waist. "Come into the house, dear. We'll have some refreshment in my parlor. Then you can rest a bit before supper."

"Thank you, Mother Flora."

Alex marveled at the instant connection Lucy and his mother made. He and his father remained at the entrance, watching their women take the staircase to the second floor.

"I think they will get on fine," John said. He looked at Hercules, still content in Alex's arm. "What's that?"

Suddenly remembering, Alex said, "Oh. Her wee dog."

"Mind it carefully. A hawk might take it for a rabbit. Come inside and have a dram."

Alex set Hercules on the floor of his father's library, where the small dog eagerly investigated everything within reach of his short snout. When he removed his coat, his father noticed his blood-spattered shirt.

"Brawling again?" John asked.

"Nae. We were attacked by highwaymen when we made camp north of Latheron."

John's eyes widened. "And?"

"Three men are dead. Two escaped." Alex's heart beat quickened. He braced himself for his father's wrath.

"You killed them?"

"We had nae choice, Da. Ask Fergus. They used deadly force."

His father scrubbed his face with both hands.

"Sorry, Da," he said. "You should know, at least one of the men was a Redcoat we had encountered earlier in the day in Golspie. Sutherland's man most likely. He was out of uniform. The man might well have shot me if Lucy hadnae been so bold."

"What?" John shook his head slightly as if he didn't hear Alex properly.

"It happened she was playing with her bow—she's more than handy with it—and when the banditi came out of the wood, two men set upon her. I cut one down. The other raised a firearm. Lucy's arrow hit him in the chest. Gave me time to finish him."

"Jesus." His father looked unsettled, and Alex had rarely seen him in that condition.

"Needless to say, she was scared. I think I frightened her more than the men who attacked us." He paused and rubbed his beard stubble. "It's odd, that."

"What's odd?" His father still didn't comprehend his story.

"Why would two men have headed for the woman? Most highwaymen would ignore the woman and take the men. There were five of them and four of us."

His father finished his whisky. "What happened next?"

"We hid the bodies in the wood, assuming those that escaped would return for their comrades. We continued north until we ran out of light."

"Lucy?"

"She was upset but uninjured." Alex chuckled. "She's a braw lassie. I dinnae ken should I be impressed or fearful." A moment of silence passed, and he added, "I'm truly sorry, Da."

"It's all right. You did what you had to do. Fergus and I will go to Thurso tomorrow morning and make a report at the magistrate's office. I'm more concerned about Lucy. Do you mind what I told you about Sutherland?"

Alex's eyes narrowed remembering his encounter with Patrick Sellar. "Oh, aye. I mind you fine. We came upon a family of Sutherland's tenants along the road. Said Patrick Sellar and his men had burned them out."

"Bloody bastard."

"When we stopped for mid-day meal in Latheron, I found Sellar in the public house."

"What was he doing in Caithness County?"

"He didnae say. I asked him about the family, about burning out his tenants. He called them liars. When I told him I'd find him out, he threatened Lucy. He said, 'Mind her carefully. The roads are crawling with highwaymen.'"

His father shot him a dark look. "Sellar's a ruthless man. If he thought Lucy was a means to keep me silent, there's no telling what he might do."

"Do you think Sellar sent those men to hurt Lucy?"

His father took another sip of whisky. "Maybe. Maybe not. They that attacked you may have been Sellar's men or highwaymen. Either way, never let your guard down. Lucy is safe here at Balforss, but go canny when you're outside the estate. Dinnae doubt Sellar's threat. Mind her carefully, son."

"If she'll let me near her."

"Oh Jesus. What have you done?" His father dropped his head and pinched the bridge of his nose.

Alex confessed his folly. Much to his consternation, his father didn't seem at all surprised.

"Dinnae fash, Alex. Women dinnae stay angry for long."

"You think she'll forgive me?"

"Aye. She'll forgive you." He added ruefully, "Mind you, she'll never forget."

Hercules whined at Alex's feet. "What do you want?"

"It's no' going to answer you," John said as if he were talking to a turnip.

Disgusted, Alex picked up the dog. "I'll feed it. That might shut him up for a bit."

It was a warm, late summer afternoon, the kind Alex didn't like to waste indoors. He carried Lucy's beastie outside and around the back of the house to the kitchen, certain the cook would find something for the dog. The smell of cooked meat and boiled potatoes floated out of the kitchen door along with the sound of Mrs. Swenson inside, banging pots and barking orders.

"Afternoon, Mrs. Swenson." He kissed the small but sturdy woman on the cheek.

"Och, ye gomeril. Stop your flirting. You know I'll feed you." She looked at Hercules with an appraising eye, as though considering whether the dog would be best boiled or roasted. "What's this you brought me?"

"It's no' for eating. It's Miss Lucy's pet." He set Hercules on the floor.

Mrs. Swenson continued to stare at it, looking confounded.

"It's a dog," he clarified.

"Best keep it indoors. A hawk's like to take it for a rabbit."

"So I've been told. Have you got anything to feed it?"

"What does it eat?"

"Dinnae ken. I saw Miss Lucy feed it scraps of meat once."

Mrs. Swenson dropped some minced beef in a bowl. "See if he'll take this, then." She sat on a milk stool and placed the bowl in front of Hercules.

Instead of eating, he gazed up at the cook with adoring eyes.

"What's the matter, dog? You dinnae like it raw?" she asked. "Shall I cook it for you first?"

Without warning, Hercules hopped onto her lap, causing the cook to let out a whoop. He tickled her chin with dog kisses. Alex had never heard Mrs. Swenson giggle before.

"Do you want someone to feed you, my wee mannie?" she said, talking to him like he was a baby. She picked up the bowl and hand-fed the bits of meat to Hercules. He chewed and swallowed, all the while gazing adoringly at the cook.

"Looks like you have a new friend."

Mrs. Swenson feigned irritation with Alex. "Och, take a cake and be gone with you."

He plucked a small raisin cake from a mound of baked goods, kissed her again, and crammed the entire thing into his mouth. On the way back to the house, he encountered Lucy. She had removed her bonnet and jacket as well as the lacy piece of clothing that covered her shoulders and chest. Some of her curly black locks of hair had come unpinned and bounced around on the swells of her breasts, leaving him spellbound.

"Where's Hercules?" she asked, as though accusing him

of losing her dog. "I have been looking all over for him."

Mouth still filled with cake, he struggled to swallow, but only succeeded in choking. Pointing at the kitchen door, Alex watched Lucy march off in a huff. At last, he swallowed a mass of cake the size of a crabapple, and wiped his mouth. He remained in the middle of the yard, waiting, half expecting to hear Mrs. Swenson and Lucy break into an argument over the dog. To his relief, Lucy exited the kitchen with Hercules and the cook, both women laughing. Mrs. Swenson pointed to the sky and Lucy nodded. Warning Lucy about the hawk?

She crossed the yard, smiling. The smile disappeared, however, when she met his eyes. She swept past him without a word, nose in the air. Some inexplicable force compelled him to follow her.

...

Lucy smiled inwardly. He'd followed her inside the house. One footstep for every two of hers echoing down the back hallway. For a reason she didn't understand completely, she liked him tagging along behind.

"Lucy," he said. Although the familiar use of her Christian name still rankled her, the tone of his soft, rumbling voice made her stop. His steps slowed. Closer. Closer, until his warm breath rippled through her hair.

"What is it?" Her words gave away the tremor in her voice.

Hercules wriggled in her arms, excited by Alex's nearness. She shifted the pup over her shoulder and patted Hercules on the back to reassure him, but he only calmed when Alex reached out and stroked his little head.

"Will you talk to me?" he asked.

The heat of his whisper burned the back of her neck. "I'm to meet your mother in her parlor. What do you have to say?"

"Please look at me."

His voice, so gentle, so sincere, touched her. When she turned, Hercules's wriggling only increased. Alex caught the pup just as she was about to drop him. He immediately relaxed in the Scot's embrace. The memory of resting in Alex's warm arms flushed across her cheeks. Lucy wanted to be angry with Alex. She wanted to punish him for his deceit. But being so near to him unbalanced her.

"Lucy. Please look at me." His intimate murmur dissolved her anger.

She gazed into his grey eyes, not the steely eyes of the soldier she'd seen on her journey here, but the soft, imploring eyes of a man who wanted her to see him.

"I'm sorry," he said. "I was wrong. I dinnae expect you to understand—"

"No. I don't under—"

"Please listen." Pleading. Alex was pleading with her.

She would have listened. Lucy wanted to hear why he had played such a silly, juvenile trick. But his eyes distracted her. A thin ring of grey around dark pupils. Delicate blond lashes, almost invisible, flitted up and down as he spoke. Ginger-blond eyebrows knit together. Wisps of tawny hair had escaped his queue. The light from the window behind him illuminated the curls creating a halo of gold around his head.

And his Roman nose—long, straight, and narrow. The only strikingly male feature on his face. It transformed the other pretty parts—eyes, brows, lips—into an utterly masculine countenance.

He smelled of the spice cake he had just eaten. A crumble of it clung to the corner of his sweet lips and she wanted to reach up and...

"Lucy?"

The sound of her name brought her back to the moment.

"Yes."

"Will you forgive me?" His question hung in the air by a thread, so tentative was his asking.

Over the last three days, he had been irritated, amused, violent, and brooding. Not once had he been uncertain. This vulnerable moment nudged at her heart, yet she wasn't ready to release him. Not until she had exacted the retribution she rightly deserved.

"You have a bit of cake," she said pointing to her own mouth.

A moment of confusion in his eyes, before Alex's tongue, pink and wet, slipped out and licked off the crumb. A corner of his mouth quirked up in a lopsided grin. "Better?" he asked.

Lucy's shoulders stiffened. By the leer breaking out on Alex's face, he knew very well the effect he was having on her. His cocksure smile reignited her anger.

Infuriating Scot.

Spell broken, she spun around on her heel and opened the nearest door. It was a storage room of some sort. Feeling foolish, she shut the door, and tried another that led to an unfamiliar room. *Merde.* She was lost in this confounded maze of a house.

"This way," Alex said, and continued down the hall. Lucy detected more amusement in his voice and struggled to disguise her irritation. She followed him out into the large entry, up the stairs, and into Flora's parlor. Alex set Hercules on the carpet and strode across the room to his mother seated by the fireplace.

Mother Flora set her needlework down and rose to embrace her son. "Alex. I haven't properly welcomed you home."

He kissed his mother's cheek. Lucy noted with a bump in her heart the tenderness in that kiss.

"Did Cook find you something to eat?" Flora asked.

"Oh, aye."

"Good. Go and wash for supper while Lucy and I take some time to get acquainted. You've had her for three days. Now it's my turn." Flora patted Lucy on the arm. "Come and sit with me, dear. Have some tea and cake."

As he passed, Alex rumbled in her ear, "We'll talk more after supper." Then he left, closing the parlor door gently after him.

Hercules went to the door and whined. "*Viens ici, mon cher*," Lucy called. He trotted back and hopped into her lap.

"I see you've found your pet. What a sweet wee thing," Flora said. "It's a dog, is it no'?"

"Yes. He's a gift from my father."

"Your father, the duke?"

"Yes. Hercules is very well behaved. Everyone loves him once they get to know him. He's not much use hunting or catching vermin like a hound or a terrier, but he's good company. I'm never lonely when Hercules is with me. He's my best friend, really." Lucy was surprised so much was tumbling out. She didn't realize how starved she'd been for female company. This was the first time since she left Maidstone Hall that she felt truly at ease.

"I can tell he's a good companion." Flora's smile was genuine rather than the plastered-on smile so many women donned at luncheons. "Will you have milk and sugar?"

"Yes, please."

Flora added a substantial dollop of milk and shoveled two heaping teaspoons of sugar into her cup, exactly the way Lucy liked her tea. The moment she had seen Flora smiling down on her from the front steps of Balforss, she'd known they would be great friends. Her handsome face was open and sincere. A rarity.

She handed Lucy the delicate china cup and saucer. "I

know you must be missing your home already. Your father, of course, and I understand you have a brother."

"Yes. His name is George. I suppose I miss my lady's maid, too. Her name is Phillipa. She's French. Like my mother." Why had she mentioned her mother? A woman she'd never known? Why open herself to the raw scrutiny of her hostess?

"I find myself lonely at times, too." Flora shifted the conversation seamlessly, as though sensing Lucy's uneasiness. As though protecting Lucy from the discomfort of an awkward topic. Never in her life had Lucy met such a gracious lady.

"My daughter Margaret's married and lives with her husband in Edinburgh." Flora sighed with real longing. "We dinnae see them but on Hogmanay and Beltane. They cannae come for the wedding as she's days away from giving birth to our first grandchild. Ian, my youngest, has joined the military like his da. We hope he will be home for the wedding. Will you have some cake?"

Flora was an attractive woman with the same tawny coloring as her son. The same kind grey eyes shone in the late afternoon light. The same blond brows and lashes. A few light red locks curled down from under her white cap. Her gown was cut from indigo wool that fit her slim figure beautifully. Although not stylish, it was well made with pewter buttons and trimmed with a fine Belgian lace collar. Pinned at the center of that collar, a charming silver adornment, heart-shaped with a tiny crown spanning the top and a rust-red stone in the center.

"What an unusual brooch."

"Thank you. It's precious to me. A token of love from John. This keepsake was first given to Alex's three times Great-Grandmother Shona from her husband James Sinclair, the first Laird of Balforss, and has been passed down to every

Lady Balforss since. You will wear it one day."

The reminder of her impending union with Alex made her cheeks redden. Lucy dipped her head and took a polite bite of her cake. She closed her eyes and uttered an involuntary, "*Mmm.*"

Flora chuckled. "I'll be sure to tell Mrs. Swenson you appreciate her molasses cake."

"It's delicious." Hercules sat up and looked expectantly at the cake. "No, you little beggar. You've had your supper." She set him down on the carpet and gave him a look of warning. "Behave yourself."

The tension in Lucy's shoulders eased. She liked Flora, and Flora seemed to like her. She didn't feel as though she had to pretend to be anything more than who she was. Pretending was so exhausting. Perhaps life would not be so awful at Balforss. Certainly better than the humiliation of returning home a failure.

Lucy took another bite of cake.

"I trust you had a pleasant journey from Inverness?" Flora asked.

Her question triggered sharp memories of yesterday's violence. She swallowed hard. "The truth is..." Lucy felt short of breath. Was this the proper time to reveal yesterday's bloody business?

Flora chuckled again. "Never mind, *a nighean*. You must be exhausted. Finish your cake. Then I'll take you to your room so you can have a rest. You'll tell me all about your journey at supper."

At her bedchamber door, Flora introduced the upstairs maid. "This is Haddie. She'll wake you in plenty of time for supper." She added before leaving, "I'm glad to have you here with us, Lucy. I hope you will be happy at Balforss."

Lucy dumped Hercules onto the bed. He found a comfortable spot and curled up.

"I'll jest put yer things awa' in the cupboard." Young Haddie was a rather ill-favored girl, impossibly thin with eyes close-set and spots on her face, but her smile was winning.

"That will be fine."

While Haddie unpacked her trunk, Lucy made herself acquainted with her bedchamber. It was a homey room. Rough-hewn wood flooring, a floral Turkish carpet by the bed, and another in front of the hearth. A large cherry wardrobe stood in the far corner of the room, with a washstand, basin, and ewer next to it.

The carved oak bed was hung with wool bed curtains embroidered in an intricate, multicolored woodland pattern. The bedchamber's one tall glazed window looked out over the front gardens blooming with lilies and daisies. A path from the garden led down through a small grove of trees, over a river and into a quiet glen. Beyond that, endless fields of green pastures dotted with sheep, and segmented by low stone walls.

"Your gowns are so lovely. It's a treat jest to touch 'em." Haddie giggled.

"Thank you."

"I'll put another brick of peat in the fire. There's a chill in the air this late in the day."

"Is this the privy closet?" Lucy asked, reaching for the knob on a narrow door to the left of the hearth.

"No, miss. That's the door to Mr. Alex's room. There's a chamber pot under the bed, and the privy closet is doon the hall. Shall I show ye?"

"Thank you, no." Lucy stood contemplating the door. "Is it locked?"

Haddie stopped poking at the fire. "Pardon me, miss?"

"Is the door to Mr. Sinclair's room locked?"

"Oh, aye. It's locked from the other side. Shall I open it for you?" The maid's eyebrows came together, nearly touching in the center of her forehead.

"Do you mean it doesn't lock from this side? Mr. Alex could—I mean, he wouldn't, but he could…"

Haddie's brows relaxed, and she glanced around the room. Spotting one of Lucy's trunks, she grabbed the side handle, and dragged the thing, empty but still very heavy, across the floor, then shoved it up against the door. She looked for confirmation from Lucy.

"Perfect." Lucy smiled her relief. Haddie could read a person's thoughts, an ideal quality in a maid.

Haddie lit a candle by the bed and closed the window shutters. "I'll be back a'fore supper to help you get ready." She left the room and closed the door without a sound.

At last, completely alone, yesterday's bloody events seized her, the smells, the sounds, the dying cries of those men, the images and sensations as vivid as they had been a mere twenty-four hours ago. Lucy lay on the bed, her body racked with tremors. She had contributed to a man's death. Was she guilty of committing a mortal sin? Would God ever forgive her?

"Oh, Hercules. I wish Nounou Phillipa were here." Too exhausted to hold on to her tears, Lucy buried her face in her pillow and sobbed.

・・・

As road weary as he was, Alex could not relax. He lay on his bed, listening to the murmurs of female voices in the next room, Lucy's bedchamber, where she would sleep, and dress, and bathe. Naked.

The sound of something heavy being dragged across the floor brought him up out of bed.

Thunk.

"She's blocked the door, the wee bizzum."

What did she think? That he would sneak in her room uninvited and take her maidenhead before they were married? The idea galled him.

He listened and waited. Silence. Hattie must have left the room. Then he heard muffled sobs. Lucy? Crying? He backed away from the door. She was unhappy here. Of course she would be. Alone among strangers in a strange place, no familiar faces anywhere, no kin, no friend, save a dog. On top of everything, she'd discovered her fiancé was an ass.

This was his doing. He had told her he was infinitely sorry, explained he'd been just as worried and nervous about their meeting as was she, that he had been wrong not to reveal himself immediately, but he hadn't meant to trick her. The ploy was a way for him to know her before they were thrust into a relationship. But Lucy hadn't heard a word he said. Or if she had, she didn't care.

He would make an attempt to explain once again tonight after supper. If she still rejected him, he would release her. If she wished to break the engagement and go home, he would not object. He tried not to think of the humiliation his failure would cause his father, not to mention the jeopardy Balforss would face should his father lose their contract with the duke. With that connection broken, Alex wouldn't be able to remain at Balforss and live with the shame. He would have to leave. Either re-activate his commission in the army or emigrate.

Unable to bear the pitiful sounding sobs from the next room, he stormed out of his bedchamber. He ignored his mother's voice calling to him. His blood was too high. He couldn't be civil to anyone in his current condition. Alex hurled himself down the stairs and out the front door. He strode purposefully to the only place he could be alone, the only spot on Balforss land where he could be with his thoughts, where he could compose himself and think clearly—the falls.

The soothing sound of water crashing and dancing down

the multi-stepped falls reached his ears a moment before the mill came into view through the trees. Already he could feel his heartbeat slow; his breath came easier, the urge to strike someone abated. He wound down the cool, tree-lined path toward his safe haven, and descended the steep stone steps at a relaxed pace until he reached the swirling pool at the bottom of the falls.

Alex was not accustomed to failure. He irritated his father all the time with his rash behavior and his penchant for fighting. But only once before had he failed on such a grand scale. Elizabeth Ulbster. Even then, her rejection hadn't laid him as low as did Lucy's now. Why?

He bent and selected a stone. With a flick of his wrist, the stone skipped one, two, three times across the pool before sinking.

Duty must be the reason. Nothing had been at stake when he had asked Elizabeth to marry him. Far more depended on the success of his and Lucy's union. To fail with Lucy was to disappoint his father, break his oath to the duke, and jeopardize the lives of everyone who lived and worked on Balforss land. One hundred and fifty years of his family's history rested on his shoulders.

And yet, that still didn't adequately explain why he wanted to beg Lucy for her forgiveness. Why would her rejection hit him harder than Elizabeth's? Why did he feel he had to regain her good favor before his heart—

Shit. His heart? Not possible. He barely knew the lass. No. No. He rejected the idea of love. What he felt must be desire. He *wanted* her. He wanted to marry her. Have her.

But did she want him?

There it was, the fear that made his insides churn. He wanted *her,* but she didn't want *him.* Or did she? Perhaps he hadn't lost her completely. Not yet. Yesterday evening, after the attack, holding her in his arms, there had been a moment between them when she'd cleaved to him. Later, by the fire, he had tried to ease her concern for having shot the man. Lucy's eyes had met his, and he remembered how the firelight licked her smooth cheek. He would have kissed her then. He believed she would have let him, too, had he not cocked everything up with his foolishness. If only he had kissed her. A kiss would have bound her to him regardless of his deception.

A kiss. That was the answer. If he could calm her ire, if she would let him get close enough, if he could kiss her, he could win her.

Later that night, Lucy swept into the dining room on his mother's arm, looking fresh and rested. No trace of her earlier distress. That was a good thing. She might be more receptive to his appeal with her mood improved. She had changed into a gown the color of a fawn, with pink stripes on the sleeves. Alex remembered his manners, thank God, and was quick to pull out her chair.

She smelled of the citrusy bergamot soap his mother made. Without her bonnet, he could see her hair wasn't a true black, more the fathomless brown of Loch Calder. She had her curls pinned into a mass of twists and whirls. Shiny dark ringlets bounced against the back of her long white neck. He wanted to touch those curls, to feel the silkiness of them in his hands. He should have worn his kilt to supper. A kilt hid a man's desire so much better than trousers.

Only the four of them were at table tonight, Ma, Da, Lucy, and he, which was unusual. Perhaps his mother didn't want to overwhelm Lucy on her first day at Balforss. Or, more likely, they had things to discuss privately. Whatever the reason, with so few people at table, their voices echoed in the dining room, adding to his nervousness.

His parents took their usual seats at either end of the long table. Across from him, Lucy sat ramrod straight, eyes assiduously avoiding his.

"Is your bedchamber comfortable, Lucy?" his father asked.

"Yes. Very," she answered with good grace. "The whole house is lovely."

"I'll show you 'round after supper, if you like," Alex offered.

Without looking at him, she answered with a hollow, "If you like."

His mother raised her eyebrows at him. Alex shrugged imperceptibly. She turned to her husband, and his father shook his head as if to say, *I'll tell you later.*

"Papa sends his warm regards," Lucy said, smiling at his father.

"They are warmly received. I trust he is in good health."

"Oh yes. Very."

Two kitchen maids entered, carrying steaming platters and bowls. They set them on the table then quietly exited. Lucy looked confused. She must be used to servants filling her plate, because she seemed at a loss as to how to serve herself.

Picking up a bowl of boiled potatoes within his reach, he asked, "May I?"

She nodded. He spooned a generous helping of potatoes onto her plate. Flora and John served themselves from different serving platters. When Flora passed her the platter of sliced roast duck, Lucy accepted it, hesitated for a moment, and then set the platter on the table. She fumbled with the serving tongs. Alex ached to help her but thought it best not to interfere. At last, she managed to get a slice of duck on her plate and returned the tongs to the platter with a *clank*. She glanced up at his father with a look of uncertainty.

"As I recall," his father said, "you had a different type of table service at Maidstone Hall. We are much more informal at Balforss."

Lucy's shoulders relaxed. The confusion she held earlier seemed to vanish. "I'm sure I will enjoy the change."

Her response to his father seemed genuine, more than a polite reply. He felt a twinge of jealousy, yet another one of his shortcomings. His father knew exactly how to put Lucy at ease. Alex looked like a fumbling idiot by contrast. He should be grateful Laird John was a good host, because Alex wanted Lucy to be happy at Balforss.

There was a lull in the conversation as they ate. Lucy examined the contents of her plate cautiously.

"Try a little of Mrs. Swenson's gooseberry preserve on the duck." Alex passed her the jam pot. She dolloped a purple glob onto her meat. When she took a bite, he was certain she smiled a little.

"Perhaps we should discuss the wedding," John said.

Lucy stopped chewing, swallowed, and set her knife and fork down, giving his father her full attention. But his mother spoke next.

"The wedding is set for a week from this Sunday."

Lucy made no comment. Her eyes flicked in Alex's direction. Did that mean he should say something?

"Erm," Alex started. "I…we…I mean, Lucy and I will discuss it, aye. After supper."

"Of course." His mother's sunny expression drooped. "Forgive me. I'm just so happy you're here."

Another lull in the conversation followed. Alex ate rapidly, wishing the meal to be over soon so he could talk to Lucy. He was about to suggest they excuse themselves when the kitchen maid entered with the clootie dumpling bathed in custard sauce. Normally, he would be thrilled at the rare sight of his favorite treat. Tonight, though, dessert was merely an annoyance.

He took some pleasure in watching Lucy inhale the

heady aroma of cinnamon and ginger. Black currant cake sweetened with treacle and covered in sweet vanilla custard was undeniably irresistible. If he couldn't convince Lucy to stay on his account, perhaps Mrs. Swenson's food would. Ah. Another discovery: Lucy loved sweets.

Supper was about to reach a successful conclusion when his father said, "Alex tells me you had a bit of trouble on the way to Balforss."

"Da," Alex blurted.

The blood drained from Lucy's face. "It's all right," Lucy said, sounding miserable. "I should tell you I'm so sorry, Laird Sinclair. I didn't mean to..." Lucy's voice quavered.

His father was quick to reassure her. "Dinnae fash yourself, *a nighean*. You had nae choice in the matter. The fault of the man's death is on him."

Lucy nodded and sniffed away threatening tears.

Flora looked from Lucy to John to Alex and back to John. "What's amiss? Did something happen?"

"It's nothing, Ma. I'll tell you later."

John reached out and patted Lucy's arm. "Alex said you dealt with the man brawly. You're quite handy with the bow, I hear."

Lucy's cheeks turned a ferocious red.

"Da, please stop," Alex said, wanting to end a conversation that was upsetting Lucy.

His father spoke more carefully. "The soldiers you talked to at the public house. Did you happen to tell them who you were?"

"Really, John. This discussion is not for the supper table." But his father paid no attention to his mother.

Lucy thought for a moment. "Yes. I introduced myself. Why?"

"No reason. Just wondering is all." His father shrugged and spooned another bite of clootie dumpling into his mouth.

"Do you think their attack had something to do with me?" she asked, alarm evident in her tone.

"No," Alex said quickly and definitively.

"Possibly," his father contradicted.

"Da, you'll frighten her needlessly." Why was his father bent on provoking his bride? "There's no need to worry, lass. You're safe here."

Flora's response overlapped Alex's with, "For goodness' sake, John. She'll have nightmares."

"Why?" Lucy looked shaken. "Does someone want to—"

"Nae, lass," he said, attempting to extinguish her worry. He could kick his father for making her anxious.

"I have a right to know." Lucy glared at him.

He sat back in his chair and cast a withering look at his father, the implication being *see what you've done now?*

"She's right," his father said. "Will you tell her, or shall I?"

Alex gritted his teeth. Barely able to control the anger boiling up inside him. "Fine. I'll tell her." To Lucy, he softened. "I'll tell you my da's concerns after."

Flora said, "Let's everyone enjoy Mrs. Swenson's pudding."

He shot his father another angry look and stabbed at his clootie dumpling.

When they left the house, a dusky light bathed the grounds around Balforss. Soft breezes tossed the leaves in the trees, making a pleasant rustling sound, a background to Balforss settling down for the night. They walked side by side at a casual pace toward the paddock. He pointed out things that might interest Lucy. The forge, the candle shed, the washhouse. She nodded without comment.

Lucy had wrapped herself in a green shawl decorated with leaf patterns.

"Are you warm enough?" he asked.

"Yes. Thank you."

"Many people unaccustomed to Highland weather complain of the cold," he said. "Not you, though. I ken you're one of those rare individuals who adjusts to her surroundings no matter the circumstance."

She glanced up at him for the first time. "If that's a compliment, then thank you."

"I meant it as a compliment."

She dipped her head. Was she hiding a smile?

Peter met them outside the stables and handed him a lantern.

"This is your new mistress, Miss FitzHarris."

"How do you do, Peter," Lucy said.

"Miss." Peter bobbed his head.

"Do you look after all these horses yourself?" she asked.

"Oh, no, ma'am. I mean, miss." Peter shifted from foot-to-foot like a boy in need of a chamber pot. "I'm just a stable lad."

"A good one, too." Alex gave him an affectionate pat on the back. Peter grinned a gap-tooth smile. "Go along to your bed, now. I'll put out the lantern when we're done."

"G'night, miss." Peter trotted off.

They entered the stables and walked down the line of horses, taking their time.

A chestnut mare named Bella stuck a curious nose out of her stall. Lucy stepped clear of the horse's reach.

"It's all right. Bella likes to be pet on her nose."

She held out a hesitant hand. Was she afraid of the horse? She stroked Bella's velvety muzzle with the tips of her fingers. When the horse snuffled, she jerked her hand away and let out a nervous laugh. She *was* afraid of horses.

"Is Peter a relation?" Lucy asked stepping away from Bella's stall.

"Nae. I found him sleeping in a corner of the market

one day in Thurso. He looked terrible. Dirty, starving, flea infested. Yet the wee laddie was feeding the remains of a piece of bread to a stray dog." Alex leaned a shoulder against a stall wall. "It made me think of the Bible story. Mark, I think it is: *For they all gave out of their abundance, but she, out of her poverty, gave all that she had.* I asked the lad where were his parents, and he said he didnae have any that he could recall. I asked if he'd like to come work for me, and he said he would. So he did."

"That was kind of you."

Alex hung the lantern on its hook and opened the flame, casting a golden glow on the wooden stalls.

"Was it a great enough kindness to make up for the disservice I've done you?"

"That was a very nasty trick, you know." She sounded peevish, an improvement over her earlier wrath.

"I told you," he said. "I was fashed about meeting you. You were nervous about meeting me, too. You told me so."

"When?" Lucy's brow crinkled.

"In the public house. You asked me if I knew Alexander—"

"And you lied to me."

"You said I was handsome." He felt as though he had just won whatever argument they were having and grinned at her.

"I most certainly did not," Lucy said, cocking an offended eyebrow.

"You most certainly did," he said, raising his own eyebrows in response. "You asked if *he* was handsome and I said *he* looked like me, and you said 'good.'"

Lucy sputtered and stuttered. "That's...that's not the same as...I wasn't implying that you were..." She stopped, took a breath, and restarted. "I was only relieved that he, *you,* had no gross deformities. *You,* in your arrogance, misinterpreted my meaning."

"Did I?" Alex was enjoying this conversation. He thought

it was tipping favorably in his direction.

"Yes, you did."

"So, you dinnae think I'm handsome?" He gave her what he knew was a charming smile, for it had worked often with other lassies. Rather than melting, though, like the kitchen maid at Ulbster Arms last spring, Lucy seemed off balance.

"I haven't given any thought to the way you look."

Alex's grin grew wider. The woman was incapable of deceit. She might be able to mask her feelings with pleasantries, but a liar she was not.

She examined him in the light. "You aren't altogether unattractive."

"Shall I tell you how beautiful you are?" He was confident now. Perhaps overly confident.

"I don't want to hear it." She turned her pretty head away.

"I think you do." He stepped closer. Closer to his target. Closer to Lucy.

She moved backward a step. "We came out here to discuss the men who attacked us."

Bella nibbled at Lucy's hair, startling her. She let out a shriek and stepped straight into Alex's arms. She gasped and looked up at him wide-eyed but made no move to escape his embrace. This was his chance. He leaned down to kiss her.

Fortunately, Alex saw the change in her expression and pulled back, catching her wrist before her palm made contact with his face.

His anger instantly ignited. "Dinnae hit me again, or I'll hit you back."

She jerked her hand away and lifted a defiant chin. "You said you would never beat a woman."

"A husband has a right to discipline his wife when she disobeys her master."

"Master?" she said, incredulous. "You see the role of husband as master? You think a wife is a mere servant, a slave, a thing to be owned by her *master*?"

Realizing he had most likely plunged into dangerous waters, he retreated. "I use the word master in a metaphorical sense, ye ken."

"And are you using the word *discipline* in a metaphorical sense?"

"I wouldnae beat you." Alex didn't like being talked into a corner. He lashed out. "But I'd gie ye a good tawsing wi' ma belt."

"You wouldn't dare," she huffed. Lucy tried to leave the stable, but he stepped in front of her, holding his arms up in surrender, careful not to touch her lest he fan the fire he had already lit.

"You're right. I wouldnae. But I *would* know this; do you want to marry me?"

Lucy's mouth opened, but no words came out.

"If you dinnae want to marry me, say so. I willnae marry someone who hates me."

"But your father—"

"It doesnae matter what he wants. What do *you* want?" When Alex got no answer, he felt his temper straining at its thin leash. His voice, like his insides, shook. "Do you want to break the engagement and go home?" Too late, Alex realized he had once again allowed his anger to supersede his better judgment.

Lucy became very still and, for a moment, he regretted having offered her the option to break their engagement. He added with less conviction, "If you want to go home, I willnae stop you."

The fire was back and raging in her eyes. "It's that easy for you, is it? Just shirk your duty the instant things don't go your way?"

"I've never shied from my duty. Ever," he said, burning with equal heat. "I made an oath to your father when I was eleven to serve and protect you. I honored that oath when he asked me to marry you."

"What?"

Oh Christ. He had done worse than anger her. He had insulted her.

The air around Lucy shimmered with rage. "Do you think he asked you to take me off his hands? That no one else wanted me? Well, you are mistaken, you…you… you horrible Scot. I'll have you know that I am wanted by a far better man than you. At least *he* is a gentleman."

"That's not what I meant. I—*who*?" Heat scorched the back of his neck as if someone had set him afire. He hadn't considered that he might have a rival. "Who else wants you? What's his name?" he demanded.

Lucy straightened. She wore the same self-satisfied look she did when she hit her mark with the arrow. "Lord Langley. He is a viscount, the Earl of Bromley's son."

Alex took a moment to absorb her revelation. He had abandoned hope of attracting the attentions of Elizabeth Ulbster and thought he might never recover. But after the duke's letter arrived, he hadn't considered Elizabeth again, all his thoughts turning to Lucy. It hadn't occurred to him that she might have left Maidstone Hall at the cost of her own heart's desire, to marry someone she might never love.

"So, you love him—this viscount—but your da made you marry me?" He was aware he was beginning to sound defeated.

Lucy looked away and folded her arms in front of her. "My father didn't make me do anything. He asked me to agree to our union, and I accepted like any dutiful daughter."

"Duty?" Alex said, nodding slightly. "This marriage is nothing to you but duty?"

She shifted again. She opened her pretty mouth to say something and closed it. What seemed like a very long silence passed between them broken only by the rustling of hay in one of the stalls.

"Well, then. I've a mind to release you from your duty," Alex said, his voice laden with resentment. "Say the word, and I'll return you to your precious viscount."

Lucy remained mute.

"I'm waiting for your answer, lass."

• • •

Lucy entered her bedchamber, trembling. She scooped Hercules into her arms and sat on the bed, allowing the warmth of the little dog to comfort her. She hadn't answered Alex when he'd offered to return her to her father because she was too proud to tell him she wanted to stay. But what if he made good on his threat to release her from her duty anyway? The thought of being sent home stung her deeply. And yet, she had begged her father for months to be released from this engagement. Now that she had what she so fervently desired, she should be overjoyed. Instead, she was distressed beyond reason. Why?

And why had she pretended Langley wanted to marry her? It had been clear by the time she'd left Maidstone Hall that he had no intention of asking for her hand. He was engaged to that ninny, Virginia. Langley's choice of bride rankled her, stung her pride, but he hadn't broken her heart.

At one time, she had believed that if she held a title, she would, at last, be impervious to the barbs of petty London Society. At one time, she would have given anything to marry a viscount. Any viscount.

Any viscount. *Oh, dear.*

How foolish she'd been with the desperate histrionics she had demonstrated daily, only when her father was watching, of course. Lucy had felt false even then, but had a childish need to get what she wanted—to get her way. How was her father faring now? Did he miss her as much as she missed him? Lucy resolved to write to Papa and reassure him of her love.

When Alex asked her if she wanted to marry him, she should have answered yes, but her pride wouldn't allow it. Pride. Phillipa had always cautioned her not to be ruled by pride.

"But what's wrong with being proud of one's accomplishments?" she had asked when Phillipa chided her for the dozenth time. "There's no harm in thinking well of oneself, is there?"

"*Non, ma petite.* But you must never let pride get in the way of your happiness," Phillipa had said. "Do you remember when your papa wanted to take you for riding lessons, but you were afraid?"

"I wasn't afraid. I just didn't want to go."

"You see? Still you hurt yourself with pride. You wanted very much to go. You know it. If you had admitted your fear, your papa would have taken extra care with you. But you were too proud. And so, you do not ride."

"*Merde.*"

Lucy flopped back on the bed and stared up at the canopy. Their conversation hadn't gone the way it was supposed to go. Alex was supposed to apologize to her. Get on his knees and ask for her forgiveness. *Beg* for her forgiveness. Instead, he had belittled her, embarrassed her, and provoked her into lying about Langley.

Beastly, beastly man.

A crash in the next room brought her up short. Lucy tiptoed across the carpet and put her ear against the door to Alex's adjoining bedchamber. Heels thudded on the floor. Alex stomping around the room, she supposed. Something banged against the door, and she let out a startled cry.

After Lucy caught her breath, she put her ear to the door again. Alex touched the other side or leaned against it, she couldn't tell which. She could hear his heavy breathing.

"Lucy," he said.

"Yes?"

There was what seemed like a long silence and then Alex said, "Good night."

The words were there, but they caught in her throat. She wanted to say good night, but she couldn't. Something strangled her—her pride. She heard Alex walk away from the door, then the creak of bed ropes.

The next morning, Alex was gone.

Chapter Seven

When Lucy joined Flora at the breakfast table, she casually enquired about Alex's whereabouts.

"He's gone hunting for the red deer with his cousins," Flora said, unperturbed by her son's departure. She passed Lucy a plate of sausages.

"Where is Laird John?"

"At the stable, most likely. Getting ready to leave." Flora took a bite of sausage and chewed.

Lucy stared at the tablecloth, shocked. So, Alex had made good on his threat after all. He hadn't even waited for her answer. Rather than returning her to Maidstone Hall himself, he'd left the chore to his father.

"Laird John will be taking me home today then?"

"What?" Flora asked, another forkful of sausage poised in front of her mouth.

"Will Laird John be returning me to Maidstone Hall? Shall I pack my things right away?"

Flora set her fork down carefully. "Why ever would he do that?"

"I thought that's what you meant when you said Laird John was getting ready to leave."

"Do you want to leave? Have we made you unhappy, dear?" Flora reached out and laid a gentle hand on her arm.

"No. I mean, I don't know. Alex is…" How much should she tell Mother Flora?

"Och, pay Alex's temper nae mind. He's hot-headed and says things he regrets later." She shoveled a heap of scrambled eggs onto Lucy's plate. Her voice didn't indicate any distress. "Have some breakfast. You'll feel better. Then you and I can spend the day together. Alex will be home tomorrow and you two can sort things then. Dinnae fash. Everything will work out."

"Do you really think so?"

"I know so. You need time to adjust to each other. That's all. Be patient."

Lucy brightened a little. "All right." Her appetite returned along with her spirits. She slathered a piece of toasted brown bread with sweet butter and strawberry jam and took a big bite.

"Good. It's settled then. We'll be making candles today." Flora had a youthful exuberance about her this morning. It must have been contagious, for Lucy felt her excitement build, too. "We'll need plenty of candles for the wedding celebration. And honey. I'll show you my hives. They're my treasure."

"You mean you make your own honey and candles?" Lucy wiped a glob of jam off her chin and licked her finger.

"Of course. How else would we come by them? Do you have a plain frock to wear? I wouldnae have you ruin such a fine gown as the one you're wearing."

After breakfast, Mother Flora helped Lucy change into her brown serge morning gown and gave her an apron to wear. She also insisted Lucy wear a dreadful white mop cap to cover her hair, explaining that, "a hairpin gone amiss could spoil a batch of honey."

They collected the necessary tools from the candle shed, and Flora led Lucy down a path past a small spring-fed duck pond to an open field of wildflowers and clover. Groupings of three to four coiled hemp beehives sat atop wooden platform benches spaced eight to ten yards apart. Flora called them skeps.

"This will be the last harvest of the summer. We must allow the bees to keep their remaining honey over the winter so they won't starve." Flora pulled the netting bunched on top of her wide-brimmed straw hat down over her face and neck. Then slid her hands into long, heavy leather gloves. "My bee armor," she said, smiling.

"Aren't you afraid you'll be stung?"

"No. That's why we harvest at mid-day when the bees are at the height of their work. There will be fewer in the hives, ken. Stand back a wee bit." Flora gave one of the skeps a sharp rap on the side and stepped backward. A flurry of bees exited, buzzed excitedly over the hive, then flew away.

"This is the delicate part." Flora turned the skep over and removed the bottom slat. Retrieving a short knife from her apron pocket, she cut several irregular waxy slabs from the hive and placed the dripping combs into the wooden bowl Lucy held.

Lucy peered into the bowl and caught the sweet scent. "We'll make honey from these?"

"Honey and candles. Come. We've more hives to harvest."

Lucy marveled at the skill and confidence Flora demonstrated as she moved from hive to hive, graceful and serene. After watching her carefully, noting each step in the process and the care with which Flora took to preserve the lives of the tiny bees, Lucy asked, "May I try?"

Flora happily transferred her bee armor to Lucy. Aside

from some difficulty removing the slat from the bottom of the skep, Lucy successfully harvested three good honeycombs from the last hive all on her own.

She basked in Flora's words of praise. The intoxicating thrill of her newest accomplishment left her breathless and beaming. If someone had told her before she left for Scotland that she would spend her first day at Balforss up to her elbows in bees, harvesting honey like a common laborer, she would have laughed in their face. Yet, here she was, out of doors, in the middle of a field of wildflowers, thoroughly enjoying herself.

She spent the balance of the day learning the arduous task of separating honey from the wax combs. The process of rendering purified honey and clean wax required a series of steps: draining, straining, boiling, and filtering. It was as much a science as an art. How much more satisfying than passing one's day in idle conversation over tedious needlework.

Exhausted and triumphant, they took their afternoon meal in the kitchen. Surprising. Lucy had never eaten in the kitchen in her life. The casual setting didn't seem at all disagreeable to Flora. It suited Lucy quite nicely, too.

Leaning their elbows on the table, Lucy, Flora, Mrs. Swenson, and Haddie ate from a platter containing a dizzying assortment of savory treats. They drank sweet tea and swapped amusing stories about Alex as a boy. Most of the stories were about Alex instigating some mischief or calamity, ultimately resulting in a spanking by his father. The walls of the kitchen echoed with shrieks of laughter. Lucy enjoyed this glimpse into her betrothed's childhood.

"Do you recall the time he tried to kiss your niece, Mrs. Swenson?" Flora asked. "I ken Alex was barely twelve and already crazy for the lassies."

Mrs. Swenson, red with laughter, said, "Och, aye. Katie was fifteen and thought herself a grown woman. I'll never forget the look on her face when Alex snuck up behind her."

"And I'll never forget the way Alex looked with a bowl of parritch on his head," Flora cried. More shrieks of laughter. Wiping her eyes, Flora added, "Oh, God. I think he thought you got a woman by stalking her like a deer."

"From what I can tell, he still believes that," Lucy said.

One breath of silence and the women erupted in laughter again, nodding and congratulating her on her astute observation.

They made no attempt to disguise Alex's shortcomings. According to his mother, Alex was bad-tempered, impatient, cranky in the morning, and prone to brawling. On the other hand, he was kind, fair, loyal, and fiercely devoted to family. Add to that his good looks and impressive size, and one could hardly do better, Lucy thought.

With each story—the formative experiences that made him the man he was today—she grew more inclined to forgive his recent transgressions. Perhaps, when Alex returned from his hunt, they could start again. That was, if he was truly repentant.

...

Alex had roused Declan and Magnus from their beds before dawn, shoving them stumbling and grumbling to the stables where he'd gathered rifles and provisions for a two-day hunt.

"But we just got here," complained Magnus, mounting his big bay mare.

"We'll need meat for the wedding celebration. Would you have my da shamed with a meager table?"

Declan said, "I thought the wedding wasnae for another—"

"We're going now," Alex said in his do-as-I-say-or-die voice.

When dawn had broken, they'd set out west with a mule in tow. They would use the beast to carry the burden of their hunt back to Balforss. The three cousins rode in silence, Alex brooding, Magnus dozing in his saddle, and Declan marveling at the rainbow arched across the moor.

"It's a good sign, aye," Declan said, turning in his saddle to look back at Alex.

"What?"

"The rainbow. It's a good sign." Declan was always prattling on about signs and dreams and the old gods. Alex never gave him chaff about it, though. Cousin Declan was prescient. He dreamed of future events with starling accuracy. Once, on the eve of a battle, Declan had dreamed where the French would attack their line. As a result, they had been prepared. His dream had saved their lives.

"My mam says it's God's promise he willnae flood the earth like he did in Noah's time," Declan said, a dream-soaked look on his face. "But her granda called it the Bifröst, a bridge to the gods only warriors most skilled in battle may cross."

"What do you think, Declan?"

"I ken it's a sign we'll have a good hunt."

"I hope you're right."

Magnus woke. "What?"

"Go back to sleep," Alex said with no particular animus. In truth, he didn't care if they were successful or not. He just needed to get away from Balforss. Put some distance between him and Lucy. He needed time to cool down. Stop speaking out of anger.

He had slept fitfully, plagued with dreams of her. It had been the same dream over and over. She was slowly sinking deeper into a peat bog. He tried to reach her, to save her. Each time he would get hold of her hand, it would slip from his grasp as though greased. His dream, of course, a metaphor for his failed attempts to gain Lucy's favor.

They stopped midday. Magnus caught two fat trout in the River Forss. They roasted them on sticks and ate them with their hands. Declan and Magnus argued amiably, Magnus poking fun at Declan's ill luck with women, Declan poking fun at Magnus's size.

"You look more like a bear than a man."

Magnus countered, "You look more like a troll than a man."

"What say you, Alex?" Declan called out.

"Few men could do better than to have a bear and a troll for friends." Alex thought tall, lanky Declan looked nothing like a troll. In fact, he wasn't a bad-looking fellow, really. And if Magnus shaved his beard, the big man would look far more presentable. He hadn't seen Magnus clean-shaven since they were fifteen.

Magnus came to sit by him on the riverbank. "How does Miss Lucy like Balforss?"

He twisted his mouth to the side and blew a sudden gust of air out his nose. "She likes the house fine. She likes my ma, my da, Haddie, Mrs. Swenson's clootie dumpling." Alex shook his head and sighed. "She likes everything but me."

"Surely she's forgiven you for—"

"Aye," he said with resignation. "She's forgiven that, I think."

"Then what's the problem, man?"

"She loves someone else. Some viscount in England. But her father, the duke, made her come here to marry me."

"Oh. I see."

"I asked if she wanted to go home."

"What did she say to that?" Declan asked, having quietly walked up behind them to join the conversation.

"Nothing." Alex rubbed at the tightening in his chest. "She gave me no answer at all. Just stopped talking. What do you ken that means? When a woman says nothing?"

"Dinnae ken." Magnus shrugged.

After a moment, Declan said, "Maybe she didnae like the question."

Magnus scratched his beard thoughtfully. "You know, for the first time, I think you might be saying something that makes sense."

"Aye. Because I know women fine, ye clotheid." Declan jabbed a thumb in his chest. "I've got two sisters."

The argument between them resumed, but Alex remained on the bank of the river, thinking about what Declan had said. Maybe Lucy hadn't liked the question. *Shall I return you to your precious viscount?* If she didn't like what he had asked, then maybe she didn't want to go home to the viscount.

The bloody viscount. He wished he could fight the sodding bastard for her. End the issue altogether. No rival. No problem. But then she'd hate him for killing her precious viscount. A picture of Lord Langley formed in his mind, a skinny, nance boy with a powdered wig and rouged cheeks. He hated him.

"Jesus, Alex. If you keep brooding, you'll make it rain," Magnus said. "Here, man. Did I tell you the story about Donald and Kyla?"

"Aye. You have. Many times." Magnus knew only one joke.

He launched into his story anyway. "Says Donald, 'Ah, Kyla, drinking makes you look so bonnie.' Says Kyla, 'But Donald, I dinnae drink.' Says Donald, 'Aye. But I do.'" Magnus laughed at his own joke as if it were the first time he'd heard it. The joke never got old for him.

Later that afternoon, Alex crawled through the grass on his

belly, Declan to his right, Magnus to his left. They were situated at the base of the mountains that bordered Sutherland, the extreme western fringe of Balforss land. The deer were near. They could hear the click and clatter of two stags battling. The wind was at their backs, but it never mattered when the red deer were rutting. Stags gave no thought to anything but fighting and coupling.

They inched forward and spotted them. Both big bucks. Magnificent beasts. Red coats gleaming in the afternoon sun. Antlers locked, heaving to and fro with grunts of effort. Powerful muscles rippling as each strained to gain ground.

Alex whispered to Declan, "You take the one on the right. I'll take the left. On three."

Snugging their rifles into their shoulders, they took aim.

Blasts followed, echoing through the glen, barely distinguishable as two. The deer fell as one. The men rose and trotted toward the kill.

"Nice shooting," Magnus said. Alex's shot had entered the neck and Declan's just below the ear. Both beasts had died instantly. In the distance, they heard the challenge of another stag's bell, a deep, hollow sounding low.

"Better reload," Alex said. "He could come upon us unawares." Magnus kept a sharp eye out while Declan and Alex cleaned their kill.

Declan was for the old ways. Alex waited for him to say the *gralloch* prayer of thanks. Then they sliced open the deer and removed their steaming entrails to leave for the corbies. With help, Alex and Magnus each hoisted a carcass around his shoulders like a yoke and headed to where they had hobbled the horses and mule. Declan, the best shot, carried the guns and kept watch for any stray stags.

They made camp in a clearing where they'd slept many times since boyhood. Although no wolves had been spotted in the Highlands for years, they tied the deer carcasses high in a tree, and then went about gathering wood for the fire.

Alex brought out the round of bread and chunk of cheese he'd pilfered from the kitchen that morning. The men put cheese between pieces of bread, skewered them on sticks, and toasted them to a light brown. The cheese oozed out of the sides and they savored each gooey bite. Magnus removed a flask of whisky from his saddlebag, took a healthy swig, and passed it to Alex.

"Do you mind the time when the white hart went after you, Alex?" Magnus asked, a string of cheese hanging from his beard.

"Oh, aye. I nearly shit myself."

"No one would shoot it for fear of hitting you," Magnus added.

Alex relived the moment of terror four years ago when a giant white stag had charged him. "I dropped my gun and ran screaming bloody murder, 'Shoot it! Shoot it!' I could feel its breath on my back, it was that close. I knew I was about to die."

"What made you stop and turn around?" Declan asked.

Alex shrugged. "I suppose I didnae want to be stabbed in the back. Better to face the beast and have done with it."

"What I've always wondered is why did the white hart back down?" Magnus asked.

"This sounds daft, but I looked in his eyes and I saw what it was thinking. He thought to himself, 'Should I kill the lad? Or should I let him live?' I just stood there with my arms out, waiting to die and praying to God I wouldnae."

"God heard you," Magnus said.

"Nae. God spoke to the white hart. Told him to let you live," Declan said.

Magnus began another pointless argument with Declan. "Have you gone daft, man? Do you think God speaks to animals?"

"The white hart spared King David of Scotland."

"That's Papist nonsense," Magnus said.

"Still, God talks to people. Why not animals?"

"Because God created us in his image. He only speaks our language." Magnus passed Declan his flask of whisky.

"That makes no sense at all." Declan took a long pull on the flask.

"You're both daft," Alex said. "I was lucky, and that's the whole of it. But I thanked God for my life to be sure." And that episode had marked his life. People thought he was blessed. But Alex knew better. He was just lucky, and so far, his luck had held. Would his luck finally run out with Lucy?

The sun dipped below the mountains, and the men spread their plaids on the ground for sleeping. Magnus poked up the fire. "Have you thought what you'll do to make Lucy want you?"

Alex darkened again. "No."

"Perhaps if you gave her something. A gift."

"What kind of gift?"

"Something a woman likes. Jewelry, a fancy bonnet, the bitty shoes they wear on their feet."

"Gowans," Declan said with certainty.

"The flowers, you mean?" Alex asked.

"Dinnae listen to him, Alex. I mean it. He knows nothing about women."

"Gowans," Declan repeated. "I'm sure of it. Hamish Clouston couldnae get my sister to look his way. He showed up at the croft with a bunch of gowans, and Margaret went all soft and started cooing for him." Declan stood up and minced around the fire, imitating his sister using a falsetto. "Och, did ye ken Hamish gave us the gowans. He's sae romantic. He kens jest what I like."

Magnus and Alex rolled about laughing.

Pointing a finger at Alex, Declan warned, "You laugh,

but I'm telling you, *gowans*."

• • •

After supper, Lucy followed Laird John into his library to search for a particular book he had on beekeeping, since she had newly taken an interest in becoming an apiarist. Stepping into the room, Lucy felt a sharp pang of homesickness, the library reminding her so much of her father's study, sizable but cozy. Not as big as her father's, but very nearly. Distinctly masculine.

The room even smelled like men; tobacco smoke, whisky, and musty old leather. Bookshelves lined three walls floor to ceiling, all fashioned from mahogany. Two tall windows faced the front garden. Flora had decorated the room smartly with wingback chairs by the fire, a massive desk, and a deep burgundy Persian carpet covering the majority of the wood planked floor. The whole room took on the character of Laird John, large and inviting. Imposing yet warm.

"Ah. Here it is." Laird John removed a well-worn leather-bound volume from the shelf. "*The Bee-Master's Companion.*"

"Thank you."

"Feel free to avail yourself of any book that interests you."

Lucy lingered for a moment, liking the room and not wanting to leave Laird John's company. He was so like the duke, and she missed her father. She wondered how they could seem so similar. The two men *looked* nothing alike. From all outward appearances, they had little in common.

"How did you and my father meet?"

"Did he never tell you?" John asked, surprised.

"All he ever said was that you were his oldest and dearest friend."

"It's a long story. Are you sure you want me to tell it?"
"Oh, yes. Please do. I'm not tired at all."
"Have a seat by the fire, lass. Sherry?"
"Yes, thank you." Lucy made herself comfortable while Laird John poured her a sherry and a whisky for himself.

"We met when we were young men, very young men. Your father was a lieutenant aboard the *HMS Prince George* headed for the Colony of New York—what is now America. I was on my way to my first commission in the army." John handed her the sherry and took the other seat next to the fire. "There was a war going on then, mind ye?"

"Of course. The American War of Independence."

"We became well acquainted during the passage across the Atlantic. He was a lot like me. We fancied ourselves men of the world. When we made port, we wandered toward the city, looking for adventure. It was our first bit of freedom since we'd left the shores of England, and we meant to make the best of it."

Laird John's gaze wandered to the peat fire as if seeing the memory play out in the glowing embers.

"Straight away, we met a man who looked a gentlemanly sort. He spotted us for strangers and asked politely would we like assistance finding our way 'round town. Seeing as the man was agreeable, we accepted his offer and joined his good company. We visited a tavern called the Bull's Head where there was much drinking and gambling. After we drank quite a lot of strong ale, the gentleman who called himself Smith, suggested we visit a bawdy house."

"That sounds like my father." She dipped her chin.

John Sinclair tugged at his stock uncomfortably. "I, of course, cautioned your da against such an unwholesome enterprise. But, as his friend, I couldnae abandon him."

"I'll bet." Lucy gave him a skeptical quirk of an eyebrow.

Laird John emitted a nervous throat-clearing before

continuing. "Aye, well. We followed Smith to a rather dodgy part of town. He led us down a narrow lane between houses, and we were set upon by villains."

Lucy couldn't stop herself from blurting, "What did you do?"

"It was dark. I ken't there were three men. One threw a sack over your da's head. I drew my dirk and stuck his attacker in the side. Your da threw off the sack and drew his sword. We faced the villains shoulder to shoulder. Aye, they were bigger, but we were quicker." John turned to Lucy again, smiling. "We made quite a racket, yelling and flailing aboot."

Laird John shook his head and laughed to himself. "Two of His Majesty's soldiers came rolling out of the whore house—swords drawn, no trousers, and drunk as hell. The braw laddies chased the blackguards awa' but not before your da and I got a bit of our own back, aye."

Lucy clapped her hands and laughed, thoroughly tickled by her father's youthful escapades. "What happened to Smith?"

"He ran," John said with disgust. "We suspected our man Mr. Smith may have been the orchestrator of the ambush."

"Did they ever catch him?"

"No. But that was the end of our adventures."

"So, you saved my father's life."

"Och, nae. The duke saw it that way, but one could also say I nearly got him *killed*." John laughed heartily then finished off his whisky.

"Thank you for telling me that story." She got up, placed the sherry glass on the table, and headed toward the door.

"My pleasure. Good night, Lucy."

She paused. "Do you think Alex will be back tomorrow?"

Laird John smiled back at her. "The thing to remember about Alex is he's exactly the way I was at his age. Brash and braw. Dinnae fash. He'll come 'round."

Chapter Eight

The next afternoon the trio rode into the yard at Balforss, filthy, exhausted, but satisfied with their hunt. Alex left Magnus and Declan to deal with the deer and entrusted his horse, Goliath, to wee Peter. He was apprehensive about how Lucy would receive him. A part of him feared she might have already left.

Christ, what will I do if she's gone?

As he walked toward the house, Declan called out after him, "Gowans."

Alex gritted his teeth. *Gowans. Nonsense.* He cursed Declan when he reached the garden, but he bent down, and picked a fist full of daisies, feeling a complete fool. Once inside the house, he called for Lucy.

"I ken she's in the candle shed with your ma just the noo," Haddie said, passing him with an armload of laundry.

He went out the back door and crossed the yard to the building behind the hatchery where his mother made her candles. The door was open. He saw his mother and another woman working over the candle wax trough.

"Hallo, Ma. Have you seen Lucy?"

"I'm right here," said the unfamiliar woman, who turned out to be Lucy. She wore a kertch on her head, and an apron like his mother's over a dull-looking gown, but her face glowed with sun-kissed cheeks and the dew of hard work. What was more, she was smiling…at him.

She wiped the moisture from her brow with her forearm and set the broche of candles she'd been dipping onto the drying rack. "Hello, Alex." She bobbed a polite curtsy.

He remembered himself and bowed, then thrust his fistful of flowers at her. "Gowans," he said.

To his utter amazement, Lucy put her hand to her chest and exclaimed, "Oh, Alex, daisies are my favorite. Thank you." She gathered them from his hand with care. "I'll go put these in water." And she skipped off to the house.

"There's a vase in the china cupboard," his mother called to her back. "Alex, shut your mouth. You'll catch flies. And go wash yourself. You smell like blood. I cannae believe you would greet—"

"Was Lucy making candles with you?"

"Oh, aye. She's got the feel of it, too. And yesterday we harvested two quarts of honey. She loves bees. Did you ken that about her?"

"So, she's staying?"

"If you can hold your temper long enough for her to get to know you. *Ooosh.*" His mother waved a hand in front of her face. "Tell Haddie to draw you a bath. I can smell you from here."

"I'll go dunk myself in the spring." He left the candle shed, happy but disoriented, as if he'd come home to a changed world. Alex encountered Haddie again, who was now hanging laundry to dry in the sun. He grabbed a clean, dry shirt and a pair of breeks from the line before heading down to the old spring that fed the duck pond. It would be chilly this time of year. Dazed as he was, though, he could use some cold water right about now. Perhaps he would come to his senses.

Damn if Declan wasn't right. The bloody gowans had worked.

...

Lucy found the vase Flora had mentioned, arranged her daisies, and brought them up to her bedchamber where she would have them all to herself, the location making them an even more intimate gift. She stood back to look at them. Alex had given her daisies. In the language of flowers, daisies meant true love.

"Perhaps he's changed his mind, Hercules." She sat on the bed next to the dozing pooch. "Surely he wouldn't give me daisies if he planned to send me home."

The dog rolled onto his back, offering his belly for a scratch. Lucy obliged him. In doing so, she caught sight of her hands. She washed, whipped off her apron and kertch, and then tidied her hair. Satisfied with her appearance again, she went downstairs to find Alex. He was no longer in the yard or at the candle shed.

She spotted Haddie hanging laundry. "Have you seen Mr. Alex?"

"I ken he went to the spring," Haddie said. "But, I'm no' so sure..."

Lucy didn't have time to stand around and dither with Haddie. She needed to find Alex and tell him... What? What would she tell him? She'd been past the spring yesterday with Mother Flora. It wasn't far. Lucy slowed her pace to give herself time to think. Would she tell Alex she was sorry? That she didn't want to return to Maidstone? That she wanted to marry him? Would she tell him she had lied about Langley?

No. He would gloat if she admitted she had lied. She was certain she couldn't endure that. She knew very well what her pride could and could not suffer. Lucy could not, would not tolerate his derision. At any rate, Alex was the one who needed to apologize.

Lucy heard splashing beyond the tall grass. She approached cautiously then stiffened. He was bathing naked in the spring. His back was to her, but she would recognize that cocky stance anywhere. Weight on one hip, shoulders at an angle, head tilted slightly in opposition. Her initial impulse was to slink away. Leave him his privacy. But her feet were riveted to the ground. She marveled at his impressive back, lean and sinewy, broad at the shoulders, tapered at the waist. He had waded in almost to his hips. She could just glimpse the top of his bum. Lucy suppressed a smile.

He had immersed himself at least once, for his hair was wet and slick against his head. Freed from its queue, it was surprisingly long. The snaky bronze tendrils clung to his back. He was shivering. The spring water must be freezing. She was close enough to see the gooseflesh on his arms.

Alex turned suddenly, caught sight of her, and froze.

She crossed her arms, refusing to look away. His private parts were well hidden beneath the surface of the water, and he made no move to cover his nakedness.

"Lucy. What are you doing here?" Alex asked with calm curiosity.

"Watching you unawares," she answered.

A wet sprinkling of ginger hair swirled across his chest, met in the center, and ran down his belly in a long dark line.

"It's not proper for you to—"

"Nasty trick, isn't it? How does it feel?"

"I see. You've made your point. Now, if you'll just turn your back—"

"No," she said. "I don't think I will."

"Lucy, it's cold. Dinnae tease me." A playful warning.

"I'm sorry," she said in mock apology. "Am I making you uncomfortable?"

His chest and belly muscles flexed and rippled with his slightest movement. "Yes," he said with unnatural patience. "I'm about to freeze my bollocks off. And if you dinnae turn your back this instant, I'm going to walk out of this pond and show you what I mean."

"Idle threats are—oh!"

Alex took one big step and Lucy ran. Once she was safely out of sight, she slowed to a walk and worked to catch her breath. In less than a minute, she heard the thump of running feet behind her and turned. Barefoot and still buttoning up the fall of his breeks, he stopped a few feet in front of her, chest heaving slightly from the brief run. His shirt clung to his wet body.

When she looked in Alex's eyes, she could see him thinking of what he should say to her. Choosing something, letting it go. Choosing something else and rejecting that. Until, all he said was, "Lucy."

"I wanted to thank you for the daisies. Gowans, you called them?"

"Aye, but I have a confession to make. I was desperate to find a way back to you. The gowans were Declan's idea." He was quick to add, "But I picked them."

"You must have missed me very much," she said, looking down.

"I did." He took a step toward her. She didn't back away. "Lucy," he said in almost a whisper. "Will you look at me?"

She did. His eyes were a soft grey in the sunlight. And his long golden lashes bounced slowly when he blinked. Now was the time he should kneel before her and ask for her forgiveness.

He took another step toward her. "Do you want to marry

me?"

She held her ground. "Your mother says we should be patient. Take some time to get to know each other."

His shoulders dropped and released a long, deep sigh as if all the air had gone out of his body. Lucy almost felt guilty for having disappointed him. When he lifted his head to peer at her, a change had come over him. His features had turned dark, causing her to take a step back.

"Do you still love...*him*?" he asked through clenched teeth.

Alex took another predatory step toward her as though hunting her, stalking her like a deer. *Run*, she thought. *Run away.* But her body would not obey. Like a cobra, he'd hypnotized her with his gaze.

Without warning, the snake struck. A flash of movement and she was in his arms, plastered against his damp chest. She felt his warm breath an instant before his soft, cool lips touched hers. Tentative at first, then he kissed her harder.

He smelled clean and sulfury, like the spring. She liked the raspy feel of his beard against her chin. She sensed his urgency. Coaxing her. Opening her. Kiss, kiss, kissing her. She hadn't remembered circling his neck with her arms, but they were there. Holding on tight.

Then she felt what she'd only heard women whisper about. Through her gown, shift, and petticoat. Solid and demanding. She wasn't appalled as she should be. It was too thrilling.

In the distance, Mother Flora called, "Loo-cy. Aaa-lex."

They separated, breathless. Shocked and shaken by the intensity of the kiss.

Reason returned, as did her ire. "You...you..." She couldn't think of a bad enough name for him. "How dare you? Get back to the spring before she sees you like that." She pointed to his trousers.

Alex looked down, seeming surprised to find his body in such a condition. "Oh, aye," he said, and started to leave, but stopped, grabbed her, and kissed her again.

When he released her, Lucy gasped. "Bastard."

Smirking, Alex shrugged an apology. A moment later, he disappeared around the bend in the path.

Struggling to pull her wits together, she marched back to the house. Bold, insolent behavior. Kissing her without permission not once but twice. She was embarrassed, too, by her reaction to his body. Alex's kiss had left her senseless. Nothing like Langley's kiss. Langley had pressed his lips to hers, briefly, the way any gentleman would do. Alex's kiss... well, it felt like he had kissed her whole body, invaded every inch of her person. She felt a tingling sensation everywhere.

Mother Flora met her at the back entrance to the house. "You look flushed, dear. Are you feeling well?"

Merde. Did the affect Alex's kiss had on her show? Had he actually branded her with his passion? Could everyone see?

"Perhaps I got too much sun. I'd better rest before supper."

...

He hoped supper would be different from the last time he and Lucy had dined together. Alex waited at the bottom of the stairs for her. He wore his best shirt and great kilt. Not his philibeg, his uniform kilt, but the green-and-blue tartan woven nearly seventy-five years ago by his great-great-grandmother and secreted away from the English in the wake of Culloden. His father wore it from time to time and had taught Alex how to wear the kilt when he was a boy. He hoped Lucy would approve.

Once again, he had angered her. She had called him

a bastard for having stolen a kiss. But oh what a kiss. Her lips told him everything he wanted to know. Alex no longer doubted her. She wanted him. Wanted to marry him. Of that he was certain. *A kiss never lies.*

Was it wrong to steal a kiss?

Yes. He would apologize to her for being impulsive.

Was he sorry?

No. Not at all.

She seemed to float down the stairs in a light blue gown of fine, shimmering cloth that made a whispering sound when she walked. The long sleeves were cleverly embroidered with daisies in a chain pattern. Did she choose this gown because he had given her daisies?

Lucy's stays pressed against her breasts, making them plump up above the neckline of her gown. A thin swatch of lace covered them, giving him a tantalizing peek at her peaks.

She wore her hair down in the back like a maid. Candlelight from the wall sconces reflected on her shiny curls, making his fingers twitch with the need to pet them. He had planned to say something flattering to her, but once face-to-face he forgot, so utterly entranced by her beauty.

"You're wearing daisies," he said, staring into eyes the same blue as her gown.

"Daisies are my favorite."

"I'll not forget." He waited a moment, then said, "I'm sorry I kissed you without your consent. I know I was wrong, but I couldnae help myself. Will you forgive me?"

Lucy pursed her pink lips and tilted her head as if considering his request. "I accept your apology, and I forgive you because you asked nicely."

"Thank you."

Lucy swept toward the dining hall, calling over her shoulder, "And I forgive you for everything else, as well."

"Everything else?" What the hell was she talking about?

"Do you mean—" Too late. The wee bizzum had already slipped away. He had to laugh at her cheek. She'd forced his apology for his previous bad behavior by forgiving him *without* his apology. Alex headed into the dining room, looking forward to continuing the conversation after supper.

A full table on this night: Alex, Lucy, and his parents, as well as Uncle Fergus and Aunt Agnes. His father had also invited Magnus and Declan to join them as thanks for the fresh venison. The table held platters and serving bowls full of venison stew, smoked fish, cheeses, tatties, and neeps. Alex and Lucy sat on either side of his father. The conversation was lively and loud, Fergus teasing Aunt Agnes mercilessly and Magnus making bawdy jokes.

His father was in excellent humor. He'd even brought out his imported sherry wine and passed it around the table. Unheard of. At one point, John took Alex and Lucy's hands, one in each of his, and squeezed. Making his father this happy brought him pleasure so acute it pained his heart.

Alex tried to stay with the conversation, but it was impossible to concentrate with Lucy looking so fetching. What was more, she looked back. She met his eyes often. Each time, he heated up inside. She hadn't yet told him she wanted to marry him, but he had kissed her. Really kissed her. And Lucy had kissed him back. A victory for him. He filled his plate and forgot to eat. All he could think of was how and where he could get Lucy alone and kiss her again. Press against her soft, willing body and hear her sigh.

Declan half rose from his chair and called down the table to him. "Alex. Did they work, man?"

"Like a charm, Declan," Lucy called back. "I had no idea you were such a ladies' man."

The room erupted in laughter. Declan blushed furiously and dropped back into his chair. Magnus delivered a few cuffs to his ears and Aunt Agnes, finding Declan's ticklish spot, poked him ruthlessly until he begged for mercy.

Declan's taunting remark was meant for Alex. He would have absorbed the blow easily, but Lucy had turned it around, clever girl. She could participate in good-natured teasing. Hold her own and return it in kind. Her cheeks were flushed with what he hoped was happiness, and her whole body seemed less contained, her movements flowing and graceful rather than rigid and self-conscious. In only a few days, she had blossomed.

What could have brought about this change in her? Surely it hadn't been the daisies, and he wasn't so arrogant as to believe his kiss alone had altered her heart. No. More likely, it was the magic of Balforss that had transformed her.

Balforss had always been like a living thing to Alex. Each stone held the power and grace of the men and women who had built it. He could reach out, touch a stone, and feel the hand of the man who had fashioned it. Draw strength from a grandfather, a great-grandfather, a great-great-grandmother. The walls of this house connected him to a proud lineage of Highlanders. They were most likely men who looked just like Alex. Yet, in his imagination, they were giants. Men and women of infinite strength and courage. They had to have been to have survived those precarious times.

His father rose, and the room quieted. When he lifted his glass, Alex expected he would make a toast to his and Lucy's upcoming nuptials. Instead, his father looked to his mother and said, "Here's to the greatest of all God's blessings, our women, who give us life, love, and a reason to be better men. *Slainte*."

After supper, Uncle Fergus detained him and Alex lost track of Lucy. He searched the house and the yard until he found her in the front garden among the gowans. She didn't see him right away, so he watched her. He liked watching her. God, how long had she watched him today when he was bathing at the spring? She must not have minded too much. He hoped not. It would be nice if she liked looking at his body.

He hadn't allowed himself to think about what she might look like naked. He'd seen the tops of her breasts. He liked those very much. She was small. Not so much short as slim. Women wore so many clothes it was impossible to tell how they were shaped. He would find out soon, though. Very soon.

"You look beautiful in the moonlight," he said.

Lucy looked up suddenly.

Now that he was closer, he could see something was troubling her. "What's wrong, lass?"

"The attack on the camp. You said you would tell me about your father's suspicions."

"I told you. There's no need to worry. You're safe here with us."

"Do you believe husbands and wives should be honest with each other at all times?"

"Does that mean you want to marry me?"

"Alex, just tell me the truth." She was making a serious request of him. He should answer her seriously.

"Do you ken the family we met on the road to Latheron?" he asked. "The people who'd been burned out of their croft?"

Lucy nodded.

"The man you spoke to at the Latheron Inn, Patrick Sellar, the one who…" Alex gestured to himself.

Lucy made a face and nodded again, understanding what he meant.

"Sellar is the man responsible for burning that family's croft and leaving them destitute."

Lucy's eyes widened. "Why?"

"He's clearing Sutherland property of all his crofters, his farming tenants. When they dinnae leave, he burns their cottages. He denies the act, of course, but it's only a matter of time before Sellar injures or kills someone. He knows my father doesnae approve and that we're watching him carefully. If we discover evidence of his treachery, we'll take him to task."

"What does that have to do with me?"

"He's threatened to harm you should I interfere with his business. But believe me, I willnae let anyone hurt you. Ever."

"Does my father know about this?"

"There's no need to trouble him. He knows you're safe here with us. That is why you must stay on the property, close to the house, unless you're with me or my men. Do you understand?"

"Yes."

"Good." Now, to bring the conversation around to his purpose. "I need to hear from your lips—and no more talk of duty—do you want to marry me?"

Lucy huffed and folded her arms under her breasts. "How do I know you want to marry me? You haven't even asked me."

"What kind of man do you think I am? I kissed you. I wouldnae kiss a lady if I didnae want to marry her." Alex dug his fingers in his hair and paced in a circle. Christ, the woman was maddening. Everything was an argument with her. He stopped his pacing and raised an index finger, preparing to make an important point. He completely forgot his important point when he saw the look of surprise on Lucy's face.

Eyes blinking, she said, "Oh." Then gifted him a dazzling smile.

Like some sort of female weapon, her smile turned his insides to jelly. "Fine. Yes. Well, shall we walk?" He offered her his arm. They made a quiet turn around the garden.

"If not for duty, why do you want to marry me?" she asked.

Alex wasn't prepared. He hadn't asked himself the

question. He'd spent so much time thinking of how to get her to want him he hadn't given any consideration as to why.

"Duty aside, if we're being completely honest with each other…" he began.

She stopped walking and turned to him. The golden light from the windows of his father's library spilled onto their faces.

"Go on," she said.

"If we're being completely honest, I dinnae ken."

A look of concern crossed her brow.

"I barely know you. We barely know each other."

She looked away. He was losing her.

"All I do know is that I want you."

She met his eyes again.

Encouraged, he went on. "I want to spend the rest of my life knowing you." He remembered his father's toast at supper. "What was it my father said? 'The greatest of all God's blessings are our women, who give us a reason to be better men.' It's like that."

The wool wrap Lucy clung to in the cool night air slipped from one of her shoulders.

He tugged her shawl back in place. "I want to care for you, protect you, fight for you. I want you to see me as a good man. To want me, and no other. To want me as much as I want you. Do you ken what I'm saying, Lucy?"

"Yes. I think I do."

"So, I'm wanting to marry you, knowing we dinnae ken each other well, but trusting that we will. I promise to be the best man I can be so that maybe one day you'll love me." Alex held her hand in his. "Lucy, will you marry me?"

She turned her beautiful face up to look at him, one side in shadow, the other shone golden in the candlelight from the window. "Yes, Alex. I will marry you."

He pulled her against him and bent to kiss her, but a

burst of laughter from the study drew her attention, and he ended with his face buried in her hair.

She pushed at his chest. "Stop. They're looking. What will they think?"

He raised his head and saw four figures silhouetted by candlelight in the window. "Don't you see? It brings people joy to see us together."

"But we're not married yet. It's scandalous to make love in public."

"Maybe that's true in England, but not here in the Highlands. Not between two people who are meant to be together." Alex glanced back at the window. "They're gone now. Let me have those sweet lips of yours." Her face was very close to his. "Let me kiss you and then kiss me back." Her eyes closed. "Let me know you want me like I want you."

He kissed her softly at first. When she kissed him back, and he felt her desire surge, he pressed on. Already aroused, he quickly became inflamed. He pulled her closer, closer. Christ, if only he could just get closer, strip aside the clothing that blocked his way to—

Lucy broke their connection. "You must stop. I can't catch my breath. My heart is—"

"Banging in your chest like a drum? Aye. I can feel it beating as strong and hard for me as mine does for you. Christ, Lucy, when you rouse me like this I feel invincible." He laughed. "Like Hercules."

He picked her up by the waist and she shrieked. "Put me down, you brute."

He set her down and steadied her.

"We will be married in less than one week," she said tartly. "If you continue like this, you will exhaust your passion and leave me with nothing on my wedding night."

"Never," he protested.

"I can see I must ration you."

"What?"

"One kiss a day. A chaste one."

"That's like asking me to live on one bite of food a day," he said in mock horror. "I cannae survive."

"I'm sorry it has to be this way. I know it's going to be very difficult for you to resist me," she teased. "But it's for your own good."

"Oh, aye. It will be difficult," he said. "But not as difficult as it will be for you."

"I beg your pardon."

"I think maybe that you will have a harder time resisting my kisses."

"I don't have any trouble resisting a man who is full of himself." Lucy turned her head.

"Oh, aye? Are you sure?" He lowered his voice and growled in her ear. "Because I think you like it when I let you feel how much I want you."

She inhaled sharply. Not so much a reaction to his bold behavior as the gasp of a woman aroused. Disentangling herself, Lucy recovered quickly.

"Swaggering, self-centered, egotistical man."

She marched off in a huff. Alex smiled. She was pretending.

As he undressed for bed, he thought he heard humming coming from the next room. He went to the door that connected their bedchambers and put his ear against it. Yes. Lucy was humming to herself. He spotted his boot on the floor, picked it up and dropped it with a *thud*. Returning to the door, he heard her lean against the opposite side.

"Lucy."

"Yes, Alex."

"Will you dream about me the night?"

"Perhaps. Will you dream about me?"

"Most definitely," he said. "I'll meet you there, in your dreams. And I'll make love to you."

"Promise?"

He grabbed himself reflexively. "Oh, God. I promise."

Chapter Nine

Lucy woke to light footsteps across the carpet.

Haddie drew aside the bed curtains with a cheery, "Morning, Miss FitzHarris."

She yawned and stretched and buried deeper under the covers. "Morning, Haddie."

The shutters creaked, the window cracked, and birdsong drifted in. Autumn had arrived on the chilly morning breeze. Lucy sat up and watched the maid poke the fire to life.

"Since you call Mr. Sinclair, Mr. Alex, perhaps you could call me Miss Lucy."

"Thank you, Miss Lucy." Haddie beamed. "Good morning, my wee mannie." She scooped Hercules off the bed and held him close to her face. Haddie had developed a fondness for Hercules, and he for her. The dog bestowed her with his kisses before she set him down on the carpet. "Will you be wanting the yellow gown this morning, miss?"

"I'll be working today," Lucy said with some pride. "The grey serge will do nicely."

Anxious to break her fast and get to work, she made a

hasty toilet and then allowed Haddie to pin her hair up in a simple twist under a white kertch. She held up her stays to be laced. "Not too tight. I need to move about while I'm working with Mother Flora."

Haddie smiled, transforming her homely face into something almost lovely to look at. After slipping the gown over Lucy's head and fastening the buttons, she stepped back to appraise her. "You look like a fine Highland lady, miss. Like you belong."

Lucy recognized the compliment. "Em…is Mr. Alex awake, do you think?"

"Och, hours ago. I passed Himself in the yard whistling and smiling like a loon. I dinnae ken what you've done to the poor lad. He's normally terrible crabbit in the mornings."

"Crabbit?"

"Aye. Bad-tempered as a wet cat." Indicating the dog, Haddie said, "Shall I take Hercules out to do his business?"

"I think he would like nothing better."

"Come on, then, poppet. Let's see what Cook has put aside for my wee prince." Hercules followed Haddie out without a backward glance. It seemed he, too, was settling into Balforss nicely.

Lucy met Flora in the hallway and they made their way down to breakfast, chatting about plans for finishing the candles in the morning and paying a visit to Aunt Agnes in the afternoon. When she stepped into the dining hall, she met Alex's eyes right away. He gave her a sweet smile that made something flutter in her belly.

John and Uncle Fergus were also at the table, discussing business. The men rose when she and Flora entered the room.

"Good morning, dear wife," John said to Flora. Lucy noticed an interesting exchange between the two. As if they shared a secret.

Flora smiled back at John. "Dear husband," she said, and

lowered her lashes.

Uncle Fergus greeted them with an individual nod. He took his leave, saying, "I'll be taking Gunn and Eagan wi' me to Thurso. Be back this afternoon."

John held out a chair for Lucy while Alex held out his mother's chair and received a kiss on the cheek for his troubles.

"Did you sleep well, Lucy?" John asked.

Lucy cast a furtive glance at Alex and met his shining grey eyes again. Her cheeks heated, but she managed a breathless response. "Yes. Thank you."

"Seems everyone had a good sleep last night," John said, eyes flicking up to his wife.

There was that look again, that wordless connection between them. Was it sexual? She stole another peek at Alex and felt a flutter in her belly again. He stared back. The look on his face was identical to that of his father's, lean and hungry.

She hoped theirs would be like his parents' union—strong, passionate, lasting. Mother Flora had said her marriage to John had been arranged. They hadn't met until the day they were married, but they had come to love each other. Somehow. So it was possible.

John ladled porridge into Lucy's bowl then pushed the saltcellar her way. "I almost forgot," he said. "You have a letter." He grinned and passed the missive to her.

A letter from home? From her father? Joy surged through Lucy's body at the sight of the folded parchment and she gasped. Surprised by her involuntary reaction, she covered her mouth. "Do pardon me."

"Dinnae fash, lass," John said, amused. "I thought you would be glad to see it."

The red wax bore an unfamiliar symbol, the head of a fox rather than the heraldic shield of her father's house. She cracked the seal, unfolded the parchment, and read.

Dear Lucy,

I have made a terrible mistake. I pray this letter arrives in time...

Before she read any more, she skipped to the bottom. It was signed: *Your Fool, Langley.* The pulse in her temples jumped and throbbed in time with her heartbeat.

"Bad news?" Alex asked, concerned.

"No." She didn't dare read more in his company. "Please excuse me." Lucy rose from the table, and the men stood. "I'm fine. Really. I just...excuse me." She left the dining room, saw the door to the library open, and went inside. She closed the door and leaned against it, knees shaking, hands trembling. Gathering her strength, Lucy went to the window for better light.

Dear Lucy,

I have made a terrible mistake. I pray this letter arrives in time. Against the wishes of my father, I have broken my engagement to Miss Whitebridge. I am come to Scotland to beg your forgiveness and earnestly hope you still hold some affection for me, wretched man that I am. Lady Sutherland, my relation, has offered me shelter and solace, so aggrieved am I that you may wed another. Until I find you and hear my fate from your lips, I will harbor love's hope.

Your Fool, Langley

Yes. She hadn't been wrong. Langley did want her. He had defied his father, broken his engagement, and traveled to Scotland to retrieve her. Langley had come to make her his. The tiny crack the viscount had made in her pride disappeared.

Lucy stared at the sweeping, arrogant writing so like Langley. She suddenly realized she hadn't thought about him for nearly two days. In fact, this letter was the last thing she had expected. She should feel elated, triumphant. She could return to Maidstone Hall vindicated, marry the viscount, and gracefully re-enter London Society.

Why, then, did she feel guilty? And why was she hiding from Alex? Had the letter arrived only two days ago, she would have been thrilled, would have waved it in Alex's face, proof she was wanted by another. Now, the letter had an oddly disturbing effect on her conscience.

The door to the library opened, and Alex poked his head in. "Is ought amiss, Lucy?"

She forced a smile and held the letter behind her back. "No. I'm fine."

"Is that a letter from your father?"

"No." Knowing what his next question would be, she answered before he asked. "It's from Lord Langley."

Alex's eyes narrowed and the muscles in his jaw flexed. He would ask to see the letter. She panicked. Though, whether she feared his reaction to Langley's intentions or her guilt for considering them, she didn't know.

"A love letter?" He spoke the words through clenched teeth, his barely contained rage frightening. An image of him, face blood spattered and eyes wild, came to her.

Lucy crossed the room and tossed the letter into the fire. Facing Alex, she said, "There. It's where it belongs."

Even though the crease between his tawny brows vanished and his tight expression relaxed, she had to fight the urge to back away when he approached her.

"Do you have regrets about him?" he asked. He was struggling to be sympathetic, she thought. But she could detect a definite note of suppressed anger in his tone.

"No," she said with as much certainty as she could muster.

"Good." He gave her a hard look as if trying to read her thoughts. "Because I'll kill anyone who tries to take you from me."

She remembered the highwayman he had cut down, and

the man he had stabbed in the throat with his dirk. He had butchered two men to save her life, but still, the hair prickled on the back of her neck, and she swallowed hard. Alex meant what he said. Given the chance, he would kill Langley.

. . .

Too enraged to remain in her company, he left Lucy in the library and set off in a blind fury. Some bloody Englishmen had the audacity to write a letter to his woman. And, yes, it had been a love letter. He knew it. There could be no other reason for her to throw the letter in the fire without showing it to him. Doubt hung over him like a dark cloud. Jesus, did she still want the bastard? Would she prove him false? Either leave Balforss and return to England, or worse, go through with their wedding and play the dutiful wife, all the while wishing she were married to another?

He stormed toward the stable, kicking anything in his path. "Peter!"

The boy came scurrying out. "Aye, sir?"

"Saddle Goliath for me, now."

"Aye, sir." Peter hunched his head down between his shoulders and ran back inside.

Alex paced in front of the paddock. If the sodding English viscount dared come for her—and he wished he would—he'd sink his dirk into the man's heart and watch him die. He'd likely hang for it, but it would be worth the satisfaction.

Christ, what was in that letter? He couldn't bring himself to ask Lucy. It would sound too much like jealousy, a weakness he despised. Yet, even now, he was drowning in it. He'd been infected with a mild case of jealousy once before when he'd been spurned by Elizabeth, but that didn't compare to the madness he felt at this moment. The degree of one's jealousy must be in direct proportion to the depth of one's affections, for the desire he had felt for Elizabeth in no way compared to that which he felt for Lucy.

Peter led the horse into the yard, saddled and ready to ride. Goliath, named so because of his size, was the tallest thoroughbred anyone had ever seen. Seventeen hands high and a deep chestnut brown. Just seeing the spirited warmblood made Alex's heart rate slow.

"Are you angry wi' me, sir?"

He glanced at Peter. The boy was out of sorts. "God, no. Why would you think it, lad?"

"You shouted at me. I thought because I couldnae pull the girth tight, you wouldnae want me for your groom." The boy's chin quivered, and tears streaked his dirty cheeks.

Alex's body strung like a bow suddenly relaxed, the tension evaporating, his rage dissolving into remorse. "Nae, lad, I wasnae angry with you. I think you're a fine groom. You know that." He searched for a way to make it up to the boy. "Here now," he said. "Go and saddle Heather. I need your help inspecting the north pasture."

"Me, sir?" Peter wiped his eyes with a filthy sleeve.

"Aye. Magnus and Declan are busy. I'll need my next best man. Will you do it?"

"Aye, sir," the boy said, the gap-toothed grin reappearing on his face.

"Good. Get yourself ready. I'll go to the kitchen and find us some food to take along."

He had intended to ride Goliath hard until he and the horse were lathered and spent. Instead, he and Peter strolled down the Seaward Trail toward the north pasture on horseback with two herding dogs named Raphe and Denny. Peter proved to be the perfect companion for Alex. He said nothing. Just smiled and swayed atop Heather, a fat lavender-grey pony with a sweet temperament.

The boy was no great horseman, but he had no fear of

the beasts and liked being around them. Naturally, the horses sensed this and tolerated Peter's attentions. Finding Peter was a lucky thing. Lucky for the boy, and lucky for Balforss.

Finding Peter had been a lucky thing for Alex, too. He was easily drawn to violence—the satisfaction of vanquishing the enemy, putting down an attacker, taking the life of a foe. That was why he had left the army. He was liking it a little too much. One shouldn't enjoy killing. It was the darker side to his nature, the part of his soul that was tarnished black. Peter was the good part of him. Evidence he might still redeem his soul.

When they came upon Old Sam Crannoch's croft, they dismounted and led the horses inside the gate to the crofter's small unkempt yard. The door to the thatched-roof croft opened and Old Sam stepped out, stooped and withered, wearing a toothless grin.

"Hallo, Sam," Alex called.

Sam lifted a hand and let it fall back to his side, the effort seeming to cost him something.

He took a wrapped bundle from his saddlebag. "Mrs. Swenson bid me bring you some of her honey cake. She asked after your health."

Sam nodded appreciatively but said nothing.

"This is my friend Peter. He's riding with me to the north pasture."

Peter waved a hand. "Hallo, Mr. Sam."

"You've got to speak louder, man. Old Sam cannae hear much."

Peter repeated his greeting with more force.

Sam motioned for the two of them to enter. They followed the crofter, Alex nearly folding in half to clear the lintel. Inside, the air was thick with smoke from the peat fire. The room smelled strongly of a full chamber pot and Old Sam's unwashed body. Alex was unable to stand up straight in the croft, so took a seat—the only seat—while Sam lay on the bed where he probably had been all day. Peter stood in the corner, twitching uneasily.

"Are you feeling poorly, Sam? Shall I tell Mrs. Swenson to come see to you?"

Sam shook his head slightly and mumbled something in Gaelic. Peter spotted the chamber pot, picked it up, and went outside to empty it. Alex was mightily impressed with the boy's courage, but supposed he might have removed the chamber pot, too, if it meant getting a gulp of fresh air. When the boy returned a few minutes later, Alex thanked him and gave him the water bucket to fill, as it was empty.

"I can see you're tired, Sam. I'll just leave the honey cake here on the table for you. I'll tell Mrs. Swenson to stop by tomorrow. Perhaps she can make you more comfortable."

Sam gestured with a claw of gnarled fingers, and Alex knelt by the old man's bed. The linens were filthy, as were the clothes he wore. He must have stopped caring for himself months ago.

Sam exhaled his words on individual breaths. "Tell… your da…he's a good…man."

John Sinclair was a good man, but to be reminded how much his father was respected by one of his oldest crofters only made Alex wonder again if he would ever measure up. When the time came for him to assume his father's role as Laird of Balforss, would he be equal to the task?

"I will, Sam. I'll send Da to see you so you can tell him yourself." He patted him on the shoulder.

Peter entered with the water bucket.

"Thanks, man. You're a kind fellow. Let's let Sam sleep now."

Once they were out of the croft, Peter asked, "Will he be all right, sir?"

"Mrs. Swenson will see to him. She's his niece, all the kin

he has left in Scotland. His sons have gone to America. A place called Kentucky."

Peter's eyes widened. "Do they have red savages that roast people and eat them in Kentucky?"

He chuckled. "Aye. But Mrs. Swenson's had a letter from her cousins, and the natives they've met thus far have been the decent sort."

They ambled up the Seaward Trail on horseback toward the north pasture, while the dogs, eager to get to work, raced ahead. Alex spotted the flock of sheep in the distant corner of the field. When last he checked, there had been twenty-eight grazing in this pasture. Now would come the tedious task of herding the sheep out of the pasture and into a holding field for the purpose of counting and assessing their health.

Peter led the horses to the far side of the trail, leaving them to munch on sweet green grasses. Dancing at Alex's feet, Denny and Raphe sensed their time for business was at hand.

"What's to do now, sir?" Peter asked.

"Denny and Raphe will herd the sheep to this gate." He opened a narrow wooden gate set into the stone fence. "It's wide enough for one sheep to pass through at a time. As they go through, we count them."

Peter bowed his head and kicked at a few loose stones.

"Do you know your numbers, Peter?"

He shook his head.

Many people living and working at Balforss didn't know how to read, but most, out of necessity, knew the basics of mathematics. Without that fundamental knowledge, one could easily be cheated.

"Right then. Time to learn your numbers."

Peter jerked his head up, alert.

"Find yourself a stick, man."

The boy ran off toward a stand of trees. He returned with

a length of branch the width of Alex's thumb.

"We'll do this the way my da taught me," he said. The trouble in Peter's expression eased. "Every time I call out *hep*, you make one scratch mark in the dirt." Peter made an experimental mark in the well-packed mud. "The counting will go quickly, so be ready."

"Aye, sir." He braced himself with the determination one might have when preparing to push a boulder up a steep incline.

"At ease, soldier. You'll be called into action soon. You can watch for a bit, aye."

Alex stepped over the stone fence, followed by two leaping dogs. "Are ye ready lads? Walk on."

The dogs took off at breakneck speed toward the flock. Alex executed a series of whistle commands. Between shepherd and dogs, the sheep were skillfully escorted toward the gate, bleating their agitation. "Get ready, Peter."

"Ready, sir," Peter called breathlessly.

"*Hep! Hep! Hep!*"

In no time at all, the sheep were in the holding field, and the counting was done. Alex spent some time examining the sheep for disease and injury. Satisfied all was well, he executed another series of short whistles and commands. The dogs herded the flock back through the gate, the sheep looking at Alex as if to say, *What was that all about?*

"That'll do," Alex called. The dogs raced back to his side. He lavished them with pats and scratches and "Good lads." Their final reward, chunks of dried beef, which they chewed enthusiastically.

"Let's see how you've done, Peter. Shall we count your marks together?"

Peter gathered himself for the task, looking as pale as a soldier before his first battle.

Alex kept a straight face, not wanting to make the lad feel

small. He held up both hands, fingers splayed, wiggling each one as he counted, "One, two, three…"

The boy held up his hands counting along, looking at his fingers as if seeing them for the first time.

By the time they reached twenty-two, Peter had the right of it. He continued hesitantly on his own with only an occasional prompting, all the way to twenty-eight.

"Well done, lad." He tousled his pupil's dirty blond hair. "Well done, indeed. It took me ages to learn my numbers, but you've conquered them in one day."

Peter blushed at the compliment. An irrepressible smile formed on the boy's face. Alex caught a glimpse of the tooth that would replace his missing milk tooth, peeking out from the gum.

"Time to celebrate." He retrieved the food Mrs. Swenson had packed for them along with an earthenware bottle of good ale. The two sat on the stone wall, eating their potato and meat-filled pastries, enjoying each bite with the satisfaction of a job well done.

They passed the bottle of ale back and forth wordlessly until it was finished, then spent some time impressing each other with how well they could belch. While they had a piss behind the bushes on the far side of the road, Peter glanced at Alex's member and back at his own with what seemed to be dismay.

"Dinnae fash," Alex said. "It grows along wi' the rest of you."

After they had stowed themselves inside their trousers and adjusted for comfort, Peter asked, "When does the hair on your parts start to grow?"

"How old are you now?"

"Dinnae ken." Peter shrugged.

"I'd say you're about ten, maybe eleven," he said, appraising the boy. "It'll start to grow in the next three years."

"Robby calls me a baby. Says I willnae be a man until the hair grows on my parts."

"Robby's lived in his father's house his entire life. He's never had to live on his wits like you. Your body may be that of a boy's, but your spirit and courage are that of a man."

"You think so, sir?"

Alex feigned indignation over Peter doubting his word. "I wouldnae take less than a man wi' me to do a man's work."

Peter smiled at him with adoration, the gap in his teeth making him look fragile. It came to Alex that this boy had never been loved. Alex felt as if he'd swallowed something too large and it would not go down. "Are you happy here at Balforss?" he asked, the words coming out with difficulty.

"Oh yes, sir."

"Do you feel safe?"

"I do."

"Good. I'm happy you are here. I consider you a good friend. One I can always count on."

Peter deepened his voice and puffed out his scrawny chest. "My word of honor, sir, I will lay down my life in your service, should you ask me."

Alex remembered the oath he'd made to the duke when he was the same age as Peter, how desperately he had wanted to be a man, how important it had been to him that his oath be taken seriously. He put a hand on Peter's shoulder just as the duke had done. "Thank you, Peter. I accept your solemn oath. You are a Balforss man now."

Tears filled the boy's eyes in contrast to his face-splitting grin.

...

Lucy lowered the broche, a long stick strung with candlewicks, into a vat of melted bee's wax. She drew it out, let it drain, then repeated the process two more times before hanging the broche on a rack to harden. She selected another broche ready for a second dipping and began the process again.

She had hoped the work would distract her, would ease the worry she'd been plagued with all morning. Some was worry over Langley's letter, but the majority was worry over Alex's reaction to the letter.

Langley was here in Scotland. In the Highlands. Nearby. How did he intend to contact her? Did he know his life would be in danger if he were to come to Balforss? And what would she do if he did? What if he were to show up tomorrow and ask for her hand? What then? Even if Alex didn't kill him as he had threatened, would she accept his proposal? Leave Balforss? Leave Alex?

Until Langley's letter had arrived, Lucy had only one choice, which, of course, was no choice at all. Now she had a choice. Marry Alex, a union foisted upon her by her father, or marry Langley, and realize her dream of becoming a viscountess. Her decision should be easy.

Then why was she struggling? Why had her peace of mind been shattered by the letter?

Lucy finished dipping the broche and reached for another.

After only a few days at Balforss, she had come to like the pace at which life bumped and tripped along in the Highlands. She liked Mother Flora. Liked collecting honey and making candles. She had purpose here. What was there for her in London? Even if she returned as Langley's bride, she knew very well a title would not stop those wicked wagging tongues.

And then there was Alex. Yes, he was irritating, impulsive, childish, and uncouth. But he was also handsome, brave, kind, and passionate. He had even given her daisies. Langley had never given her daisies, and he didn't kiss like Alex kissed. He never made Lucy feel like she wanted to curl up on his lap like a cat. Alex may not have a title to offer her, but she preferred the Scot.

The proper thing to do would be to write to Langley, politely decline his offer, and ask that he never contact her again. Why then did she want to see him? The answer shamed her. The answer was as wicked and vindictive as Lucy felt. She wanted to see his face when she spurned him. She wanted to witness his pain, the same pain she had experienced when he had abandoned her.

Lucy selected another broche of candlewicks and began the dipping process.

She imagined several scenarios involving her chance meeting with Langley. Each featured a moment where Langley went down on his knees before her and begged her to marry him. Each time, she would state with noble sympathy that she could not marry him. Her heart belonged to Alex Sinclair, her handsome, brave Highland warrior.

Unfortunately, all the scenarios careened out of her control, ending in unhappiness. In one, Langley killed Alex, and she lived alone for the rest of her life, a martyr to love. In another, Alex killed Langley and was promptly hanged for the offense. The worst was the most probable scenario. Alex discovered Lucy and Langley talking, said he could never trust an inconstant wife, and sent her home shamed and heartbroken.

The broche slipped from her grasp and the rod with the six half-finished candles fell into the vat of hot beeswax. She reached reflexively to retrieve it.

"No," cried Flora, too late. Lucy stuck her hand halfway into the wax before jerking it out.

"*Merde!*"

A quarter of an hour later, Lucy lay on her bed, a damp cloth on her forehead, her right hand submerged in a bowl of cool water sitting on a stand next to her bed. Hot beeswax,

Mother Flora had told her, caused no lasting injury. "By tomorrow morning, you'll be right as rain."

The incident had, however, left her with a beastly burning sensation that throbbed, making any movement of her fingers painful. The accident had been entirely her fault. Flora had warned her to remain attentive at all times, but she'd let her mind drift and so had paid the price.

Perhaps it was God's punishment for being prideful. For wanting to personally deliver her rejection instead of writing a polite letter. For wanting to restore her pride after Langley had failed to return her affections. For wanting 'a piece of her own' as John Sinclair would put it. *That's spiteful and petty.* She didn't see herself as a spiteful person. Yet, that's what she was. How had she become so utterly wretched?

A sudden commotion echoed in the entry. Who was shouting? Footsteps thundered up the staircase.

"Lucy! Lucy!"

Her bedchamber door flew open, and Alex launched himself to her bedside, dropping to his knees, out of breath, fear tightening his features.

"Ma said you burnt your hand. Are you all right, lass?"

Overwhelming remorse snuck up on her. "I'm sorreeee," she keened. Tears rolled down her cheeks like rain. She covered her face with her good hand to hide from Alex.

"Hush, lass. It was an accident."

The bed dipped. She felt the comforting warmth of his body next to her. He removed the damp cloth and caressed her forehead with his lips.

Lucy sniffed, took a few gulping breaths, and tried to speak. "It was my fault. Everything is my fault. I'm sorry about the letter, Alex. I don't want to marry Langley. I want to marry you, but I don't want you to kill him." She fell apart again, blubbering, sobbing so hard her shoulders shook with the effort.

"*Wheesht*, now. *Wheesht*. Dinnae fash. I willnae kill him."

"How can you want to marry me? I'm awful. I'm spoiled, and prideful, and nasty to you." She considered her appearance and wailed, "And I look terrible."

Alex chuckled.

"Don't laugh at me," she blurted. Even as she said it, she knew he wasn't laughing at her so much as her histrionics. She was being dramatic, as her father would say. Exactly as she had as a child. She wiped her eyes and nose on the bed linens, then struggled to a sitting position and made herself stop crying.

"Better now?" Alex asked.

She nodded and sniffed.

"Listen to me. You are not awful. You're a bonnie, braw, and canny young lass. And I want to marry you for all those reasons."

"What do you mean?" An unladylike hiccup escaped.

"You're bonnie because you're spoiled, but you came to Balforss, rolled up your sleeves, and learned to make honey and candles wi' my ma. You're braw because you're prideful. You're full of dignity and courage, and you willnae compromise what's most important to you. You're canny because you're nasty to me. No one else dares." He smiled, teasing her now. "You challenge me. You stand up to me." He looked abashed and lowered his voice. "And you point out when I'm wrong. When I'm being an ass." Alex softened and touched her cheek. "And you dinnae look terrible. You look like a woman who has toiled all day for her family. That's a beautiful and noble thing, aye. You're a true Highland beauty."

She stared at him with her mouth half open. Did he really see her faults as assets?

"Show me your hurt hand," he said.

She placed it on his outstretched palm, wet and looking

small by comparison.

He bent and pressed his lips to the top of her hand where it wasn't red. "I'll take my daily ration now, if you please." He placed a soft kiss on her mouth. "I'll see you at supper."

...

Alex bid Lucy good night straight after supper. His poor wee lass was tired as a lamb after the incident with the hot wax. Thankfully, Lucy had said the pain in her hand had passed. She would sleep well tonight.

He and his father retired to the library, where they took a dram of whisky and talked of plans for purchasing another two hundred cheviots, sheep prized for their excellent wool. Listening to his father speak of Balforss's domestic future soothed Alex. His father was preparing him for the role of laird he would one day assume, slowly easing the mantle of responsibility down upon his shoulders. Still, Alex wondered if he would ever acquire the strength and wisdom necessary to bear that weight.

A knock on the library door interrupted their peaceful discussion.

"Come," his father called out.

Uncle Fergus entered, his face an angry red.

"What troubles you, *bràthair-cèile*?" his father asked, using the Gaelic for brother-in-law.

"There's a lad outside would have a word with you."

"About?"

"Patrick Sellar." Uncle Fergus spit out the name like a bad taste.

His father set his whisky down and slipped on his waistcoat. "Bring him in."

Moments later, Fergus coaxed the lad through the library door. The boy's eyes darted about the room then widened when they landed on Laird John's imposing figure. Soot covered the lad's clothing and ringed his face near his nose and mouth. He held his hat in hands wrapped in filthy bandages.

"What's your name, son?" John asked.

"Callum Mackay, sir."

"He walked here from Rosal Village," Fergus said. "Took him three days. Tell the laird what you saw, lad."

"Aye, sir." On the brink of manhood, his voice faltered from low to high and back again. Alex estimated he was no older than fifteen. "Last week Mr. Sellar telt my grannie her croft was to be fired. She could leave it or burn wi' it. He didnae care."

In a low voice, Fergus inserted, "His granny's Margaret Mackay. Lives near Strathnaver about twenty miles west."

"When Mr. Sellar and his men come three days ago, Granny wouldnae leave and…well…"

"Ah, Jesus. They didn't." The muscles in his father's jaw jumped and flexed, a sure sign he was enraged.

"Aye, they did. My ma and me come to help her move and found her croft afire just as the men rode awa'. We pulled her free of the croft in time, but I dinnae ken she'll live. She's awful bad."

"Has a doctor come?"

"There's a healer with her now, doing what she can." The boy stepped closer to John, hands fisted, his birdlike frame shaking with anger. "Mr. Sellar's men barred the door, wedged a log against it, set fire to the croft, then rode away laughing. It was pure luck we were there. They meant to kill her, sir," he said, his voice breaking. "I come to you because folk say you're the only laird brave enough to go against the Sutherland and get justice for my Granny Mackay."

John placed a hand on the lad's shoulder. "You did right coming to me. First thing tomorrow you'll take us to your granny, aye. Mr. Munro will show you to the kitchen. After you've eaten, he'll find a place for you to sleep."

"Thank you, sir."

"Fergus, have Mrs. Swenson look at the boy's hands, as well."

Fergus led the boy away.

Alex said, "By the looks of him, he hasnae eaten a good meal in a long while."

His father made no response, just paced in front of the fire, one hand propped on his hip, the other rubbing his forehead.

"Da, you know what we must do," he said. "This is the proof we need to stop that bastard, Sellar."

John continued his pacing. He freed his queue and swiped a hand through his hair.

"We cannae let this stand," he said with more vehemence. Again, no answer from his father. "If you willnae do something, then I—"

"Enough." John held up a hand.

Alex stilled under his father's heated gaze. He knew instantly he'd misread him. He'd misread calculation for indecision. John Sinclair would never let this injustice stand.

"Go tell the men we ride to Strathnaver tomorrow before dawn. Then ask Mrs. Swenson to have provisions set aside for us. We'll be gone two, maybe three days." Before Alex headed off, his father said, "You know what this means, son. When we bring charges against Sellar, we make ourselves a target. I dinnae ken what the man will do, but you can believe Sellar will fight back."

Alex stopped himself from smiling. He welcomed a chance to go head-to-head with Sellar and his men. The rat-faced bastard had threatened his woman. Sellar was a man who needed killing, and he wanted to deliver the fatal blow.

"We'll be ready, Da."

Chapter Ten

The next morning, a Saturday, Alex sat atop Goliath, head bent and leaning into gale force wind. An early winter storm blew in from the North Sea, making conditions for travel less than ideal. The men, heads hooded with plaids to shield against the sleet, made decent progress along the coastal trail, despite the weather. By sunrise, they crossed into Sutherland and took the bridge at Bighouse over Strath Halladale waters. They wound their way around Melvich, passing through Strathy around noon.

Riding single file, his father led, and then Callum, Fergus, Magnus, and Declan followed in that order. Alex brought up the rear. All six men rode silently, cold, wet, and uncomfortable.

They had a grim task ahead of them. His father would inspect the remains of Margaret Mackay's croft in Naver. Then, if she still lived, he would gather what details he could from Granny Mackay. If his father had further plans, he had not yet revealed them to him. Whatever came next, Alex had faith his father would do the right and honorable thing no matter the risk.

Alex appreciated the quiet ride. His mind drifted often to his betrothed. Lucy was nothing like the woman he had dreamed he would one day marry. Oh, she was bonnie, had a comely figure, and a sweet mouth. But she was not the biddable lass he had imagined. She was strong-willed, outspoken, argumentative, and often infuriating. To Alex's surprise, he found her spirit arousing. Just as he appreciated a worthy sparring opponent, Alex enjoyed the challenge of his difficult woman.

Lucy had been abed when they'd left Balforss. Ill at ease about leaving without a farewell, he had deliberated for several minutes with a quill poised over a blank sheet of parchment. What to write? Words of devotion, regret, desire, reassurance? Running short of time, he'd scribbled five words.

He smiled remembering his message, words that would spark equal feelings of passion and anger in the wee bizzum. He wished he could be present when she read his note. It seemed the sharper her temper, the more passionate her kisses.

The storm dwindled to a fine mist by the time they took their mid-day meal at a tavern aptly named *Tabhairne Nabhair*, Gaelic for Naver Tavern. Alex tucked into a good bowl of smoked haddock soup—good because it was hot.

Young Callum grilled Declan and Magnus for details about the army. The lad was eager to join a Highland regiment. King George was fighting wars on two fronts, France and America. No doubt the army would take him, despite his age. Perhaps Callum would be better off. The boy's life would be in no more danger on the battlefield than starving and homeless in the Highlands.

"Where's Uncle Fergus?" Alex asked his father.

"I sent him to Invernaver to collect the bailiff, a man named Innis Clyne."

"Why?"

"He'll pen the statements made by the witnesses and swear to them. I'll present the statement to the Chief Magistrate and request a warrant for Sellar's arrest."

"Do you ken the bailiff will come willingly?" he asked.

"He's the brother of Aunt Agnes's half sister's husband. He'll come."

Alex smiled to himself. Family ties were strong in the Highlands, no matter how stretched or how thin.

Two hours later, Fergus arrived at the tavern with Innis Clyne, a small man with whispy white hair, a bulbous nose, and eyes that crinkled shut when he smiled. The bailiff looked a comical sight dressed in waistcoat, breeks, stockings, buckled shoes, and wide-brimmed hat, sitting atop a shaggy, fat-bellied pony.

"Thank you for coming, Mr. Clyne," his father said after Fergus made introductions.

"I'm pleased I can be of service, Laird Sinclair. Munro tells me I'm to record the testimony of several witnesses. May I ask what this is regarding?"

"Murder, Mr. Clyne," John said. "It's best you dinnae speak of the details to anyone."

The smile slowly faded from Innis Clyne's cheeks. "Does this have anything to do with Sutherland's…improvements to the land?"

"You've got the right of it. Any reservations about lending your services?"

"Nae," Clyne said, sitting taller in his saddle. "Lead on, sir."

• • •

They came upon the remains of Granny Mackay's croft late afternoon. Blackened stone walls and hearth outlined where once had been a one-room shelter. Nothing inside the croft had survived the blaze. Sellar's men had also fired the open cow byre and trampled the kale yard.

The Sinclair men circled the property on horseback, seeing no need to dismount. Mr. Clyne, however, clambered down off his pony, opened his leather satchel, and removed the instruments of his trade—ink, quills, parchment, and a writing board. He walked around the perimeter of the croft, making quick, short notes. Then he stepped inside the burnt walls, lifted a few mangled tools, and turned over a charred bucket. His quill scratched away after inspecting each item.

"Did your granny own any livestock?" Clyne asked Callum.

"Oh, aye. A cow and six chickens."

"Where are they now?"

"Dinnae ken. Run off. Or maybe the men took 'em."

Clyne made another note, examined the kale yard, made more notes, and then returned his writing tools to his satchel.

"Have you finished here, Mr. Clyne?" John asked.

"Aye. I've seen what I need to see."

"What was it you were writing, sir?" Callum asked. The question hung on the lips of every man, yet Callum was the only one willing to risk looking ignorant.

"The croft belongs to Lady Sutherland. The livestock, the produce, and the possessions lost in the fire belong to your granny. I've made an inventory so that she might recover their value should Patrick Sellar be found guilty of willful destruction of property."

"How did you know Patrick Sellar was responsible?" John asked.

"He's responsible for clearing all of Sutherland. That alone is no crime. Our task will be to prove he ordered the croft fired with Mrs. Mackay inside. That's the only way we can get him for attempted murder."

"Right, then," John said, turning his horse eastward. "Take us to your granny, Callum."

On the way to see Granny Mackay, Callum explained that his father had died two years ago. Since then, the boy had been working the potato fields, or tattie rigs, as he called them, alongside his mother. The foreman had recently informed all the Rosal Village crofters this would be their last harvest. By winter, Callum and his mother would lose their croft, as well.

"I'd join the army," Callum said. "But I worry aboot me mam. I cannae leave her alone."

"Dinnae fash yourself, son," John said. "We'll sort things once Mr. Clyne has finished with his writing."

Alex marveled at his father's ability to interact with strangers both highborn and low. He had an uncanny way of making people feel at ease in his presence, yet all the while maintaining his air of command. Friends and enemies alike respected John Sinclair. Was his da born a leader or had John Sinclair learned the skill from *his* father, Laird William? Once again, the question of whether he had the proper temperament to be Laird of Balforss ate away at Alex's confidence.

The afternoon sun at their backs created elongated shadows on the dirt road before them, eerie dark images of apocalyptic horsemen, a mesmerizing sight.

Magnus urged his horse even with Goliath. "Seems you and Miss Lucy are on good terms again."

Alex snapped out of his trance. "Oh, aye. She likes me well enough."

Hearing the exchange, Declan turned in his saddle. "The gowans worked, did they not, Alex?" He lifted an I-told-you-so chin to Magnus.

"She liked the gowans fine, but she likes my kisses even more."

Magnus gave a lusty laugh. "Ye gomeril. I ken she liked you from the start. Did you no' mind the way she looked at you on the road from Inverness?"

"Nae. When did she look at me?"

"Mostly when you werenae looking at her. And when she was deviling you for being such an ass—"

"You calling me an ass?" Alex shot a hot look at Magnus.

Magnus pointed an accusing finger back at him. "Dinnae deny it. You know you were a horse's ass playing her for the fool."

Declan laughed, and Alex shouted for him to shut the hell up.

From behind them, Fergus added, "Magnus is right. You were a horse's ass."

"I dinnae need your opinion, Uncle."

Is everyone set on riling me today?

"Anyway," Magnus said, "my point is, anyone could tell by looking at the two of you that you never had cause for concern. You were made for each other, man." The white of Magnus's teeth flashed through his black beard, quelling Alex's mounting agitation.

"Fine." Alex blew out a gust of surrender. "I was an ass, and I paid for it dearly." He waited a few seconds before he smiled and said, "But I ken she likes my kisses, too."

Their party reached Rosal Village near sunset. Callum's croft was similar in size to Granny Mackay's, one room with a roof barely tall enough for a man to stand upright. The lad scrambled down off the horse John had loaned him for the journey and ran to the door, calling for his mother. The remainder of their party dismounted. Declan led the horses and Mr. Clyne's pony into a clearing where they could graze.

When Callum motioned for Mr. Clyne and John to step inside the croft, Alex followed them into the tiny space. He got no further than the threshold. His father's broad shoulders blocked the view of the suffering woman, but he could hear her moans of agony. He sniffed the air. Callum's mother must be roasting meat for supper. His mouth watered.

Hunger turned to bile instantly when his father bent to one knee, and Alex saw the horribly burned body of Granny Mackay. Both arms, hands, and legs were blackened and blistered. One side of her face had been burned, leaving only a few wisps of grey hair trailing from her oozing red scalp. A light-weight flannel had been draped over her middle for modesty's sake. Granny Mackay's entire body shook uncontrollably. The pain from her burns must be unbearable.

Mr. Clyne asked Callum's mother, "Can she speak?"

Mrs. Mackay shook her head, then lifted her apron to her face and wept.

Overwhelmed, he stumbled out of the croft into the dusky light. He bent over, thinking he might vomit. After a few gulps of fresh air, he straightened. Fergus, Declan, and Magnus stood before him grim-faced.

Alex bared his teeth. "I'm going to kill Patrick Sellar."

. . .

"Is it raining?" Lucy stretched and rubbed the sleep from her eyes.

Haddie swept the bed curtains aside, allowing the sun's cold gray light into her chamber. Hercules, excited to greet Haddie, raced up and down the length of her bed, trampling over Lucy's belly with tiny paws.

"Gonnae no' dae that, ye numpty." Haddie plucked Hercules off the bed. "Oh, aye. It's a dreich day."

"What?"

"It's cold and wet. A miserable day to be traveling," Haddie said, poking up the fire.

"Traveling? Are we going somewhere?"

"Och, nae. It's the Laird and Mr. Alex what's gone awa'."

Lucy tossed aside the bedclothes. "Haddie, you're not making sense this morning. Do you mean Alex and Laird John have left Balforss?"

"Aye. Will you want your grey gown, miss?"

Growing more impatient by the second, she said, "Mr. Alex didn't say anything about a trip. Where did they go?"

"Dinnae ken. Och. I almost forgot. Mrs. Swenson telt me to tae gie ye this." She held out a folded piece of parchment.

Lucy snatched the note from the maid's hand and read.

Dream of me. Your Master

The back of her neck went up in flames. "Impertinent Scot," she mumbled. "Master, my behind. Infuriating."

"What's that, miss?"

She sucked in her cheeks to keep from smiling. Alex wanted her to dream of him while he was away. A romantic thing to ask of a woman. Still, of all the brazen, disrespectful, rude—Alex wrote this to provoke her.

"*Merde.*"

"Are you all right, miss?"

"I'm fine, Haddie. Take Hercules out for me. I'll manage dressing on my own this morning."

Twenty minutes later, she found Mother Flora seated alone in the dining room.

"Good morning, Lucy dear. Is your hand better today?"

"Yes, thank you. Where are Alex and Laird John?" She tried and failed to sound casual.

"Sit, *a nighean*. Have some breakfast and I'll explain. There's no need for alarm."

Lucy swallowed hard and took a seat. In her experience, the words *no need for alarm* always preceded distressing news. Could Alex have gone in search of Langley? He'd promised not to kill the viscount, but he hadn't promised not to hurt him. Her heart banged away inside her chest.

"They have gone to the home of a crofter in Sutherland. John is looking after the welfare of some tenants recently affected by an incident on their property."

Flora revealed what little else she knew of their journey. She noticed how carefully Mother Flora chose her words.

"Will there be danger?"

"There is always an element of danger outside our borders," Flora said.

All Lucy's earlier irritation with Alex and his impertinence vanished, replaced instead with worry for his safety.

"I share your concern." Flora placed a hand over Lucy's and smiled kindly. "They are capable men, dear. Fergus, Declan, and Magnus are with them. They will return in two days' time."

Anxiety over Alex's welfare only partially assuaged, Lucy had little appetite for breakfast. She nibbled some dry toast at Flora's insistence. Two days without Alex. Two days worrying about his safe return.

As if reading her mind, Flora said, "We've so much to do for the wedding feast, there'll be no time to fret. Come. We'll finish the candles this morning. If the weather clears, we can harvest the remaining herbs in the garden and hang them to dry."

True to her word, Flora kept her busy all day Saturday. Lucy had never worked so hard in her life. Oddly, none of the chores felt like work. Candle-making was a new source of pride. Creating something useful for the residents and guests of Balforss had an exhilarating effect on her. She found working in the garden rewarding as well. They harvested the last of the cooking herbs for Mrs. Swenson, tied them into bundles and hung them from the ceiling in the pantry cupboard to dry.

At supper, she practically fell asleep in her bowl of stew.

Flora gently coaxed her out of her chair and guided Lucy to her bedchamber. Haddie was there to help her remove her gown and turn down the bedclothes.

"Will you wake me if Mr. Alex returns?" she asked dreamily as she slipped under the covers.

"Oh, aye. Will you be wearing your yellow gown to kirk in the morning, miss?"

"*Mm-hm.*" Lucy snuggled close to Hercules. "Alex will be home soon, *mon cher.* There's no need to worry."

Chapter Eleven

Alex slept under the roof of a small cow byre crammed side-by-side and head to toe with Declan, Fergus, Magnus, and Mr. Clyne. His father spent the night inside the croft, insisting he relieve Callum's mother from her vigil at Granny Mackay's side.

Alex was in awe of his father's fortitude. It took amazing strength of will to remain in the oppressive atmosphere of the croft with Granny Mackay suffering so. John Sinclair had spent ten years in the army, as opposed to Alex's two, and had witnessed much human suffering when fellow soldiers had been wounded in battle. Perhaps his father could endure their pain because his heart had hardened to such things. Or more likely, John Sinclair's heart held an unfathomable well of empathy for the suffering of others. Whichever the case, Alex was proud of his father. A man's talent with a sword was important, but kindness and compassion make a great man. And Laird John Sinclair was a great man.

After breakfast, Alex spotted three riders approaching. Uncle Fergus went to alert Laird John inside the Mackay croft, while Alex, Declan, and Magnus walked toward the road, all three making certain their swords and pistols were on display. The lead rider reined in and called a halt to the riders behind him. Alex's hands fisted when he recognized Patrick Sellar.

"You again?" Sellar said. "What the hell are Sinclairs doing on Sutherland property?"

"We've come to see what's to do about Granny Mackay," Alex said. "Seems someone tried to murder her five days ago. Set fire to her croft with her inside. Do you ken who that someone is?"

"Feeble-minded old woman probably set her own croft afire. I should charge her for the damages." Sellar removed a rolled document from inside his coat. "I've come to serve a notice of eviction to the occupants of this croft."

A voice boomed behind him. "I'll take that." Alex's father strode forward.

"Laird John. Why am I not surprised to see you here?" Sellar looked down his beak-like nose at Alex's father. "Just as well. Give this to the tenants. I doubt they can read. Tell them they must be out seven days hence."

"Certainly. Right after I finish taking statements from those that witnessed your men fire Margaret Mackay's croft," John said.

The smug smile vanished from Sellar's face. His upper lip curled into a sneer. "I've had enough of your meddling, Sinclair. I'll teach you not to stick your nose into my affairs."

At the challenge, Alex drew his sword, with Declan and Magnus drawing a half second following.

"Halt!" John called.

"Having trouble controlling your men, Sinclair?" Sellar taunted.

The desire to obey his father warred with Alex's need to spill blood. He gripped the hilt of his sword so tight his arm shook. "He's a murderer, Da. The blackguard cannae go unpunished." Alex, Declan, and Magnus advanced one step. "We can take them—"

"Stand down!" his father shouted.

Alex and his cousins froze.

Sensing the mounting tension, Sellar's horse danced under him. The man laughed then spun his gelding around, nearly trampling Alex's father in the process. All three riders took off at a gallop. John Sinclair's jaw worked while he watched them ride away.

"Da! Why did you stop me? We had them. We had them!"

His father grabbed the front of his coat and yanked him until they were nose-to-nose. "Because I don't countenance murder!" he shouted, then shoved him away. A vein in John's temple pulsed with anger. "We no longer settle scores by the sword in the Highlands. We will take Patrick Sellar down, but we will do it with the law." His father cocked a warning eyebrow at him. "Do you understand?"

Declan and Magnus sheathed their swords. After a few seconds, his bloodlust somewhat abated, and his breathing recovered, Alex sheathed his, as well. "I understand, father." He swallowed the remainder of his rage even though it threatened to choke him.

A woman's baleful cry split the morning air, calling the men's attention toward the croft. Mr. Clyne stepped out, leaving the door ajar. "Mrs. Mackay has passed," he said.

"She's free of pain, now. May she bide in God's good hands," John said.

They bowed their heads and murmured a chorus of "Amen."

John turned to his men. "Fergus. You, Declan, and Magnus see Mrs. Mackay receives a proper burial. Then help Callum and his mother gather their things and escort them to Balforss. I'll find a place for Mrs. Mackay. Alex, you and I will return Mr. Clyne safely to Invernaver. I want everyone gone from Strathnaver by noon today. Understood? I've ruffled Sellar's feathers, and he's bound to take action. Be on your guard."

Well after dark, Alex and John strolled their horses into the yard at Balforss. They had seen Mr. Clyne to Invernaver, thanked him, and continued eastward. But Alex and his father hadn't spoken to each other the whole way home.

All of Balforss was asleep. Not a candle lit. Alex pulled Goliath to a stop and dismounted. His father groaned as he swung a long leg over his mare. After two days in the saddle, both men were road weary and longing for their beds.

"I'll see to the horses."

"Where's that wee groom?" John asked.

"Fast asleep, nae doubt." Alex headed off toward the stable without bidding his father good night. Their disagreement over Sellar had not been resolved. According to his mother, he and his father were as stubborn as rocks. They often butt heads about stupid things, and Alex was always the first to back down because his father was always right. But on this, John Sinclair was wrong. If they waited for the law to deliver justice, others might suffer at the hands of Patrick Sellar. Someone had to act now. Someone had to protect those unable to protect themselves. If his father refused to do it, then Alex would take care of the sodding bastard himself.

The horses followed Alex into their stalls without protest and patiently waited to be released from their trappings. He fumbled next to the door where the lantern and flint were normally stored.

"Damn."

"You looking for the lantern, sir?"

"Is that you, Peter?"

"Aye."

"Where's the damn lantern?"

"The rain was getting to it, so I moved it to the other side."
"Thanks. Go back to bed."
"I'll help you."

Alex held a dry bit of hay and struck the flint several times. A moment later, the lantern cast a golden glow around the stable and its occupants. Peter stood in his nightshirt and boots, rubbing his eyes.

"See to the laird's horse. I'll see to Goliath."

"Mrs. Swenson said you and the men went on an adventure."

"Did she, now?" Alex peered over the stall wall at Peter. The boy had to stand on a stool to remove the mare's bit.

"Aye. She said you were venturing into Sutherland on a dangerous mission."

"There was some danger, to be sure." He dug a wooden scoop into a barrel of oats and dumped the contents into the feeding trough.

"Did you see any pirates?"

Alex chuckled. Whether it was the stable surroundings, the boy's company, or sheer exhaustion, he felt the tension of the last two days slip away. "Oh, aye. But not the regular sort of sea pirates. We saw land pirates."

Peter sidestepped out of the stall, grunting with the weight of a saddle larger than himself. He hoisted the saddle onto a rail and, huffing with exertion, asked, "What did they look like?"

"Ugly as sin." Alex launched into a stream of dramatic embellishments for the boy's entertainment. "Their faces were covered in weeping boils. Their mouths hung open, slathering and drooling, and one of them's teeth were filed to sharp points. Another had hair that looked like nothing but long, black snakes. The biggest had a silver ring pierced through his nose just like a bull. Och, they were a lowpin' looking lot. Their horses were prettier than them."

"And did you do battle with them?" Peter's eyes were big

as robin's eggs.

"We came close. But I drew my sword and let out a war cry that could frighten a banshee."

"Then what?"

"They turned tail and ran awa' like scared rabbits." He laughed and ruffled the boy's dirty hair.

"Will you teach me to use a sword?"

Alex unsheathed his dirk and made a notch on the side of the stable door approximately five feet from the floor. "When you're this tall, we'll begin your training. Now get to bed."

Peter flashed a brilliant gap-toothed smile before scampering off toward the bunkroom in the back of the stable. *He's a good lad.* He was very happy for having brought Peter to Balforss.

Alex entered the house through the back door and groped his way down the dark corridor, through the dining room, and into the entry hall. He paused at the foot of the stairs. A faint light flickered through the open door to the library. Most likely his father was having a dram before bed. They should reconcile, put this disagreement to rest. He went inside to apologize.

Instead of his father, he discovered Lucy curled in the wingback chair, fast asleep, an open book on her lap, and her wee dog snoozing before the dying fire. His eyes flit from Hercules back to Lucy. She was wearing a robe of some sort with lacy edges and pink ribbons, which meant she wasn't wearing all the stiff sorts of things underneath that guarded women's soft parts like armor. Alex felt a stirring below his belt. His heart thumped so hard in his chest he woke the damn dog.

Hercules barked a greeting, and Lucy's eyes fluttered open. She looked at Alex for a half second as if determining he was real, then she launched herself out of the chair, the book slipping from her lap to the carpet with a *clump*. Alex saw a blur of bouncing curls before her body thudded against his. He let the rush of gladness wash over him when she flung her arms around his neck and buried her head under his chin. He placed his palms on her slender back and, for the first time, he felt the give of her soft form under his hands, the warmth of her skin through her clothing, the press of her plush breasts against his hard chest.

"You feel so good." He wished he hadn't spoken.

Spell broken, Lucy pushed herself away from him and folded her arms over her bosom. "You were supposed to be home hours ago. You had your mother worried half to death."

Alex grinned, liking the pink patches on her cheeks. "I'm sorry." Christ, he was always apologizing to her. "I didnae mean to worry you."

Lucy unfolded her arms and looked at the floor—something she did when she told white lies. "I wasn't worried. I was angry you weren't more considerate of your mother's feelings."

"Did you get my note?" Alex reached for her. She made a half-hearted attempt to free herself before allowing him to embrace her like before.

"You smell like a horse," she said, sounding petulant.

"You smell like Heaven." He nuzzled her neck and inhaled deeply. "I thought of you all day and dreamed of you all night," he whispered.

She melted against his body. In an instant, he was rock hard, painfully so. Jesus, she made the most intoxicating sounds when he squeezed her.

• • •

Lucy made an involuntary *mm* sound when his velvety beard stubble brushed against her cheek. Then Alex placed his soft lips on hers. By some unspoken command, her mouth opened to him, inviting his tongue to delicately probe the inside of her mouth, slipping in and out just like she imagined—oh dear. That was *exactly* what he was doing. Demonstrating how he would—his hands slid down her backside and cupped her bottom—a roguish thing for him to do, but dear Lord, it felt so deliciously wicked.

Alex and his roving hands seemed determined to undo her, and if she lingered in his arms one more moment, she might let them. Lucy pushed herself away again.

"I'm glad you're back," she said, catching her breath. "Good night." She fled through the library door with Hercules at her heels, both of them bounding up the stairs. She narrowly made it into the safety of her room and put the latch on. Once she had her breathing under control, she listened to Alex's unhurried footsteps, his bedchamber door opening, closing, then a soft scratch on their adjoining door. Smiling, she put her ear to its surface.

"Did you dream of me while I was gone?" Alex asked.

"Yes."

"Oh God, Lucy. I cannae wait to marry you."

"Only one more week."

Her bed was cold. The hot stone Haddie had left had lost all its heat. Lucy snuggled close to Hercules, her body trembling. Though, whether from the chilly bedding or from her recent encounter with Alex, she couldn't tell. She liked Alex's kisses. A lot. She liked the feel of his big hands on her back. And when he squeezed her bottom...

One more week. Only one more week and she would be Alex's wife. In seven days, she would sleep in the same bed with Alex. He would see her naked. She would get to see him naked again. All of him. Lucy's nipples tightened. Did all brides feel this way before their wedding? Would Lucy have felt this way if she were marrying Langley?

She didn't think so. It was Alex who made her shiver. Only Alex, her fierce Highland warrior, could make her feel so...*wanton*.

Chapter Twelve

Lucy spent most of Monday morning trying to learn how to knit. Aunt Agnes and Mother Flora were extremely patient with her. She was, it seemed, utterly hopeless when it came to knitting. After several hours of dropping stitches, losing count, and battling with tension, Lucy gave it up for lost.

"Nae mind," Aunt Agnes said. "My niece never took to knitting. She's fine with a krokr, though. Would you like to try hekling?"

"What's that?"

"It's a way to make lacy things. Only instead of tatting, you use a krokr or a small hook. I ken French folk call it crochet."

"I know what that is." Lucy conjured delicate lace collars and cuffs. She liked the idea of making those more than making dull woolen socks.

"Here, I've got a krokr in my basket and a spool of cotton," Agnes said.

A volley of shouts interrupted the serenity of Mother Flora's parlor. Out of curiosity, Lucy went into the hallway to investigate. The shouts were coming from Laird John's library. Loud Gaelic curses, biblical invectives, accusations involving animals and dung heaps—all very nasty sounding words and most of them from Alex's mouth.

"What's going on down there?" Lucy asked.

"Och, pay them nae mind, dear," Flora said. "John and Alex quarrel constantly. If they ever stopped, I'd call the doctor to have them looked at." She and Aunt Agnes laughed.

"But why? Alex worships his father."

"Because they're two sides of the same coin. Or had you not noticed?"

Lucy startled when the library door slammed. She went to the top of the stairs in time to see Alex storm out the front door. So, someone else could whip Alex into a fury as easily as she could. She darted back to the parlor and snatched her shawl from the back of her chair. "I'm going after him."

"You do at your own peril," Flora called. "Dinnae say I didnae warn you."

When Lucy had riled Alex on previous occasions she'd seen him disappear down a path through the hedgerow. Flora had said the path led to the mill. She suspected that was where she would find him now. The dense stand of trees let little sunlight through their branches, and the path grew dark and silent but for the dried pine needles crunching under her slippers. Gradually, the roar of the falls grew louder, and louder, until it drowned out all but the creak and groan of the mill's giant water wheel. Still, no sign of Alex. She faltered. Had she taken the wrong path?

The trees opened up on a steep stone staircase set into the side of the embankment. Lucy peered over the edge, calculating the risk. Someone would have to be a mountain goat to manage them. If she lost her balance and fell, it might be days before anyone found her. Even if she called out, no one would hear her over the falls. Nevertheless, she picked up her skirts and started down, determined to find out what Alex and his father had quarreled about.

At the bottom, she took a moment to congratulate herself for not breaking her own neck, and then paused, spellbound, bewitched, transfixed by the falls. The bouncing, crashing, splashing River Forss—the torrent from which Balforss drew its name. She understood why Alex would choose this place for his refuge. One look at the falls and anyone could forget their problems.

Having acknowledged its majesty, she tore her gaze from the mesmerizing sight and walked down the bank around the bend in the river. There he stood, a good ten yards away with his back to her. By the set of his shoulders, he was still steaming.

She watched him hurtle stones one at a time as far down the river as his arm could throw. Burning off his anger, she thought. She could sneak up on him so easily. He'd never hear her with the falls drowning out all other sounds. Just then, though, he paused and turned his head, not at all surprised to find her, as if he knew she was there all along. He didn't welcome her, but he didn't warn her off, either. He just nodded slightly, turned away, and resumed his violent stone tossing.

Once he'd exhausted his supply of projectiles, he let his arms fall to his side. His head dropped forward and his shoulders slumped. Defeat? How could that be? Her heart skittered. Alex—her Alex—could never be defeated. He was her protector, her valiant knight, her fierce Highland warrior.

She went to him, wanting to shake him out of his ill humor, but stopped herself in time. Heat radiated off him like a furnace and his entire body, strung taut like her bow string, vibrated. She'd heard people use the expression shaking mad, but she'd never seen it until now.

"He says I'm—" Alex cleared his throat, clouded by

strong emotion. "He says I'm rash. That I dinnae consider the consequences before I act. He says I endanger everyone around me."

It took strength and courage to say those words. Courage *she* never had. A marvel, really. His willingness to reveal himself to her, to lay down his weapons and expose his soft parts. She stood perfectly still, afraid to shatter the moment.

He cast her a sidelong glance so sharp she caught her breath. "Are you sure you want to marry a man like me?"

"Yes," she said without hesitation. "I want to marry a man exactly like you. One who is decisive and quick to act. Because only a man like that can protect me no matter the danger. I know when I'm with you I'm safe."

Alex turned to her, his shoulders and spine molding back into his characteristic cocky stance. A slow smile spread across his handsome face, and cool grey eyes fixed her to where she stood.

"Do ye now?"

Apparently, her answer had a healing effect on him. A moment ago, she'd felt like a brave mouse removing a thorn from a lion's paw. Now, though, the lion turned his hungry gaze on the mouse. He took a step toward her, and she squeaked.

Alex laughed. "Every time I think I know who ye are, you do or say something that knocks me back on my heels."

Relieved she was no longer in danger of being his lunch, Lucy folded her arms and fired back a pert, "I certainly hope so. I would never want anyone to say I was predictable."

"Nae lass. No one could ever say that about you."

Still grinning profusely, Alex plopped himself down on the grassy riverbank and rested his arms atop his knees. He plucked a long stem of grass and chewed the end contemplatively. Then, as if suddenly remembering she was still present, he darted a look from her to the spot next to him—an invitation to sit. And so, she did.

"Did you follow me down here because you were afraid I'd toss myself in the river?"

"I didn't follow you. I... Well, I followed you, but I wasn't..." Lucy huffed. She didn't like being cornered with double-edged questions.

"Ah. You just wanted to be near me."

Lucy let out an exasperated growl. "Why must you be so impossibly full of yourself? I've never met such a self-centered, self-important, supercilious braggart in all my life."

Alex drowned out her tirade with a belly laugh and stretched his long body out on the grass with his arms folded behind his head and his legs crossed. Infuriating man. She refused to look at him. They stayed quiet for a while, listening to the falls in the distance, the birdsong, and the river burbling by.

"Thank you," he said.

She twisted around to see if he was indeed as sincere as he sounded. "For what?"

"For coming to find me. For putting me in a better temper."

"You're welcome."

"Do you ever wonder what it will be like?"

"What what will be like?"

"Being married."

This was new. They were having a serious conversation. One in which they weren't arguing and he wasn't vexing her. "Do you mean what will the wedding be like?"

"Nae. I mean what will we be like together. Will we be happy? Will we like the same things?" He hesitated for a moment and asked in a softer voice, "Will we have children?"

The mention of children warmed her from the inside. "Would you like children?"

"Oh, aye."

He tickled her neck with the tasseled end of the grass stem he had been chewing.

"Sometimes I lie in my bed and I wonder how it will be to sleep next to you. I've never slept next to someone in a bed before."

Something fluttered in her belly before she realized he wasn't talking about making love. He was talking about sleeping, honestly concerned that he might not be able to sleep with her in his bed. "Do you want me to sleep in my own room?" she asked, not meaning to sound so incredulous.

"I do not," he said, as if laying down a royal decree. "I will have *my* wife in *my* bed and no other." He backed off his declarative tone and added, "I was just wondering what it would be like, is all."

"Oh, well…" Lucy reclined on her back next to Alex. "I imagine it will be a lot like this." She adjusted her position until her right side aligned with his left. Heart beginning to thunder in her chest, she asked, "Is this all right for you?"

"Oh, aye. How is it for you?"

"It's quite nice, actually." Truthfully, it was thrilling lying next to the large, powerful, and very warm body of her almost-husband. And if she was completely honest with herself, she was looking forward to Alex's bed and all that came with it—the mattress, the man, and the other things.

Alex rolled to his left and propped his head up to look down at her. "Sometimes I like to sleep on my side."

Their bodies touched and she could almost imagine what his skin would feel like against hers. "I suppose I might be in danger of you rolling over in your sleep and squashing me."

"Like this?" He slung a leg over hers and draped an arm across her belly, then snugged his head into the crook of her neck and breathed in her ear. "Am I crushing you?"

"I'm very comfortable, thank you." She rather liked the weight of him. Her nipples tightened to the point of aching.

They were almost married. Would it be so bad if they started now, instead of waiting until Sunday?

...

The raven-haired beauty wanted him exactly as he was, in spite of what he was—rash, hot-headed, and prone to violence—because she felt safe with him. Contrary to what his father had said, she believed he could protect her from danger. Lucy wanted *him*. And, God save him, he wanted her, needed her, had to have her now.

He buried his nose in her hair and breathed in. "So good," he rumbled. "You smell so good." She turned her head and their lips met. His Lucy was no delicate flower. When she wanted something, she let him know. Sometimes with a look. Sometimes with a word. Sometimes, like now, with a kiss. Breath hot, lips parted, tongue alive and seeking. Oh God, oh God, yes. His cock leapt to attention so fast, his balls ached from the strain. Needing contact, friction, anything to press himself against, he took hold of her ample bottom and pulled her tight against his hips. She answered him with a moan, low and languid. But when she tangled her leg with his, he came close to losing himself.

Their lips disengaged, and Lucy, eyes closed and lips swollen, let her head fall back. He ran his mouth down the side of her neck, laying kisses along the way and resisting the insane urge to bite her.

"Lucy. I want you. I want you as my wife right now. Right here. Will ye have me?"

"Don't stop. Please don't stop."

He took a moment to gaze at her beautiful face, one last look before they joined, before they made love and everything changed. He couldn't help taking time to admire the way her stays pressed against her breasts. He wanted to free them. To see them. To see her skin bared to the sunlight. Should he risk being caught in the act out in the open, the two of them naked? He would like nothing better than to remove her gown, release her stays, strip off her shift and…shit. No time. He was desperate. He'd ruck up her skirts and plunge in now.

"Yeck."

Alex halted abruptly and looked at Lucy. She frowned back at him.

"Is something wrong, love?"

A young voice asked, "Are you two kissing?"

They craned their heads around, searching for the intruder.

Damn.

Lucy extricated herself from under him and sat up immediately, tidying her hair and straightening her skirt. "Hello, Peter. What are you doing here?"

"Lady Sinclair sent me to fetch you for dinner."

"Tell her we'll be there soon," Alex said, not bothering to disguise his irritation.

Peter jammed his hands in his pockets and rocked back and forth from foot-to-foot. "I checked the candle shed first, but you werenae there."

Alex ground his teeth. "Fine. You found us. You can go now."

"But Lady Sinclair said I was to bring you back with—"

"Bloody hell, man, leave us!" he roared.

The boy ran for his life.

Lucy got to her feet, laughing, whereas his aching balls could find nothing funny about this moment. Shouldn't she be just as frustrated as he by the interruption? She reached a slender hand down to help him up. He had half a mind to yank her to the ground again. He was still more than ready to ravish her.

But the moment of Lucy's surrender had come and gone,

and the family waited for them at the dinner table. It took a monumental effort to stand. He'd known ninety-year-old men who sprang to their feet faster.

"I suppose I should thank Peter for saving me," she said.

"What do you mean by that?"

Lucy dimpled. "I have you to protect me from the world, but who will protect me from you?"

Bloody hell. The wedding wasn't for another six days. What the devil was he going to do with this throbbing walloper in the meantime?

...

That evening, Lucy met Alex for a walk in the garden, a custom they'd fallen into naturally, during which they would share the happenings of their day. Alex, having reached a tentative truce with his father, had been gone for much of the afternoon, visiting one of the crofters living on the property. He returned home with the sad news that the crofter, a man well into his seventies named Old Sam, had passed away in the same cottage in which he was born.

"Old Sam thanked my da for not making him move off the land. It was a kindness not many lairds offer their crofters these days."

"I'm glad to hear he doesn't turn people out of their homes. I was upset when I learned what had happened to the family we met on the road near Golspie."

"My da's nothing like that cruel bastard, Patrick Sellar."

"The odious man I met in the Latheron Inn?"

"Aye, that's the one I told you about before. Lady Sutherland's factor. He manages her property."

Sutherland. That was Langley's relation. "Is Lady Sutherland a bad person?"

"Dinnae ken. I've never met her. Da says she doesnae

care about the people that live on her land. She only cares about the money she makes from her sheep farms."

According to Alex, his father was a unique Highland laird. While most Scots who owned large properties had moved to Edinburgh or London, leaving their factors to manage the daily operation of their estates, John Sinclair had chosen to remain on his land and forgo life in Society with all its cultural and domestic fineries, in favor of living the life of a real Highlander.

"It's the land, ye ken. The land is what gives us our strength. Here, we have the freedom to behave like Scots. London Society requires one to..." He shook his head, looking for the right word. "Conform," he said with a measure of contempt. He must have seen her bristle. "Sorry. I didnae mean there's something wrong with that way of life. It's just not the way we live. You've been here long enough. You must see the difference."

"I do. How do you know the difference?"

He gave her a crooked smile. "I've been to London, Lucy."

She felt the color rise in her cheeks. "Oh, yes. I forgot." She recovered quickly from her brief gaffe. "You're very proud of your father, aren't you?"

"He's the finest man I know," he said. "It's no small thing to be the son of a great man, as you must know, being the daughter of a duke."

Lucy was pleased Alex had pointed out that last part about her father. Had he not, she would have.

"I, em..." Alex paused and Lucy gave him her full attention. "I worry sometimes."

"About what?"

"I worry I may never be as good as my da. Good enough to be Laird of Balforss."

She sensed what it cost Alex to admit his fear. At that

moment, she would have done anything to erase his doubt. She put a hand to his cheek and waited until he met her gaze. "In my eyes, you are a giant among men."

Alex exhaled and let his forehead meet hers.

"We had a narrow escape this morning," she said.

He trailed his lips to her ear and whispered, "Lucy, I want—" He jerked away suddenly, his eyes trained on Haddie rushing toward them, apron clutched to her bosom. "Mr. Alex, Mrs. Swenson says you're to come quick as you can. Wee Peter's looking peely-wally."

Alex sprinted toward the kitchen, and Lucy picked up her skirts to follow in his wake, wondering what the devil peely-wally meant. She soon found out. Inside the kitchen, still warm from the fires used to cook the evening meal, Peter stood swaying before Mrs. Swenson, fighting to keep his eyelids from shutting.

"What's the matter?" Alex asked, kneeling down beside Peter, turning him to get a better look at his face.

The change in Peter since earlier in the day alarmed Lucy, but she thought she recognized the problem. "Alex, don't go near Peter. I suspect he has the mumps, and if you've never had them, you could get very sick."

Alex stood and stepped away while Lucy took his place before the boy.

"What makes you think it's the mumps?" Alex and Mrs. Swenson asked at the same time.

Mrs. Swenson added, "He's got no swelling."

"I've had it, and my brother." Feeling his forehead, she asked the boy, "Do you have a headache?"

"My head hurts me something terrible, miss," he said, obviously in pain.

"What else is different, sweetheart?"

Peter's eyes opened upon hearing the endearment. "I'm so tired all the sudden, and my arms and legs pain me right down to the bone."

Lucy rose. "I'm very sure you have the mumps, Peter. The good thing is you'll get better. The bad thing is you'll have to stay in bed for some time." She turned to Alex. "Can he stay in one of the guest rooms in the house? It will be easier for me to care for him there."

The worry on Alex's brow smoothed. "Did you hear that, man? Miss Lucy will be seeing after you." He reached automatically to ruffle the boy's hair, but Lucy stayed his hand, shaking her head.

"You and Peter will have to be separated for at least a week before you are out of danger." She put an arm around the boy. "Come with me, sweetheart. The first thing you need is a bath."

Lucy received raised eyebrows from John and Mother Flora when she walked past the parlor with her patient in tow. At Lucy's request, Haddie brought up enough hot water to fill the small bathing tub. She gave Peter strict instructions to scrub every inch of his body thoroughly.

"Use soap," Lucy said firmly. She could never understand why boy children had such an aversion to soap. "And wash your hair, too. You smell like a sweaty horse." While Peter bathed, Lucy fetched a mug of beef broth from the kitchen. According to Mrs. Swenson, he had eaten nothing at supper. With the mug in one hand, she knocked on the door with the other. "May I come in, Peter?"

Peter opened the door tentatively. Now clean, he was almost unrecognizable, with his blond hair still wet and plastered to his head. Lucy thought he was quite a handsome child. He would probably grow into a good-looking man. Right now, he looked like a waif, drowning in the nightshirt Alex had lent him.

She examined behind his ears. "You did a good job of washing. Hop into bed. I want you to drink some broth before you sleep."

Peter pointed. "You want me to sleep in this big fancy bed?"

"That's the only bed in the room, so yes, that's the bed I mean." She pulled back the linens and Peter climbed in.

He looked around the room wide-eyed. "Does your room look like this?"

"Yes. Very much like it." She helped prop him up with pillows at his back.

"And Mr. Alex's room looks like this, as well?"

"I've never seen Mr. Alex's room, but I imagine it looks similar. Here." She handed him the mug of beef broth. "Try drinking some. It's not too hot."

Peter dutifully gulped it down in one breath. He gasped when he finished, handed her the mug, and wiped his mouth with the back of his hand. "Thank you, Miss Lucy." A soft belch escaped.

"You're excused," Lucy said.

"What?"

"Whenever you burp, you're supposed to say 'excuse me.' It's not polite to burp, you see."

"It's not?"

"No. You should try not to burp in front of people, but if you do, you must say 'excuse me' or 'pardon me.'"

"But Mr. Alex burps," Peter said, and added, "He showed me. He can burp loud and for a very long time. You should ask him to show you."

"Yes, well, I imagine polite rules don't apply when it's just men." Lucy pulled the bedclothes up, allowing Peter to slide down under them. "Go to sleep now. There's more willow bark tea for your headache right next to the bed."

"Wait." Peter's call stopped her from pulling the bed curtains. "Could you leave them open, miss? I'm not used to being closed in when I sleep."

"Of course. Good night. I'll see you in the morning."

Alex was waiting for her in the hall outside Peter's room. "How does he fare?" he asked.

"He'll be fine. It just takes time. Will you send for a doctor just to be sure?"

"I have. He'll be here tomorrow."

"Right now, he's fascinated with the inside of the house, but I'm afraid he'll become bored very soon. It might be difficult to keep him in bed."

"A week, you say?"

"It's best to keep him quarantined to prevent others from catching it. Haddie had mumps when she was a girl. She and I can care for him."

"Thank you, Lucy. It's kind of you. He has no one, you ken."

"He has you. That's no small thing."

"There's so many of them." Alex seemed to focus on something far away. "Hundreds of children roaming about with no home and no parents. Starving. Suffering. Even dying."

His kindness moved her. He had taken off his waistcoat and stock, leaving his shirt open at the neck. She laid a hand on his shirt and felt the soft, springy curls of his chest hair at the opening. "It's late. You should be in bed," she said.

"I couldnae. I need more medicine."

"What?"

He slipped a hand behind her back, and pulled her close, holding her firmly against his body. "Your kiss. It's what keeps me alive. It's what makes me strong."

He kissed her long and urgently. She resisted only for a moment, then melted into him, let his whiskers bristle her chin, inhaled the smell of the long day on his skin. When Alex released her, she staggered, and he swept her into his arms in one sudden motion. Circling her arms around his neck, she rested her forehead on his cheek as he carried her down the hall.

He set her down in front of her bedchamber door, and said, "It takes every last ounce of my strength to keep from following you into this room, barring the door, and taking you."

His thick and velvety words thrilled her, stirred her desire. She lost her will to fight and let her body surrender. She pulled open his shirt glowing white in the night hallway, making the rest of him look dark by contrast, and lay an impulsive kiss on his chest.

He shivered. "Jesus, woman. Are you trying to make this even more difficult for me?"

"Why do you stop?" she whispered.

Her words had the effect of a slow match to a fuse. In a sudden burst of passion, he pushed her against the wall and yanked up the side of her skirt with one hand. Shaking with desire, he kissed her, caressed her, consumed her. He let his rough hand roam from her bared hip, down her thigh, and back up the inside of her leg toward her...oh God. He was almost...she needed him to...just a little farther. Lucy's involuntary response to his rough advance should have made her blush. Instead, she answered his unstoppable need. Only the sound of a door opening down the hall brought them to an abrupt stop.

Out of the dark end of the corridor, they heard, "Alex? Is that you?"

"Yes, Ma. Just...erm, saying good night to Lucy," he groaned.

"How is our patient?" Flora asked.

"He's fine," Lucy said a little feebly. Then added, "He's asleep, I think."

"Oh, good. Good night, then," Flora said.

"Good night," Alex and Lucy said in unison.

Flora lingered in the doorway. Realizing she would remain there until they, too, said their good nights, Lucy stifled a giggle.

"Night, Alex."

"Night, Lucy," Alex said through clenched teeth.

They entered their respective bedchambers. Lucy closed her door, then ran to the trunk still barricading the entrance to Alex's room and put her ear to the cool surface. He was there, as she knew he would be. She could hear his breathing.

"That was close," she said.

"Very close. A few more seconds and I wouldnae have been able to stop."

"Will you dream of me?" she asked.

"I already am."

Chapter Thirteen

Alex spoke to Dr. Farquhar the next morning, a Tuesday. The doctor confirmed Lucy's suspicion. Peter had a case of the mumps. As a precaution, he had the doctor check the other lads working on the property. No one else presented symptoms. A relief. Mumps could spread like wildfire throughout Balforss, bringing the running of the estate to a grinding halt.

Lucy allowed him to stand at the boy's door and talk to him from a distance. He was relieved to find the boy's health improved after only one night's rest. Hercules served Peter well, keeping his spirits high and boredom at bay. The two became great friends immediately.

By Tuesday evening, the lad looked a comical sight, like a chipmunk with his neck swollen just below his cheeks on both sides. He also looked like a prince propped up in the bed with clean hair and face. Alex had mentioned to Lucy that Peter could neither read nor write and had only a limited grasp of basic mathematics. She took it upon herself to teach him his letters and reported Peter's progress at supper. As

Alex suspected, the clever boy proved to be a willing and able student.

On Wednesday afternoon, he found Peter in an enviable position, propped up in bed with Lucy seated next to him, her arm around him as she read.

"As you value your pence,
at the hole take your aim,
chuck all safely in,
and you'll win the game."

Peter glanced up at the doorway. "Mr. Alex."

"I recognize that," he said, and rattled off the rest of the children's tale.

"Chuck-Farthing, like trade,
requires great care;
the more you observe,
the better you'll fare."

He smiled. "*The Pretty Little Pocket Book.* That was my favorite when I was a wee lad."

"Miss Lucy is teaching me to read. I know my letters and I can count to one hundred. I can even write my name. Want to see?"

Lucy brought him the slate tablet upon which Peter had been practicing his writing. He smiled at the boy's childish scrawl but recognized the achievement as significant. She'd spent only two days with him. He was like a sponge. The time Lucy spent teaching Peter had a positive effect on her, as well. She was continuing to blossom. It occurred to him, for the first time, that she would make an excellent mother.

"I'm proud of you, Peter," he said.

Peter's chest inflated. "I'm proud of me, too."

Haddie appeared behind Alex in the hallway with a tray, and he moved aside to let her into the room.

"I've got your dinner, Peter. Mrs. Swenson's made mince and tatties."

"Wash your hands first," Lucy said in a low voice. "And Haddie, will you please take Hercules out to do his business?"

Peter slid out of bed and dutifully scrubbed his hands in the washbasin. After Haddie had finished laying out the table, the boy pulled out a chair for Lucy, who in turn took a seat. He made a gentlemanly bow then proceeded to take his own seat.

She turned to Alex and explained, "We're practicing our manners."

Haddie exited with Hercules, her lips sucked in and pressed tightly together in an effort to keep from laughing.

Alex leaned against the door jam, arms folded across his chest. He'd seen Peter eat in the kitchen in the past, always hunched over his plate protectively, holding a spoon in a death grip, and shoveling food into his mouth as fast as he could. Witnessing what followed was entertaining, but also disturbing.

Peter picked up a serviette, tucked it into the collar of his nightshirt, and delicately collected a fork in one hand and a knife in the other. The boy proceeded to eat—a slow, if not clumsy process—with occasional admonitions from Lucy.

"Take your time."

Lucy demonstrated patience she'd never offered Alex before.

"Chew before you swallow."

If he didn't know better, he might be jealous of the attention she lavished on Peter.

"Elbows off the table."

When Peter finished, he wiped his mouth on his serviette, placed it back on the tray, and said, "May I please be excused, Miss Lucy?"

After tucking Peter back into bed, Lucy turned toward the doorway and said, "Close your mouth, Alex."

He jerked to attention and tipped his head toward the

hallway. "Could I have a word, Lucy?"

"You forgot to say please," Peter said.

Cheeky bastard correcting his manners. Christ, Lucy was creating a monster.

She leaned over Peter and whispered, "It's not polite to correct adults, sweetheart," and then kissed him on the forehead. "Sleep well." She swept out of the room past Alex and down the hall.

He took one quick look at the smug child in the bed before he turned and stomped after her calling, "Lucy. I'll have a word, *if you please*."

The fact that he had to chase her all the way downstairs and into the library only added to his irritation. He found her searching for more books with which to educate the cur occupying the guest bedchamber. Lucy looked beautiful, as always, serene and self-assured.

Maddening.

"He's not a pet, ye ken." He used the voice of authority, a tone he'd often heard his father use when confronting his mother.

Lucy lifted an eyebrow. "I beg your pardon?"

"What you're doing with the boy. It'll be hard for him to go back to the stables after you've taught him to be a wee gentleman," he said a little unkindly.

She lifted her chin to scan the bookshelves. "Maybe he doesn't need to go back to the stables. Perhaps he would be of more use in the house as a footman, or an underbutler, or as your man."

"My man?"

"Your valet. You know, to take care of your things and help you dress."

"I am not a woman," he said, his Highland accent becoming more pronounced with his rising anger. "I dinnae need help dressing myself. And we dinnae have butlers and footman at Balforss."

Lucy tore herself away from the bookcase to look at him. "Why not? Is there a law against having footmen in the Highlands?" She gave him a sweet smile. It's what she did when she said something sarcastic. He hated it.

"Look," he said, trying to maintain his temper. "I dinnae mind you teaching him his letters, but I'll ask you to stop teaching him to bow, and say please and thank you, and calling him sweetheart, and—"

"Alexander Sinclair. Are you jealous?" Lucy advanced on him with a predatory look.

He backed away a few steps and fetched up against the desk. "Dinnae be daft. Of course, I'm not jealous of…of…" Alex had never seen her look at him this way, half amused and half…what? Hungry? She leaned against him, and his traitorous body responded in opposition to his brain.

"Are you sure you're not just a little jealous?" she whispered very close to his mouth.

He felt himself surrendering. "Well, you never call *me* sweetheart."

"That's because I have another name I call you." She placed light kisses on his neck.

"What name is that?" His question came out as a groan.

"I can't tell you until after we're married." Then, she kissed him full on the mouth.

He was struggling not to lose track of the conversation. Her bold behavior shocked him, but he liked it. A lot. She pushed herself away from him, laughing, then glanced down at the bulge in his trousers. Lucy was in no way disquieted. Quite the opposite. He saw a flush of pink creep up her chest. She was pleased with what she'd done to him, the minx.

"Come help me select another book for Peter."

He was about to protest, but she put a finger to his lips.

"Dinnae fash, Alex," she said, using the common

Scottish phrase to tease him. Then, more seriously, "Peter gets impatient with the etiquette quickly. It's just a game to him. He likes learning to read and write, but he's eager to get back to the stables. He loves horses. That's all he talks about, really. Horses and you, whom he admires above all other men. When he gets back to the stables, I'm sure he'll chuck all his manners. But he'll have them if ever he needs them."

Speechless, he gave her an apologetic look. She returned a look of complete forgiveness. And he felt the last tumbler fall into place as his heart unlocked. He was in love with her. Completely, immutably in love with Lucy.

Should he tell her? Did he have the courage? Would she laugh? Perhaps if he whispered the words in her ear... He reached to pull her close, but the rumble of hooves and rattle of harness pulled his attention away from his purpose. He went to the window to see who had arrived. One look at the occupants of the carriage and he backed away immediately.

"Oh, Christ. Dig me a grave."

...

Utterly baffled by Alex's reaction to the carriage, Lucy asked, "Why? What's the matter?"

"My mother's kin come for the wedding."

"But the wedding's not until Sunday."

Flora called from above stairs, "Alex! John! Cousin Diana is here with Sir Ranald. Alex, where are you?"

Looking like a cornered animal, he whispered, "Dinnae tell her where I am." He folded himself into the wingback chair facing the fire so he couldn't be seen. Just then, the door to the library opened and Alex's father John slithered inside, holding a finger to his lips. He went straight to the wingback chair and, finding it occupied, said something in Gaelic that sounded like a curse word.

"Get out of my chair," John said.

"I got here first," Alex hissed.

"Well, it's my chair." John attempted to remove his son bodily from the seat. A scuffle ensued with much grunting and growling and, Lucy thought, some laughter.

"What is going on with you two loons?"

Lucy, John, and Alex whipped their heads around to see Flora, hands jammed on her slim hips.

"Fighting like a couple of weans when you should be out greeting our guests like proper hosts." Her scolding evoked shamed faces from the men, whereas Lucy was bewildered by everyone's behavior.

Seeing her confusion, Flora said, "My dear Cousin Diana and her husband Sir Ranald of Ulbster have arrived. I wonder if they've brought Liam and Elizabeth wi' 'em. Come with me, Lucy. I cannae wait to introduce you." Flora turned and glared at the men. "And you two, get out there and greet our guests. Now."

Flora, John, Alex, and Lucy lined up outside the front door to Balforss while the driver helped the passengers disembark. A big woman, both in size and volume, was the first to emerge from the carriage. Lucy guessed the woman was Cousin Diana. She and Mother Flora embraced. At last, Diana released Flora and proceeded down the receiving line, giving John a bear hug he half-heartedly returned, and planting at least six kisses on Alex's face, all the while talking to him like he was a baby.

Extricating himself from her grasp, Alex said, "Cousin Diana, this is my fiancée, Miss Lucy FitzHarris."

Lucy bobbed a curtsy, and Diana let out a startling cry. "Ooo hoo hoo hoo *hoo*. There you are. Aren't you lovely. Just lovely." Diana called to her husband, who was making his way down the receiving line in a much more sober manner. "Ranald. Ranald. Isn't she lovely?"

Lucy bobbed a curtsy Sir Ranald's way.

Sir Ranald smiled genially. "How do you do, my dear? Yes, yes. Very lovely indeed. Congratulations, Alex. Well done."

She found it curious that neither Diana nor Sir Ranald had the Scottish burr she had become used to. Were they English?

Diana was a statuesque woman of about fifty who had maintained her good looks. She wore a gown of lavender lawn cloth trimmed with brilliant fuchsia and yellow ribbon rosettes. A green bonnet with red ostrich plumes and long red kid gloves accented her gown. Her ensemble was blinding. Just like her personality.

Diana swept Lucy along with her on her way into the house, Sir Ranald trailing behind. In doing so, Lucy missed being introduced to...what had Flora said their names were?

"Perhaps you'd like to go directly to your room and rest after the journey?"

Ignoring her suggestion, Diana whipped off her bonnet and tossed it on a chair. "Thank God we got here in time for dinner. I'm absolutely ravenous."

Diana's voice echoed around the entry hall, making the picture frames rattle. Without waiting for further invitation, she walked into the dining room and plopped herself into what was normally John's chair. Sir Ranald looked around the entry hall and then at Lucy. He smiled stupidly and nodded, as if nothing out of the ordinary had just happened.

"Won't you please follow me, Sir Ranald. I'll see about the meal." She led him into the dining room. Instead of sitting, Sir Ranald stood in a corner, admiring a small framed engraving of a ship. Diana emitted loud sighs, signaling her hunger and fatigue.

"Excuse me, Lady Diana, while I go talk to Cook."

"Aren't you a darling. Thank you."

She hurried out of the dining room and down the back corridor. By the time she reached the kitchen, Mrs. Swenson was already loading trays and boiling water.

Mrs. Swenson waved her off. "Dinner'll be ready in a trice."

"Did someone tell you Sir Ranald and Lady Diana—"

"Dinnae have to. I heard her coming." Mrs. Swenson gave a slight roll of her eyes.

Lucy smiled. "You've met her before, then."

"Aye. She's loud, but she's harmless. Dinnae fash. She'll no' stay forever." Mrs. Swenson filled a platter with cold sliced beef. "Sir Ranald, now, he's a quiet man but very deep. Always thinking and planning what's best to do for Scotland. You'll like him."

"Do you recall the names of their son and daughter?"

Mrs. Swenson suddenly stopped what she was doing. "They brought Liam and Elizabeth?"

"Yes. That's it. Liam and Elizabeth."

The cook brushed nonexistent crumbs from her apron as if her life depended on it.

"Is anything wrong, Mrs. Swenson?"

"Och, nae," she said, snapping back to her bubbly self. "I'm sure everything will turn out fine." Lucy sensed a strong note of uncertainty in the woman's voice.

When she returned to the dining room, she found Flora sitting at Diana's elbow, listening to her chatter. Diana stopped long enough to ask if she brought her anything to eat, and Lucy assured her food was on the way.

Laird John, Sir Ranald, and a well-groomed younger man, who must be Liam, stood in the corner, also chatting, but at a much lower volume. Lucy remained standing for some time before Liam noticed her and introduced himself.

"So you're the one Alex will marry. I'm Liam Ulbster." Liam made a courtly bow, and she matched him with a curtsy.

"I'm very pleased to meet you, Mr. Ulbster."

"You must call me Liam. We'll be family now." Taking her un-offered hand, he kissed it with wet lips. He dressed like a London dandy—fawn-colored pantaloons, Hessian boots, navy tailcoat with brass buttons, and an elaborately tied cravat with ruffles bursting from a silk waistcoat. At one time, she had found this mode of dress attractive. Now it seemed effeminate compared to her kilted Highland warrior. There was something Lucy did not like about the man, despite his stylish dress and manners.

"By the looks of you, no one had to twist Alex's arm to marry you." Liam let his eyes travel up and down her body. That, along with his comment, offended her.

"I assure you, Mr. Ulbster, no one had to twist anyone's arm," she said, her voice as brittle as autumn leaves.

Liam laughed, a nasty, unholy laugh.

"You sound English," Lucy said. "But not like any Englishman I've ever met."

"Elizabeth and I spent most of our lives in England. I was educated there. We only come to the Highlands once or twice a year for brief stays."

At the mention of Elizabeth's name, she glanced around the room. Alex and Elizabeth were not to be seen. If Elizabeth was anything like her mother or Liam, she ought to go rescue Alex.

She made to leave the room, but Flora called to her. "Oh, Lucy, do join us."

"I'm just going to find Alex."

Diana bellowed, "He's with Elizabeth. Leave them be, dear, and talk to us."

Against her better judgment, she joined Flora and Diana at the table. When Mrs. Swenson and two kitchen maids entered with the meal, the men took their seats. Unfortunately, Liam took the seat right next to hers and sidled up to her.

She half rose saying, "I should tell Alex and Elizabeth dinner is served."

"They'll be along." Diana motioned for her to sit. Goodness, everyone seemed determine to leave Alex to his fate.

Liam buttered a scone vigorously and leaned toward her. "Worried about Alex and my stepsister, are you?"

"Of course not. Why should I be?"

"Surely he's told you about him and Elizabeth?"

Lucy felt her cheeks flame.

"*Oooh*," he said chuckling. "I do apologize. I've spoken out of turn. Well, I'll leave it to him to tell you."

She wanted to stab him with her fork. He wasn't sorry at all. He relished telling her—and what the devil was the disagreeable fop implying?

"I'm sorry. Did I spoil your appetite?" Liam bit his scone.

At that instant, the men rose to their feet, and Alex entered the room with Elizabeth draped on his arm. They seemed alarmingly familiar with each other. Lucy felt a swell of jealousy. Elizabeth was stunning—blond, perfectly coifed, not a hair out of place. *Merde*. How did she do that? She'd just gotten out of a carriage, for goodness' sake.

Elizabeth wore a pastel green gown with lace overlay, long sleeves, and low square neckline. She laughed at something Alex said, as though he was the most entertaining person in the world.

How dare she?

Lucy stood and prepared herself for introductions.

"Miss FitzHarris." Elizabeth bobbed and gave her a cool smile.

"Miss Ulbster." She bobbed and mirrored her exactly.

The exchange lowered the temperature in the room ten degrees. All conversation came to a halt, the room deadly quiet but for the rustling of Elizabeth's skirts. Alex pulled out her chair with a screech that made Lucy's teeth buzz inside her head.

John, bless him, engaged Elizabeth in conversation. Soon, the room began to hum again. Alex had the presence of mind to help Lucy back in her seat before taking the last chair available. Next to damn-her-eyes Elizabeth.

Throughout the meal, Elizabeth monopolized Alex. Diana and Flora were deeply engaged, as were John and Sir Ranald at the other end of the table. She wished Liam was a polite conversationalist but, truth be told, the man turned her stomach. When she couldn't stand his innuendo any longer, she excused herself, explaining that it was time for her to check on Peter.

As she quit the room, Lucy heard Flora talking about the groom's convalescence at Balforss. She ran up the stairs and down the hall to Peter's room. Knocking, she heard Hercules bark.

"Come in, thank you," Peter called.

She smiled. Peter was trying so hard to please her. "Did you sleep at all?" Lucy arranged her skirts and sat on the bed next to him.

"No, miss. I couldnae. There's such a stramash down there. What's going on?" A shrill cackle reverberated through the floorboards. "Are we being raided by pirates?"

Lucy had to stifle a laugh. That's exactly what it sounded like.

"No. Mr. Alex's cousins have arrived for the wedding. They're having dinner in the dining room. Your room is just above, so, unfortunately, you can hear everything." More wild laughter vibrated the floor.

"Maybe I should go back to the stables so I can get some rest?" He sounded hopeful. It had taken only twenty-four hours for the novelty of his room to wear off. Since then, Peter had been pestering her about when he could return to the horses. Lucy's best efforts to keep him entertained had not been diversion enough. She felt for him. Two days in bed and he was bored silly.

"When your temperature goes down, and the swelling in your neck disappears, then you can return. But you don't want to go back and give Robby the mumps, do you?"

Peter's eyes slid sideways, as though he considered the prospect a good one. "Well, no," he said with some reluctance. "I suppose not."

"Try to sleep. I'll be back after supper to read you a story."

"Do you have any stories about pirates?" His eyes glittered with excitement.

"I'll see what I can find in the library." She scooped up Hercules and left Peter's room.

More laughter from below echoed up from the staircase. She didn't want to go back to the dining room. Instead, she went to her own room and closed the door. The fire was nearly out, so she added another brick of peat and poked up the flames. She hazarded a glance in the glass above the washbasin. Not too bad, she thought. Her hair was reasonably in place. Complexion clear and rosy. She smoothed her brows and bit her lips to plump them.

Lucy wasn't wearing her best gown, but at least she hadn't had on her grey serge and apron when they arrived. They would have mistaken her for a servant. She hadn't brought many gowns with her; two morning gowns, and the navy wool for every day, the light blue gown she was wearing, the brown silk, the yellow silk, the beige cotton, and the white gown made of lawn cloth. She'd brought her hunting jacket and skirt, the outfit she'd had made two years ago with the hope that she might be asked to participate in a hunt. Alas, she had never gotten around to riding lessons and so had not had an opportunity to wear the ensemble. And, of course, she'd brought the gown she would wear for her wedding. Made of silk chiffon, it was the most beautiful cream color, like rich vanilla custard, with delicate gold roses Phillipa had embroidered on the bodice.

"*Charmante!*" Phillipa had said when Lucy tried on the gown. "Your husband will think he marries a princess. *Oui?*"

Lucy hoped Phillipa was right. She hadn't realized until this moment how much she wanted to please Alex. Until now, she had only been concerned with whether he could please her. A tiny thread of self-doubt crept into her consciousness. Would he come to love her the way that John loved Mother Flora? Would they have a happy marriage? Or was there someone else Alex preferred?

And what the devil did that insufferable man mean by, "Surely he's told you about him and Elizabeth?" Liam's salacious tone and waggling eyebrows seemed to imply there had been a romantic relationship between the two. She pulled Hercules onto her lap and let him kiss her face. He was, as always, a comfort to her.

The door to her room burst open, and Elizabeth stepped inside. Hercules barked his head off at her until Lucy managed to quiet him.

Elizabeth made a face. "What is that thing?"

"This is my dog, Hercules, given to me by my father." She lifted her chin and added, "The Duke of Chatham."

"You're quite certain he's your father?"

She nearly gasped at Elizabeth's crass reference to her parentage, but she refused to take the horrible woman's bait.

Elizabeth looked around. "They've put you in my room."

"Your room?"

The woman let her eyes slide to the adjoining door and back to Lucy. Smiling, she said, "Yes. I usually stay in this room."

The nastier side of Lucy surfaced and took possession

of her faculties. "Yes." She let *her* eyes slide to the adjoining door and back to Elizabeth. "I don't doubt that you do."

She had the extreme pleasure of seeing rage flare in Elizabeth's eyes before the woman spun around and stomped away. The hollow sound of her heels echoed down the hallway. As quickly as satisfaction filled Lucy's bosom, it evaporated. The heavy realization that Alex had been romantically involved with that awful woman practically crushed her.

She wondered if he had protested as long and hard as she had when his father announced that he had to abandon Elizabeth and marry a stranger. Most likely he had. Except he most assuredly had not carried on like a child the way Lucy had. He'd probably born the burden stoically and did his best to accept his lot. *His lot*, she thought bitterly. This morning she was to be his beloved wife. Now she was just his lot.

Lucy's better nature felt pity for her betrothed. Poor Alex. He had tried to make the best of the situation. He had tried to make her feel like he wanted her. Like she had been his choice. He had pretended they had a reason to hope for happiness.

And just that quickly, Lucy's pride reared its ugly head. She faced an impossible situation, a conundrum, a choice between two evils. To marry a man who, no matter how hard he tried, would always love another was something she could not endure. On the other hand, to walk away from the engagement, lose to that awful, spiteful, damn-her-eyes Elizabeth? Unthinkable.

She held the dog up to her face and vowed, "We will not lose, Hercules. Alex will choose me. I will make him fall in love with me. This is *my* room. Now and forever."

. . .

Alex and his father managed to escape the house after the

midday meal. His head ached from Diana's nonstop blethering. The pitch and sheer volume of her voice threatened to make his ears bleed. He was certain the only reason Sir Ranald could live in the same house with the woman was because he was almost deaf. Then again, it was likely Diana's talking had made him deaf.

Sir Ranald was a pleasant man. Interesting to listen to. Hard to talk to, though, as one had to shout into his left ear. A generous man, as well, charitable and kind. The best sort to be representing the concerns of Scotland in Parliament. How could Liam, a selfish, vain, and dishonorable man, be his son?

Even as a boy, Liam had been unlikeable. He'd lied, cheated at games, and teased smaller children mercilessly. He had enjoyed seeing Alex get in trouble and had always wanted to watch while John took a strap to his backside. He chafed at the attention Liam had given Lucy at dinner. It didn't look as if she welcomed his company, but if Liam persisted, Alex would have to get physical with the bastard.

"Lord save us all," his father said.

"Indeed," Alex agreed.

The two headed for the falls. The mill was in full operation today, the huge water wheel churning steadily with the current. They made their way down the steep stone staircase set into the embankment a hundred and fifty years ago by Alex's three times great grandfather, James Sinclair.

Alex regarded his father's back, broad like his own, his carefully plaited queue swaying as he walked, comfortable in his favorite well-worn kilt. His dark hair showed only a few threads of silver, and his step was as light as a young man's. John Sinclair's long career as a soldier had kept him fit. He couldn't imagine his father ever getting old.

At the bottom, they found their hiding place, an alcove carved out of the riverbank. Captain Sinclair was buried here, Alex's great-great-grandfather. A giant granite slab covered his grave. John lifted a piece of slate and withdrew a tin flask from beneath. They sat, their backs against the rocky embankment and sighed. They didn't talk at first. Just passed the flask back and forth in silence. Each golden sip of whisky loosened another muscle in Alex's neck until, at last, he could breathe freely again.

He let his gaze travel a few yards down along the river bank where, only two days ago, he and Lucy had lain in a passionate embrace. He'd almost had her. Almost reached that heavenly place between… Jesus, he should have broken Liam's Goddamn arm for daring to breathe on his woman.

"Did ya see that mingin' bawbag, Liam, yaffin' wi' Lucy?" Alex said.

"You should be more concerned about Elizabeth."

"Aye. She never paid me much mind when I was courting her. Now she's saying how I'm so clever, so handsome, so fine. She spurned me not six months ago." Alex shook his head. "I dinnae ken what she's playing at."

"It could be she's had a change of heart." His father's cool voice had a calming effect on him. "Sometimes people cannae see the value of something until someone else wants it." John took another sip of whisky. "It's equally as likely the vain creature needs to have the attention of every man in the room to herself."

Alex laughed. His father was so right about that.

"But, knowing the spiteful bitch as well as I do," John said. "I'd bet money this has nothing to do with you. I ken she just wants to humiliate Lucy."

He scoffed at his father's speculation. "Och, Elizabeth cannae be that ugly inside."

"Oh, aye? You never met her natural father, Diana's first husband, Nathan Campbell. He was Captain of Dragoon's. I have never seen a man enjoy flogging another as much as he did. His men hated him. Officially, he died in battle, but I suspect his men killed him. And I wouldnae blame them. Elizabeth takes after him, to be sure."

"Why did you no' tell me this when I was courting her?" Alex asked.

"You dinnae believe me now. Would you have believed me then?" His father cocked his head in the same direction as his eyebrow.

Whether his father was right about Elizabeth or not, her rejection no longer bothered him now that he had Lucy. He was glad to know, too, he had no more feelings of desire for the woman. In fact, he couldn't recall what he'd found so beguiling about her in the first place.

He and his father were quiet for a while, enjoying the mesmerizing sound of the falls. Something occurred to Alex, and he asked, "How did you know Lucy would be right for me?"

"I ken her father well. He's a just and honest man who knows the value of friendship," John said. "He's also intelligent, braw, and the most headstrong man I've ever met. I saw those qualities in Lucy when she was only nine years old. You met her yourself then. Do you no' recall?"

"I remember bits of it. I remember the duke took out his sword and named me Lucy's champion and protector."

"Do you recall why the duke named you thus?"

"I ken it was because I fished Lucy's wee ball out of the pond."

"Nae, lad. That's what got you the tawsing. That and bloodying her brother George's nose." John laughed at the memory. "Nae. Lucy begged her da not to let me punish you. Said you rescued her ball and defended her. Insisted you were brave and should be rewarded. That you were her protector." John laughed loud and hard. "Oh God, Alex. I still remember you standing next to Lucy, righteous and dreekit. Ready to take your punishment. And you were so scairt when the duke took out his sword, I thought you'd piss yourself." John wiped his eyes. "But then, after you swore to protect Lucy, well...I was right proud of you."

"And Lucy? What did she do?"

"Och, she was bold as brass with her da. Standing by you. Demanding justice for you. After you made your oath to the duke, you tried to pledge your allegiance to Lucy like a gentleman. But she ran and hid her face in the duke's coat. I ken she was embarrassed when the attention was on her."

Alex could remember some of the pieces but had to fill in the holes, imagining Lucy as a lass. He did remember thinking she was lovely even then. Perhaps that's why he'd wanted to show off for her by fighting with her brother and retrieving her ball from the pond. He also remembered *wanting* his father to give him a tawsing. Taking a beating for being gallant would only be further proof of his manhood.

"It's four days until the wedding. Four days with the Ulbsters under foot. What should I do about Elizabeth?" Alex asked.

"Dinnae do anything about her. It's Lucy who needs you. Stand by her. Serve and protect her like you promised the duke. If she kens you're on her side, she'll be impervious to Elizabeth's wicked tongue."

Later that night, Alex knocked lightly on Lucy's door. It was time for supper. He wanted to escort her to the dining room. That way he could choose Lucy's seat. Be a buffer between her and Liam.

"Lucy. It's Alex. Are you ready to—"

"There you are, Alex, darling." As if by magic, Elizabeth appeared at his side. "Come, take me down to supper."

"Go on without me," he said pleasantly. "I'm waiting for Lucy."

"You wouldn't let me go down without an escort, would

you?" She used her *poor little me* voice.

"Perhaps your stepbrother Liam will be along soon, aye? I'll be taking Lucy," he said firmly.

"Oh, Alex, you are a slave to your duty." Elizabeth waltzed away. When she was out of earshot, Alex knocked on the door again.

"Lucy, she's gone. Will you come out?"

The door opened, and Lucy stepped into the candlelit hallway, looking more beautiful than ever with her plump pink lips, rosy cheeks, and large, wide-set eyes. Her hair had been swept up and twisted into a fetching knot with a few errant curls tickling her neck. Glowing pearl ear bobs dangled above alabaster shoulders aching to be kissed, and a string of tiny pearls encircled her long, slim neck. Her rich, chocolaty brown gown sported a daring neckline revealing the swell of her breasts. He remembered the salty taste of her skin and wanted to be alone with her. Damn. If he didn't have a houseful of guests, he'd take her right now.

He snapped out of his trance and straightened. Although it bothered him that Liam would surely devour Lucy with his eyes, he admired her competitive streak. Alex placed his bet on his thoroughbred bride. She would make Elizabeth run for her money tonight.

Chapter Fourteen

Lucy had taken extra care in the mirror to make certain she was at her best. It was important to her that Alex think her pretty. He confirmed her success with his appreciative look.

"Ready?"

"Wait. I want to ask you something."

"Of course."

"Why did you never mention Elizabeth?"

Alex shifted his weight to his other foot, took a deep breath, and released it. "Do you mind when you got the letter from the blasted viscount and I was so angry?"

"Yes."

"Well, it occurred to me then to tell you, just to make you jealous, ken?" He scratched the back of his neck and squinted one eye shut. "But I reckoned that would only make us both miserable, so I didnae." He shifted again and reached toward her, pinching the fabric of her skirt and rubbing it between his fingers in a half-curious way. "And then...well"—Alex stopped fidgeting and looked her straight in the eye—"I just forgot."

He looked so boyish and so earnest, she believed him.

"Fine then. Just so long as she stays forgotten."

He gave her a broad smile, and she slid her hand into the crook of his elbow.

"One thing," Alex said. "I sit next to you from now on."

"I think that is an excellent idea."

They were the last to arrive at table. When Lucy entered, the gentlemen rose, and her heart fell. Two chairs remained empty. Elizabeth sat between them.

John, seated in his usual chair at the head of the table, stepped aside. "Alex, take my seat so that you may sit next to your Lucy. I'll sit on the far side of Elizabeth."

Elizabeth's smug smile faltered, but she recovered quickly. Alex gave Lucy's hand a light squeeze before she took her seat.

Supper started well. John made a warm and welcoming toast to his guests, after which Sir Ranald made an equally gracious toast to his hosts. Liam sat directly across from Lucy. She avoided eye contact with him despite his repeated attempts to engage her in conversation. Each time he asked her a pointed question Alex would answer for her or change the subject.

Alex, her champion.

As she had during dinner, Diana dominated the conversation at the other end of the table through sheer volume. Fortunately, Diana's diatribe discouraged the need to chat with Elizabeth to her left. About a quarter of an hour into the meal, she felt a friendly foot nudge her under the table. She glanced at Alex. If he were flirting with her, he would surely signal her with his eyes. He did not. It was Liam playing footsies under the table. She tucked her feet under her chair to avoid further disturbance.

Moments later, Alex jerked. She heard a dull thud under the table and saw Liam wince. An impish grin appeared on

Alex's face while he continued to stare straight ahead down the length of the table, feigning interest in Diana's oration.

Alex, her protector.

Lucy sucked in her cheeks and tried not to laugh.

At the height of Diana's story, which included hand gestures and impersonations, Elizabeth spoke to Lucy.

"I'm so sorry," Lucy said, indicating she couldn't hear her.

Elizabeth repeated her question, even though Lucy *had* heard her the first time. The witch had asked, "Who did you say your mother was?" This was her code for, "I know your father never married your mother."

She had always been an easy target for women like Elizabeth. Again, she shook her head and repeated, "I'm sorry." Usually, people would give up after the second try. If their barb never hit its mark, they never scored.

Elizabeth leaned in and asked her question again, louder, as if she were speaking to a child. For the third time, Lucy shook her head.

"My God, Alex, she's as deaf as my stepfather." At that precise moment, Diana paused for dramatic effect. The whole table heard Elizabeth's snide remark insulting not only Lucy, but Sir Ranald as well. Jaws and silverware dropped.

"I do apologize," Lucy said sweetly. "I didn't want to miss any of your mother's story."

At this, Liam broke into a rather vicious laugh. Apparently, he liked it when his sister stumbled publicly. Lucy's brother George enjoyed teasing her mercilessly. But he never, ever humiliated her in front of others. These two siblings were loathsome individuals.

Diana took up her story again, calling attention back to herself. Everyone else resumed eating. Feeling victorious, Lucy enjoyed the sensation of Elizabeth's hot, hate-filled glare on her shoulder.

Mrs. Swenson entered the dining room and placed a full platter of juicy roast beef and vegetables on the table in front of Laird John, who served himself. He held the steaming platter for Elizabeth. After serving herself, Elizabeth took the platter from John and held it for Lucy. However, when Lucy picked up the serving tongs, the platter slipped from Elizabeth's hands, and its contents—scorching hot beef, potatoes, and carrots—emptied into Lucy's lap.

The hot juices immediately seeped through the delicate silk of her dress and she cried out. Alex leapt to his feet and pulled her out of her chair, brushing away the scalding food.

"Oh dear," Elizabeth said. "I am so sorry. Please forgive my clumsiness."

Lucy pulled herself together and said through gritted teeth, "Not at all."

"Excuse us," Alex said. He wrapped a protective arm around her and led her out of the dining room. "Are you all right, sweeting?"

"Take me to my room." She felt tears of pain pricking at her eyes. *Merde.* She would be damned if she let that horrible woman make her cry.

He escorted her above stairs, opened her bedchamber door, and brought the candle from the hallway inside.

"Lucy, are you hurt?"

"Get Haddie for me." Her voice and her body shook uncontrollably, though from anger or from the struggle not to weep, she couldn't tell.

"Please, love, are you hurt?"

"I won't know until I take off my gown."

"Let me see." He reached for her hem.

"*Stop it.*" She batted away his hands. "Leave me be and just...go get Haddie." She couldn't let him see her like this. So out of control.

"I cannae leave you alone."

"Go away!"

...

Alex flew down the stairs, through the back hallway, and around to the kitchen where he knew he'd find Haddie. "Miss Lucy needs you, lass. Go to her. And bring some of Mrs. Swenson's burn ointment with you, just in case."

Haddie found the earthen jar of salve and sprinted out of the kitchen.

"What's happened?" asked Mrs. Swenson.

"There was an accident." Alex leaned against a breakfront, trying to catch his breath, his heart thundering in his ears. "And Lucy may have been hurt."

"Did Miss Elizabeth have anything to do with this accident?" Mrs. Swenson asked, the anger in her voice unmistakable.

Alex confirmed her suspicion with a sharp nod.

The cook made the sign of the horns with her fingers to ward off evil spirits, then whispered, "The spawn of Satan."

She surprised Alex. As kind and fair a woman as his mother, he'd never heard Mrs. Swenson utter a mean word about anyone. His father had pointed out Elizabeth's dark side earlier in the day, and now, Mrs. Swenson—two people who were sound judges of character. How could he have been so blinded by Elizabeth's charms not to notice her true nature?

He left the kitchen and headed back to the house. Finding the dining room empty, he assumed the men had settled themselves in the library for a whisky. He heard Diana's voice coming from his mother's parlor upstairs. No doubt Elizabeth was with them. Damn her.

Worry over Lucy plagued him. Seeking refuge from his relatives, he slipped out of the house and wandered into the garden Lucy liked so much.

Gowans. Gowans might make her feel better.

He'd bring her more gowans, and she would smile again. As he reached down to pluck a few stems, he heard Elizabeth.

"Oh, Alex. I am so sorry. I feel awful."

She stepped out of the house and crossed the yard to him, wiping her eyes and sniffing. Alex gritted his teeth.

"I hope she's all right. I don't know how I could have been so clumsy. Please, please forgive me, Alex. The platter slipped from my hands." Her voice had a small, helpless quality quite unlike any he'd heard her use. She fell against his chest and sobbed. He was always at a loss when women cried. She seemed genuinely distraught. Perhaps it had been an accident after all. The platter was heavy and so full it could have happened to anyone.

"It's all right. No one blames you," he said, patting her on the back.

"But the way you looked at me. Like you hated me. Alex, I couldn't stand it if you hated me." She sounded truly contrite.

"I dinnae hate you."

She let the length of her body lean against him, the lavender in her silky blond hair tickling his nose. His body remembered the last time he'd held her like this, and he became aroused despite his mind telling him *you are betrothed to another.*

The woman's hands slid from his chest up to his shoulders. "I made a terrible mistake sending you away. I didn't realize how much I loved you until I saw you today. My heart will break when you marry Lucy."

Before he knew it, her lips were on his, kissing him with a passion she had never demonstrated before. He pulled away from her mouth.

"Kiss me again, Alex. I can tell you still want me. Kiss me

once more, plea—"

"No." Alex grasped her by the shoulders and held her away from him.

She smiled a joyous smile. Six months ago, he would have done anything to make her smile like that. When she turned her face up to the second story of the house, Alex followed her gaze. Lucy stood at her window, staring down at them, her beautiful face twisted in agony. At first, Alex thought she must still be in pain from the accident.

Then Elizabeth laughed. "Oops." And she covered her mouth.

For a second, he forgot how to breathe. Then the horrible weight of understanding nearly sent him to his knees.

Lucy. Oh God, Lucy. Bloody hell, what have I done?

...

Liam waited in the shadows until Alex went inside the house before he started to applaud. "Well done, dear stepsister," he said, grinning. His admiration for Elizabeth's malicious nature deepened.

She rounded on him. "You can go to hell."

Liam was less intimidated than aroused by the venom in her tone. "I'm congratulating you. You've played your part expertly."

"Do you know how humiliating that was for me? Prostrating myself at that oaf's feet?"

"Keep your voice down." Liam took her roughly by the arm.

She yanked her arm away but followed him to the side of the house where they would not be seen. "You'll have to give her the letter. She won't take anything from me now."

"Give it to me. She'll be needing solace tomorrow, and I will be there to give it to her."

Elizabeth removed a folded parchment from her reticule. She handed the missive sealed with red wax bearing the emblem of a fox to her stepbrother. "I want my letters back. *Now.*"

"I don't have them with me, dear heart. But don't worry. You'll get them just as soon as my business is done." He reached up and pinched her nipple through the bodice of her gown.

His stepsister took a vicious swipe at his face with her claws. "If you ever touch me again, I will kill you," Elizabeth spat. She turned on her heel and marched into the house.

Liam tucked the parchment into his waistcoat and patted it gently. If all went according to plan, within forty-eight hours his financial troubles would be behind him. He touched his face. No blood, but her nails would leave a mark, three welts, rising as steadily as his cock.

Chapter Fifteen

"I'm fine, Haddie. No need for the salve," Lucy assured her.

Haddie helped Lucy into her nightgown. The tender skin on her thighs was red and angry-looking, but thankfully, she was not burned.

"Will you bring me some willow bark tea?"

"Aye, miss."

After Haddie left the room, she wandered to the window, restless. When Alex had helped her from the dining room, she'd been furious and in so much pain, she hadn't had it in her to be the least bit tender toward him, whereas he had been nothing but attentive toward her. The moon was out, affording her a magical view of the front garden. Everything looked different in moonlight. As if fairies had cast a blue dust on all the flowers.

Alex stood in the garden among the daisies, looking downcast. Feeling a pang of regret, she put her hand to the windowpane. She was about to open the latch and call to him when another figure stepped out of the house and into the garden. Icy fingers skittered up her spine. Lucy stood transfixed as she watched Alex take the horrible Elizabeth into his arms and hold her. Then he kissed her. *Oh, God, he kissed her.* The two lovers looked up at her window…and laughed. Lucy clapped a hand over her mouth and backed away from the window.

Haddie stepped into the room. "Miss? Are you all right?"

She staggered forward and grabbed the bedpost to keep from crumpling to the floor. "I'm not feeling well." She shut her eyes tight. The scene in the garden exploded into sharp fragmented images. They stabbed at her brain and melted into red and yellow spots behind her eyelids.

She was only vaguely aware of Haddie helping her into bed.

"Drink the tea. It'll help you sleep." Haddie tucked the bedclothes tight around Lucy. "I'll leave the lamp burning and check on you in an hour."

There was a sharp knock on her door. Lucy's eyes flew open wide.

"Lucy. It's Alex. May I come in?"

She shook her head violently. Haddie nodded her understanding and went to the door. As she exited, the maid said, "*Wheesht.* You'll wake her. She's sleeping now."

"Is she hurt bad, Haddie?" he asked.

"No, but it pains her. Best let her sleep."

Lucy heard them walk away. A few seconds later, though, Alex scratched at the door joining their rooms.

"Lucy. I ken you're no' asleep. Will you talk to me, please? It's not what you think."

She shut her eyes and covered her ears. No more lies. She didn't want to hear any more lies from Alex. His betrayal cut her to the bone. The truth crystallized in her mind so suddenly it made her ill. She was living a nightmare, surrounded by people who did nothing but lie to her. Alex didn't want her. His father John had arranged this marriage with her father for financial gain. His mother Flora was probably just being nice to her to make her think she was welcome here. What would things be like after she married him? Would his true nature surface? Would they all turn against her? Was Balforss to be her prison?

An even more horrifying thought came to her. What if, once the marriage was complete, Alex planned to do away with her so he could be with Elizabeth? No. No, Alex would never do something like that. Or would he? There were the men he'd cut down, slaughtered savagely, without a second thought.

Her frightened mind jumped from one paralyzing conclusion to another. What if those men who attacked them on the way here had been Langley's men trying to rescue her? She had helped kill one of them. How could she have been so gullible? She had to stop crying and think.

Hercules, always able to sense her distress, whined for attention. She hugged him close and whispered to him. "We can't marry Alex, *mon cher*. We have to leave this place." But how?

Langley.

Was it too late? Was he still nearby, hoping to see her? In his letter, he said he was staying with the Lady Sutherland. Somehow, she had to get a message to Langley or convince someone to take her to him. Langley would save her.

Her head swam with visions of Alex kissing Elizabeth. The two of them making love under her nose while laughing at her. When she fell asleep, she dreamed fitfully. Nightmares of men trying to kill her brought her to consciousness. When she lapsed into sleep again, she dreamed of Alex placing a smothering kiss on her face, and she woke covered in perspiration.

My God. I nearly let Alex ruin me.

Sometime during the night, Haddie had come into her

room and extinguished the lamp.

Haddie is good. Haddie will help me escape in the morning.

• • •

Well after midnight, Alex lay on his bed still dressed. He couldn't sleep. Wouldn't sleep. Not until he got Lucy to listen to him and understand. Growing angrier by the minute, he launched himself out of bed, reached for the handle on the door adjoining their rooms, and stopped. She was still upset. He knocked instead.

"Lucy," he called. "Talk to me." Nothing. He went into the hall and rapped on her door. "Lucy, please. I'll knock this door down if you dinnae open it now."

"Alex?" His mother called to him from the opposite end of the corridor. "What's the matter? Is Lucy all right?"

"Nothing, Ma. Go back to bed." He was in such an agitated state he couldn't disguise the anger in his voice.

His reply had been far too short for his mother's liking. She marched down the hall toward him, tying her robe around her as she went. He could tell by the sound of her footsteps she was boiling mad. Barely speaking above a whisper, she said, "I will not have you creating a fuss in the middle of the night. Go to bed and leave Lucy be. You can resolve whatever is troubling you tomorrow."

Thoroughly disgusted with himself and his miserable situation, he stomped past his mother and barreled down the staircase. If he couldn't settle things with Lucy tonight, he'd find relief in a bottle. He flung open the library door, strode to the cabinet, and poured himself a long shot of his father's best whisky, then tossed it back. He nearly spit the whole mouthful out when he heard an unseen individual speak.

"Something bothering you, brother?"

A head popped out from behind the wingback chair.

"Ian."

Alex embraced him, pounded him on the back several times, and then shook him by the shoulders. His troubles evaporated in an instant, replaced with pure joy at seeing his brother. It had been nearly a year since he'd been home last. He stepped back to get a better look. Ian was dressed in full uniform, dust covered and road weary, but looked as happy as Alex felt.

"When did you get here?"

"Just the now. Someone is sleeping in my room. I didnae want to wake Ma, so I thought I'd sleep down here and surprise her in the morning." Ian pointed to the whisky bottle. "May I join you?"

Alex retrieved another glass and poured them both a tot. They settled down at the card table.

"I'm glad to see you, man," Alex said. "*Slainte*."

"I wouldnae miss my big brother's wedding."

His smile faded. "If there is a wedding." He took another swallow of the golden liquid. It was helping, but he wouldn't sleep until he was dead drunk.

"Sounds serious," Ian said. "Is something amiss?"

"Aye. Lucy willnae speak to me."

"Why?"

"She saw me kiss Elizabeth."

"Christ, man." Ian bolted to his feet. "Have you lost your bloody mind? Days before your wedding and you're kissing Elizabeth?" He paced around the library, sending looks of disgust Alex's way.

"She kissed *me*." Alex protested.

"I fail to see the difference."

He proceeded to tell Ian everything, starting with his first embarrassing blunder on the road from Inverness to Balforss.

"You did what?" Ian asked, dumbfounded by Alex's stupidity.

"I revealed myself to her before we got home," he said, again on the defensive.

"And she forgave you?"

"Aye." He continued to tell him about their subsequent misunderstandings regarding the love letter and offering to call off the wedding. Ian shook his head in disbelief.

"Things were going well for a while. She was responsive, ye ken?" Alex said, seeking understanding from his younger brother.

"Aye. I ken well enough."

"Lucy liked me. She wanted to marry me. Until Cousin Diana and Sir Ranald arrived." When he got to the part about Elizabeth injuring Lucy, then tricking him into kissing her, Ian covered his face.

"I need more whisky," Ian said, holding out his glass. "I dinnae ken how you will dig your way out of this. You've done some serious damage."

"What should I do?"

Ian shook his head. "Be prepared to spend tomorrow on your knees, brother."

Alex folded his arms on the table and laid his head down.

"You say she's handy with a bow?"

"Aye," Alex said, his voice sounding muffled with his head buried in his arms.

Ian patted his brother on the back. "Dinnae fash. I have an idea that just might work."

• • •

The pleasant morning sounds of Balforss coming to life teased Lucy awake. She stretched. Then memories of last night's terrible revelations descended upon her, pinning her body to the bed as if she were staked to the ground. Unable to move, unable to open her eyes, or lift her head from the pillow. How could she? How could she face the sunlight, much less the faces of those people who had betrayed her? Elizabeth, Liam, John, Flora. Was everyone in league with Alex?

Haddie slipped noiselessly into her bedchamber. "How are you this morning, miss?" Hercules danced on his hind legs and pestered Haddie to take him outside.

Was Haddie a part of Alex's deception? No. Haddie was far too guileless.

"Perfectly fine, thank you," Lucy said. "No damage done."

She managed to drag her body from the bed and stagger to the washbasin. As she performed her morning ablutions, Lucy considered the risk involved in asking her maid for help. She wanted desperately to get away from Balforss—today, if possible. Asking Laird John outright to be returned home would tip her hand. If they had planned to force the union and imprison her here as she suspected, she might lose her only opportunity to escape.

The young woman fastened the back of the grey serge gown Lucy used for everyday.

She probed her maid with caution. "I think of you as a friend, Haddie. I feel as though I could count on you if I were in trouble or needed help."

Haddie examined her face with an intensity that made her uncomfortable. "I would surely help you whenever I could. Is ought amiss?"

"No. Of course not. Not exactly." She was about to broach the subject of escape, when Hercules became adamant about his personal needs.

Haddie smiled down at the dog and her face transformed, the plain girl becoming appealing. "I'll see to him, miss." She swept Hercules up off the rug and trudged out of the room.

Lucy surveyed the bedchamber, once a happy place, now a room full of sadness. If she were leaving today, she would need to pack her things. She wouldn't be able to take everything. Maybe one gown, her jewelry, and her night rail. She would have to leave her bow and arrows behind. Lucy would regret their loss more than her gowns.

She gathered the things she would take and stuffed them into a small satchel. Perhaps she could pilfer a few food items from the kitchen this morning for the trip. Thank goodness she had coin of her own. Enough to pay for lodging and passage to London.

There was a knock on her bedroom door. She quickly hid the satchel under her bed. "Who is it?"

"It's Flora, dear. Are you well enough to come down for breakfast? There's someone I want you to meet."

"I'll be down soon. I want to check on Peter first." Lucy put her ear to the door. Certain no one was in the corridor, she slipped out and down the hall to Peter's room.

"Morning, miss," Peter said, getting up from his breakfast. He bowed dutifully and pulled out a chair for Lucy to join him.

"My, you are turning into a real gentleman."

"Thank you, miss. I'm feeling much better today. I've no fever and the swelling in my neck has gone down. I'm not feeling gun-tay-shus at all."

"You mean contagious?"

Peter nodded solemnly.

The boy was so earnest. She hadn't realized until now she had grown fond of him. "I'm relieved to hear it."

"I ken mayhap I should go back to the stable today. The horses'll be missing me sorely, and with the wedding and all, I wouldnae want to leave Mr. Alex shorthanded. Miss? Miss? Why do you cry, Miss Lucy? Have I said something wrong?

Did I forget my manners?"

She scrubbed away tears and said, "No, sweetheart. You didn't do anything wrong." Lucy held out her arms. Peter stepped into her embrace and allowed her to hold him. It felt like holding a bird. His rigid little body relaxed after a moment. He patted her gently on the back.

"Dinnae feel sad, Miss Lucy. Everything will be fine. Mr. Alex will make everything fine," he said with absolute certainty.

She released him and gathered herself. "Yes. You're right, of course." If only Peter were right. If only Alex could make last night disappear, never happen. But that was the furthest thing from reality.

Liam Ulbster appeared at the door to Peter's room. He was one of the last people she wanted to see this morning, third only to Alex and Elizabeth.

"Excuse me, Lucy. I have something for you." He held out a folded piece of parchment with a red seal. Lucy's stomach flipped. She rose and took the proffered missive from Liam. It bore the emblem of the fox—Langley's seal.

"Where did you get this?"

"Read it."

Lucy cracked the seal and unfolded the parchment. Excitement and fear battled with each beat of her heart.

Dearest Lucy,

The bearer of this message is my agent. You may trust this person. If you still hold fond feelings for me, as I fervently hope you do, I beg you fly to me on love's wings. I will never know true happiness without you.

Yours, Langley

She refolded the letter, hands trembling. "Excuse me for a moment, Peter." Lucy stepped into the corridor and closed Peter's door. "I ask you again, where did you get this?"

"Langley is a dear friend," Liam said. "He begged me to

bring this to you. I will be leaving Balforss this morning. If you are inclined to join me, I will deliver you to him."

She eyed Liam with suspicion. Something told her not to trust this man.

"It's your choice. You can go through with this ridiculous marriage, or you can come with me." When she didn't reply, he continued, "I will be leaving in an hour. I'll wait for you in my carriage about a mile down the lane. If you aren't there by ten o'clock, I'll leave without you. As a precaution, I suggest you tell no one." He walked away without looking back.

She tucked Langley's letter in the pocket of her gown and peeked inside Peter's door. "I'm going down for breakfast, sweetheart. I'll come back later, and we can talk about you returning to the stable tomorrow."

Upon entering the dining room, Lucy noticed a new face at the breakfast table. John and Flora were seated in their usual places. Elizabeth was conspicuously absent as were Sir Ranald and Lady Diana. Apparently, they were late sleepers. Alex spotted Lucy and stood. The remainder of the men rose automatically.

"Lucy, are you well?" Alex asked.

As always, her body responded to the soft rumble of his voice. She turned away, afraid that if she looked into his eyes she might lose her resolve. "I'm fine."

"This is my brother, Ian."

"How do you do?" She bobbed a curtsy without really seeing the man's face. He, in turn, made a suitable bow but did not reply. She sat as far away from Alex as possible, taking a seat to Flora's left. Lucy pushed eggs and sausage around on her plate while pretending to listen to Flora babble about how glad she was Ian could be here for the wedding.

After an acceptable amount of time, she quietly excused herself from the table. Unfortunately, her departure was punctuated by all the men rising to their feet. It seemed perverse to her that they chose now to demonstrate such impeccable manners.

Lucy's body moved, making all the necessary arrangements to leave Balforss, yet her mind resisted. She shouldn't trust Liam. He was a despicable person. On the other hand, he would transport her away from this nightmare, away from Alex into the arms of Langley. What did it matter how she reached Langley? All that mattered was that she leave Balforss today.

She begged a few food items from Mrs. Swenson, making up a story about a pretend picnic with Peter in his room. On her way back, Alex accosted her. She clutched her bundle of food to her chest.

"Lucy. I'm stalking red deer today." Alex spoke in the soothing tone he used for his horse. *Blast him.* "Will you come with me and bring your bow? I ken you would be most helpful on the hunt."

She almost laughed in his face. Lucy had longed to go on a hunt for years. Now, at the very moment of her departure from Balforss, the man she hoped never to lay eyes on again offered her the one and probably only chance to participate in a hunt.

Merde.

Thoughts sparked around her brain like flashes of lightning. She needed to get to her room, gather her things, and get away from the house as soon as possible. If she refused his offer, Alex would follow her around all day.

"Yes," she said flatly. "I would be glad to go hunting with you."

Alex's handsome face broke into a heart-stopping smile.

She looked away, unable to bear his false kindness. "I have to change into my hunting costume and collect my bow. I'll meet you at the stable in an hour." Lucy made a move to leave, but Alex gathered her up by the waist.

"I want you and no other," he said.

She cast her eyes downward. She would not allow herself to be tricked by this monster again.

"Do you hear me, Lucy?"

"Yes," she said. Alex kissed her with lips soft, insistent, crushing her to his chest. She felt the same stirring she always did when he held her. How could Alex kiss her so passionately when he desired another? Lucy gathered her wits and pushed him away.

As she hurried toward the house, he called to her. "I will find a way back to you, Lucy."

She focused her mind on her objective rather than the dull ache in her chest, willing her body to keep from rattling apart. When she reached her bedroom, she locked the door and collapsed on the bed. Her darling Hercules scrambled across the bedclothes and licked her face.

"Am I doing the right thing, Hercules?"

The dog put his head down between his paws and looked at her with soulful eyes.

"Come on, my little man. No time to lose."

She struggled out of her grey serge and donned her hunting costume. Fortunately, it was possible to dress herself without assistance—a white blouse, a brown velvet jacket cut very much like a man's style, and a black wool skirt full enough to ride. She completed the ensemble with a well-tied cravat, light brown kid gloves, and a small, black beaver hat.

A fortuitous twist that Alex should invite her on a hunt. Not only did it give her the time away from him she needed for her escape, but the hunting costume would also be better for travel, and no one would question why she was carrying her bow case and satchel full of lunch. Clever, and yet, so tragic.

"Come, Hercules. We're leaving now."

...

Alex leaned against the paddock fence, chewing the sweet end of a blade of grass. Last night he thought Lucy might never forgive him. This morning he had hope. She had agreed to go hunting with him—Ian's idea.

Whether they brought anything home or not, he would be alone with her. Away from the witch, Elizabeth, and her foppish stepbrother, Liam. He would have Lucy to himself for hours. She couldn't stay mad at him forever. Alone with her, he could explain what had really happened. Then he would apologize, she would see reason, and forgive him.

"Alex," Ian called. "How is it this morning?" His brother approached the stable with Declan and Magnus trailing behind. Alex met him half way. Embracing forearms, Ian said, "You look like a man who's just been saved from hanging."

"Thanks for the idea. She's going hunting with me. I'm waiting for Lucy now."

"I heard what happened," Declan said. "You sure you want to be alone with the lass? She's deadly with the bow."

"If he comes home gutted and tied to the saddle, we'll know who did him in." Magnus laughed and congratulated himself on such a fine jest.

Ian moved to inspect one of the horses Alex had saddled for the hunt. "What have we here? He's a new one."

"He's my wedding gift to Lucy." Alex slapped the white thoroughbred on the neck. "She's afraid of horses. I chose the gelding for his even temper. I ken they will get on fine. I was going to give him to her on our wedding day, but I thought maybe today would be better, aye?"

"He's a beauty to be sure. What's his name?" Ian asked.

"He came with the name Atepomarus, but I renamed him Apollo for Lucy."

"How long you been waiting for her?" Magnus asked.

Alex glanced at the sun. Lucy should have returned by now. In fact, she was very late. Had she lost track of time? "She must be detained with Peter or Ma. I'll fetch her. Will you wait with the horses, Ian?"

She was nowhere to be found. Not in her room, Peter's room, the library, his mother's parlor, the dining room, the kitchen, or the candle shed. Alex scratched his head. Lucy had said she would go hunting with him. He was sure he had understood her clearly. He returned to the stable, but Ian hadn't seen her. Alex retraced his steps, checking every room a second time, concern plucking at the edges of his thoughts.

"Haddie, have you seen Miss Lucy?"

"Not since this morning when I helped her dress."

He stopped his mother on the staircase. "Have you seen Lucy?"

"Not since breakfast."

"If you see her, tell her I'm looking for her."

He trotted down the hall to Peter's room once again, this time venturing a few steps inside. "Peter, have you seen Miss Lucy?"

"Aye. She said I may go back to the stable tomorrow."

"When was the last time you saw her?"

Peter looked up as if he might find the answer somewhere on the ceiling. "I ken it was a couple hours ago. Maybe longer."

"Did she say where she was going when she left?"

"Oh, aye. She went to breakfast. Said she'd be back after, but she never came."

Alex pinched the bridge of his nose. This search had scrambled his thoughts and made his head hurt. Lucy's trail kept circling back to where he started.

"Miss Lucy was sad," Peter said. "But then the man came to the door and gave her something."

Alarm jolted Alex back to clarity. "What man?"

"I dinnae ken. I never seen him a'fore."

He forgot Lucy's ban on Peter's company and went to the boy's bedside. "What did the man look like?"

Peter's description sounded suspiciously like Liam.

"What was it he gave Miss Lucy?"

"I didnae see, but I ken whatever he gave her made Miss Lucy feel better."

Alex tore down the stairs, looking for his mother. He found her in the kitchen with Mrs. Swenson.

"Where the devil is Liam?" he shouted.

His mother gave him a tongue lashing for using bad language before she finally explained that Elizabeth felt unwell.

"She and Liam left for Ulbster before breakfast," Flora reported. "I saw them off. It was only the two of them in the carriage."

That was a bit of good news. Lucy hadn't left with sodding Liam. He didn't imagine she would. He certainly didn't think she'd climb into a carriage with Elizabeth. That would be like dropping two angry cats into a bucket of water.

Alex initiated a proper search for Lucy, enlisting the entire Balforss household. Declan, Magnus, and Ian spread out to cover the grounds around the house in case she'd gone for a walk with Hercules and the dog got away or she'd twisted an ankle. Alex ran down the path toward the duck pond. An Ophelia-like vision of her floating in the water appeared in his head. "Please, please let her be safe." He was relieved to find the pond empty. *But where in God's creation is Lucy?*

The men met in front of the house an hour later. It was now half two in the afternoon. The last time anyone had laid eyes on Lucy was approximately five hours ago. Alex forcibly tamped down the panic rising in his chest.

"It's apparent one of two things has happened to her," Alex said. "She's either run away, or someone has taken her."

"Her dog's gone," Magnus said.

He let the meaning of Magnus's words sink in. If someone had taken her, they wouldn't have bothered with the bloody dog. Lucy had left voluntarily.

Haddie ran out of the house, waving something in the air. "Mr. Alex. I found this. It was in the pocket of her grey gown, the one she was wearing this morning."

He unfolded a parchment with a broken red seal and read.

"I'm going to kill him!"

Chapter Sixteen

Lucy reached the carriage, shaking and out of breath. Liam stepped out and helped her load her bow case and satchel. When she climbed inside clutching Hercules to her bosom, the dog lost his little mind. Her stomach lurched. Elizabeth sat in the seat across from her.

"What are you doing here?"

Instead of answering, Elizabeth said, "I see you've brought your pet."

She struggled to control Hercules, who was writhing in her arms. "Stop your fussing, little man."

"Keep him away from me. He's dirty, and he smells." Elizabeth lifted a perfumed handkerchief to her nose.

Liam climbed in next to his stepsister and banged on the side of the carriage, signaling the coachman to drive on. "This is cozy," he said, a false cheeriness in his voice.

"Where are we going?"

"We're taking you to Langley, of course."

"Where is he? Why didn't he come himself?"

Liam and Elizabeth exchanged a look Lucy was unable

to interpret. The look made her uncomfortable. But then, simply being in the company of these two people made her queasy.

"We're on our way to Dunrobin Castle in Golspie. He's with Lady Sutherland," Liam said.

Why had Langley chosen such a disagreeable person to trust with her safety? He must have been so desperate to retrieve her anyone would do, even Liam Ulbster. That thought gave her some comfort. Langley wanted her, and soon all this nasty business with Alex would be behind her. When she returned to Maidstone Hall, she would explain to her father the terrible events that had befallen her in the Highlands. Her father would beg Lucy's forgiveness and grant Langley permission to marry her.

"Did you tell anyone at Balforss of your plan to leave?" Liam asked.

"No. No one. I'm confident no one saw me."

"Excellent," Liam said. "The thought of seeing your Langley must leave you tingling all over."

Lucy resented the wicked implication in his comment. "If you don't mind, I'm tired. I'm afraid I'm no good for conversation at the moment."

"Of course," Elizabeth said. "I'm sure everyone would benefit from some quiet."

Lucy closed her eyes, thankful not to have to look at or speak to them. Attempting, or at least pretending sleep, she tried to imagine how it would be when she would at last be delivered into the viscount's arms. Unfortunately, she had a difficult time remembering what Langley looked like. Every time she tried to conjure him, it was Alex's face that invaded her mind. In every one of her fantasies, she would fling herself into Langley's embrace only to find herself kissing Alex.

"*Merde.*"

"I beg your pardon," Elizabeth said. Did she know how

ugly her scornful countenance made her look?

"Excuse me. Talking to myself."

Hours passed as the carriage rocked and rattled southward down the narrow road. Liam's carriage was well appointed. Much more comfortable than the wooden coffin in which she had traveled to Balforss. Black leather cushioned seats, black lacquered finishes, and glass windows with curtains. They also made much better time in this carriage than the lumbering Balforss crate.

Her stomach growled, reminding her that she'd had very little to eat today. The uncomfortable fact that she needed to relieve herself also pecked at her nerves.

"Will we be stopping soon?" she asked Liam.

"In another hour. I want to put plenty of distance between us and Balforss."

"Do you think he will come looking for me?" Lucy asked, aware that she sounded almost hopeful.

The question amused Liam. "You mean your other puppy, Alex? Yes, I have no doubt your pet will be hunting for you, nose to the ground, just like a dog."

Elizabeth doubled over laughing. *Monstrous woman.*

Lucy lifted her chin. "He's not a puppy, and he's not my pet."

"Don't worry," Liam said. "I will take every precaution to make certain you reach Dunrobin Castle."

At last, the carriage pulled to a stop at one of the rare patches of forested land. The copse of trees popped up out of nowhere, looking out of place amid vast stretches of rolling fields, clumps of gorse, and endless moors. Was this the same spot where they had been attacked? Where she had shot that man? She gazed at the tree line and shuddered.

Liam and the driver made haste to the trees on one side of the road while Elizabeth and Lucy searched for a secluded spot to relieve themselves on the other. Hercules, concluding his business in short order, must have thought it safe to inspect Elizabeth, for he helped himself to a sniff while she was in a compromising position.

Elizabeth screamed, "Get away from me, you filthy mutt," then stood and kicked little Hercules.

He yelped and scampered into Lucy's arms. She stomped over to the other woman, bloody murder pounding in her heart. "If you ever touch my dog again, so help me, I will…"

Elizabeth narrowed her eyes. "You'll what?"

Lucy wanted to slap the sneer off of her face but resisted. It was more important that she get to Dunrobin Castle without incident. She marched back to the carriage, holding Hercules protectively in her arms.

Another coach, not as fine, but near as handsome as Liam's, jangled toward them from the opposite direction and slowed. When Liam emerged from the forest, the coach's occupant called for his driver to stop.

"Ulbster!" a man inside the coach shouted.

Elizabeth muttered a curse. "It's the Sinclairs from Stempster. Just nod your head and keep your mouth shut." All smiles, she hurried to the new carriage, calling, "Harriet, George, how wonderful to see you."

Once she had climbed aboard, Lucy overheard Elizabeth explain to Harriet and George how it was necessary for them to leave Balforss early.

"Our dear friend is ill and needs to return to Ulbster. It's best you not get too close in case it's catching."

The carriage occupants wished Lucy a swift recovery. They said their farewells, but before the coach continued on its way, Hercules erupted into another barking fit.

"Shut that thing up," Elizabeth snapped.

For the next three hours, Lucy tried to make sense of Liam's investment in her escape. He had promised his friend Langley he would deliver her to him. He couldn't be all bad if he were Langley's friend. Loyalty and friendship were good qualities in an individual. If Liam completed his mission successfully and she reached Langley without incident, she would thank him graciously. In the future, she would maintain a good opinion of Liam and forgive him his minor social ineptitudes.

Elizabeth was an altogether different case. First, she had been rude. Second, she had attempted to embarrass Lucy by calling attention to her illegitimacy. Third, she had intentionally dumped the hot platter on her lap, ruining her gown and almost causing her physical harm. She was a mean, spiteful, graceless woman. Why Alex would be attracted to her was mystifying.

She remembered something Nounou Phillipa used to say. *Penser avec sa bite.* Thinking with his cock.

Lucy's stomach tightened, remembering the feel of Alex pressing against her body, how he became aroused by her kisses. It had made her light-headed. She missed the Alex she had known before Elizabeth came to Balforss and bewitched him. If only he was the real Alex. She would have been happy with that man as a husband. The thought of Alex pressing himself against this woman upset her.

She supposed she should thank her for revealing the true Alex before she made the monumental mistake of marrying him. Her pride, however, made it difficult to be civil to the woman, much less grateful to her. The sight of Elizabeth kissing Alex was painfully burned into Lucy's memory, and it made her angry to admit how much he'd hurt her.

The puzzling aspect of this whole endeavor was Elizabeth's presence. Why hadn't she remained at Balforss? Why would she take part in her escape? She doubted it had anything to do with loyalty to her stepbrother, Liam. They seemed to detest each other.

Lucy could understand if she were, at the most, indifferent.

Was it possible Elizabeth was uncertain of Alex's affections? So uncertain that she was desperate to rid Balforss of Lucy, thus ensuring the marriage would not take place?

Merde.

She couldn't care less about Miss Damn-Her-Eyes' insecurities. What rankled Lucy the most about her was that the nasty woman had won.

• • •

Alex gave his mother's shoulder a slight shake. "Where's Da?"

"I ken he's at the forge with—"

"I need him. Please, Ma. Get him, now."

Flora dashed away, skirts aflutter.

No matter how deeply he inhaled, Alex couldn't get enough air. How was it possible to suffocate in the out of doors? "Magnus, Declan, sound the alarm. Gather as many men as can be ready to ride in half an hour. Tell them to arm themselves." Alex turned to his brother. "Ian, will you help me?"

"Of course. Go and get ready. I'll bring Da to the library, and we'll meet you there to plan the search."

Ian's words steadied him. His brother's calm presence eased the storm of rage and fear churning in his belly. At last, his breathing slowed. "I've got to get her back."

"It looks as if she's left on her own accord," Ian said.

"Aye, that's how it looks. But until I hear it from her lips, I willnae believe it."

Alex dressed and armed himself, fumbling with his belt and cursing his trembling hands. He took the painted miniature of Lucy from his table, rubbed his thumb over it, and closed his eyes. "Please God. Let me find her before it's too late." He dropped the miniature into his sporran.

He located Haddie in Lucy's room and questioned her further. She listed what items of Lucy's were missing; her jewels, a yellow gown, and the wooden case containing her bow and quiver. She believed Lucy was wearing her hunting costume and described the outfit from boots to black hat.

Had she been kidnapped, Alex might have ransomed her. But the evidence was clear. She had packed and left willingly. Either the bloody viscount or someone else—possibly Liam acting on Langley's behalf—had met her and hastened her away. Her life was not in immediate danger. That fact brought him a small measure of comfort. Most likely, she was only in danger of her own misjudgment. Alex's greatest fear was wrought from the idea that he might never see her again.

Why make her stay against her will? A week ago, he would have let things be, allowed her to go, and admitted defeat. He would have accepted that she didn't want him, let her have her lover, and to hell with her. But that was before he had kissed her. Before he had held her in his arms and felt the sincere passion she had for him. Alex knew better. Lucy would not have left him had he not driven her away.

His father and Ian stood in the library, grim-faced and heads bent in contemplation. Alex expected them to try to convince him not to go after her. He was surprised to find that they were equally determined to find the lass.

"Her abductor will want to secret her out of the country by ship as quickly as possible," his father said. "I propose I take half our men and cover the port cities to the north—Thurso, Dunnet Head, and Keiss. Alex, you and Ian take Declan and Magnus and ride south to Latheron. From there, head east to Ulbster. We'll meet in Wick."

"Agreed," Alex said. "They've got a good half day's jump on us, but they'll be traveling at a slower pace." Alex gave his father a detailed description of what Lucy was wearing, hoping it might help in their search.

Flora appeared at the library door, wringing her hands in her skirts, worry etched on her face. "What shall I do when the other wedding guests arrive?"

"Beg their forgiveness and send them home, I'm afraid," John said.

"I'm sorry, Ma. This is all my fault," Alex said.

Diana's voice echoed in the entry hall from above stairs. "Flora, what's all this fuss about? Where is Haddie? I haven't had my tea."

"Go, Flora," John said. "Keep her upstairs until we're away. I cannae have her adding to the frenzy."

As Flora left, Sir Ranald wandered into the library, looking lost. "I take it something's gone amiss, John," he said, eyes roaming around the room. "Ian. Good to see you, man. On leave from the army, are you?"

"Aye, sir." Ian spoke louder for Sir Ranald's benefit. "It's good to see you, as well."

Alex wanted to be off. They were wasting time blethering when they should be looking for Lucy. Hardly able to contain himself, he cast a look of distress his father's way.

"Sorry, Ranald," John said. "We cannae stay. Alex's bride Lucy is what's gone amiss. We must look for her straight away." John abandoned Sir Ranald and asked Alex, "One thing more before we leave, son. What can you tell us about this Langley fellow?"

"Langley, did you say?" Sir Ranald startled the other men with his question. Usually, Sir Ranald grasped half of what anyone said and only when one shouted directly at him. Alex suspected Sir Ranald Ulbster wasn't quite as deaf as he let on.

"You know the name?" Alex asked.

"Yes. I believe so," Sir Ranald said. "I'm trying to recall where I've heard the name. Oh, yes, of course. The Earl of Bromley. Yes. Yes. Langley is an acquaintance of Liam's.

They met at school."

Alex, Ian, and their father exchanged looks. Bloody Liam was the culprit who took Lucy from Balforss.

"Why?" Sir Ranald asked. He dodged aside as all three men rocketed out of the library, calling after them, "Have I said something wrong?"

...

Lucy woke when the carriage jolted suddenly. It must have hit a large stone in the road. Her neck ached from having slept in such an odd position. She rubbed it with one hand while patting the seat cushion next to her with the other, mildly alarmed to find it empty.

"Hercules?"

Liam and Elizabeth were dozing on the opposite bench. She lifted their lap blankets and searched.

"Hercules?" She made another desperate search around the inside of the carriage. "Stop the carriage. Stop the carriage!"

Liam roused himself enough to ask, "Why?"

"Hercules is missing. Stop the carriage now."

Liam lowered the glass window and banged on the side of the door. The carriage lurched to a stop. She flung open the door, jumped out, and ran back down the narrow road calling to the dog. "Hercules!" She kept running. Kept calling. Running and calling over and over. She refused to believe her dearest companion was lost. If she called his name loud enough he would come, wouldn't he?

Lucy stopped to listen for his familiar bark, her chest heaving, unable to catch her breath. Nothing. Silence. From her vantage point, she could see miles and miles down the road until it disappeared into the horizon. No Hercules. Lucy felt her knees buckle as her loss sliced its way into her heart.

She wept bitterly.

"Lucy, get up," Liam ordered.

She couldn't. She was bereft without her little man. Hercules was her only friend, and now he was out in the open, abandoned. How frightened he must be. He could be hurt or hungry.

"Lucy, get up, I say. We cannot tarry."

"Turn the carriage around," Lucy screamed, her voice ragged from calling for Hercules. "Turn it around now. We have to look for him."

"I'm sorry you lost your pet, but we can't."

She got to her feet and glared at him. "You're not sorry at all."

Elizabeth poked her head out of the carriage and called, "What the devil is going on?"

"You did this." Lucy pointed an accusing finger at the evil witch. She marched back to the carriage, fists clenched and shaking with rage. "You hated him. You're a cruel hag, and I hope you die a horrible, painful death. Just like my—oh God, Hercules." Lucy covered her face and sobbed.

"Temper, temper," Elizabeth taunted.

"Quiet, Elizabeth," Liam shouted. "Don't make matters worse." He put a hand on Lucy's shoulder to comfort her, but she batted it away.

"Don't touch me."

"Get in the carriage, Lucy." Liam's normally saccharine tone turned ugly. "We must be on our way. There's no time to lose. Langley is waiting, but he'll only wait so long."

"No. I'm going to find Hercules. I'll walk if I have to."

"No, you won't." Liam grabbed her roughly by the shoulders, spun her around and shook her once hard, making her neck snap painfully. "Stop your nonsense and get back in the carriage before I toss you inside!"

Dazed from his abuse, Lucy climbed back into the evil

conveyance, sat down, and stared blankly at the empty space next to her. Hercules was lost. She was alone. Completely alone.

Grief stricken, she fought back bouts of weeping. Her tears amused the witch. She seemed to feed on other people's misery. In all her life, Lucy had never known a more loathsome person. London Society teamed with despicable people. Most of them women who, whether from envy or boredom, entertained themselves by spreading wicked lies about others. But she had never known someone who would deliberately harm an innocent creature. Her hatred of Elizabeth doubled.

They reached an inn before nightfall, the one she had visited on their way to Balforss. Lucy refused supper, unwilling to be seated at a table with her tormentors. Instead, she went to her room and locked the door.

Once there, she felt the loss of Hercules acutely. Were he with her, he would jump on the bed and make himself comfortable. When she retired, he would snuggle close to her, and they would share their warmth. She was never frightened when Hercules was with her. Tonight, though, she started at every footstep, every creaking floorboard, every muffled voice.

She removed her jacket, boots, and hat, then washed her face and brushed the road dust from her clothing. Lucy had little appetite. She nibbled on the bread and cheese Mrs. Swenson had given her. This morning felt like a hundred days ago.

For the first time, she began to doubt the wisdom of her decision to run away. If she had stayed at Balforss, Hercules would still be with her. Had she been rash? Prideful? Dear Lord, was her foolish pride the reason Hercules was lost to her? Fat tears rolled down her cheeks unchecked.

Memories of Alex holding little Hercules in his arms

soothed her anguish. Alex had been kind to Hercules, treated him like the treasure the dog was to her. Once, she had come upon Alex unawares. He had allowed Hercules to stand in his lap and lick his face. No doubt the dog had wanted to taste his handsomeness. Alex had laughed and called Hercules "wee beastie." The little man had looked so tiny in Alex's big hands.

She closed her eyes and touched her lips. She missed Alex—his voice, his smile, his smell. She even missed his temper. But it had all been a lie right from the start. The effort it must have taken to pretend to want her. How could she have been such a fool? Was she so desperate to find a kind and loving husband that she had overlooked his deceit? And yet, there had to be some truth behind those kisses. No one could act a part that well. Perhaps he had, after all, liked her a little.

The image of Alex kissing Elizabeth, the image that had permanently burned itself into her memory, drifted to the front of her mind. She pounded a fist on her thigh. *Stop it. Stop imagining that he ever cared for you.*

Feeling too vulnerable to change into her nightrail, she lay down on the lumpy bed fully clothed. Tomorrow, she kept telling herself, tomorrow she would see Langley. He would sweep her into his arms, tell her how much he missed her, and beg her to marry him. Tomorrow, they would sail away to England, to Maidstone Hall, to Papa, and George, and Phillipa.

But try as she might, she could not remember what Langley looked like.

...

Alex gave Goliath his head and raced south toward Latheron. He swore to himself he would beat Liam Ulbster until his face was unrecognizable if he had harmed a hair on Lucy's head. If Lucy lost her life on this escapade, he would see both Liam and Elizabeth hanged. In any case, he planned to remove Langley's arms and legs, one by one, once he found him. What kind of a scoundrel steals another man's bride, days before his wedding?

He felt better than he had earlier today when he'd had no idea where Lucy was or how she'd disappeared. He was certain now that Liam and Elizabeth were taking Lucy to the viscount. Most likely, they would meet him at their estate in Ulbster, or the docks in Wick. Nevertheless, his father took Uncle Fergus and three men to cover the ports along the northern road. Alex, Ian, Declan, and Magnus headed south. Two hours into their race to Ulbster, he confirmed they were on the right trail when they met George and Harriet Sinclair of Stempster on their way to Thurso. Alex summarized his current dilemma. George Sinclair said they had indeed encountered stepbrother and sister in the company of a dark-haired woman with a dog.

Four hours later, the sun hovered over the western ridge. They were still twenty miles away from Latheron. Alex wanted to press on.

"We cannae ride this road in the dark, man," Ian said. "One of our horses is like to go lame."

"Just a few miles farther before we stop. There's still light."

"Alex, please. The horses need rest and water. We must stop now."

Alex pulled back his reins. His brother was right. They had ridden hard all afternoon. They would be doing themselves no favors by riding their horses until they collapsed under them. With reluctance, he called for his men to dismount and make camp.

"There's a burn several yards to the right. We can water

the horses there. I'll gather wood for the fire whilst there's still light," Alex said.

"What's that?" Declan cocked his head to the side.

"What do you mean?" Alex asked.

"That sound. Do you hear it? It sounds like…" Each man trained an ear in the direction in which Declan pointed. A tiny yelp.

"Wee Hercules!" Alex ran toward the yipping sound. "Hercules! Here boy! Come here to me, laddie. That's a good boy." Pure joy surged through Alex when he managed to make out the dim outline of the tiny dog bounding down the road.

When the screech of a white-tailed eagle pierced the air, his joy turned instantly to cold hard fear. Alex saw the dark shape of the eagle hurtling downward. Scooping up a few rocks, he flung them at the bird, all the while running toward the pup. The other men took his lead and started hurling stones at the bird, and calling for Hercules, but he was still yards away.

Seconds before splayed talons reached the dog, a stone connected with the raptor and it faltered, giving Alex enough time to dive to the ground and cover Hercules with his body. He felt the *whoompf* of the eagle's wings as it swooped skyward, abandoning its hunt.

Alex gathered Hercules into his arms and held the trembling dog. He murmured comforting words and petted him gently. "There, there, Hercules. You're all right now. I've got you."

Ian stood over his brother. "Is that Lucy's wee beastie?"

Alex ignored his brother's question and inspected the dog for injuries. "He's frightened and hungry, but he'll do." Alex got to his feet and deposited Hercules into Magnus's big hands. "Find something for him to eat. I'll search down the road for Lucy."

Ian followed Alex at a trot. "You said yourself she would not part willingly with her dog. This does not bode well."

Alex rounded on his brother. "I ken that," he snarled. Alex instantly regretted his outburst. A moment of silence passed between brothers. "Sorry."

"No mind. Let's keep looking."

After three fruitless hours calling her name and searching the dark roadside with torches, Alex lay in the grass, gazing up at the stars. Praying for Lucy's safe return, he made bargains with God, promises to God, declarations to God. All the while, he held the warm bundle of fur that was Lucy's beloved Hercules close to his heart.

Alex had thought Lucy ironic to name the wee thing after a powerful legend. But little Hercules had demonstrated the courage and strength of his namesake. No doubt he had survived many hours alone in the Highland wilderness.

Guilt, worry, and anger gnawed at the back of his mind, making sleep impossible. How could he eat or sleep when Lucy might be hurt or frightened? At last, he convinced himself that although he was a despicable cad, Liam would not harm a woman. And if Langley had gone to this extreme to retrieve Lucy, he certainly wouldn't put her in danger, either.

He made one last bargain with himself before he closed his eyes. When he found Lucy, if she heard his apology and still wanted to leave with the viscount, he would not stand in her way. He would, however, personally see Lucy safely returned to England. Alex had given her father his oath to protect his daughter. He would guard her life until the Duke of Chatham released him from that oath. That was, if he found her. If she was still alive.

...

Liam walked back to the inn from the carter's office, where he had arranged for a driver to take them to Dunrobin Castle in the morning. Elizabeth would take their carriage east to Ulbster House. If Alex and his men from Balforss were searching for them, Elizabeth would lead them in the opposite direction.

An odd feeling that someone was following him tickled the spot between his shoulder blades. He glanced over his shoulder into the darkness for the third time. Liam heard and saw nothing but quickened his pace back to Latheron Inn.

This ordeal was almost concluded. By afternoon tomorrow, he would hand over Langley's precious Lucy, Lady Sutherland would release him from his debt, and he would be off to London with money in his pocket. Why his friend would go to such extremes to retrieve Lucy FitzHarris was beyond Liam's comprehension. No woman was worth that amount of effort, as far as he was concerned, least of all this ridiculous chit.

Lucy FitzHarris was nothing like the wenches and courtesans with whom Langley normally carried on. If he planned to wed her, the duke must have provided her with a respectable dowry, perhaps an annual stipend, as well. Still, the embarrassing stink of her illegitimacy would forever follow her around like old fish. Absolutely baffling.

Exhausted, Liam put an end to the tedious conversation with himself. The reasoning behind Langley's intentions interested him little. His goal was plain. Freedom. No more fear of debtor's prison. No need to face his father with failure. All his difficulties erased with a few day's work.

He stepped through the door into the warm reek of the tavern. It smelled of roasting meat mingled with various body odors and peat fire smoke. Do these people never bathe? Lord, he hated Scotland.

Liam found Elizabeth seated in the corner table by the

fire, spooning pudding into her pretty little mouth. The bitch hadn't waited for him to return. She had gone ahead and eaten her supper without him. Typical. Just another offense added to the pile of insults, injuries, and abuses his stepsister heaped upon him. Yet, he was drawn to her unspeakable cruelty.

"Oh. It's you." She sneered. She looked radiant in the firelight.

He took the seat across from her. "I'm wounded you didn't wait to dine with me, dear heart," he said, matching her animus.

"I didn't want to lose my appetite."

"Will you be eating?" A large woman loomed over Liam. "We've beef stew."

"That sounds divine, my dear lady. I shall have a tankard of ale, as well." Liam's attempt at charm seemed to fall short with the woman. She harrumphed and lumbered off toward the kitchen. "That was a needlessly spiteful stunt you pulled with Lucy's pet."

"That smelly little cur gave us away. Do you think George and Harriet won't report having met us? Do you think she won't mention the dog?" They were rhetorical questions, of course.

"Still, the damage was done. Why upset the silly wench when we're so close to success? She nearly lost her mind."

"The dog draws attention to us. If Alex comes here searching for her, people are more likely to remember us with the dog."

"I beg you to stop baiting the girl. I can't risk failure."

"If you hadn't frittered away your money on gambling and your sexual perversions, you wouldn't be in this situation." Elizabeth popped the last spoonful of pudding into her mouth.

The large woman returned and deposited a bowl of stew,

a chunk of bread, and a tankard of ale in front of Liam with a *ka-clunk*. She held out a grubby hand. "Thrupence."

Liam pointed to his stepsister. "The lady will pay."

Elizabeth shot him a look of sheer malice before handing the coin to the woman. When the woman left, she lowered her voice to a hiss. "After this is over, the only money you will get from me will be the pennies I place on your eyes when they bury you."

"Goodness, Lizzie. You make my willie go all stiff and tingly when you talk to me like that." It was the truth. He was growing harder by the second.

Elizabeth rose from her chair and whispered in Liam's ear. "Speak to me like that again, you pathetic worm, and I will place your willie in a vice and turn the screw."

Left alone, Liam chuckled to himself. She was so delicious. He dug into the stew, noting it was also quite tasty. A moment later, he sensed someone watching him again. Looking around the room, he saw a collection of peasantry and low gentry, no one he would consider a threat. Still, the sooner he was safely locked in his chamber, the better he would feel. As quickly as possible, he finished his stew, drained his tankard, and took the stairs to the guest rooms two at a time, the tingling spot between his shoulder blades feeling like a target.

Chapter Seventeen

Lucy woke before dawn and stretched, anticipating wet kisses on her cheek from Hercules. That was how he roused her in the morning. When the wet kisses didn't come, the nightmare of losing her most precious companion returned. Sorrow like she had never known clutched at her heart.

"Oh, Hercules. My dear little man. Where are you?"

She clung to the hope that someone would find him and take him in, love him as she did, and care for him. If Alex found Hercules, he would care for him.

She sat up in bed, a small flame of an idea sparking hope inside her. If Alex were looking for her, as Liam said he would, perhaps he would find Hercules on the road. If so, he could return the little dog. That is if he knew where to find her.

Lucy heard stirring in the taproom below, the tavern mistress preparing breakfast for the guests. She scrambled to her feet and gathered her things.

An hour later, as Lucy was finishing her last bite of egg-soaked bread, Liam descended the stairs and sauntered into the dining area.

"My, you're up early. Anxious to see your precious Langley, are you? He is a lucky man to have found such an eager bride." Liam plucked an uneaten bit of sausage from her plate and tossed it into his mouth.

Lucy wanted nothing more than to be shut of his smug face and suggestive remarks.

"I've hired a driver to take us to Dunrobin. Get your things and follow me."

"What about Elizabeth?"

"She's taking our carriage to Ulbster. I'll be delivering you to Langley alone."

She should be glad to be rid of the vicious woman. She hoped never to lay eyes on that monster again. Still, traveling alone with Liam did not sit well with her. He must have seen the reluctance in her face, for the next thing he said spoke to her uncertainty.

"Don't worry, my dear. You are the last woman on earth with whom I'd make amorous congress."

Before Lucy exited the Latheron Inn, she sent one last look to the tavern mistress, and prayed the woman would be true to her word.

...

Alex and Ian burst through the door to the tavern, upsetting the maidservant. Her tray of pewter tankards crashed and clanged to the floor. Chairs screeched and toppled over as startled patrons got to their feet.

"Has anyone seen a young lass with dark hair?" asked Alex. "She would have been traveling with another man and woman."

The inn patrons returned blank stares. Some shrugged apologies and sat down again. Others finished their ale, making to leave.

In a much less threatening voice, Ian said, "Please. The lass may be in danger. If you know anything, we would be much obliged."

Out of the corner of his eye, Alex saw the maidservant shift her gaze to a large woman standing near the door to the summer kitchen. Those two knew something but were afraid to speak out. He was certain of it. Alex gave an apologetic nod to the room in general as he backed out of the inn with Ian. "We didnae mean to interrupt your meal. Please forgive us."

Once outside, Alex said, "Ian, wait here with Magnus and Declan. I mean to speak to the tavern mistress. I ken she knows a thing or two about Lucy."

"Go gently," Ian cautioned.

Alex paused at the remark. His brother was right. Go gently. And if that didn't work, he'd wring the information he craved out of the woman with his bare hands.

He walked around the tavern to the small structure located behind the main building. The large woman, presumably the tavern owner's good wife, stood just inside the entry to the kitchen, waiting for him. She did know something.

"Good afternoon, mistress." Alex gave the woman a deferential nod. "Do you have something you'd like to tell me?"

She motioned for Alex to step inside. "What is your name?" the woman asked.

"Alex Sinclair of Balforss. Miss Lucy FitzHarris is my fiancée. She's been taken from my house."

"Are you so certain she wants you to find her?"

"I believe the people who took her may mean her harm. Please, what can you tell me?"

The woman remained mute. Alex pulled a sovereign from his sporran and held it up for her to inspect.

She withdrew a folded scrap of parchment from the pocket of her soiled apron and handed it to Alex in exchange for the coin. The unsealed scrap of paper was addressed to him.

"She gave it to me in haste. Asked me not to tell the gentleman she was with about it," the tavern mistress said.

Heart pounding, hope mounting, he unfolded the parchment.

Alex,

I am to Dunrobin Castle. From there, on to London posthaste. Due to treachery, poor Hercules is lost. My heart breaks for him so frightened and alone. If, by some miracle, you find him, I beg you to set aside your anger and return him. He is innocent in all this. I would be forever in your debt.

Lucy

Shit. Dunrobin. Sutherland. Patrick Bloody Sellar. As if written in larger letters than the rest, the words *treachery, frightened,* and *alone* leapt off the page. The words cut him, lanced his chest open, exposing his heart. It was Lucy who was frightened and alone, surrounded by treachery. Most awful was the word *anger*. Did she think he was angry? With her? Surely it should be the other way around. He'd allowed Elizabeth to kiss him.

"Are you well, sir? You look a wee bit peely-wally." The young maidservant he'd seen earlier in the tavern had entered the summer kitchen without his notice. He snapped out of his stupor.

To the tavern mistress, he demanded, "When did they leave?"

"But an hour ago," she said.

Alex raced to the horses and flung himself into his saddle. "Liam has taken her to Dunrobin. We have to find Lucy before Sellar gets his hands on her. Magnus, ride east. Find my father and his men. Meet us at Dunrobin as quick as you can." Hercules, still tucked within the sheltering folds of Magnus's plaid, poked his wee head out. "And guard the dog with your life, man."

"Aye."

Magnus turned east toward Wick at a gallop, and Alex, Ian, and Declan spurred their horses west. It was twenty miles to Dunrobin Castle. A good two-hour ride if the weather and the horses held up. Chances were slim they'd find Liam and Lucy before they reached Dunrobin. And if they didn't…

It would take Magnus twelve hours at best to find his father and return with them to Dunrobin. More likely, it would be mid-day tomorrow. What was worse, Alex had no plan. They would not be welcome at Dunrobin. They would likely meet with hostility, but he must speak to Lucy. He had to find her. He would let nothing stop him from that single goal.

And if Sellar laid a hand on her, he would lose that hand, and then Alex would end the bastard's life.

...

Lucy and Liam made the journey along the coast in silence, stopping once for personal needs. Liam made only one attempt at conversation.

"What do you have in that wooden case?"

"None of your business."

He laughed. "Whatever's inside, it must be precious. You've never let the case out of your sight this entire trip."

"If you must know, it contains a gift from my father. It has no value beyond what it means to me."

Lucy turned her head away and feigned interest in the scenery. In truth, all she could think about was Hercules. Chances were slim she would ever see her beloved pet again. So many stars had to align for her prayer to be answered.

Hercules had to survive on the moor. Alex had to find him. The tavern mistress had to give Alex her note. And what if Alex hadn't even bothered to come after her?

No. He *would* come. Even if he cared nothing for her, he cared about his blasted honor, his promise to her father, his oath.

The driver called something out, a cry of distress. "What did he say?" she asked Liam. Before he could answer her, she heard the thunder of horses approaching fast from behind.

Liam leaned out the window. Spotting whoever was behind them, he shouted to the driver, "Drive on, man. Drive on! We're being pursued!"

One crack of the whip and the tiny coach jerked forward, sending Lucy tumbling out of her seat into Liam's lap. She scrambled to her seat again, searching his face for some explanation as to what was happening. Liam looked stricken with panic.

"Who's chasing us?"

He offered no answer. As the driver picked up speed, the greenery outside the windows blurred past. The whip cracked again. Hooves striking the muddy road grew nearer.

Again, she called to Liam. "Is it Alex? Is Alex chasing us?"

A loud *bang* and the coach jumped. Lucy bounced once before her bottom hit the seat and sent her ricocheting upward, her head hitting the ceiling of the cabin. Again, she fell against Liam, her forehead striking his shoulder.

Fear dulled the pain. Rather than helping her to her seat, Liam wrapped his arms around her. They swayed to and fro, careening violently from side to side along the road, each time making a wider and wider path.

"Hang on, Lucy."

...

They had traveled a little over half the distance to Dunrobin when Declan raised his hand. His cousin studied the tracks on the road.

"Look here, man," Declan said. "Where the prints dig deeper and the mud from the road is disturbed."

"Aye, I see." They trotted farther down the road, examining the tracks.

"And here. Where the carriage wheels swing right, then left," Declan said, pointing.

Realization dawning, Alex kicked Goliath hard. "They were chased!"

Goliath galloped another half mile to a sharp bend in the road. Horse and rider narrowly made the turn without crashing sidelong into a stand of trees. Just ahead, Alex spotted the wreck toppled on its side with an agitated horse tangled in the twisted harness. Hope and dread rippled through his body as he flung himself off Goliath and sprinted to the broken coach. He peered inside. No one. Only a small black derby. Lucy's hat.

"She's not here," Alex blurted. He reined in his fear. "Quick, search the brush. She may have been thrown clear.

Declan did his best to detach the crazed carriage horse from its harness, while Alex and Ian thrashed through the undergrowth lining the road.

"I found the driver." Ian shouted.

"Alive?"

"Nae. Shot dead."

Panic bit Alex in the side. Lucy. Where was Lucy? She had to be alive. He wouldn't accept any other outcome. He saw a rustling in the brush farther up the road and ran toward the movement. Liam, crawling on his belly, the back of his coat soaked in blood. "Over here," Alex called. Alex knelt beside Liam.

"Where's Lucy?"

"Help me. I'm shot." Liam's voice sounded strangled. His breathing was labored, and blood was leaking from his mouth.

"Turn him over," Ian said.

Liam yelped when Declan and Liam rolled him onto his back.

"Where's Lucy? Was she hurt? Did someone take her?" Alex demanded.

Ian waved Alex off. He unbuttoned Liam's waistcoat and tore open his shirt. A hole the width of Alex's thumb bled profusely. Ian removed Liam's cravat. Using the balled-up material to staunch his wound, he asked, "What happened, man?"

"They took her," Liam managed to say.

"Who? Who took her?" Alex leaned closer for the answer.

"Two men." Liam grabbed Alex's sleeve and coughed, spraying blood. "Shit. I'm dying."

"What did they look like? Which way did they go? *Tell* me, Goddammit."

Liam closed his eyes and shook his head.

"Is there anything I would say to your da for you?" asked Ian.

Liam choked, unable to catch a breath. He kicked and grappled, clawing at his throat, then at Ian's arm. His eyes filled with terror, a disturbing sight. At last, after nearly a minute of struggle, his flailing abated. Liam went limp, and the blood ceased to seep from his wound.

Alex bent over in agony. "This is Sellar's doing," he growled.

"I'd say the same, if I were to guess. What makes you so certain?" Ian asked.

"I saw Sellar last week. He threatened to harm Lucy if I didnae stop interfering in his business. We saw him again when we went to see about Margaret Mackay. He knows Da has what he needs now to have him arrested."

"But why kidnap her? Liam was delivering her to Dunrobin," Ian asked.

"To throw suspicion elsewhere!" Alex cried, losing control. "To frighten Da into backing down!"

"Easy, brother."

Alex took a deep breath. "With Liam dead, he could deny any knowledge of her whereabouts."

"What about this Langley fellow?"

Alex shook his head and paced. He didn't care about Langley. He wanted Lucy.

"Do you think Sellar has her at Dunrobin?" Ian asked.

Coming to a stop in front of his brother, Alex said, "I'll bet my life on it."

"It rained last night." Declan pointed to the road. "We can follow the trail. Two horses plain as day. If it leads to Dunrobin, we'll know for certain."

"Right the coach, and help me put the bodies inside," Ian said. "We'll take the horse. We may need it."

"There's no time." Alex cried out. His brother's lack of urgency was maddening. Lucy had been lost to him for twenty-four hours. Didn't Ian know every second they wasted she would slip farther and farther from his grasp? He seized Goliath's reins and lifted a boot to the stirrup. A heavy hand on his shoulder stopped him.

"Let me go, Ian. I dinnae want to hurt you." He shook himself free.

Ian made a grab for his arm. Pure reflex took hold of Alex. He spun around and slammed his fist into Ian's jaw. Ian's head snapped back before he fell on his ass. Instant remorse hit him full on at the sight of his brother sitting in the mud, wiping blood from his split lip.

"Christ. I'm sorry."

Ian cursed under his breath. "Think, man. *Think*. They've taken her to Dunrobin Castle. Sellar willnae harm her until he has what he wants from Da. If you go riding into the yard sword drawn, as I know you want to do, you'll jeopardize Lucy's life."

As usual, his brother was the voice of reason. Da had always said Alex was the brawn and Ian the brain. He held out a hand, and Ian grasped his forearm with caution before Alex yanked him into his embrace.

"I'm sorry, brother," Alex said.

Ian thumped him hard on the back twice, signaling he was forgiven.

But Alex hadn't forgiven himself. This was all his fault. All of it. From beginning to end. His rash, impulsive behavior had brought them to this desperate point. That was what Lucy meant. *I beg you to set aside your anger.* She knew her disappearance would drive him to the brink of insanity. He had to let go of his anger or he might lose her forever.

Declan approached, holding an empty blue satchel in one hand and a yellow gown in the other, both Lucy's. "Found these strewn about. I ken they took anything else of value. Her bitty bow case is still inside the carriage."

Alex swallowed hard, on the brink of frustrated tears. "She'll want her bow. It's precious to her."

"We'll find them," Declan said, baring his teeth. "And we'll slit their bloody throats."

Chapter Eighteen

Blindfolded and gagged, hands bound behind her back, Lucy endured a painful ride on her belly, slung over a saddle in someone's lap—a very smelly someone reeking of fish, stale beer, and urine. He maintained a rude grip on her behind. With the saddle's pommel digging into her ribs, and the sour tasting rag in her mouth, she was slowly suffocating.

Blood rushed to her head, making her drift in and out of consciousness. At one point, she sensed the horses slowing.

"She awake?" a man asked.

"Nae," answered the man above her.

"Not dead is she? We won't get paid if she's dead."

Her fetid saddle mate grabbed a fist full of her hair and lifted her head. Her shriek of pain merely a muffled squeak.

"Nae. She's still alive."

Someone had ordered her abduction. Who and why? And would they ransom her or kill her?

"Shall we have a bit of fun before we deliver her?"

Fun? What did that mean? Would they violate her? Lucy's heavy limbs jerked to life. Kicking. Thrashing. Unable to connect with anything.

"See what you did? She was still until you opened your fat mouth."

Lucy growled like a rabid animal until a boot swiped her hard against the side of her head. Lights flickered behind closed eyes, her lids having been sealed shut by the pressure of a blindfold tied so tight her head throbbed. The cup of her ear pulsed with searing pain. Was she bleeding?

"Shut up, or next time I'll cut your pretty face."

Lucy must have lost consciousness again, for when she resurfaced, the motion had ceased. Cool, wet stone pressed against her cheek. No sounds of horse hooves and creaking saddle leather. No sounds at all. Instead of the bruising pain of the pommel against her ribs, the points of her shoulder and hipbones ground against a cold hard surface. She lay curled on the floor, hands still bound behind her back.

She attempted to ease the pressure on her wrists, the rough rope having rubbed her skin raw. Aside from a general throbbing sensation in her palms, she couldn't feel her fingers. The blindfold remained in place, as did the gag. Taking stock of damages, she flexed her ankles, testing, then straightened her legs. No broken limbs. She rubbed her forehead on the stone floor, trying to remove the blindfold, but to no avail.

Lucy righted herself, grunting with the effort. The shift in position caused her head pain, a nauseating pulse as if her brain might burst her skull open. After taking a few deep breaths through her nose, the bilious feeling subsided.

Think, Lucy. Stay calm and think.

Her father had often said those who kept their heads in battle lived. To lose one's head meant certain death. She must stay calm to survive.

Blind, mute, fingers numb, only her ears and nose served to sense her surroundings. No more rank human smell. Only a damp musty odor similar to her father's wine cellar. And the sea. A strong smell of the sea. No sounds save her own breathing. She was alone. Left in a room below ground? If so, there must be a door.

She whimpered. *Stop it. Stop crying. Crying will get you nowhere. Get on your feet and get out.*

Lucy struggled to stand, staggering a little. She tested the ground with a tentative foot before shifting her weight. Three, four, five steps and her toe hit a surface. A wall. Unable to feel with her fingers, she placed her cheek against rough, cold, damp, hard…a stone masonry wall.

The echo of distant footsteps reached her. Heels against stones. Then a jangling of…was it keys? Was someone coming to release her?

Lucy cried out, "Help," but only made an ineffectual muffled grunt.

A key inserted into a lock turned, and then the creak of a door. She twisted her head right, then left. Which direction? Someone was entering. She could smell him. Lucy backed away from the footsteps, fetching up hard against another wall. Two dull clunks. She flinched.

"Stand still," a deep voice commanded. Lucy froze. A rough hand tugged off the blindfold. She blinked, her eyesight blurry. Torchlight flickered behind a massive figure. She flinched again when he reached behind her head to untie the gag. He fumbled with the knot.

"Bloody hell," the voiced hissed, angry, impatient. "Turn around." He turned her roughly by the shoulders and pressed her forehead against the stone wall. "Don't move a muscle or my hand may slip and take off an ear."

Lucy felt another jerk on her gag. It loosened, and she spit it out. She swallowed and moved her tongue around her mouth, trying to work up enough saliva to speak. Peering over her shoulder, she could see better now. Well enough to spot the glint of a long dirk in his hand. She screamed a ragged cry.

"Quiet. I'll no' kill you. I'm here to free your bindings. Stop your screaming."

Lucy panted, certain her life would end at any moment. She felt the searing pain of the ropes cutting into her wrists again. "Please," she begged. "Please let me go." A snap and her hands fell to her sides, heavy, throbbing, starving for blood. Sudden spiteful pain surged from her wrists to her fingertips, at once brutal and welcome.

Gently massaging her hands, Lucy faced the man. He pointed to the floor and said, "Piss bucket, water bucket. Dinnae get them confused." He sheathed his dirk and headed out the door of her windowless chamber. Any glimmer of hope that the man was there to rescue her evaporated. This man was her jailer.

"Why am I here?" Lucy called. "Stop. Please let me go." She took three steps toward the door before he slammed it shut, leaving her in total darkness.

Lucy pounded an aching fist against the solid door. "Please. Don't leave. My father is the Duke of Chatham. He'll pay you handsomely for my life. Please."

A jangle of keys, the *clunk* of the lock, and footsteps faded to silence. Lucy stepped back from the door and blinked. Darkness. Eyes open or shut made no difference. For a moment, she felt disoriented, as though she floated in a black void. She reached for the door again, seeking to anchor herself in space.

Stay calm. Stay alive. Stay calm. Stay alive.

· · ·

About a mile before they reached Dunrobin Castle, Alex, Ian and Declan left the road and led their horses deep into the wood.

Alex turned to Declan. "Walk back to the road and confirm the trail leads to the castle then report back. Keep yourself well hidden, aye?"

"Got it."

He watched Declan's back as his cousin snaked his way through the dense stand of firs. Alex's jaws ached from grinding his teeth together. His imagination painted terrifying scenes of Lucy in chains, Lucy injured, Lucy bleeding, his woman violated...dead. Terror and rage waged a fierce battle within his chest. He wanted to kill the bastards who had taken her. Cut off their limbs one by one, hear them scream and beg for mercy before sinking his dirk into their chests.

"Brother?"

Alex whipped his head around, reaching for the hilt of his dirk. He relaxed fractionally when he met Ian's gaze.

"You cannae lose your head," Ian said. "I ken you fear for Lucy, but a rash decision willnae save her."

"I know, brother. I know." But Ian had no idea the effort it took to shed what was instinctual for Alex, to fight against his nature...to be different. "I should think what Da would do."

"Nae, brother," Ian said, a hint of a smile teasing his lips. "This situation takes more than Da's logic. This problem needs a creative solution. One only a mind like yours can conjure."

Alex closed his eyes and leaned his back against a tree, releasing a chestful of wrath in one long breath. A creative solution. Jesus, since when did his creative solutions lead to anything but disaster? Still, his brother's belief in his abilities buoyed his self-confidence. Lucy believed in him—*had* believed in him. Once. It had meant everything to him that day by the river when she'd said she knew he could keep her safe no matter the danger. He couldn't let her down now. He had to prove to her he was still the best man, the *only* man for her.

"I have to find her. Not knowing where she is or if she's in pain—it's killing me."

"You love her," his brother said, a statement of fact, not a question.

He scrubbed his hands over his face, drawing them down his cheeks until his palms met under his chin in a gesture of supplication. "I do. I love her. She may not love me. She has good reason to hate me." He dropped his hands to his side and closed his eyes. "Doesnae matter. I just need to find her. If, God willing, I find her unharmed, I can bear all else."

Ian clapped a hand on Alex's shoulder. "When Declan returns, we'll plan what to do."

Declan was a canny bastard and the best man for reconnaissance. Able to move silently through cover, slim as a birch tree, Declan was known to get close enough to the enemy to overhear conversations and return with the exact number of their ranks. Alex and Ian spoke very little while they waited and waited and waited. Time seemed to creep along. With the sun cloaked heavily by clouds, Alex had difficulty determining the hour but was certain at least three had passed. He feared Declan might have met with disaster.

"I'm going after him," Alex said.

Ian grabbed hold of his arm. "Nae. Listen."

He heard the familiar call of a curlew, then Declan materialized in front of him. Irritation with his cousin swamped his initial relief. "Where the hell have you been, man?" his voice rasping and furious.

"Got anything to eat?" Declan asked. "I'm famished."

"Never mind your empty belly. What did you find out?"

Ian extracted a piece of dried beef about the size of a chestnut from his sporran and handed it to Declan.

His cousin popped the whole of it in his mouth and talked around the hard chunk as he chewed. "The tracks definitely lead to Dunrobin. As long as I was at the castle wall, I learned what I could about their strength."

"What did you see?"

"Two men at the gate by the road. Six men guard the entrance to the castle. There's two stationed in the back by the old entrance to the keep."

"Anything else?"

"For what it's worth, the masonry crew working on the new construction create such a din, you cannae hear a thing. Plus there's plenty of coming and going, what with materials arriving by the cartload."

"Do the guards question the deliveries?" Alex asked.

"Nae." Declan chewed and swallowed. "Just wave 'em on through."

Alex smiled for the first time in two days. "You did a fine job, Declan. Rest now. I need time to think."

Declan uncorked his flask and drew a long swallow of whisky. He wiped his mouth with a dusty sleeve. After a few minutes, he asked, "Have you got a plan, yet?"

"Aye, I'm working on one. We'll bide here the night. First thing tomorrow morning, we'll put my plan into action."

Ian asked warily. "What do you have in mind?"

"A bit of highway robbery, brother."

...

Shrouded in a silent darkness, Lucy battled with despair. Where was she? How long would they keep her? Would they feed her, or let her starve to death? And who were *they*?

Feeling her way around the space, she estimated the dimensions to be roughly nine feet wide by twelve feet deep. It was deathly cold in her cell. Her bones ached, her shoulders shivered, and her teeth chattered. To keep the cold at bay, she walked the circumference of the room, using her fingers on the wall as a guide. She counted her strides, each one roughly three feet. When she became dizzy, she changed direction.

Each time she stopped to think about what was happening to her, what *would* happen to her, the urge to scream and beat the walls threatened to take hold of her reason. So, she concentrated on the steps, the counting. Her mind often drifted to thoughts of Alex. Would he search for her? Would he find her? Would he rescue her from this hellhole? Liam had seemed certain Alex would follow them.

Liam.

Was he dead? Should she feel sorry for the man? After the carriage had overturned, a man had dragged her from the wreck and made her lie face down in the dirt road, his knee pressing into the middle of her back while he tied her hands together. She'd seen the driver run away. Another kidnapper had lifted a pistol and fired at the fleeing man. A *crack*, a puff of smoke, and the driver had crumpled to the ground. Then the blindfold had been wrapped around her eyes and yanked tight. Lucy had heard Liam pleading, "No, no, don't shoot." She'd cried out to him, her call drowned out by another crack of gunfire. Liam had spoken no more.

She was glad she had not seen Liam's shooting. As much as she didn't like him, she would not want him dead. Elizabeth, on the other hand…

Lucy stopped her pacing. Alex had been right to warn her about English soldiers. The man in the glen who had tried to kill Alex had been an English soldier, her captors were English soldiers. But why? Who would order the King's men to perform criminal acts?

Something else tickled her memory. Something Alex had said when they spoke in the garden about the first attempt on her life. Patrick Sellar, the man she met in the tavern. He had said Patrick Sellar threatened to harm her should the Sinclairs interfere with his business.

"Alex interfered with Sellar's business when he went to see Granny Mackay," Lucy said out loud.

Her voice pinged back from the wall in front of her, carrying with it a new and terrifying thought. It hit her like a fist in her belly. If Sellar was behind her abduction, he wouldn't ask for ransom. Sellar would do away with her as a means to punish Alex and Laird John.

She whispered a prayer, "Please God. Don't let me die." Lucy started walking again, this time quietly chanting, "I'm not going to die. I'm not going to die. I'm not going to die."

This was definitely *not* the great adventure her brother George had in mind. None of this was good. It was all bad. The cold, the dark, the rustling sound coming from the corner. *Rats*. She shuddered. Even more disquieting, she didn't know the time of day. How many hours had passed?

As if in answer to the question, Lucy heard her jailer enter the hall outside her cell. Hope blossomed in her chest while fear churned in her belly. Hope that the man was coming to release her. Fear that he was coming to kill her. She backed into the far corner and waited for him to unlock the door.

A dim shaft of light spilled inside her cell. "Supper," her jailer announced, and dropped a tin plate containing something brown on the floor. "And here's a blanket."

Lucy stepped forward and snatched the wadded blanket from his outstretched hand. "May I have a lantern, sir?"

The big man's features were hidden in shadow, but he seemed to hesitate. Maybe the man held some sympathy for her. She could appeal to his better nature. Maybe he would help her escape.

She asked nicely without whining. "Please, sir. I'm frightened in the dark."

He slammed the door shut and turned the lock, dashing her hopes of freedom.

Groping on her hands and knees, Lucy found the plate

of food, some sort of stew containing mushy vegetables and grizzly chunks of beef. She ate it with her hands and licked her fingers clean. Rats were present, and the smell of food would draw them in. She placed the empty plate on the floor in one corner. Then Lucy wrapped herself in the scratchy blanket and sat in the corner farthest from the plate.

God might bless her, watch over her, but he was not going to save her. She whispered another prayer to the only one she knew could rescue her. "Please, Alex. I'm sorry I was such a proud fool. Find me. Save me." She closed her eyes, repeating her prayer.

How long she waited, she couldn't say. She'd lost her sense of time. Lucy roused at the sound of keys. The jailer was back. The door creaked opened a crack and one arm reached inside and set a chamberstick with a lit candle on the floor.

"Thank you," she said in a voice that sounded unintentionally childlike. "You are very kind." The door shut. Without another word, the lock turned and the jailer walked away. How long did she have? How many hours? Would Alex find her before someone came to take her life?

Chapter Nineteen

Alex and Ian spent the rest of the evening formulating a plan based on Declan's information. The plan, of course, relied heavily on luck. But by mid-morning the next day, they had accomplished the first step. They had jacked an ox cart of flagstone, stripped the driver and his man of their clothes, then gagged and bound them to trees deep in the forest.

"You'll not be harmed," Ian assured the two men. "When we complete our mission, we'll return your cart and give you silver for your troubles."

Declan and Alex disrobed and donned their captives' clothing. Unfortunately, even the largest of the two pair of breeks were a snug fit for Alex, leaving little room for his private parts to rest comfortably.

"Cover yourselves with stone dust," Ian said, and gave Declan a good sprinkling.

Alex tucked his red-blond queue into the driver's filthy bonnet, then rubbed stone dust on his face and forearms. He doubted the guards would recognize either of them. Chances were more likely the other workers might peg them as strangers. When questioned, the driver had revealed they were from a stone quarry in Spittal. The other masons would know Alex was lying if they posed as workers from the same quarry.

"Remember," he said to Declan. "If anybody asks, we're from Achanarras Quarry. Ian, you wait here for Da and the others."

"What would you have us do once they get here?"

"To tell you the truth, Ian, I havenae thought that far ahead. But be ready. If we find her and can get her out, you can best believe Sellar's men will be hot on our tail."

Armed only with dirks, Alex and Declan climbed aboard the cart. Declan took up the reins, gave the oxen a snap on the rump, and the cart lurched forward. The mile-long journey was agonizingly slow-going. When they turned off the road down the tree-lined lane leading to Dunrobin, nearly an hour had elapsed. The oxen paused in front of the gates at the castle wall, waiting patiently for them to open. Two guards granted them entry without question.

The cart trundled noisily into the yard. Sweat trickled from Alex's forehead, tickling his cheeks and dripping off his jaw. He glanced at Declan, looking cool and untroubled. How he loved his sleekit cousin.

One of the armed guards lingering in the yard in front of the keep directed them toward an entrance to what looked like a courtyard. The sound of stone-cutting and hammering emanated from within the enclosed space. Most likely where all the construction was taking place. Declan maneuvered the oxen toward the entrance.

A chilling voice called, "Halt."

Declan pulled on the reins. "*Stad!*" The Gaelic for stop.

A second guard strode over to their cart. "You there. I've never seen you here before. Who are you?"

"Got a load from...from..." Alex's mind went blank. He

shot a panicked look at Declan.

"We're from Achanarras Quarry," Declan said.

God bless his cousin's perfect memory.

"Achanarras? Dunrobin trades with Spittal Quarry." The guard removed his rifle from his shoulder, a slow, almost unconscious movement, but a sign of suspicion. "Who sent you?" the guard demanded.

Alex sensed Declan lifting his shirt to gain easy access to his dirk.

"Dinnae ken." Alex shrugged. "Quarry manager ordered us to deliver the stone."

"Let me see your inventory paper," the guard said, holding his hand out and flicking a crooked finger impatiently.

Shit. No bloody papers. Alex felt Declan tense beside him. *Shit, shit, shit.*

"What paper, sir?" He attempted to sound as stupid as possible.

The guard stepped back, holding his rifle in both hands. "Get down. The job foreman will want to speak with you."

Shouts and the sound of horses trotting into the yard drew the guard's attention away from Declan and Alex.

Laird John Sinclair bellowed, "I demand to see Patrick Sellar!"

Every one of the six armed guards, including the one interrogating Alex, scrambled to form a line in front of the main entrance to Dunrobin Keep and trained their rifles on Laird John. Magnus, Ian, and Fergus edged their horses forward, hemming in the guards.

Laird John lifted his head to the second story. "Patrick Sellar, come down and face me like a man."

Alex's brilliant father had timed his arrival with military precision, allowing them the diversion they needed to slip past the guard without inspection. Declan snapped the reins, and the oxen lumbered into the courtyard, squeaky wheels protesting and stone rattling in the back of the cart.

The courtyard buzzed with construction activity. At least two-dozen masons and carpenters were in the process of erecting the foundation and framework of a large addition to Dunrobin. Alex had never seen such an ambitious construction project, the cost of which must be in the thousands. This, he thought, would be the chief reason Lady Sutherland was so intent on increasing her sheep farming and wool production.

Alex tensed when a worker approached. He was going to have to speak with the job foreman after all. The man waved a friendly greeting then ordered two other workers to begin unloading the stone from the cart.

"You're late," the man said to Alex. "You'll find the foreman in the kitchen. Hurry or you'll miss second breakfast." He pointed to the servant's entrance to the castle.

"Thanks." He and Declan hopped down off the cart and made for the door.

Once inside the dark hallway, he took his bearings. The sounds and smells of breakfast came from the right. Down the corridor to the left, the flicker of a torch illuminated what looked like the entry hall to the keep. Alex turned left, signaling for Declan to follow.

Their plan was to search the lower levels. That was where holding cells were most often located in castles as old as Dunrobin. Just before they reached the archway to the keep, Alex heard footsteps. He and Declan plastered themselves against the wall, out of sight. The front door to the keep opened and daylight spilled into the hall.

Alex's father shouted, "Call off your dogs, Sellar!"

"Laird John, to what do I owe the honor of your visit?" The sticky voice and the feigned pleasantries belonged to Patrick Sellar.

"Where's Lucy FitzHarris?" John demanded.

"Whatever do you mean?"

"Miss FitzHarris left my home yesterday. I believe she is here at Dunrobin."

"You've lost your son's bride? She's only just arrived. Awfully careless of you."

"I'm in no mood for nonsense, Sellar."

Alex smiled to himself. His father was an excellent actor. Anyone who didn't know the man would believe his outrage.

"Why would you think Miss FitzHarris is here?" Sellar, also a decent actor, played innocent.

"She received a letter instructing her to meet Lord Langley at Dunrobin Castle."

"I don't know any Langley, and Miss FitzHarris is not within these walls. But I welcome you to search the castle yourself."

"Thank you. I will. Ian, come with me."

Three sets of footsteps clattered up the keep's winding stone staircase. The front door to the keep closed, leaving the entry hall in torchlight again. Declan slithered into the entry and snatched the torch from the wall. He led the way down the stairs to the lower level, the dungeon. It was cold, dark, and dank when they reached the bottom. Alex shuddered at the thought of Lucy being held in such a place. She would be frightened half out of her mind.

"See any light, Declan?" Alex whispered.

"Nae. No voices, either."

They continued down a corridor, casting about with the torch, looking for chambers or likely places where a hostage might be secreted away. It seemed obvious to Alex this level hadn't been used for anything but storage for some time. Nevertheless, they made a thorough search.

Frustrated, he called out, "Lucy." No answer.

"She's no' here," Declan said.

"Come on. Da will be searching the second and third

floors. Let's return to the main floor and see what we can find."

As he and Declan reached the landing at the keep entrance, Alex heard his father striding up and down the halls above, cursing in a way that would singe most people's sensibilities.

"Lucy. Goddammit, woman! I ken you're hiding from me. Come out here this instant. I'll have a word with you."

Declan laughed. "He's a sly devil, your da. Acting like it's Lucy's choice to be here. Not letting on about her kidnapping."

Alex headed down the corridor with Declan right behind. Finding an unlocked door, he opened it, took the torch from Declan, and peered inside.

"You there. Stop."

The unfamiliar voice made them freeze in their tracks. Alex slowly turned to face the voice. A small man wearing a powdered wig, dressed in pink and white livery, stood in the hallway behind them, scowling with disapproval.

"Just where do you think you're going?"

Alex went blank. Fortunately, Declan maintained his wits.

"Looking for the kitchen, sir," Declan said, assuming the proper tone of an underling.

"Straight down the hall. You'd better hurry. Second breakfast is almost over."

"Yes, sir. Thank you, sir. We'll just be on our way," Declan said, bobbing his head as he backed away.

"Wait," the man in livery called.

Alex and Declan froze again, hands on their dirks.

"Put that torch back where you found it."

"Right, sir. Sorry, sir." Declan took the torch from Alex and did as the man asked. When he strode back, Alex saw a smile on Declan's face and wanted to smack him. This was not a lark. This was a matter of life and death. His cousin must have seen the irritation in Alex's face, for he straightened his own.

"Come. Maybe one of the servants knows something," Alex said through gritted teeth. He gave his cousin a shove in the back, urging him forward. "Hurry."

Heads turned to greet them when they stumbled into the steamy kitchen, all three faces rosy-cheeked from the heat of the pots bubbling over the fires, all three pates covered in white kertches, and all three women looked boiling mad.

"We've just finished second breakfast. You've missed it. Be off with you," the matron of the trio said.

Alex smothered his anger with charm. "But we've just arrived, and your cooking smells so good." He approached the woman slowly, a hand on his belly. "My wame is growling at me. He's saying, 'Feed me one of the bonnie lassie's bannocks, or I'm like to die.'" He dropped to one knee before the matron who appeared to be the head cook, and smiled up at her.

The cook's beefy cheeks flushed even redder. "Och, stop your flirting and sit yourselves down. Tess, get the lads something to tide them over until dinner."

Declan and Alex sat on a bench by the wall while the comely Tess heaped two plates with bannocks, chunks of cheese, and brown bread dragged through bacon grease. Alex consumed the welcome and much-needed scran, and considered his next move. One could count on servants knowing everything that went on in a household, but how to ask them without drawing suspicion?

"You worked for Lady Sutherland long, miss?" Alex asked the cook conversationally.

"Near fifteen years," she said, turning her attention to a pot about to bubble over.

"Must be a chore serving all us workers."

"Nae. I've got my Tess and Elspeth to help."

The girls giggled at the mention of their names.

"Did you hear that lunatic upstairs yelling for some lass?" Alex asked. "What the devil is he on about?"

"Dinnae ken. What goes on up there is none of my concern." The cook lifted her eyes to the ceiling and shook her head. "I just feed them."

Tess piped up. "He's calling for someone named Lucy. He sounds powerful mad."

"Who's Lucy?" Alex asked.

Tess and Elspeth shrugged.

Declan nudged him with an elbow and chucked his chin toward Alex's left. A large man wearing a long black coat, black britches, and black boots seemed to appear from nowhere. He paid Alex and Declan no mind. Without a word, he approached Tess, held up two fingers, and waited while she loaded two plates just as she had done for Alex and Declan.

The hulking figure retraced his steps across the room. He opened an almost invisible door set into the oak wood paneling of the kitchen wall and slipped into a dark corridor.

"Who's he?" Alex asked.

"Mr. Boatman," Tess said.

"Why'd you give him two breakfasts?"

"He asked for two plates last night, as well. He wouldnae answer me when I asked him why. Must be he has help minding the docks."

"Where's that door lead?"

"You're awfy nosey," said the cook, giving Alex a sidelong look.

"I'm a mason," Alex said by way of explanation. "The construction and layout of these old castles interests me."

"It's a passage to the docks. Used it a hundred years ago for quick escapes. Now we use it for deliveries straight up from the water's edge."

...

Lucy woke in darkness, shivering violently. The sour smelling blanket hadn't offered much warmth. She remembered sitting earlier with her knees hugged to her chest, leaning against the wall and fighting back sleep. She must have lost the battle and shifted to a curled position on the freezing stone floor.

The candle stub had burned out. Had she slept long? Was it morning? The jailer had brought the candle to her quite some time after her last meal. By the length of its stub, she had estimated the wax would give her at least three hours of light. She groped along the floor with one hand, found the chamberstick, and touched the wick. Cold. It had been out a while.

Despair swept over her, a feeling unfamiliar to Lucy. She had never felt this hopeless and afraid. Lucy straightened abruptly.

"Do not cry. To cry is to lose."

Having spent many years as the target of her brother George's nasty pranks, she had learned a valuable lesson: the first one to cry loses. She supposed she should be thankful to George. His teasing had made her tough. In George's games, the loser wasn't the weakest or the slowest. The loser was the first one to cry. Tears equaled shame and defeat.

In Lucy's mind, it was acceptable to cry if one was sad for someone else. It was acceptable to cry if one was injured. But one did not cry when one felt sorry for one's self. Wallowing in self-pity was the same as accepting defeat. She would rather die than lose. If the object of imprisoning her in this cold, dark hell were to make her cry, *they* would lose.

Lucy flung away the blanket. Every muscle in her body protested when she unfolded her legs and forced herself to stand. It was difficult to find her balance in total darkness. She reached out, found the cold, stone wall with one hand,

and resumed her circuit around the cell.

I will not cry. Let rage burn away self-pity. Let anger kill fear. I'll use my wits to get me out of this. Think. How to survive? How to escape?

What tools did she have? The pewter chamberstick holding her candle, a smelly blanket, the empty tin plate, and two wooden buckets—nothing she could use as weapons. Lucy reached into her pocket and felt the three flimsy hairpins she'd removed from her hair last night, far from lethal. If she had the strength, she might hit the jailor over the head with a bucket. But he was a big man, solid and tall. No doubt, she would only make him angry. There had to be another way, another weapon. Without strength, what weapon did a woman have? What was it Phillipa had said?

"Le charme d'une femme est sa seule arme." A woman's charm is her only weapon.

Lucy snorted. Charm worked well in the drawing rooms of London. Dear Phillipa had never prepared Lucy for the dungeons of Scotland. What good would charm do her here?

What the devil time was it? And why was knowing the time of day so important? She'd never considered time before, beyond punctuality. Even without access to a timepiece, one always had some notion of the hour based on the amount of daylight. Without light, how could one measure the passage of time?

Her stomach growled. Hunger. She hadn't eaten in a while. Her last meal would have been considered supper. Her next would be breakfast. She was taken yesterday morning, so…one day, one full day in captivity and she was already going mad. How did prisoners survive years in a cell?

What day was it and why was it so important that she keep track? Cousin Diana and Sir Ranald had arrived on Wednesday. She'd left Balforss the next morning and had been abducted the next. "Saturday." She blinked back sudden tears. "Tomorrow is my wedding day."

The jangle of keys. Her jailer was back. Lucy stood in the center of her cell, facing the doorway and waited, heart thumping in her chest. Footsteps, a *clunk* as the door unlocked, then a shaft of light outlining the big man.

"Good morning," she said, schooling her voice to hide her mounting fear. "It is morning, isn't it?"

The jailer held out a plate of food without answering.

"Thank you. I'm Lucy. What's your name?" she said, accepting the plate.

Silence. The man stooped to collect her empty plate from yesterday's dinner, as well as the chamberstick.

"I only ask so that I might address you properly."

He set the items on the floor outside the door.

"It was kind of you to allow me the candle. May I have another? It's so dark, and I'm afraid of the rats."

As the door closed, Lucy pleaded, "Please, sir. Don't leave me. I don't like being alone. Just stay and talk to me for a little while. Please?"

The lock went *clunk* and Lucy's shoulders slumped. So much for her charm.

She touched the food on her plate. Bread with something smeared on it. Jam? She lifted the bread chunk to her nose and sniffed. Bacon. She tasted a corner of the bread and savored the grease-soaked mouthful. In no time, she devoured every crumb. Lucy felt the remaining contents of her plate. A smooth, hard wedge. Cheese. And…what were the last two things? Crumbly lumps about the size of a scone. She'd felt something like this before. Yes. Oatcakes.

Bannocks. Alex called them bannocks. She let her knees buckle and sat down hard on the stone floor, forgetting the rest of her breakfast. The last thing Alex had said to her was, "I will find a way back to you, Lucy." She hadn't believed him. She hadn't believed him when he'd said Elizabeth had tricked him into kissing her. But Lucy had seen them with her own eyes.

As she had done too many times to count, she replayed that dreadful scene in her head. Alex standing in the garden. Elizabeth walking to him, leaning against him. He hadn't resisted. That fact stung. Worse, Elizabeth standing on tiptoe and kissing him. How long had the kiss lasted before they'd looked up and laughed. One, two, three heartbeats?

Merde.

She heard the jangle of her jailer's keys. Lucy stuffed the cheese and bannocks in the pockets of her skirt and stood. The jailer opened the cell door and replaced her buckets. Before shutting the door, he produced another candle, this one twice as tall as the last. Lucy breathed a sigh of relief. She would have light. For a little while, at least.

She exchanged her empty plate for the chamberstick. "Thank you for your kindness," she said. "Won't you please stay a while? I wouldn't feel so frightened if I had someone to talk to."

The jailer hesitated at the door. "I'm not supposed to talk to you."

"I won't tell anyone. I would never tell. No one would know."

He stood silent for several seconds.

"You don't have to talk. You could just listen. That way you won't break any rules. I know lots of good stories." Lucy paused for a response. None came. "I know. You can sit in the doorway while I tell you a story." Still no movement or sound. She searched her mind frantically for a story that might appeal to the man. A story featuring Scots as heroic might be best.

"Do you know the story of King James V and clan Douglas?"

"My mam was a Douglas," he said.

Good. He'd taken the bait. Now, to set the hook.

"Then you'll love this story." Lucy sat on her blanket a reasonable distance from the door and held the candle closer so her jailer could see her face. "Please. Sit down. It's a good story."

The big man folded his arms across his chest and leaned against her doorway, looking skeptical. He waited for her to begin. Unable to recall the exact words of the poem, Lucy narrated *Lady of the Lake* using what words and phrases of Walter Scott's she remembered.

"A great stag lived in the forest on Uam-Var Mountain near Stirling Castle. He was the largest and most noble of stags, and though he had been chased many times, no huntsman had ever been able to come near him."

Lucy recounted the tale of the hunt, describing the stag as "a regal giant of the forest." How one hundred huntsmen and their hounds chased the great stag across rivers, through glens, over heather, and up mountains, while the stag never tired, never stopped for a drink.

"The worn and weary huntsmen slowly dwindled in number until the once one hundred was but one."

The jailer nodded as if he approved of the single hunter who wouldn't give up the hunt. He lowered himself to the floor and waited for more of her story. The next part Lucy remembered well, for it had moved her when she'd first read the lines.

"Close on the hounds, the hunter came,
to cheer them on the vanished game,
but stumbling on a rocky dell,
his gallant steed exhausted fell.
The impatient rider tried in vain
to rouse his horse with spur and rein.
The good steed, his labors over,
stretched his limbs to rise no more."

The jailer uttered a mild oath at the huntsman's foolishness. Parched, Lucy palmed a mouthful of stale water from her bucket before resuming her tale. Using many of her own embellishments, she told the story of James Fitz-James and Ellen Douglas. Throughout the telling, her jailer remained still. Occasionally he would make sounds of approval, or grunts of agreement, and once a knowing chuckle.

Lucy paused for breath and saw her jailer lean toward her as if urging her to continue. The candle had dwindled by half when her tale was interrupted by voices echoing in the distance. The jailer scrambled to his feet.

"No, wait."

"Quiet," the jailer said. He left her cell and locked the door.

What should she do? Scream? Did the approaching voices belong to men who would rescue her? Lucy listened. Her jailer sounded as though he was having an argument with someone—with two someones. She could barely make out the words.

She recognized the deep voice of her jailer shout, "Nae."

"It'll take but a minute or two. In and out, as they say."

"Come on, man, just a wee tup. No one will be the wiser," another said.

Lucy caught her breath. She knew what the vulgar word "tup" meant.

"Nae," her jailor bellowed. "No one's allowed to talk with her. Be gone with you."

Some laughter. "We'll nae say a word. Tuck and I are real quiet fuckers."

The two other voices were those of her abductors. They had returned and wanted to do her harm. Her heart beat so hard she felt it in her fingertips. She backed away from the door. Would her jailer let them into her cell? The argument seemed to continue farther down the hall until she could hear no more. Cowering in the corner, Lucy waited. Who would be the next to enter? Her jailer or her kidnappers? Minutes turned to hours as the candle burned lower.

"Please, Alex. Please find me. Take me away from this place. Save me."

Liam had been certain Alex would search for her. Would Langley be looking for her, too? He said in his letter he would wait at Dunrobin Castle with Lady Sutherland. What had Alex said about Lady Sutherland? Ah yes. Lady Sutherland employed Mr. Sellar—

Lucy's hand flew to her mouth. Patrick Sellar was Lady Sutherland's factor. He was a bad man. Alex had told her, warned her, Sellar might use her to harm his family. *Oh, God.* Why hadn't she put these things together before?

"How could I be so stupid?" she said out loud. "I'm a fool. I trusted Liam over Alex. I believed damn-her-eyes Elizabeth over Alex. This is all my fault. My stupidity. *My pride.*"

Hercules, Alex, her freedom, all lost because of her pride. Lucy gave in to self-pity and choked on her sobs. She had lost.

When she woke, the liquid beeswax welled in the bottom of the chamberstick as the candle guttered for a moment and then expired. Based on the length of the candle, six, maybe seven hours had passed. It might only be mid-afternoon. Hours until supper. She withdrew the cheese from her pocket and nibbled. She wouldn't want food on her person in the dark. The rats might be too bold.

Footsteps outside her cell. She tensed. Keys jangled. Her jailer returning for his story? The cell door opened.

"You're back. Would you like to hear the end of my story?"

The jailor placed a bowl on the floor, shut the cell door, and locked it.

"Please," she called. "Please don't leave me alone. My candle's gone out. Please come back." Lucy paused. Waited. No response.

Then she heard the jailer say, "I'll bring another taper soon."

"Thank you."

He returned about a quarter of an hour later with a candle, shorter than the last one, but taller than the first. He lit the candle from his lantern and twisted it solidly into the base of the holder. Then he produced a spoon from the pocket of his long dark coat. Lucy wiped it on her skirt and the big man resumed his seat on the floor. She took up her story while she ate her supper, a very good bowl of chicken and leek soup with bits of bread soaking in the broth. It had been several months since Lucy had read *Lady of the Lake*. Remembering the details of the poem might have been difficult had the story not left a deep impression on her.

She took her time, preferring to share the jailor's questionable company rather than be alone with her fear. Hours passed, but her voice never failed her. At the penultimate point in the story when James Fitz-James and Ellen Douglas presented themselves at court to beg for her father's release, Lucy paused.

"You still haven't told me your name," she said.

Though her jailer remained shadowed by the torchlight behind him, she thought she heard a smile in his voice when he said, "James."

For the first time in days, Lucy laughed. "No wonder you like the story." She waited another breath or two before she asked, "Who were those men before? What did they want?"

"Criminals and they wanted nothing good. I willnae let them near you."

"Thank you, James."

Lucy picked up the story again.

"Ellen entered the throne room with James at her side. She searched but saw no one who resembled a king. All in the room, to their knees did bend and remove their hats. Only one man, James Fitz-James, dressed in simple green, remained standing with his hat on, all eyes upon him. Bewildered and amazed, tears filled Ellen's eyes. James Fitz-James brushed them away with a gentle hand. Her brave knight was none other than Scotland's King James V."

A gasp of surprise escaped Jailer James. "The Knight Fitz-James was King James all along?"

Lucy nodded.

"What did she do when she found out?"

"Ellen laid herself at her monarch's feet, unable to speak. King James smiled, lifted her up and said, 'Yes, my fair Ellen. Poor wandering Fitz-James claims the fealty of all Scotland. Ask not for your father's freedom for he and I have already forgiven each other. Instead, claim your seat beside me as my queen."

That wasn't the way *Lady of the Lake* ended, but Lucy liked her ending better than Walter Scott's. And besides, she was the one stuck in a jail cell. She could tell the story any way she liked.

"Was Ellen angry with James for deceiving her?" Jailer James asked.

The memory of Alex and his silly prank came to her. What she thought was an unforgivable act at the time, now seemed...like something a prince might do.

"Do you think she should have been angry?" she asked, her voice faltering.

"Nae. He had good reason," James said with absolute certainty. "He would win her love as a man first before he wed her as a king."

Lucy sniffed. "A brave knight once fooled me. When I discovered he was a prince, I was angry. I punished him."

Lucy's shoulders shook and her words tumbled out on her sobs. "Now, I wish I hadn't. I wish I had been nice to him."

"Och, dinnae weep, lassie. I'm certain all will be well."

She wiped her tears away with the dirty sleeve of her coat. "Do you think so? Will I be released soon?"

Jailer James stood. "It's late. Sleep now. I'll be back in the morning." He shut the door to her cell and locked it.

Remaining seated on her blanket, she listened as the big man walked away. A few seconds later, though, she heard a commotion. James bellowed, "Nae. Nae! You'll not pass. Get out!" More confused yelling and then coarse whispers.

"Get the keys, get the keys," one said.

Two sets of footsteps, running. Was it Alex? Was Alex finally here?

"Not that one. Try the other one." The voices were right outside her cell.

"Alex? Is that you?" she called.

Trying to get to her feet, Lucy stepped on her hem, tripped, and banged her head on the stone wall. The door flung open. Two figures swayed in the doorway.

"She looks like a scairt rabbit, Tuck."

"Remember us? We've come to pay you a visit as we had no time to sample your wares yesterday."

No. No. No. The soldiers. Her kidnappers. Oh God, no. In a panic, Lucy lunged for the slop bucket and tossed it. The first man ducked. The bucket hit the man behind him square in the face.

"Och, you bitch."

She grabbed the water bucket by the handle and swung it at the first man. He caught the bucket, wrenched it from her hand, and tossed it in the corner. Only then did she remember to scream bloody murder. Pinwheeling her arms at the advancing man, she connected a few blows to his face and head before he had both her wrists. She kicked at his knees and shins.

"Give us a hand, dammit."

The second man got hold of first one ankle, suffered a good kick to the side of his head, then latched on to the second. These men had rape in mind, and she wasn't going to submit without a fight. They stretched her body horizontally while she continued to squirm and screech and writhe.

"I'll kill you," she screamed. "I'll kill you!"

The threat drew laughter from her attackers. They pinned her to the floor. One man knelt on her thighs, his full weight grinding into her muscle and bone. She let out a yelp of pain different from her screams of terror.

The other man held her wrists above her head. "Open her front, Ned. I want to see her titties." He reeked of alcohol and giggled like a lunatic.

The contents of her stomach churned. She was about to vomit. The other man, Ned, continued to crush her thighs with his weight. He tore open her blouse, sending its buttons pinging across the stone floor. He slid his blade from his waist and held it in front of her face.

"Stop your fighting, or I'll stick you. I can give it to you dead just as easy as alive."

She willed herself to stop struggling, but her body would not obey. Nor could she stop shrieking when the man lowered his knife to her bodice. He cut the laces to her stays with a few quick flicks. When he finished, he drew aside the boned garment and yanked down the front of her shift. She felt cold air hit her chest. Filthy, rough hands fondled parts of her no man had ever touched. Oh, God, no.

"Make 'em jiggle."

"Like this?"

"Aye, that's good."

Lucy screamed, "Stop. Stop." Out of breath, terrified, her screams became whimpers. "Please don't. Don't touch me."

Tears streamed down her temples and caught in her hair.

The man on top of her suddenly arched his back and then fell forward on top of her like a sack of grain. The air in Lucy's lungs escaped on a *hoomph!* His body covered her face, making it difficult to breathe. The one holding her arms released her and shouted, "Who the hell are—" A strangled gurgling sound followed. Oh, God, what was happening?

She grabbed at the heavy weight on top of her and pushed until she wriggled out from underneath the body. Gasping for a lungful of air, Lucy scrambled to her hands and knees and blinked her vision back into focus. Alex had one of her attackers by the throat, pinned against the wall, his legs dangling. He thunked the man's head against the stone once and released him.

"No. No. We was just having a little fun—"

Those were the last words the man uttered before Alex slit his throat, nearly removing the man's head. Blood spurted out, drenching the front of Alex's shirt as the man slumped to the floor. A growl and a flash of movement caught her attention. The man who had been on top of her got to his feet and lunged for Alex with his knife.

She called out, "Alex!"

He spun around and dodged right. Lucy thought she saw the knife enter Alex's side, and she screamed. In the next instant, he buried his dirk in the man's belly with a vicious upward thrust. Slowly, the surprised look on the man dissolved. Alex pulled his dirk from the man's chest and tossed him aside, then wiped the bloody weapon on the dead man's clothes. Sheathing his blade, he turned to her with the same feral look in his eyes as the day he'd killed the highwaymen. Only this time, she was overjoyed to see it.

"Lucy. Are you all right?" Strong arms helped her to her feet. She teetered unsteadily, the pain in her thighs still throbbing.

"Alex?" She sobbed his name.

"It's all over, sweeting." He buttoned her jacket closed over her ruined shirt with shaking hands.

"You came for me. You found me."

"Of course I did. You're mine."

He looked angry. Angrier than she had ever seen him, and she had angered him often. But the quaver in his voice betrayed his fear. He swept her up and held her tight to his chest, his arms the only thing keeping her boneless body in one piece.

Declan, his voice once irritating, now welcome as sunshine, said, "Go on, you two. Ian waits for you in the boat. I'll be right behind you."

...

Alex strode down the tunnel toward the sea, his treasure cradled in his arms. The man the kitchen maid called Mr. Boatman lay unconscious. He stepped around him. He would have liked to cut his throat as well but refused to let go of Lucy. They weren't out of danger, yet. They must get well away from Dunrobin before he could let his guard down.

"Dinnae make a sound, love," he whispered. "Not until I tell you. Sound carries on water."

Declan trotted up behind him and signaled him to stop at the gate leading to the docks. After making certain no other guards were about, they crept down a steep embankment to the water's edge. He transferred his precious burden into his brother's arms and stepped into the small skiff. Ian returned Lucy to his lap and draped his coat over her. The skiff glided into the water and Declan hopped in.

Lucy fell asleep shortly after they left the shore and remained so while Ian and Declan took turns rowing all night. They were silent the whole way, until Ian said, "Almost there, brother." Campfires flickered off the coast of Helmsdale in the distance. "How does she fair?"

"Well as can be. I should have fetched her sooner. She was so frightened."

"What happened?"

"There were two of them holding her down," Alex clenched his teeth. "Touching her. I killed them both."

"Same ones that nabbed her. I found her jewelry on one of them," Declan said in a low voice.

"Did they—"

"No." Alex cut his brother off before he could ask the dreaded question. "We got there just in time."

"Da and the others are watching the road. They'll intercept Sellar's men, if they give chase."

"After we reach Helmsdale, take Lucy back to Balforss for me," Alex said. "I'm returning to Dunrobin."

"What for?"

"I'm going to kill Patrick Sellar."

"No you aren't." Ian stopped his rowing. "Da says—"

"I ken what he says, but the man needs to die," Alex growled out.

"Don't be a fool. You'll be hanged for murder and all Da has worked for will be lost."

"Try and stop me."

"Ye cannae do it," Declan said.

Alex looked over his shoulder at his cousin. "Why not?"

"I dreamed you and Lucy have a girl child," he said, as easily as if he was commenting on the weather.

Alex had learned from past experience to pay attention to his cousin's dreams. However, that didn't mean he couldn't kill Sellar *and* leave a child behind. It would be tricky, but...

Chapter Twenty

The light of dawn never seemed to creep the way the setting sun did. One moment it was dark and the next it was light. Alex looked down at Lucy. He'd been showered with the blackguard's blood when he slit his throat. Some of that blood had gotten on her, tainting her perfect skin. Blood would wash away, he told himself. It would take an ocean to scrub away the memory of these last few days.

Lucy's eyes fluttered open, blinked, then locked on his.

"Good morning," he said, forcing a smile.

"Where are we?"

"Safe away from Dunrobin."

"Alex, I'm sorry I was angry when you pretended you were a soldier. I didn't know you were a prince."

"A prince?" He chuckled. She must be delirious. "I'm no' a prince, love. Believe me."

"I ran away because I thought you didn't want me."

Alex had difficulty swallowing. "Never," he said, forcing the word past the lump in his throat. He laid a gentle kiss on her forehead.

Two lads from Helmsdale Village waded into the water and helped pull their skiff ashore. Helmsdale was the rocky strip of shoreline Lady Sutherland had bequeathed her displaced tenants. The once-farmers now had to make their living from the unforgiving North Sea with no tools or knowledge of fishing. Alex had visited Helmsdale last year. Scanning the shore this morning, it looked to him as though its population had doubled.

Ian took Lucy from him and deposited her at the water's edge, keeping an arm around her, as she was still unsteady. Alex climbed out of the skiff, winced, and clapped a hand to his left side. When he withdrew his hand, he saw it was covered in fresh blood. His blood.

"You're injured." Lucy stumbled toward him, looking alarmed.

He covered his side again with his hand. "I'm fine. A scratch. Dinnae fash yourself."

"Let me see." Ian brushed away his hand and tore open his blood-soaked shirt. Alex felt queasy at the sight of the gaping four-inch wound on his lower ribcage. Ian tugged the stock from around his own neck and bunched it up. "Hold this and press hard."

He did as his brother commanded. He must have lost a considerable amount of blood, for he was admittedly light-headed. Ian dug his shoulder under his right arm to steady him. Lucy flanked his left side, and together they guided him away from the beach toward the village.

Looking back over his shoulder, Alex called to the lads who had helped them to shore, "Use the skiff for firewood, aye. If Sellar's men catch you with it, he'll accuse you of stealing."

Ian shouted, "I need a healer."

"Mrs. Murray's the one you need," a lad said. "Her place is this way, sir."

They followed the boy toward one of the ramshackle huts that passed for housing in Helmsdale. A white-haired woman stood at the entrance and gave Alex a toothless grin.

"He's been cut bad," Ian said. "Can you help him?"

"It's no' so bad," Alex protested.

"Set him down out here where I can see him in the light."

Lucy spread Ian's coat on the ground for him.

Sitting hurt like the devil, and he had to grind his teeth together to keep from crying out. Once his ass hit the ground, a short yelp escaped. "Shit."

"Lay down all the way, ye big numpty. Let me take a look." Mrs. Murray pried his hand away from his side and removed Ian's bloody stock. "You're right. It's no' so bad. I'll have you stitched in no time. Someone get me some whisky."

Alex thanked the Lord. He needed a swig or two of whisky to settle himself. Hell, he could use a whole bottle. Declan produced a flask from within the folds of his plaid. He reached for the flask, but to his dismay, Mrs. Murray snatched it away and took a long pull. She wiped her mouth and, without warning, poured whisky on his wound. He jerked to a sitting position and howled. The searing pain would not abate. It felt like being stabbed with a hot poker.

"Hold him down," Mrs. Murray ordered.

Ian and Declan immediately pressed his shoulders to the ground. He inhaled, and his breath caught. The act of expanding his lungs only increased his agony. He was reduced to short, quick panting like some wounded beast. But he supposed that's what he was. Lucy's soft hand caressed his forehead, distracting him from his torment for a moment.

"Come here and help me, lass," Mrs. Murray said. "Hold out your hands." Alex turned his head to face his next torture. The old healer poured whisky on Lucy's hands then emptied the rest of the whisky on her own. "Press his skin closed while I stitch him up."

Lucy positioned herself on her knees at his side. "I'm sorry this hurts. Put your arm around me and hold on."

He wrapped his arm around her slim hips. The pleasing sensation of her delicate fingers pressing against his side momentarily overrode the pain of the whisky eating at his wound like acid. Lucy kept her eyes locked with his, her brow deeply creased with concern. He was only vaguely aware of Mrs. Murray and her busy hands.

"Will you take me home after this?" Lucy asked.

Alex felt his heart seize up. "To England?"

"That's not my home. Balforss is my home."

Releasing a breath through gritted teeth, he smiled. "Yes."

Her features smoothed, and the trace of a smile played with the corners of her mouth. All the reassurance he needed. She still wanted him.

Mrs. Murray was mercifully swift with her business. Lucy managed to shock Alex when she removed his dirk, lifted her skirt, and sliced away the bottom half of her shift for Mrs. Murray to use as a bandage.

Alex flashed a warning at his comrades. Ian cleared his throat and looked away. Declan, his cheeks flushed red, excused himself to go find the rest of their party, mumbling something about Laird John being anxious to learn of their success.

"You're a braw laddie." Mrs. Murray patted his chest. "You lay here and rest. I'll take the lass inside for a wash."

Lucy helped Mrs. Murray to her feet and followed her into the woman's hovel.

"Help me up," Alex said, lifting a hand.

"But she said—"

"Never mind what the old witch said. I cannae lay here another minute."

"You're in a rare state," Ian said, steadying him.

The two wandered toward Mrs. Murray's door and leaned against the outside wall. Alex surveyed the pitiful village of Helmsdale. A hundred or more people had taken residence on the rocky coast, just out of reach of high tide. A terrible gale could easily scour the beach and wash away all trace of Helmsdale. Crofters were, by virtue of their status, poor. The people of Helmsdale were dirt poor. Particularly disturbing were the haunted looks the hollow-cheeked children gave them. Alex wished he could do something.

As if reading his mind, Ian said, "You cannae save them all, brother."

"Aye, but I can ease their suffering a little."

"How?"

"Dinnae ken. I'll think of something."

A good while later, Mrs. Murray stepped out of her scrap heap of a home, followed by Lucy. She had fared remarkably well. All traces of the blackguard's blood had been sponged away, and her clothing brushed out. Lucy's hair was wet but combed and plaited in a gleaming queue that hung halfway down her back. Refreshed, smiling, and steady on her feet, Lucy embraced Mrs. Murray and thanked her.

Alex felt a swell of pride for Lucy. She had good manners—not the parlor room manners of a socialite, but the manners of a gentlewoman worthy of the title Lady Balforss. He pressed a sovereign into Mrs. Murray's palm, then experienced a moment of confusion when she handed it back to him.

"Will you take my grandson?" She gestured to a boy of no more than ten years standing near the edge of the water, poking at the sand with a stick. "His ma and da are dead, and I willnae make it through this winter. He'll have no one."

He was an impossibly thin lad. Clothes, face, and bare shins covered in dirt. His coat must have been a cast-off from a much larger man, possibly his father. His filthy hair would, of course, be hopping with lice.

"He'll work hard for you. I promise," Mrs. Murray said.

Christ. What level of desperation would drive her to give away her grandson? "What's his name?"

"Gilchrist. Gilchrist Murray. We call him Gil."

Alex raised a hand and called to the boy. "Gil. Come here to me, lad."

Gil immediately dropped his stick and ran toward Alex, tripping and stumbling along the way, his boots too big and lacking buckles.

"Aye, sir," the boy said, out of breath.

"My name is Alex Sinclair of Balforss. This is my bride, Miss Lucy, and this man is my brother, Captain Ian Sinclair of His Majesty's Highland Regiment."

Gil remained silent, nodding to Lucy and Ian as they were introduced.

"Would you like to come work for me at Balforss? You'll eat regular and have a warm place to sleep at night."

His eyes lit up. Then he turned to his granny, and his face fell. "I'm sorry, sir. I'm needed here to take care of my gran."

Alex thought his heart might break. For the second time that morning, he struggled to swallow a fist-sized lump in his throat. "We'll be needing your gran to come work for us, as well."

Gil beamed first at Alex, then at his grandmother. Lucy slipped her hand into Alex's and squeezed, a warm, soft reassurance that he had done the right thing. He just hoped his father wouldn't kick up too much of a fuss.

"God bless you, Laird Sinclair," Mrs. Murray said.

He was about to correct her when her words hit him square in the chest like a battering ram. So, this was how his father felt when someone addressed him, choked with responsibility, strangled by duty, suffocated by the weight of people counting on him to make the right choice, to do the right thing. God, how did his da bear it?

Alex cleared his throat. "We'll take Gil with us today and send a wagon back for you and your things later in the week, Mrs. Murray."

"Come on, lad," Ian said. "You'll ride with me."

They met Laird John and the others waiting at the side of the road, and Lucy fell into his father's arms.

"I'm so sorry. I'm so, so sorry. It's all my fault," she repeated over and over.

Alex's da patted Lucy on the back. "*Wheesht* now. None of this was your fault. You were duped by an evil man who used you to manipulate me. But he failed." John turned to Alex. "Are you well enough to ride, son?"

"Aye. I'm fine. I'm going back for Patrick Sellar."

"No, you're not."

"Don't try to stop me, Da."

"I ken you want to make him pay," John said. "But we'll let Sellar answer to the law. The Chief Magistrate will be delivering a warrant for his arrest."

"He kidnapped my woman. You cannae deny me my revenge. It's a matter of pride!"

"Stop!" Lucy shouted and came to him. "Alex, enough." She twined her fists in his bloody sark. "Please listen to me. I know what pride has cost me. I let my pride take control and look what happened. Men are dead, Hercules is lost, and I almost—" She choked on a sob. Alex held her close to him, wanting to console her, ease her pain. She drew away. "I know the price of pride, and it is too great. I will not lose you because of it. I love you. If you love me, listen to your father. Don't go back to Dunrobin."

A moment ago, he would have cut his way through the gates of Dunrobin and flayed Sellar alive. A moment ago, nothing mattered to him but blood. Nothing would sate his appetite for vengeance but the death of Patrick Sellar. That was a moment ago. The moment before Lucy declared her love, a declaration that seemed like the hinge on which the door to Alex's future opened. Now, in this moment, with the certainty of her affection shining down on his new world, Alex found the serenity for which he had prayed for so long. Suddenly the wisdom and restraint that came so easily to his father found its way into Alex's breast like a second heart. Today he was a new man, the man who would one day be Laird of Balforss.

Something black and ugly lifted out of his chest, hung in the air for a moment, then drifted away on the wind. He felt weightless. As if he'd become untethered. As if he might float away. The only thing that kept him attached to the earth was the look in Lucy's eyes, eyes shining with love, love for him.

"God, I love you, lass. I love you more than life. More than my own damn pride. I'll leave Sellar to the law and surrender myself to you, if you'll have me."

Lucy flung her arms around his neck, and he covered her mouth with a kiss, a kiss he never wanted to end. Because if he could have her, if she would let him give himself to her, the devil could take the rest of it and he could bide in her love forever. A horse stomped impatiently, Ian sniffed, and Declan, blast him, snickered into his sleeve. Alex lifted his head and barked, "Will you three gomerils leave us the hell alone."

Hercules nudged his head free of Magnus's plaid, whining and writhing, desperate to get to his mistress. Lucy freed herself from Alex's arms and walked trance-like toward Magnus as though she couldn't believe her eyes. Alex thanked the Lord they'd found the beast. Maybe someday, Lucy would be as happy to see him as she was to see Hercules returned to her, unharmed.

Lucy held the dog and spoke to him like a baby. "Hush, *mon cher. Je t'aime. Je t'aime.*" She favored Magnus with a smile. "You found him. Thank you, Magnus."

"Wasnae me. Thank Alex. It was he who saved your wee beastie."

She turned her smile on him, the same smile the nine-year-old Lucy had given him when he'd retrieved her yellow ball from the pond. Beautiful then. Even more beautiful now.

"We found your bow case, as well," Alex said.

Lucy's smile crumpled. She came to him and pressed her face into his chest, a squirming Hercules trapped between their bodies. For the first time since her rescue, Lucy wept openly. He wrapped his arms around her slender shoulders, gently twisting back and forth in what he hoped was a comforting motion.

As if sensing Alex and Lucy needed a private moment, the men from Balforss mounted up and headed down the road at a leisurely pace.

They made the ten-hour journey back to Balforss, stopping only twice to rest and water the horses. His Lucy demonstrated courage and endurance like Alex had never witnessed in a woman. Although fearful of Goliath, she shared the saddle with Alex, never once complaining.

For the most part, she was quiet. There was much about her ordeal she wouldn't discuss with others around. He hoped, when they finally got home, she would tell him everything. He needed to apologize for triggering the disaster, but he also needed to understand why she left. That she willingly went to meet the viscount troubled him still.

They were about an hour away from home—a hot meal, a hot bath, and a warm bed—when Lucy asked, "Did you kill Langley?"

"I dinnae think Langley was ever in Scotland, love. They used his name to lure you away from Balforss."

"But the letters."

"Forgeries."

"*Merde.* I'm so stupid."

"Not you. Me. I'm the clotheid. I let Elizabeth dupe me. I swear, I'll make her pay for her part in this."

"No, don't. I'd rather you didn't go near her again. Just leave that evil witch to her own miserable fate."

"I ken it makes no difference, but I didnae want her to kiss me."

Lucy squeezed his thigh. "I know." After a long silence, she asked, "Is Liam dead?"

"Aye. Shot. When we found him, he was still alive. He told us you had been taken. That was all. My da made certain the bodies of Liam and the driver were returned to their homes. He sent one of the men back to Balforss to inform Sir Ranald of his son's death."

"I think he truly thought he was taking me to Langley," she said. "I don't think he meant me harm."

"If you expect me to forgive him, you're mad."

"No." After another pause, Lucy asked. "Do you forgive me?"

"For what?"

"For leaving Balforss with Liam."

"It's me that needs forgiveness, love."

"Then I forgive you, if you forgive me."

"Done." He marveled at how easy it was for him to ask for forgiveness, how effortlessly she gave it. Was it because they weren't facing each other eye to eye? He always had an easier time saying difficult things to Lucy when she wasn't looking straight at him. Or maybe, just maybe, pride no longer stood between them.

"I'm not sorry you killed the men who tried to rape me. But I am sorry you killed the jailer."

"I didnae kill the jailer. He was already out cold when we entered the passage."

"Oh, good."

"Why?" Why would she concern herself with the well-being of a man who kept her incarcerated in a windowless cell for two days?

"He was kind to me. The experience could have been worse, but he gave me a blanket and a candle. And he let me talk to him when I was lonely." She twisted around in the saddle and asked, "Have you ever read the poem *Lady of the Lake* by Walter Scott?"

"Nae. Cannae say as I have."

"It's very good. I'll write and ask Papa to send me his."

Amazing how her mind seemed to hop from one unrelated thing to another. Jailers and poets. Pranks and princes.

A half hour later, Balforss came into view. Lucy exhaled on a sigh. "Home."

"Do you ken what today is, love?" Alex asked, his lips touching the delicate shell of her ear.

She turned her cheek into his kiss. "No."

"It's our wedding day."

Chapter Twenty-One

"Alex. *Alex*."

He lifted his head and let it loll backward. His eyelids seemed to be sealed shut with heavy weights.

"Are you going to sleep through your wedding night, too?"

He rubbed his eyes open and worked to focus on the person hovering over him, gently shaking his shoulder.

"Ian?"

"You fell asleep in your bath."

Alex had nodded off. For how long, he didn't know, but the bath water was cold. Folded in two and wedged into the wooden tub, he struggled to haul himself out with little success. Haddie must have given Lucy the larger of the two upstairs bathing tubs.

"Give me your hand," Ian said, sounding bored.

"Christ." He grasped Ian's forearm and let his younger brother yank him free of the tub. Ian tossed a drying cloth at him. "That was embarrassing."

"Wasnae my favorite moment, either," Ian said chuckling.

"Get yourself shaved and dressed. Everyone's waiting in the library."

Alex blinked. *Why is everyone waiting in the library?* He should remember. Ian seemed to think it was very important.

"For your *wedding*," Ian said, talking to him like he was thick-headed.

A jolt of adrenaline surged through Alex, and he jerked to attention. Bloody hell. He stepped out of the tub, caught his foot on the edge, and tumbled into a heap on the floor.

"Jesus," his brother cursed.

He shook his head and scrambled to his feet, clutching the linen over his privates. "I'm fine." He tucked the cloth around his waist as he staggered to his washbasin.

"Stand still," Ian said, holding out a roll of cotton. "Ma sent me up to put a fresh bandage on you. Did you get your stitches wet?"

"Nae." He raised his arms and let his brother wind the long strip around his chest several times before tucking in the end. "Thanks."

Alex thought his brother understood his implied dismissal, but Ian remained in the room, leaning against the door, arms folded across his chest. He finished soaping his beard and cast a sidelong look at him. "I said I'm fine." The man didn't move. He looked in the mirror, turned his cheek, and lifted his chin, his straight razor poised and waiting for his hand to stop trembling.

Ian launched himself off the door. "Sit," he ordered pointing to a chair. "Give me the—"

"I can do it."

"No, you can't."

Alex considered his brother for a moment, fought the need to strike him, then reluctantly handed him the straight razor and sat. He clamped his mouth shut and allowed Ian to scrape away his whiskers. He hadn't slept last night and had only slept a few hours the night before.

"Did you sleep at all since we got home?" Alex asked, trying to keep his jaw still.

"I got a couple hours."

"Declan?"

"Last I saw, he was asleep on the library floor."

Alex laughed. Declan could sleep anywhere, anytime.

"Stop laughing or I'm like to slice your throat." Ian continued shaving him with sure strokes, pausing to rinse the blade every so often. "Da says they've arrested Sellar. He's to be tried for murder."

Alex grunted his approval. "They'll sell tickets to his hanging."

"We can only hope." Ian finished and handed him a towel. "Are you ready for this, brother?"

"Oh, aye."

"Have you ever bedded a virgin before?"

Alex leaned back and buckled his brow at Ian.

"One. Why? Have you?" he asked his brother incredulously.

"Aye. One," Ian said, cocking a defiant eyebrow at him.

"Who?" He'd never given much thought to the idea of his brother, three years his junior, having had carnal knowledge of women.

"The butcher's daughter in Thurso."

"Gertie MacDonald?"

"Aye." Ian sounded a bit on the defensive.

Alex tried to suppress a laugh. "She told you she was a virgin, did she?"

"What do you find funny about it?" Ian asked, looking like he was going to clobber him at any moment.

Practically doubled over, Alex finally managed to sputter, "She told me she was a virgin, too."

Ian joined Alex in what was perhaps the funniest joke

they'd ever heard. Their laughter rolled on and on with pointing and knee slapping, and gasping for air. Alex held his injured side. "Oh, God, that hurts." At last, wiping tears from his eyes, he said, "It seems neither of us has bedded a virgin, brother."

Their laughter was cut off abruptly by a sharp rap on the door. Not the bedroom door. Rather the door connecting his room with Lucy's. Haddie's terse voice came from the other side.

"We can hear everything you say, ye numpties."

"Shit," Alex and Ian whispered in unison. They turned to each other, their faces mirroring shock and horror.

Ian helped him dress quickly and silently.

Alex asked, "How do I look?"

"Like something that's been beaten, dragged by a horse for forty miles, and left for dead. But you'll do."

"Go on without me. I want a word with Lucy."

Ian flashed him a set of fine white teeth and quit the room.

He knocked lightly on the adjoining door. "Lucy?"

"I'm almost ready."

"Are you sure about this?"

"Of course."

"It's not as we planned. We were supposed to have a church wedding."

"It doesn't matter."

He placed a hand on the door. "But all you've been through these last few—"

"Alexander Sinclair, are you changing your mind?"

He caught the warning in her voice. "N-no."

"Are you going back on your promise to marry me?"

"I…no…I—"

"Need I remind you of your duty? Your solemn oath to my father?" Lucy asked, working up a head of steam. "You promised to marry me, and I expect to be your wife."

A long silence passed. "Lucy," he asked softly, "are you sure?"

"Yes, Alex. I'm more certain of this than anything." Calm again, her voice sounded reassuring, confident, even sweet. "I want to be your wife now and forever."

When Alex entered the library, he found his father, Uncle Fergus, Ian, Magnus, and the barrister, Ewan MacBeath, having a dram.

Magnus nudged Declan with his boot. "Wake up, ye gomeril. It's nearly time."

"I thought we missed the wedding," Declan whined from the floor. "Where's the clergyman?"

"I'm here to officiate," Ewan MacBeath said. "The wedding contract the duke signed specifies today's date. Unless Alex wishes to wait until another contract is signed…" MacBeath glanced at him over his spectacles. He shook his head. "…we must complete the bond before midnight this day."

Magnus handed him a tot of whisky. "Here, man. You need this. You look like you're about to rattle apart and die."

"Nae. Alex looks handsome as ever." His mother swept into the library with Aunt Agnes at her side. Flora gave him a kiss on the cheek.

"Thanks, Ma. You're looking lovely yourself." He meant it. His mother had always been a beauty, but she looked especially nice this evening in a fine, dark green gown.

"Lucy'll be down any minute," she said. "After the ceremony, Mrs. Swenson has a grand feast waiting for us in the dining hall. Most of the guests left this afternoon, along with the vicar, thinking there would be no wedding. I dinnae ken what we'll do with all the food Cook's prepared."

Alex's stomach grumbled, and he remembered the starving children he'd seen this morning. "Da, can we share our abundance with the people of Helmsdale? I ken they'll make good use of it." He expected his father to dismiss his impulse. Instead, Laird John nodded his approval.

Ian, having witnessed the exchange, smiled and shook his head. "Perhaps you will save them all, brother."

...

Haddie finished placing the last pin in Lucy's hair and stood back. "You look like a princess, miss."

Lucy smoothed the silk chiffon folds of her cream-colored gown and traced the flowers Phillipa had lovingly embroidered on the bodice. She wished Phillipa were here with her now. She took a deep breath. No room for sadness. Only joy. Today was her wedding day.

"Thank you, Haddie."

Laird John waited for her in the hallway. "Are you ready for this, hen?" John asked, smiling down at her and offering his arm.

"More than ready."

"Alex is a lucky man to have you as a wife, just as Flora and I are lucky to have you as our daughter."

"Thank you, John."

"I ken you can call me Da now, aye?"

"Thank you, Da."

Haddie handed her a nosegay of white heather. "This is for you, for luck."

Bagpipes growled to life and wailed throughout the hall below—a baleful cacophony. John led Lucy downstairs to the entry hall where members of the household lingered outside the library door—Mrs. Swenson, Peter, the blacksmith Mr.

Gareth, as well as Gilchrist Murray, who looked marginally cleaner than he had when Lucy met him this morning.

Callum Mackay and his mother were there, as well. According to Haddie, Ian had offered to take young Callum with him when he returned to duty, and Laird John had found Mrs. Mackay work at the mill.

The group parted, allowing John to lead her through the grand entry into the library. Many heads turned toward her, but the only face she saw was Alex. Clean shaven, light red hair plaited in a queue, his clear grey eyes shining. He was wearing what looked like his dress uniform, a dark green, almost black kilt, red jacket with black cuffs and gold brocade, and a long black-and-white horsehair sporran hanging from his waist. Alex, her Highland warrior, her brave knight, her prince.

They walked at an agonizingly slow pace toward the fireplace where her betrothed was standing. She gripped John's arm to anchor herself. Between the lack of sleep and the excitement of the moment, she thought she might float away. When at last she was standing in front of her soon-to-be husband, John peeled her fingers from his arm and transferred her hand to Alex. The sound of the bagpipes mercifully expired.

A strange man standing near them called attention to himself by clearing his throat. "My name is Ewan MacBeath, Esquire. I'm very pleased to meet you, Miss FitzHarris.

"Mr. MacBeath is here to marry us," Alex said.

"Oh good." Lucy was aware how dimwitted she must sound. "I mean, I'm glad to make your acquaintance."

Mother Flora had visited her room while she was bathing and explained a few of the finer points of Scottish Marital Law, assuring her their bond would be legal. Apparently, a church wedding was not necessary as long as one held a binding contract.

"If we're ready, we can begin," Mr. MacBeath said.

Mother Flora took the nosegay of heather from Lucy. Standing face to face with Alex, both hands clasped, she could feel him tremble. Her brave knight was nervous, and for some reason, that pleased her.

"Alex and Lucy," MacBeath began, "do you come together of your own free will to bind yourselves in matrimony on this day?"

"We do," they answered in unison. Alex squeezed her hand, and Lucy, vibrating with happiness, stifled a giggle.

"Do you, John Michael Sinclair, and you, Ian Allen Sinclair, bear witness to the union of Alexander and Lucy?"

"We do."

"Then I ask you, Alexander James Sinclair, do you take Lucy Ann FitzHarris to be your wife, to be her constant friend, her partner in life, and her true love? To love her without reservation, honor and respect her, protect her from harm, comfort her in times of distress, and to grow with her in mind and spirit?"

"I so do." Alex gazed down at Lucy, firelight flickering in his eyes.

"Do you, Lucy Ann FitzHarris, take Alexander James Sinclair to be your husband, to be his constant friend, his partner in life, and his true love? To love him without reservation, honor and respect him, protect him from harm, comfort him in times of distress, and to grow with him in mind and spirit?"

"I so do."

"You may place the ring on your bride's hand," MacBeath said in a much less formal tone.

Alex twisted a simple gold band off his finger and reached for her, fumbling for the correct hand.

"The left," MacBeath offered kindly.

He slipped the ring, seven sizes too large, on her slender

finger.

"And now for the binding," MacBeath said.

John Sinclair stepped forward. "Cross your right hands at the wrist." They did, and John tied what looked like a scrap of tartan around them.

"Now you are bound one to the other with a tie not easy to break," he said. "May you grow in wisdom and love, may your marriage be strong, and may your love last in this life and beyond. You may kiss your wife."

Alex placed his lips on hers. His kiss, so tender and loving, held a promise of devotion. Through the fog of her joy, she heard applause and congratulations. The piper took up his bagpipe, this time with a jauntier tune, the kind one might even dance to.

He broke their kiss and said, "We're married."

"I know. I can hardly believe it."

"Considering everything that's happened, it's a miracle." He kissed her again.

Mrs. Swenson entered the library, holding a tray filled with glasses of whisky, and passed them around as Laird John spoke a blessing.

"A thousand welcomes to you with your marriage. May you be healthy all your days, may you be blessed with long life and peace, may you grow old with goodness, and with riches."

The walls echoed a hearty, "*Slainte mhath*."

Flora called out, "Everyone into the dining hall for the feast."

On their way out of the library, Alex leaned close to Lucy's ear and whispered. "You promised to tell me your secret name for me once we were married. Will you tell me now?"

She whispered back, "When you take me to your bed and make me your wife, I will call you *master*."

He sucked in air through his teeth, quick and sharp, then groaned, "Oh, God."

...

Throughout his twenty-one years, Alex had experienced sexual frustration on a number of different levels. During his early teens, he had little to no control of his body's responses. The mere mention of breasts would make his soldier stand at attention. His years in the army had afforded little privacy. He sometimes went for weeks without any release, while in the constant company of his fellow soldiers. Since Lucy had arrived at Balforss, it had been an ongoing struggle to contain the desire she stirred in him, despite their frequent conflicts.

None of that compared to the ball-aching agony he had experienced during their journey back to Balforss. Lucy seated in front of him in the saddle, with her soft bottom bumping gently against his crotch, had nearly driven him to the brink of madness.

Now, though, sitting next to her at the head of the table, surrounded by friends and family sated with their wedding feast, Alex had developed a case of nerves. He'd been with women before, of course. But the objective of those encounters had been *his* pleasure. In a matter of minutes, he would be called upon to please his wife, and he hadn't a bloody clue how to do it.

"Alex?"

He turned abruptly to his bride seated on his right.

"Is something wrong?" she asked.

Magnus began another in a seemingly endless round of toasts, first to the married couple, then to the Laird and Lady Balforss, then to Ewan MacBeath. At the moment, Magnus was toasting Hercules for his courage and strength. If this continued much longer, Alex would be too drunk to bed his wife.

"Nae lass. Nothing's wrong." He lifted his glass to the dog. "How do you fare, love?"

"It's well past midnight. Do you think anyone would notice if we slipped away?" She placed a warm hand on his thigh, and he roused instantly to her touch. Apparently, his soldier had no doubts about its ability to please his wife.

He cleared his throat. "Father, Mother," he announced, gathering the attention of those at the table. "Family and friends, Lucy and I thank you for your love and well wishes. We are lucky to be blessed with your presence at our wedding table. Stay and enjoy my father's whisky for as long as it lasts. It's time for my wife and me to retire. Good night."

Alex endured a few congratulatory slaps on the back while he waited for Lucy to kiss his parents good night. It was no easy thing for a man to announce to a room full of people he was about to bed his wife, but he thought he had done it brawly.

Alex and Lucy left their wedding guests behind, laughter echoing throughout Balforss. How many Sinclair men before him had spent their wedding night under this happy roof? His parents, his grandparents, his great-grandparents? Five generations, at least. He led his wife upstairs without a word, his heart thrumming inside his chest. Once inside his room, he latched the door. Someone, Haddie most likely, had lit at least a dozen candles and placed heather on the pillows.

"What do we do now?" Lucy asked, her eyes reflecting the same excitement Alex felt.

"First, I must tell you something."

"I'm listening."

"Good because this is important. I mean it's important I tell you this."

"Tell me what?"

"I love you."

"I know. And I love you," she said.

"No. That's not what I mean."

"You've changed your mind?"

"Yes. I mean no," he said, and held her steady. "This is not coming out right. Let me start again."

"All right." She looked very concerned.

"I had two worrisome days to think of nothing but you. I always assumed I would fall in love with you *after* we married. I was so wrong, Lucy. Because you see, I was already in love with you. I have loved you since the day I met you." He saw tears glistening in her eyes and hurried to finish. "When I was a boy of eleven, I must have known even then I would be the one to love and protect you. Do you remember the oath I made to your father?"

"You and my father both mentioned the oath, but I don't remember."

"I gave him my solemn oath that I would serve and protect you with my life. I meant it then, and I mean it now. I ken I was as much in love with you then as a boy could be. It was as if I pledged my troth to you that day. I was too young to see the oath as a promise to marry you. But it's clear to me now."

Tears streamed down Lucy's cheeks. He used his thumb to wipe them away.

"I had to tell you before I take you to my bed and make you mine forever. I've made so many mistakes because I've been a coward. I love you. I have always loved you. I will always love you."

"Oh, Alex." Her chin dimpled. "I was too proud to tell you I love you. Think of all the pain we could have avoided if—"

"*Wheesht* now. Dinnae think of what might have been. It's all behind us, and we're the better for it. Think only of the future."

When Alex kissed her, Lucy's body seemed to melt against his. As their kiss deepened, he ran his hands down her back and cupped her bottom, pulling her to him. They parted lips long enough for him to whisper, "God, Lucy. You make me want you so much. I cannae wait any longer. Will you have me?"

...

The room had already begun to spin even before Alex asked, "Will you have me?" four words that scorched their way down her body and settled between her legs.

"Yes, Alex. Make me your wife."

She trembled both from anticipation and nervousness. He seemed to sense her trepidation and loosened his grip on her behind.

"As it's your first time, we'll go slow," he said. "If I do anything you dinnae like, you'll tell me, aye? And I'll stop."

Lucy nodded.

"And if I do something you *do* like, you'll tell me, aye? That way, I'll know to do it more. I want to please you."

"I want to please you, too."

"First," he said, touching his lips lightly to her forehead. "We undress each other. Very slowly. Would you like that, wife?"

"Yes, please." She felt as though her body was becoming liquid in her husband's hands.

"Turn around, love. I'll start with your buttons."

She bent her head and pulled the locks of curls that had escaped her coiffure aside. He mumbled a few mild oaths as he struggled with the tiny buttons. Thankfully, there were only five. When he finished, he trailed warm kisses from her shoulder to her ear, making her shiver with delight.

He undressed her slowly, deliberately, mindfully. As each

article of clothing dropped from her body, he laid kisses on her newly bared skin. Neck, chest, shoulder, wrist, the inside of her elbow. The process was so deliciously slow that, when at last her shift floated down and puddled at her feet, she felt liberated by her nakedness. Flushed with sexual freedom. Freed from guilt over her desire for Alex.

She stepped back from her husband to allow him a better look, a brazen act but so, so exciting. She raised both arms and turned a full circle for his benefit. When she faced Alex again, he stared at her legs, looking crestfallen. She dropped her arms and covered herself.

"You don't like what you see?" she said, suddenly feeling like she wanted to run away.

Alex shook his head. "You're beautiful, but the marks those animals made…" He dropped to his knees in front of her. Looking down, she saw the ugly bruises on her thighs where the man had held her down. "I'm so sorry," he whispered. "I should have come sooner." He caressed her thighs and gently kissed the bruises.

Lucy laid a hand on his head as he trailed soft wet kisses up her left leg to her belly. "Cuts and bruises will disappear," she said. "Our love will last forever."

Alex paused, inhaled deeply, and said, "You smell so good."

She tugged the ribbon from his queue, freeing the braided red hair, and raked the fingers of both her hands through.

He stood. "Will you take your hair down for me?"

One by one, Lucy pulled out the combs and hairpins holding her curls on top of her head until the dark mass fell down her back and over her shoulders.

Alex let out his breath in one whoosh. "Lovely."

"My turn, now."

Her husband wasn't nearly as biddable as she. Undressing an octopus would have been easier. While she struggled with his stock and waistcoat, he was busy fondling her breasts with fascination. Very distracting. Not until she applied nimble fingers to unbuckling his kilt, did his attention stray from her pebbled nipples to the progress of her hands.

Once freed, his member sprang away from his body and bobbed joyously between them. Lucy gasped. She didn't expect it to be so…animated. Before she had an opportunity to explore his part more carefully, Alex lost patience with the process. He tore his shirt over his head, toed off his boots, and plastered his bared chest against her. They sighed in unison when they connected skin to skin.

"Does your wound pain you, Alex?" She brushed her hand lightly over his bandaged side.

"Believe me, love. I dinnae feel anything but you right now."

He slid his big hands down her back, splayed his fingers around her bum cheeks, and squeezed, as if testing their ripeness. Following his lead, she cupped her hands around his smooth, hard buttocks. The sound he made, a cross between a groan and a growl, pleased her, as did the feel of him pressed against her belly. He was hard as brass.

Alex released his hold and pulled back the linens, wordlessly ushering her into his bed. His breath quick and his movements urgent, Lucy complied, sinking deep into the downy mattress. He crawled cat-like onto the bed, nudged her legs open with a knee, and hovered over her.

Shadowed in the candlelight, he appeared much larger. Big and threatening, like an animal. The way the light caught in his eyes gave him an almost demonic look. Uneasiness swept through her. The image of the horrible man in the cell flickered in her memory.

"Alex?"

The beast growled and lowered his head to bite her breast.

"Stop."

The looming body froze. "I'm sorry, love. Did I do something wrong?" Alex asked, his voice warm and solicitous.

Reassured that the broad shoulders belonged to a man and not a monster, the tension in her body released. "No. I just got a little scared." She reached a hand to his cheek to make certain the man was really Alex.

He shifted his body to lie next to her, allowing the candlelight to reach his face. "I went too fast. I'll slow down." He bent his mouth to hers, his tongue teasing her lips with a sweet, soft kiss. When he drew back, he lifted to his elbow and propped his head in his hand. "I want you too much. Every part of my body wants..." He played with a lock of her hair, drawing it out, letting the silky tress slip through his fingers.

"What does your body want?" she asked, feeling light-headed.

"You," he said, his voice low. He brushed the back of his knuckles across her nipples, making them tighten and ache.

Lucy drew in a sharp breath and let it out again slowly. He raked his eyes the length of her nakedness, then dragged the tips of his fingers down the middle of her chest, her belly, and paused at the triangle of curls between her thighs. She liked the way he looked at her. Hungry. As if he wanted to devour her. He moved his head down and placed his mouth on her right nipple and sucked. Shocked at the intense sensation, Lucy writhed involuntarily.

Alex released her nipple. "Is this good, love?" At her moan of agreement, he bent his attention to the other. Her hips began to move in answer to his ministrations.

"I'm ready to try again," she said, realizing every part of *her* body wanted *him*.

He positioned himself between her legs again, cradling his hips against hers and propping the bulk of his weight on his elbows. His arms and legs, trembling with effort or need, made the mattress beneath her vibrate. His brow furrowed with intense concentration.

"Alex," she whispered. His eyes met hers. "Kiss me."

She felt his body relax against her, a comforting weight. He covered her mouth with his, slipping his tongue past her lips, her teeth. Was he mimicking with his tongue what he would do when he took her? A throbbing need centered between her legs demanded she let her thighs spread farther apart.

"Oh, God, yes." Alex pressed against her, seeking entry. Lucy raised her knees. "That's it, love. Wrap your legs around me."

He pressed inward, withdrew, and pushed further in. Lucy felt a sharp pinch and yelped.

Alex froze, breathing hard through his nose. Eyes shut tight in concentration. "Sorry, love. Does it still hurt?"

From the way he spoke, it sounded like he was the one in pain. "No. I'm all right."

Slowly, carefully, he began moving, establishing an increasing rhythm. The new and exotic feel of him inside her erased the initial sting of his invasion. Gradually, her hips moved in answer to his. The throbbing sensation grew more intense each time their bodies met at that slippery junction. And oh, how lovely, how very, very, warm and lovely—

"Let go, Lucy. Surrender to me. Let me please you."

Her lips formed a taut *O* but no sound came out. Lucy fisted the bed linens and held on as the sensation rose, crested, and crashed over the edge, sweeping her body and all reason away with it.

"*Alex.*" She breathed his name again. "Oh, Alex." With each surge of ecstasy pulsating inside her, she cried out, "Oh, oh, oh."

Alex released what sounded to her like a cry of victory before jerking once, twice, and stilling. Hovering above her, he panted. Beads of perspiration glistened on his forehead and sweat sheened his torso like a hard-ridden horse. Or perhaps she was the horse and he the rider?

Once he caught his breath, a wide smile spread across his face.

"Did I serve you well, wife?"

"Yes, *master.*"

Alex laughed and buried his head in Lucy's neck. "Jesus, God, Lucy. Feel my heart."

She laughed. "It's beating so hard. Are you sure you're not dying on me?"

"If I do, I die a happy man."

...

He made love to her twice more. Slowly. Lazily. She surprised him with her enthusiasm and curiosity. He lasted longer each time they joined. And with each joining his vixen bride's cries of pleasure brought him home.

When dawn keeked through the shutters, Lucy slept on her side, cradled in his right arm, her hands curled under her chin and her right leg slung over his. The bedclothes lay twisted and tangled around their limbs, making it difficult to tell where his body began and hers ended.

He hadn't slept at all last night. How could he when he was so conscious of the person lying next to him? He'd never shared a bed with a woman before. Who knew sleeping with one's wife would take so much getting used to?

She stirred and then rolled away from him without fully waking, settling herself in a secluded corner of his big bed, offering him a glorious view of her backside.

Alex covered her body with the linen before getting out of bed, then dressed himself as quickly and quietly as possible. With boots in hand, he tip-toed to the door. Just as he reached for the knob, he heard, "Alex?"

"Go back to sleep, love."

She rose to one elbow and rubbed her eyes. "Where are you going?"

"I've something to see to before breakfast."

"What?"

"It's a surprise."

Lucy closed her eyes and burrowed into the bedclothes. "*Mm*. I like surprises," she purred.

At the bottom of the stairs, he pulled his boots on. Mrs. Swenson and one of the kitchen maids were setting the table for breakfast. He'd have to hurry before the whole house came alive.

Trotting toward the stable, he called out for Peter.

The groom emerged from the stable with curry brush in hand and a smile on his face that warmed his heart.

"All recovered, man?"

"Aye, sir." Had the boy grown since he last saw him?

"I have an important job for you this morning. I want you to give Apollo a good grooming—a wash and a brush. Make his tail and mane shine. Then saddle him and bring him 'round to the front of the house after breakfast. Got that?"

"Aye, sir. You can count on me," Peter called, already running back toward the stable.

When Alex returned to his room, he was disappointed to find his wife no longer in his bed. Instead, he found Haddie tidying the bedchamber.

"Where's Miss Lucy?"

"In her room, taking a bath." Haddie pulled the bed linens off the mattress.

When he caught sight of a red splotch as she dragged the sheet off the bed—the blood from Lucy's maidenhead—he called out a little too sharply, "Wait."

Haddie's eyes dropped to the linen and bounced back up to meet his, immediately understanding what he was about.

People often saved the linens from their wedding bed—some as proof of the bride's purity, others as trophies. Alex wanted to save the precious linen so that he might never forget the best night of his life. Haddie left the bedchamber, closing the door behind her. He folded the sheet carefully and tucked it away in the bottom drawer of his chest, where he kept all his most treasured possessions.

He smiled at the humming coming from the next room. A songbird she was not. He knocked on the door connecting their rooms. "Lucy, can I come in?"

"I'm bathing," she called.

Alex chafed at her refusal. "I know. I want to come in and talk to you."

"After I'm done bathing."

Maddening. Lucy was his wife now. She was obligated to obey him. "I'm coming in."

"No."

He pulled the door open and hurdled over the chest blocking his entrance. Lucy sat folded into the wooden bathing tub, only her head, shoulders, and knees peeking above the water's surface. He took an odd delight in her shocked expression, blue eyes wide and pretty mouth open.

"But the door was…" She huffed. "You mean you could have come in at any time?"

"Aye. And I didnae because we werenae married. But as you're my wife, and I am your master, from now on, I forbid you to shut the door between our rooms. And I willnae tolerate you disobeying my—oh."

Lucy rose up out of the tub, water sluicing down her curves and soapsuds clinging to her breasts.

Speechless, Alex stared at his naked wife.

"Close your mouth, Alex."

His teeth clacked together.

"What were you saying about a surprise?"

...

"Keep them shut." Alex led Lucy outside by the hand. "No peeking."

She shuffled hesitantly, testing each step. He positioned her in front of Peter and the snow-white gelding.

"All right, then. You can open them now."

He watched her carefully, not wanting to miss her reaction. She opened her eyes, blinked, then looked to him, clearly confused.

"This is Apollo," he said. "My wedding gift to you."

Her eyes darted back to the horse. Alex tensed. He couldn't tell yet if she was surprised in a good way or a bad way.

"Mine?" she said in a small voice. "My own horse?"

"Aye. He's all yours."

She approached Apollo cautiously and laid a hand on his neck.

"He's beautiful." She turned a brilliant smile his way.

He felt himself breathe again, relieved his gift had pleased her. "I ken you dinnae ride, but I'll teach you. I'll enjoy teaching you."

"But I didn't get you a wedding present."

Alex put his arms around her. "Aye. You did. You gave it to me last night. I liked it very much."

"I love you," she said.

"And I love you." He kissed her, a long, thorough kiss. Alex looked up when he heard a groan from Peter. The boy rolled his eyes to heaven and tapped his foot impatiently.

He released Lucy's lips and said, "Someday, Peter, you will fall in love—"

"Yeck. Never." Peter thrust a belligerent chin at him.

"And I hope I'm there to remind you of this day."

Chapter Twenty-Two

Alex knew marital bliss couldn't last forever. Not with such a headstrong wife as Lucy. Nevertheless, he thought it might last longer than the two short weeks during which it seemed he could do no wrong and she was the Goddess of Love made flesh.

Now, knee deep into their first serious disagreement as husband and wife, he was having trouble remembering why he had been so eager to marry. His Goddess of Love had become a difficult and irritating woman.

"I said no." He continued walking with purpose toward the stable, Lucy hot on his heels.

"Why?"

"Because I said no." Alex nodded a curt good morning to his Uncle Fergus. He chose to ignore the smirk on the man's face. Evidently, his uncle found his connubial difficulties amusing.

"That's not a reason," she said, tugging at his coat.

He whirled around to face his shadow. "It should be reason enough." He had spoken too sharply. His wife's perfect face crumbled. "I'm sorry, love. I didnae mean to speak so harshly."

Too late. Tears welled in her eyes. Lucy pressed her lips together and tried valiantly to fight them back by looking sideways and breathing through her nose. He never knew what to do when women cried.

"Please dinnae weep. It willnae change my mind. It'll just make me feel like a jackass."

She harrumphed and folded her arms. Apparently, she agreed with his self-assessment.

Alex bent his knees and leaned his head sideways to look into her eyes. "Will you forgive me?" Tears having abated, she became petulant. He could handle a petulant Lucy.

"I don't understand why I can't come along with you on the hunt," she said, still refusing to look at him.

"I told you." He remembered to maintain his patience. "We'll be gone two, maybe three days. It wouldnae be proper to bring a woman along with a group of men. We'll be sleeping rough and—"

"I don't see anything improper if I'm with my husband. Many women accompany their husbands on such excursions. I know I won't slow you down. You said yourself my riding lessons have been going well. I can manage Apollo fine. And I'd be an asset. I'm handy with a bow. Plus you promised you would take me on a hunt. Don't you remember?"

"That was different. That was just the two of us. Look…" He searched for a new way to explain things to her. "I will take you hunting, just you and me, but this hunt is men only." He shifted, not wanting to admit the real reason, yet all the while knowing she wouldn't relent until he did. He lowered his voice to almost a whisper. "It would be difficult for me, ken? To be the only one who brings his wife. The men would think I couldnae go anywhere without—they'd think you had me by the—they'd say I was hen-pecked."

To his relief, understanding washed over Lucy's face. *"Ooooooooh."*

He straightened and assumed what he thought was an air of command in an effort to regain his dignity, one fist jammed on his hip, the other resting casually on the hilt of his dirk.

"We can't have that." She stepped close and retied his stock.

"No?" he asked, a little unsure.

"No. We can't have them thinking you're not a real man. Not after you proved your manhood so ably in our marriage bed." She batted her eyes at him.

Good. He had made her see reason, albeit at the expense of his pride.

"I'll miss you, you know. The bed will be very cold at night," she said, pressing the length of her body to his.

"I'll miss you, too." His response to her had become automatic. One arm circled her shoulders. The other slid down her back and rested on her right buttocks.

"I won't have your big warm body to curl up with." Her clever hands slipped inside his coat. He moaned involuntarily. "Will you think of me when you're out there sleeping alone in the cold?"

He closed his eyes and smiled. *"Mm-hm."*

She whispered in his ear. "Will you remember that lovely thing I did that you liked so much?"

Alex felt his soldier spring to life and opened his eyes to look at his wife. Just moments ago she'd been a burr in his side. Now she was a vixen. "Aye, I'll think of it, if you like."

"Will you do that thing and pretend it's me?"

"What? Are you talking about—" He glanced around in case anyone was listening. "Are you talking about self-abuse?"

"I wouldn't call it abuse. I thought it was quite nice."

"I cannae do that with Magnus sleeping not five feet

away from me." He was shocked he was even having this conversation with his wife.

"I'm going to think of you," she said. "And pretend you're doing it to me."

"Touch yourself, you mean?" He spoke too loud and Lucy placed a finger on his lips.

She gave him a wicked smile and nodded.

"You cannae do that. You need me to do that," he said, feeling a proprietorship over his wife's sexual pleasure.

"Well, you'll be gone. What else am I to do?" She sounded quite innocent.

"I forbid you."

Lucy tilted her head to one side. "Really? How do you plan to enforce that command, *master*?"

So choked with frustration, his words backed up in his throat, and nothing came out but incoherent sputtering sounds. The back of his neck went up in flames. He released his wife and rubbed his neck while pacing back and forth in front of her. He made several attempts at a response using hand gestures, but still, no words. At last, he took a deep breath and let it out in defeat.

"Christ, woman. Go get your things and meet me at the stable."

"Peter's already packed my things and saddled Apollo." She took his face in her hands, stood on tiptoe, and kissed him. "Thank you, husband. I love you."

He watched her skip away and called after her, "I love you, too," then shook his head and mumbled, "Ye wee bizzum."

Epilogue

Lucy blew her nose and checked her reflection for any telltale traces of tears. The ache in her lower back yesterday signaled the arrival of her monthly. She had hoped she was mistaken, but this morning confirmed she was not pregnant.

It had been seven months since their wedding. Shouldn't she be with child by now? Was there something terribly wrong with her womb? What if she couldn't get pregnant and Alex stopped loving her, cast her aside in favor of a fertile bride? Fresh tears rolled down her cheeks.

"Lucy?" Alex stood in the doorway of her dressing room. "Is ought amiss?"

She would like to hide her concern from him, but he probably already suspected he had a defective wife. "I'm not pregnant." She collapsed on the chaise and buried her face in the pillow.

The chaise creaked from Alex's added weight and his big hand warmed her back. "*Wheesht* now. I ken you're eager for bairns, but there's time."

She sat up, sniffed, and hiccupped. "I'm afraid you'll send

me away if I can't give you babies."

He laughed. She couldn't believe it. He was laughing at her misery. Temper ignited, she swatted his arm. When that had no effect, she pinched his thigh until he yelped.

"Stop laughing at me, you giant Scottish oaf."

He captured her wrists to ward off further assaults. "I'm no' laughing at you. I'm laughing at Declan."

"What does that beanpole have to do with me? With us? With *anything*?"

"Tell you in a minute, but first I want you to know something." He let go her wrists, and put an arm around her. "I would never, ever send you away. Not for any reason. You're my wife and my life. I can do without a lot of things, but I cannae do without you."

He kissed her, sweetly at first. Then deeply, passionately. Until all her doubt seemed to float away. She was essential to him. They were essential to each other.

He released her lips on a sigh. "Have I made myself clear?"

She managed a breathy, "*Unh-huh*."

"Good. Now." He adjusted the front of his trousers. "There's no need to fash aboot us becoming pregnant because I know with certainty we will have a girl child, at least."

"And you know that how?"

"Declan dreamed it."

"What?"

"Declan dreamed we will have a lass of our own."

"And you believe him?"

He made a solemn nod.

She jumped up and whirled on him. "Your idiot cousin Declan told you that?"

"Dinnae be fooled by his awkward behavior, love. Declan is a canny one. Sleekit and lethal. He has eyes like a hawk. Nothing gets past him. And he's prescient. His dreams never lie."

"Alexander Sinclair, that is the most ridiculous thing I've ever heard you say. Are we consulting fortune tellers about the honey harvest now? Should we ask a sorcerer to cast a spell on our sheep?"

When he laughed again, Lucy huffed and stormed out of the room.

"Where are you going?"

She called back, "To fetch Dr. Farquhar. You need your head examined."

Later that morning, she and Apollo took their daily ride. She rode Apollo astride because Alex wouldn't allow her to ride sidesaddle like a lady. He said it was too dangerous. *I cannae afford to lose a wife. I'll never find another one as good as you.*

She was still agitated by him and his nonsensical tale about Declan's uncanny ability to tell the future through his dreams. *Merde.* She'd never heard such a pile of rubbish in her life. But Alex had been so adamant, so certain. He had absolute faith in Declan's vision and, truth be told, she was desperate enough to want him to be right.

She and Apollo arrived in the clearing where Declan had begun construction on a whisky distillery. The tall, lanky, dark-haired Scot was engaged in his hammering and didn't notice their arrival at first. Declan wasn't handsome the way Alex was handsome but, seeing him shirtless, she had to admit he did have a certain sinewy appeal, lean and defined. Alex said his cousin was sleekit, meaning cunning or sneaky, but sleekit also meant smooth and shiny, an apt description for his mess of dark curls.

She called to him, and when he looked up, he smiled and dropped his hammer.

"Ho there, Lucy. Are you well this morning?" He struggled into his shirt for her benefit.

"Very well, cousin. And you?"

"My day's much improved with your arrival." Declan strode to her side and reached up to help her dismount. "Did you come to see my malting shed?"

Lucy smiled to herself. Scots were forthright about most things. About others, they were very adept at talking around a subject. Declan wanted to know why she was here, alone, in the middle of the day, but was too polite to ask, so named the most innocuous reason.

Her feet touched ground, and she smoothed the folds of her riding skirt into place.

"Actually, Declan, I came to talk to you."

He looked puzzled and plucked nervously at his shirt where it stuck to his sweaty chest. "Oh, aye?"

They left Apollo to graze and walked toward the malting shed. He indicated an upended crate for her to sit and offered her a dipper of water, which she refused.

"Whisky then?" He reached for his flask.

"No thank you. Please sit with me, and I'll get right to the point."

He carefully lowered himself to a tree stump, never breaking eye contact, as if she might spring an attack on him at any moment.

"It's about your dream."

"Aye," he said, and squinted his left eye, still suspicious.

"I would like to hear about your dream."

"The dream I had about building a distillery?

"No..."

"The one about building a house for my wife?"

"You have a wife?"

"Nae. But I dreamed I would have a wife one day."

More's the pity for the woman.

Lucy closed her eyes. Dealing with Declan always required more patience than she possessed. "No, cousin.

You told Alex you dreamed we would have a girl child," she clarified.

Declan leaned back with sudden understanding, "Oh, that dream."

Lucy waited. Declan smiled back at her stupidly.

Struggling to conceal her temper, she said, "Would you mind telling me about your dream?"

Declan's eyebrows arched.

Merde. This was like pulling teeth.

"Because, you see, Alex believes in your dreams. He says they always come true exactly the way you dream them, and I would just like to know…" The quaver in her voice alarmed her. Lord, would she start to blubber in front of blasted Declan? "I would like to know what you dreamed, exactly what you dreamed because…" She was going to lose control if she didn't stop soon. She blurted, "Because I want to believe your dreams, too."

Declan nodded, made himself more comfortable on the stump, and leaned forward, elbows on his thighs, hands clasped, settling in to tell a long story. He glanced up at the clouds as if remembering. "I had the dream the night before we rescued you from Dunrobin. Seems I always have these kinds of dreams before something big like a battle."

She nodded, encouraging him to continue.

"I dreamed me and Gullfaxi—that's my horse, ye ken—I dreamed we were waiting in front of Balforss House early one morning. I was there to collect Alex. We were going hunting for grouse. And I called out, 'Alex! Are ye coming, man?' And he came out of the house, smiling like I never saw him smile before." He looked up, his gleaming black eyebrows pinched together. "Which was odd because he's normally that crabbit in the morning, ye ken."

Lucy chuckled. "Yes, I ken. Go on."

"And he said to me, 'Morning, cousin. It's a grand day, is

it not?' And I agreed because it was indeed a fine day. And then you stepped out of the house, looking your usual bonnie self," he smiled at his sly compliment. "And I was that pleased to see you because you were standing there in a yellow gown holding a bairnie on your hip."

Lucy gasped and covered her mouth.

"A wee lassie no more than two years. She was still half asleep, sucking on her finger, her head on your shoulder. And you said, 'Wave good-bye to Papa, sweetheart.' And the peedie girl lifted her head and waved to her da."

There was no way to hold the tears back. She let them roll down unchecked because Declan wasn't looking at her anymore. He had his eyes closed, reliving the dream.

"And her hair, *Jeeeesus*, that head of blazing red hair glowed like a torch in the morning sun."

Lucy bent over and sobbed with joy, relief, gratitude. The feelings melded into one and threatened to overwhelm her.

From behind her, Alex's voice boomed. "Declan! What the bloody hell did you say to my wife?"

Declan snapped to attention and held his hands up in a gesture of innocence. "She wanted me to tell her the dream, so I told her the dream."

Lucy gathered herself and embraced her big Scottish husband. "I'm all right, Alex. Everything is all right now. We're going to have a daughter."

He held her close and patted her back. "I know, lass. I know. And she'll be a bonnie wee thing."

Author's Note

There was a woman named Margaret Mackay who lived in Strathnaver and died when her cot was fired. All other details about her death herein were invented to suit the story. Patrick Sellar, one of the most notorious historical figures related to the Highland Clearances, was arrested and tried for Margaret Mackay's death, but later acquitted. My description of Dunrobin Castle is loosely based on drawings of the keep before Lady Sutherland made her improvements. Today, one can visit the beautiful Dunrobin Castle in Sutherland or hike to Badbea, the Clearance Village on the rocky hillside overlooking Helmsdale.

Acknowledgments

My sincere thanks to the following for their help and support: Kim Suhr, Robert Vaughan, and the members of Red Oak Writing Studio, the members of Wisconsin Romance Writers, Dave Rank, Lisa Lickel, Phil Martin, S.J. Rosen, Margie Lawson, publicist Krista Soukup at Blue Cottage Agency, web designer Corey Kretsinger at MidState Design, editor Erin Molta at Entangled Publishing, and my agent Cassie Hanjian at Waxman Leavell Literary Agency. And to my husband Richard (my Beta reader), and my son Nick (my best creation) my unending love.

About the Author

Jennifer Trethewey is an actor-turned-writer who has moved her performances from the stage to the page. In 2013, she traveled to Scotland for the first time, where she instantly fell in love with the language, humor, intense sense of pride, and breathtaking landscape. Her love for Scotland has been translated into her first series of historical romance novels, the Highlanders of Balforss.

Trethewey's primary experience in bringing the imaginary to life was working for one of the most successful women's theater companies in the nation, where she was the co-founder and co-artistic director. Today she continues to act, but writes contemporary and historical fiction full-time. She lives in Milwaukee with her husband. Her other loves include dogs, movies, music, and good wine.

Discover more Amara titles...

HIGHLAND REDEMPTION
a *Highland Pride* novel by Lori Ann Bailey

Skye Cameron has no idea why she was kidnapped, but the last thing she wants is to spend any time with her rescuer, Brodie, the man who broke her heart. She's promised to another in a political marriage and must fight to keep from falling for her handsome childhood sweetheart again as they dash across Scotland in an attempt to elude her captors and stay alive.

THE LADY AND MR. JONES
a *Spy in the Ton* novel by Alyssa Alexander

Jones, born in the rookeries, was saved as a young boy and trained to be an elite spy. He serves His Majesty in espionage, hunting rogue spies. Cat Ashdown is a baroness. She knows every detail of every estate that commands the largest income in Britain—yet her father placed her inheritance in trust to her uncle who is forcing her to marry against her will. The baroness's battle against law and convention leads her to Jones and results that are surprising...and possibly unwanted.

THE MAIDEN'S DEFENDER
a *Ladies of Scotland* novel by E. Elizabeth Watson

Madeline Crawford is a daughter of the disgraced Sheriff of Ayr. Fierce Highlander Teàrlach MacGregor was her father's head guardsman. They dream of a future together. Those dreams come to naught when Madeline is betrothed to the son of her warden. Madeline and Teàrlach's love is forbidden but Teàrlach vows to fight, even the king, to make her his.

Printed in the USA
CPSIA information can be obtained
at www.ICGtesting.com
LVHW091810191023
761576LV00001B/85

9 781979 604246